She'd been genuinely surprised at Evan's suggestion that they take one last look at Dylan's death. While she refused to delude herself into thinking that they'd solve the case, the fact that Evan understood, that he made the gesture, endeared him to her even more. She hadn't been exaggerating when she'd told him that finding him, realizing that she could find love again, had stunned her. She'd not even considered looking, assuming that she'd spend the rest of her life alone. She had pretty much made her peace with that. No one, she'd figured, had the right to expect that kind of total love, total devotion, more than once in a lifetime. It had shocked her to learn it could happen—and that it had happened to her.

She was so deep in thought that she missed the call on her cell phone. She picked it up and looked at the screen. Her brother. She hit the automatic-dial number and Connor answered on the first ring.

"Hey, sorry. I missed your call by about one ring," she told him. "Where are you?"

"Now, you know that if I told you, we'd have to kill you."

By Mariah Stewart

COLD TRUTH
HARD TRUTH
DARK TRUTH
FINAL TRUTH

DEAD END
DEAD CERTAIN
DEAD EVEN
DEAD WRONG

UNTIL DARK
THE PRESIDENT'S DAUGHTER

A Novel

DEAD END

MARIAH STEWART

BALLANTINE BOOKS • NEW YORK

Dead End is a work of fiction. Names, characters, places, and incidents are the products of the author's imagination or are used fictitiously. Any resemblance to actual events, locales, or persons, living or dead, is entirely coincidental.

2006 Ballantine Books Mass Market Edition

Copyright © 2005 by Marti Robb
Excerpt from *Final Truth* copyright © 2006 by Marti Robb

Published in the United States by Ballantine Books, an imprint of The Random House Publishing Group, a division of Random House, Inc., New York.

BALLANTINE and colophon are registered trademarks of Random House, Inc.

This book contains an excerpt from the forthcoming hardcover edition of *Final Truth* by Mariah Stewart. This excerpt has been set for this edition only and may not reflect the final content of the forthcoming novel.

Originally published in hardcover in the United States by Ballantine Books, an imprint of The Random House Publishing Group, a division of Random House, Inc., in 2005.

ISBN 0-345-48382-0

Cover design and art: © Tony Greco

Printed in the United States of America

www.ballantinebooks.com

OPM   9   8   7   6   5   4   3   2   1

I have been blessed for ten glorious, fun-filled years to have had the most wonderful, incredible women in my corner. Love and thanks to my personal dream team—Kate Collins, Linda Marrow, Gina Centrello, and, of course, St. Loretta the divine.

"Talk of devils being confined to hell, or hidden by invisibility! We have them by shoals in the crowded towns and cities of the world.

Talk of raising the devil! What need for that, when he is constantly walking to and fro in our streets, seeking whom he will devour."

—Anonymous

PROLOGUE

Cortés City, Santa Estela
Central America
December 2002

AN UNHEALTHY DAMPNESS CLUNG TO THE SHACKS OF
corrugated tin and rotted wood in the poorest section
of a poor city. Beyond the mean dwellings, the river
moved lazily to the ocean just a few scant miles away.
Between the windowless shacks and the river stood
a series of ramshackle warehouses—long abandoned
by the banana trade—and several decaying docks
where only the most dangerous or the most desperate
dared to venture after the sun went down.

A street fair earlier in the evening had lured the residents of the shacks to the town center some blocks
away, where reggae had blended with salsa and hip-
hop to flavor the night. At this late hour, however,
even the most die-hard revelers had staggered home,
drunk and exhausted, leaving the unfriendly streets to
the rats and little else.

The rattle of the old panel truck as it made its way
toward the docks might have drawn attention had
not the local population celebrated themselves into a
stupor. Slowing as it came to the alley between the
last two warehouses, the truck jerked to a stop, but

its engine remained running. Within minutes, a black SUV with tinted windows pulled boldly behind the truck and made a half U-turn. The drivers of both vehicles got out and conversed in hushed tones, their gestures speaking more loudly than their words, as they negotiated a mutually agreeable amount for the truck's cargo. Finally, a deal struck, the driver of the SUV motioned toward his car, and several more men got out. One carried a briefcase. The others carried rifles and made a semicircle around the driver of the SUV.

The truck's cargo door began to rise as flashlights were trained on the opening. No fewer than forty children, stunned in terrified silence, turned their heads to avoid looking directly into the beams as the lights made their way from one dazed young face to the next.

A lone witness watching from the shadows between the buildings debated what action to take. The children—boys and girls, the youngest of whom appeared to be no more than five or six, the oldest perhaps twelve or thirteen—were obviously all headed for slavery or would be filtered into the international child-sex trade before the end of the week. Whichever hardly mattered at that moment to the observer, who knew only that something had to be done, and quickly. But he was wise enough to recognize that caution had to rule. There was one of him, and at least six of them, perhaps more inside the truck.

He'd come upon the scene by accident as he'd

made his way to the last dock, where he was to be picked up by a small boat and whisked away to a larger craft, upon which waited the helicopter that would take him to a small airport in Mexico. From there, he'd be shuttled back to the States. His mission—totally unrelated to the scene unfolding around him—was now complete, and he was expected to give a full report to his superiors at Quantico at eight o'clock the next morning.

From downriver, he could hear the first hum of the boat's motor and knew that he had to make a decision, and fast.

The driver of the SUV directed one of the men to shine the light onto the contents of the briefcase, and as he did so, his face was illuminated as well. The man in the shadows had more than enough time to study the well-lit features. A thin face, sparse dark hair that receded from his forehead, making him appear older than he probably was. Round dark eyes, small and wide set. A nose made flat by at least one run-in with a well-aimed fist. A humorless mouth.

The sound of the boat came closer, though the men in the alley appeared not to hear over the drone of the truck's engine. The man in the shadows counted the rounds in his gun.

He heard a faint shuffle behind him and flattened himself against the wall of the warehouse, his gun drawn, hoping he wouldn't have to fire and call attention to himself. He raised the gun as another shadow eased around the corner where he himself had earlier emerged, then lowered it as he cursed softly.

"Jesus! What the fuck are you doing here?" he growled.

"I might ask you the same question," the newcomer whispered.

"Are you on this? You're working this?"

"Yeah. Been following them for weeks. No one told me you were part of the operation."

"I'm not. I'm supposed to be picked up in about three minutes down on the dock. I'm to brief the director in the morning on—" He caught himself. "On another issue."

"Well, I suggest you get yourself down there, or you're going to miss the boat."

"You're on this, though, right?" He grabbed the newcomer by the arm. "You know what's in that truck, right? You know what's going down here, what's going to happen to those kids? And you're going to take care of it?"

"Hey, relax. I said I was on it. Don't worry, they'll never get the truck out of the alley. We're just waiting for the deal to be completed, then we'll get them all."

"You have backup . . . ?"

"More than enough. Go on, man, get going. Don't miss your boat. The engine's cut, they must be right down at the shoreline. But I'd suggest you go out the way I just came in, down through the little stretch of woods to the water."

"That's one ugly son of a bitch, down there. Don't let him get away."

"Don't worry." There was a pause, then he asked, "You saw him? Saw his face?"

"It's a face I'll never forget. See you back in the States," he said as he slipped into the darkness.

The man remaining in the alley leaned back against the wall and exhaled, a long tired breath laden with anxiety. He wiped the sweat from his forehead with both hands and wondered what the hell he was going to do.

The man with the receding hairline and the flat nose took an envelope from inside his jacket pocket and passed it to his companion, whose eyes darted around the outdoor café.

"Not to worry. No one here cares what we do," he said as he signaled for the waiter to bring another coffee.

His companion merely nodded.

"All right, Shields," the man demanded, "out with it. What's on your mind? Not having second thoughts about our little bit of commerce, are you?"

"Someone saw you last night."

"What do you mean, someone saw . . ." His small eyes grew even smaller. "Saw me?"

"When I came around the building, someone was there, watching you."

"And you left his body where?"

"It's not quite that simple."

The waiter silently traded the old cup for a new one and disappeared back into the café.

"Explain to me what is complicated about getting rid of a witness."

"It wasn't just any witness. He's with the Bureau and he's . . ."

"He's an agent? Another agent saw me with a truckload of kids . . ."

"I told him I was on the case. I told him I was handling it. He doesn't know who you are."

"What the hell was he doing there? That's your job, to make sure that no one else in the Bureau noses around."

"He was on his way to a pickup, on his way back to the States. He just happened to be getting picked up on the docks at the same time you were concluding the deal."

"And the reason you didn't kill him . . . ?"

"If he hadn't made the boat, there'd have been five or six coming ashore to find him. He was supposed to be meeting with the Director this morning. There was no way he wasn't going to be missed immediately."

"All right." The man took a sip of his coffee and tried to calm his thoughts. "You're certain he saw me?"

"Yes."

"Okay. We can handle this. He doesn't know my name, he doesn't know you're involved."

"He thinks I'm shutting the operation down."

"Well, that's fine. You're due back in the States in another few weeks, right? You were reassigned?"

His companion nodded.

"So, you find him, you take care of him then. I'm due back in two months. I can't run the risk that he'll recognize me, Shields. I want him gone. Permanently." The index finger of his right hand tapped methodically on the table. "You know him, right? You know where to find him?"

"Yeah, I know him. And finding him won't be a problem." He rubbed his hand over his mouth, which had gone dry. "He's my cousin."

____CHAPTER____
ONE

Lyndon, Pennsylvania
August 2005

WHAT COULD POSSIBLY BE GOING THROUGH A MAN'S mind at the moment he decides to take the life of a child?

Detective Evan Crosby stared down at the twisted body of Caitlin McGill and wondered.

The young girl's blank eyes stared endlessly at the sun, her mouth open in its final scream. Her thin arms stretched outward, bent at the elbows, to form perfect *L*s. Her feet turned in, toes touching.

"Pigeon-toed."

"What?" Evan turned his head slightly, though his eyes were still on the girl who lay at his feet.

"We used to call people whose feet turned in like that pigeon-toed," one of the crime-scene investigators noted. "How old was this one?"

"Not even fourteen," Evan replied.

"Just like the last one." The CSI shook his head. "Crazy. Just plain damned crazy. She was a real cute kid."

"They were all cute kids."

"This is what, the third? Fourth? In the past two months?"

No one responded to the question, which was rhetorical. Everyone on the scene—from the Avon County, Pennsylvania, detectives to the CSIs to the local police to the medical examiner—knew exactly how many others there'd been since the first of May.

Four.

Jamie Kershaw.

Heidi Fuhrmann.

Andrea Masters.

And now Caitlin McGill.

All between the ages of twelve and fourteen. All pretty girls who attended one of the many private schools that flourished in the Philadelphia suburbs. All with dark red stains down the front of the white cotton shirts that were standard school-uniform attire.

All of them barefoot.

"What's up with that, anyway?" Joe Sullivan, Evan's onetime partner at the Lyndon Police Department, came up the hill from the playground and stopped three feet behind Evan. "Whaddaya suppose he's doing with their shoes?"

"Your guess is as good as mine."

"Poor kid." Sullivan shook his head. "What's your old lady say about it?"

"I haven't had a chance to talk to her yet. She's been away." Evan let the "old lady" comment ride. He'd had that conversation with Joe on more than one occasion. It had never done any good—Joe was Joe and wasn't about to change.

"Guess they keep those FBI profilers pretty busy, eh?"

"Never a shortage of psychos, Joe, you know that." Evan nodded to Dr. Agnes Jenkins, the Avon County medical examiner, as she hurried past.

"Can't remember anything like this, though. But at least he left them where they'd be found quickly." Sullivan's voice was flat, emotionless.

The M.E. bent over the body and began her ministrations. Evan looked away. Over the past eight weeks, he'd had more than his fill of young girls who'd had their throats slashed. He took a few steps back, then turned and went back to his car. The crime scene would be turned over to him once the M.E. was finished, but for now, he'd use this time to check his phone messages, return those calls he could. Start the paperwork on this latest homicide. Get as much work done as he could while he could. It had all the makings of another very long night.

It was well after three in the morning when Evan arrived at his townhouse in West Lyndon. Bone weary, he left his car parked out front, and bleary-eyed, let himself in through the front door. He ignored the pile of mail on the hall table—when had he put that there?—and pretended not to see the blinking red light on his telephone. Messages could wait. He was simply too tired to deal with anyone or anything.

Too tired, too, to make it up the steps, so he let himself drift backward onto the living-room sofa, fully clothed. He'd just closed his eyes when he heard the soft footfall on the stairs. Dismissing it as little more than wishful thinking on his part, he continued to sail toward sleep.

"Evan?" a voice called from the doorway.

More wishful thinking, surely.

"Evan." The voice, gentle, filled with concern, drew closer.

Soft hands caressed his arm. He sighed and smiled in his state of almost-sleep.

"Evan, don't sleep down here. Come up to bed." The voice was in his ear now.

He reached out and touched skin.

"Annie."

He felt her weight as she sat on the edge of the sofa and leaned over him, her lips pressed against the side of his face.

"When did you get here?"

"About nine." She snuggled next to him, and he felt himself relax for the first time in days.

"Why didn't you call me?"

"I heard on the scanner that another body had been found. I didn't want to disturb you. I figured you'd be home when you were finished with what you had to do."

"How long can you stay?"

"I'll be in town through Tuesday. Have you forgotten that my sister is getting married on Friday?"

"Oh, shit. I did forget." He stared up at the ceiling. How could he have forgotten that?

"It's okay. I'm here to remind you. Thursday night, rehearsal dinner. Friday night, wedding. Saturday, sleep until noon. Saturday night, just me and you. Sunday through Tuesday, I'll be staying with my niece, until Mara and Aidan get back. Not much of a honeymoon for them, but at least they'll have a few days to themselves."

"Rewind back to Saturday. Saturday sounded real good." It had been weeks since they'd had a night together alone. There'd been something every weekend for the past month. Four weeks ago, it had been Mara's wedding shower. The past three, either Annie or Evan had been working.

Maybe on Saturday night they could have dinner at their favorite restaurant, he was thinking, then catch a movie. Or maybe they'd just stay at home, just the two of them. That sounded even better.

She lay against him, her head on his chest. His fingers trailed lightly through her soft blond hair.

"How old was she?" she asked softly.

"Thirteen. Almost fourteen."

"Same as the others?"

"Yes."

She fell silent, and he knew that she was working it through. As a psychologist and one of the FBI's most skilled profilers, Annie—Dr. Anne Marie McCall—couldn't help but sort through the pieces.

"Shoes?"

"Missing," he told her through a fog of fatigue. "Just like the others."

"Odd trophy," she murmured.

"I wanted to ask you what you thought about that."

"Tomorrow." She sat up. "We'll talk about that tomorrow. Right now, you think you can make it up the stairs?"

"Doubtful."

"Okay."

She stood, and cool air replaced her warmth. His hand searched for her in the dark, but she had already moved out of reach.

"Where are you going?"

"I'll be right back."

Moments later she returned. He felt the soft flow of a blanket drift over him, the comfort of a pillow under his head.

Bliss.

"Move over." She slid under the blanket and wrapped her arms around him, her body molded to his in the dark.

"Annie . . ."

"Shh. Tomorrow. There's nothing that can't wait until the morning."

He wanted to say something, but his tired brain had stopped communicating with his mouth. Effortlessly, he sailed off into the darkness, where he dreamed of endless closets filled with small bloody shoes that frantic mothers tried to match into pairs.

CHAPTER TWO

"EVAN! HOW'S IT GOING?"

A hand slapped him on the back, and Evan turned to find Will Fletcher, a friend of Annie's from the Bureau, leaning against the bar.

"Some wedding, huh?" Will gestured around the tent with one hand, the other hand wrapped around a glass of champagne.

"Yeah. Beautiful. Glad the weather held for Mara and Aidan. The reports this week weren't too promising." Evan declined the flute offered by a tuxedoed young man and opted for a pilsner of beer.

"That's one beautiful bride." Will nodded at Mara, who, with her tall, handsome groom, was making her way around the room.

"No argument from me," Evan agreed.

"Great idea, don't you think, to have Annie and Julianne give the bride away?"

"Well, since Mara's parents aren't alive, having her sister and her daughter there for her was a really nice touch."

"The kid—Julianne—looks like she's survived her ordeal pretty well."

For a moment, Evan had forgotten that Will had been there when Julianne had been returned after spending seven years living under an assumed name with her father, Jules Douglas. Unable to forgive Mara for having divorced him, Jules had done the one thing he knew would hurt Mara the most. He took their five-year-old daughter, and disappeared.

After years of tracking, the FBI was finally led to the Valley of the Angels, a Wyoming ranch that was part of the network of one self-proclaimed evangelist who called himself Reverend Prescott, whose mission in life was to "rescue" young drug-addicted runaways from the streets, only to clean them up and sell them to the highest bidder on the Internet. Jules's mathematical wizardry had come in handy when it came to cooking the reverend's books. Jules was currently in prison awaiting trial for kidnapping and a host of other charges related to his work at the Valley of the Angels. Julianne had been present when her father was arrested, just a few days after she'd been reunited with her mother. All in all, it had been one hell of a year for everyone involved.

"From all accounts, Julianne seems to be doing just fine. She seems to be accepting Aidan as a stepfather—Mara would have postponed the wedding if she hadn't been able to handle it—and Annie has been keeping tabs on her. She thinks Julianne's doing great." Evan's searching eyes found Annie, halfway across the tent.

He willed her to look at him, and eventually, she did. She smiled and winked, and continued her conversation with one of the guests.

Will said something else, and Evan nodded and excused himself. The band was starting to play an old ballad from the forties and he wanted to dance with Annie, wanted to feel her arms around him, wanted to feel her pressed against him. He smiled at the person she was chatting with—a man he vaguely recognized as someone from her office—and took her hand.

"It's time to dance with your guy," he told her as he led her to the dance floor.

"Gladly." She moved into his arms and swayed with him.

"What's with this forties music?" he asked.

"Mr. Shields asked them to play it."

"He asked them to play the last two sappy songs. Since when does the father of the groom get to submit his own playlist?"

"Since no one has told him he couldn't."

Out of the corner of one eye, Evan watched the Shields clan gather. They were all now, or had been at one time, in the FBI. Aidan, the groom. Connor, his older brother and best man. Thomas, their father, and Frank, their uncle and Thomas's brother, both now retired. The cousins—Frank's kids—Andrew, Brendan, Grady, and Mia, the lone female in the family. Two generations of FBI, eight in all.

But of course, there had been nine. It was the ninth

Shields—Thomas's middle son, Dylan—who was on everyone's mind right then.

"Annie!" Grady shouted over the heads of the other dancers. "We need you!"

Evan thought he'd felt her stiffen slightly, but she smiled and kept on dancing.

"We're about to drink a toast to Dylan, Annie"— Brendan made his way through the crowd and took Annie's arm—"and we can't do it right without you."

Annie appeared slightly uncomfortable, as if unsure what to do, but did not protest when Brendan tugged her along.

"Evan, do you mind . . . ?" she asked.

"You go on," he said. "It's okay . . ."

"If you're sure . . . ?"

"Sure." He shrugged, and watched her disappear into the crowd.

A few minutes later, Thomas Shields asked the band to stop playing so that he could propose a toast to his son.

Not Aidan, the groom. But Dylan, the one who'd been killed in an undercover drug deal gone bad more than two years earlier.

Dylan, everyone's favorite, the best of the Shields brothers. Best athlete. Best student. Best friend. Best agent. The golden boy whose memory would forever remain untarnished to those who had known and loved him.

Dylan, who had been engaged to marry Annie.

Evan signaled the bartender for a beer, then leaned

back against the bar and took a long drink while listening to the tributes, one after another, being paid to the fallen hero.

"If they keep this up much longer, they'll turn the wedding reception into a wake," he muttered.

"What?" The man next to him leaned forward, thinking Evan had been addressing him.

"I said, nice that they're remembering Dylan," he said dryly.

"Oh, hell of a guy. Damn shame, what happened to him." The man shook his gray head. "Just a damn shame. And him all set to marry that pretty little Annie McCall. Broke her heart, the day he died, I can tell you that. Just a tragedy."

The man appeared to wipe a tear from his face, and Evan fought an urge to roll his eyes.

"Friend of his, were you?" the man asked.

"Ah, no. We never met. I'm actually a friend of the bride."

"Then you must know Annie."

"Yes, of course. I know Annie."

"They sure do love her, don't they?" He nodded to the cluster that the Shields family made on the opposite side of the room. "But then again, what's not to love about Annie, right? Damn shame she had the love of her life snatched away from her like that."

Evan's stomach began to knot. He put the beer down on the bar and started to excuse himself, but his companion kept talking.

"Makes it worse for everyone, not knowing, you know?"

"Not knowing what?"

"Not knowing who pulled the trigger. Never did find the shooter. I think that would have helped everyone, if they had closure, you know?"

"I'm sure the Bureau investigated thoroughly."

"They did, but nothing came of it. Sometimes it happens like that. It's not always like it is on those TV shows, you know."

Evan knew.

The eulogies finally over, the band began to play again. Evan looked around for Annie, but found her still surrounded by the Shields family. When he saw Mara standing along the edge of the dance floor chatting with a girlfriend, he put his beer down and made his way to her.

"May I have the honor of dancing with the bride?" He held out his arms.

"I thought you'd never ask." Mara smiled and joined him on the dance floor.

"Beautiful wedding, Mara," he said.

"Oh, thank you. I'm so glad it didn't get humid. You know how it gets here in Pennsylvania in the summer. It can really swelter."

"Well, you lucked out, all around." He moved her around the dance floor in time to the music. "Everything is perfect."

She nodded somewhat absently, and he caught her looking over his shoulder.

"What?" he asked.

"We should be leaving soon, but I'm afraid it's going to be hard to tear Aidan away from his family."

"On his wedding night? I doubt it."

"It's been a difficult day for them—for Aidan and his dad and his brother and the rest of them. This is really the first big family event since Dylan died, and they're all missing him so much." Her eyes flickered, and she looked up at him. "Probably not so easy for you, either, but for a different reason, right?"

He shrugged.

"The Shieldses are a tough group, Evan," Mara said, as if that were all the explanation necessary.

"Honey," he said softly, "it's your wedding. They should let you have your day and not turn it into a memorial service for a man who's been dead for more than two years."

Her cheeks flushed, and he instantly regretted his words.

"I'm sorry, Mara. I shouldn't have . . ."

"It's okay. And you're right. I know I should say something, but they are just a little intimidating when they're all together. And I don't think any of them ever got over him dying like that, the way he did. I know Aidan is still having a lot of issues because of the way he died."

"Look, how about if I go on over there and see if I can get Aidan's attention."

"That would be great. Thanks, Evan. Maybe just

let him know that he needs to watch the time, and that I'm ready to leave whenever he is."

He left Mara with the same friend she'd been chatting with earlier and somehow managed to breach the edge of the circle that was gathered around Thomas Shields and his two sons. Between Aidan and Connor sat Annie, looking very much a part of the clan. Evan managed to catch Aidan's eye and mouthed that Mara needed to talk to him. A quick glance at his watch reminded Aidan why. He nodded and excused himself quietly. Evan stepped back to let him pass, pausing, trying to decide the best way to get Annie's attention. But she was absorbed in a story Grady was telling about one time when they were younger and he'd had the bad judgment to challenge Dylan to a pitching contest, the prize being Grady's new bike. Dylan, who'd been scouted by several pro baseball teams as a senior in college, had all but taken his cousin's head off with his fastball and, at the end of the exercise, had driven off on Grady's bike, whistling "Take Me Out to the Ball Game."

Evan stepped back and away from the crowd. Still on the fringes, he watched Annie for a few more minutes, but she never glanced his way. He walked out of the tent toward the parking lot and disappeared into the night.

He drove around for forty minutes trying to decide what to do. When his phone rang, he answered on the first ring.

"Crosby."

He listened for a moment, then turned his car around in the next parking lot.

"I'm on my way."

He headed for Belle Mead, a small town four miles away, where another young girl lay dead, and tried to ignore the fact that his first reaction had been relief of sorts for having been provided with an excuse for having left the wedding.

He knew that it was Annie he'd left behind, and that sooner or later he'd have to deal with that. For now, he could simply tell her he'd been called away, and rather than making a scene at the wedding, he'd thought it best to just slip out quietly. Surely she'd understand. She was, after all, with the FBI.

She's also a shrink, he reminded himself, and more likely than not would see right through that smoke screen.

Well, so be it. He'd deal with it.

And sooner or later, they'd both have to deal with the fact that while Dylan Shields was gone, he sure as hell wasn't forgotten.

____CHAPTER____
THREE

ANNE MARIE SAT AT THE RED LIGHT AND SPEED-dialed Evan's cell phone for the fourth time. He always had his phone with him, and it was always turned on. Why wasn't he picking up?

Maybe he's in a meeting and has the volume turned down. Or maybe he's at a crime scene and can't take the call. She glanced at the clock on the dashboard. It was almost two in the afternoon. He could be home, sleeping. Maybe he'd been out on a case all night and had only been home for a few hours. Not unusual for a homicide detective to play catch-up during the day if he'd been up for more than twenty-four hours.

She'd find out soon enough. She was less than six miles from West Lyndon and Evan's townhouse.

She closed up her phone and tossed it onto the passenger's seat, and tried to ignore the uneasiness that had been haunting her since she'd looked for Evan at the wedding and found that he was gone.

That had been three days ago. She hadn't heard from him since, despite having left several messages for him on his home, office, and cell phones.

Not a good sign. Definitely not a good sign.

As she turned the corner onto Evan's street, she was surprised to see his car parked out front. Annie pulled into the space behind his and turned off her engine. Walking alongside then in front of his car, she placed her hand on the hood. It was cold. The car had been there for a while.

Okay, so I was probably right about him sleeping.

She slipped the key he'd given her three months ago, when their relationship passed from occasional to steady, into the lock. Assuming that he was in fact asleep, she opened the door and quietly entered the townhouse then paused in the foyer. From the basement, she could hear music. Loud blues, which grew louder with every step she took in the direction of the steps leading downstairs.

"Evan?" she called.

"Yo!"

Well, if nothing else, he was awake.

She descended the steps into the long, narrow space Evan had been working on for the past year. His goal was to have a fully operational family room—complete with wide-screen TV, a bar, and a built-in stereo—before next Christmas. For months, he'd barely had time to work on it. Today, he appeared to be determined to make up for lost time.

In the center of the room, Evan stood over a table saw. At his feet, a pile of two-by-fours was stacked unevenly. He turned on the saw and proceeded to cut first one, then another, of the lengths of wood until they were all of a uniform size. Annie sat on the third step from the bottom, watching the pile grow, making mental bets with herself as to how many minutes would pass before he would turn around and talk to her.

Finally, she stood up, unplugged the saw, and turned off the radio.

"Why, yes, I was able to find a ride home from the wedding, nice of you to inquire."

"Any one of a dozen people would have been more than happy to see you home on Friday night. I knew you'd have no problem getting a ride." No longer able to cut, he started to stack the wood in an obsessively neat pile, an attempt on his part, she knew, to concentrate on anything other than her.

"That's it? That's all you have to say?" Her eyes narrowed. "You knew someone else would take me home after you dumped me?"

"I didn't dump you. I got called out."

"Not another . . . ?"

"Yup."

"Same as the others?"

"The same—but different this time."

"Are you going to elaborate?"

"Same MO. Throat slashed. Vic is the same age as the others, but no one seems to know who she is. No ID. No one's reported her missing. And she's Hispanic. The others have all been white, reported missing before the bodies were found. This girl, it's like she came out of nowhere. I'm not sure what to make of that."

"You're sure it's the same guy?"

"Like I said, same MO. Same cause of death, the missing shoes—"

"Any chance of a copycat?"

"We never released the details, no one outside the investigation knows about the shoes."

"I realize this is an important case, but you could have taken one minute on Friday night to tell me you were leaving."

"I couldn't have gotten to you even if I'd tried."

"What's that supposed to mean?"

"It means you were in the Shields zone. No outsiders allowed."

"That's ridiculous."

"Is it? I did come over to the table, but I couldn't get through the throng. Couldn't even get your attention, you were so caught up with whatever story whichever Shields was telling at the time."

"If I didn't know you better, I'd think you were jealous."

"Maybe you don't know me so well, after all."

"Are you serious? You're jealous?"

"Let's just put it this way, Annie. It's really tough having to compete with a dead man for your attention. Especially when that dead man was, by all accounts, an absolute paragon of—"

"Stop it, Evan. Just . . . stop it."

She turned her back and started toward the stairs. She got up to the second step and turned back to him.

"I will say this one time, so listen up." She took a deep breath. "If you are waiting for me to tell you that I did not love Dylan, you are going to be very disappointed. I did love him. I loved him with all my heart. I planned to marry him and grow old with him. When he was killed, I thought I'd never feel that way about anyone, ever again. I accepted that."

"Annie . . ."

"Don't. You started this, you will let me finish."

She came down off the steps.

"The first time I met you, I knew how I was going to end up feeling about you. Don't ask me to explain it because I can't. But I met you, and I thought, Well, now, how about that? Lightning can strike twice, apparently. Then we began dating, and for a time, I was confused, because I wasn't sure I understood how anyone could be lucky enough to find that kind of love more than once. And I knew that I loved you, pretty much right from the time we started seeing each other. There was just something in you . . . something so good and honest, something that just spoke to my heart." She took a long breath.

"Don't take this the wrong way, but there was something else I saw in you that I saw in Dylan as well, and I don't mean this to sound as if I'm comparing you to him. I'm not. It wasn't that you were alike. It's more in the way he cared about what he did. It might sound corny, but he took the whole business of fighting crime very seriously. He was always on the side of the victims, always stood for those who couldn't stand for themselves. I loved that in him. I saw all those same things in you—that same determination, that same dedication—and I loved it in you, too. I really felt that in spite of what had happened, I would have my happily-ever-after. With you."

Evan rubbed the back of his neck, then shoved his hands into his pockets. He just didn't know what to say.

"I'm sorry that you felt left out on Friday. I have to be very honest with you—I did feel uncomfortable, after a while, the way Dylan's family was turning my sister's wedding into a sort of memorial service. But you have to understand that this is a very close family. In some ways, they are still trying to come to grips with Dylan's death. His father will probably never accept it. He's still reeling from it. I feel bad for all of them. It hasn't been easy."

"You didn't seem to be protesting too much when I saw you."

"What was I supposed to do, Evan? Tell them all to just get over it, to get on with their lives?"

"You didn't have to sit there all night and be part of the wake. It looked to me that you fit right in."

"I did not know what else to do, Evan. I did not know how to gracefully walk away. They see me as a link to him. Especially Thomas. Dylan loved me; they have to love me, too. If he hadn't died when he did, I'd have been one of them."

"You are one of them."

"This is a family that has been shattered by a death they believe wasn't supposed to happen. It makes it all the more difficult for them to accept because they still don't really know what happened that night. That wound is still festering. That one of their own was murdered, and none of them—none of the big bad FBI Shieldses—has been able to bring his killer to justice."

"Someone else said something like that, someone I was talking to near the bar. He said that the FBI still didn't know what went wrong."

"True. And it haunts everyone, everyone who knew him."

"Are you haunted by him, Annie?"

"Not *by* him, maybe, but *for* him, I guess. I wish I did know what happened that night. I wish I did know who killed him, and why. I wish there could be justice for him. It was set up to look like it was part of that undercover drug deal, but no one ever thought that felt right, and no one has been able to come up with an alternative that makes any sense, either."

"What didn't feel right? It's not unusual to have an undercover op go bad."

"The dealers Dylan and Aidan were meeting didn't arrive until after Dylan had been shot. They pulled into the alley just after, and of course, the agents in the building across the alley opened fire, and—"

"So you're thinking if the dealers had been onto the op, they wouldn't have shown up at all. If anything, they'd have sent their henchmen to kill Dylan and Aidan and simply disappeared."

"Exactly. But these men came to the buy, just like they'd planned. And they all denied having known that Dylan and Aidan were law. They all swore they had no clue."

"Of course they'd deny it. No one in his right mind admits to setting up the FBI."

"True. But no way, if they'd shot an FBI agent minutes before, would they have shown up at all. That's just plain stupid, and these guys have been at this a long time. They're far from stupid." She shrugged. "And that's what's so hard to accept for everyone. Dylan's killer got away with murder, and no one has the slightest idea who he is. That's what keeps it raw, keeps it stuck in everyone's craw. Not knowing why, or who."

"Does anyone really think they'll ever answer those questions?"

"Realistically, no. But they'll never stop asking, never stop talking about it."

Evan shook his head somewhat vaguely.

"What?"

"I'm sorry for what happened to him, I swear I am. But I can't fight them for the rest of my life, Annie. There are just too damned many of them. Your sister married into the family; they're always going to be around." He took a deep breath. "I'm always going to feel as if I'm sleeping in a dead man's bed. I'm just not sure how long I can go on doing that."

"Oh God, Evan, I had no idea you felt that way. I'm so sorry. I'm sorry I can't change the situation," she said softly. "But I can't change what was or what is. I'm so sorry, for both of us. I was hoping that you and I . . ."

Her voice trailed off and she made a gesture—a sort of "I give up" flutter of her hands—before going up the steps and directly to the front door. Once in her car, she sat quietly for a few moments, trying to compose herself, fighting back the tears that had been threatening to fall, trying to stop the hollow feeling inside her from spreading, but it soon engulfed her. With a sense of sorrow and regret, she put the car in gear and headed toward the airport. It was going to be a long trip back to Virginia.

Evan sat on his back steps, his forearms resting on his thighs, mindlessly peeling the label from his bottle of beer, dropping the little scraps of paper at his feet. The deck he'd started building in the spring was just as he'd left it two months ago, mostly frame, some lit-tle bit of floorboard. Incomplete, like the basement.

Like his life.

Well, he'd almost had it all, hadn't he? The girl, the job, the future he'd always dreamed of. Then, of course, he had to go and let that green-eyed monster take over his intellect, had to go and open his big mouth. Well, that was the end of that. Shit, he must have sounded like a bratty adolescent who'd caught his girl walking with another guy to her locker.

He blew out a long breath that was filled with exasperation and self-doubt. He had some big decisions to make, and he'd have to make them now, before things between Annie and him got any worse.

Like they could get worse.

He went inside, dropped the empty beer bottle into the glass recycling bin, and got himself another, then went back outside. He walked the deck frame, balancing carefully as he followed the narrow supports that would eventually be covered with flooring.

If I get that far.

He stood at one end, the end where he'd planned on building steps that would go into the narrow backyard. A few months ago, back in the early spring, he and Annie had stood out here and discussed flower beds. She'd been excited about the prospect, and they'd spent an afternoon talking about how he would go about digging beds around the entire perimeter of the yard so that she could plant her favorites—roses, peonies, hollyhocks. All the staples of an old-fashioned garden, she'd told him, just like the one her mother had planted in the tiny yard of their twin home in Philadelphia's University City back when her father was a professor at Drexel. Annie's cheeks had flushed with the joy of that memory, and her eyes had sparkled at the prospect of re-creating her mother's garden.

Evan had dug up one section that weekend, a short piece across the back face, and the following day,

Annie had gone to the nursery and bought three peonies, which they'd planted together.

"The man at the nursery said that they won't bloom for a few years, but that's okay." She'd smiled up at him. "We can wait them out together. Just think how much we'll appreciate those first flowers when they finally bloom . . ."

That had been the last time they'd worked on it. The responsibilities that came with both their jobs had intervened. Now Annie's garden lay before him, just one more loose end in his life. Just one more thing he'd started, but never got around to finishing.

Evan put the beer down on the back-porch steps and went into his garage. He emerged a minute later, carrying a shovel. He went straight to one side of the fence, walked off a depth of three feet, and began to dig. When he finished with one side, he began to dig along the other, until the entire fence was framed with a newly dug bed.

He stood in the middle of the yard, panting slightly from exertion. If she came back, the garden would be ready for her to plant.

He leaned upon the shovel handle and asked himself just how likely it was that she'd come back.

"Fat chance, Crosby," he muttered aloud. "Why would she?"

Because she loves me. His inner voice spoke without hesitation.

Dragging the shovel, he walked back to the porch,

took a long swig of lukewarm beer, and told himself something he already knew.

The ball is in my court. First, I need to decide how I feel about her.

Do I love her? Yes.

Do I want her? Yes.

How far am I willing to go for her?

As far as it takes . . .

But how, he wondered, could they plan a life together, with the specter of her dead fiancé standing between them?

As long as questions about Dylan's life remained unanswered, Evan knew he and Annie could not move forward, could not plan a life together. It was as simple as that.

"Okay, then. So that's the bottom line." He muttered the words aloud, acknowledging what had to be done.

Maybe he'd known all along. Maybe Friday night had just brought it all into focus.

He dialed Annie's cell phone and was disappointed when he got her voice mail. Taking a deep breath, he began.

"Annie, I'm sorry. I acted like a fool. A very immature fool. I'm trying to put myself in your place, and I guess maybe I'd feel the same way. If something happened to you . . . well, I doubt I'd ever rest until I found the truth. I'd owe you that much. Just as you owe Dylan. So. We need to talk."

He paused, then added, before he hung up, "I love

you, Annie. With all my heart. I'm not willing to spend the rest of my life without you. If finding Dylan's killer is what we need to do in order for this thing to work between us, then let's do it. Let's try to figure it out so that Dylan can be at peace. And so can we . . ."

He tried to think of something else to say, then realized he'd said it all. He disconnected the call and slipped the phone back into his pants pocket. There was still another hour or so of daylight. The local nursery was only ten minutes away. Maybe he'd have time to pick out a rosebush or two.

On his way to his car, his phone rang.

"Crosby." He smiled, anticipating the sound of her voice.

"Evan, we need you. We've found another body . . ."

"Where?" His adrenaline began to flow, and Annie's garden was, once again, forgotten.

____CHAPTER____
FOUR

IT WAS FOUR IN THE MORNING BEFORE EVAN HAD A chance to check his messages. His message to Annie had been received—apparently well received, since she'd asked him to return the call, regardless of the time.

"Hi." She answered the phone on the third ring, her voice heavy with sleep.

"Hi."

"You still on the job?"

"Yeah." He glanced around at the crowd of law enforcement personnel that seemed to grow by the minute.

"Like the others?"

"Like the others, but different. Same difference as the last one."

"She's Hispanic. No ID. And no one reported her missing."

"Right. 'Course, maybe by morning, we'll have gotten a call. Someone might be looking for her by now, or maybe someone thinks she's at a friend's house . . . there could be a hundred maybes when you're dealing with a kid, you know?"

"I know. I saw your chief on TV yesterday."

"The press has been all over this. It's national news. The grandfather of one of the victims is an ambassador."

"I saw him on CNN."

"So did I. He had some harsh words for the D.A."

"Yeah."

The awkward pause he'd been avoiding settled in. It was now or never.

"Look, Annie, I . . . I had this idea. I'm thinking that, well, I'm thinking maybe we should take one more look at Dylan's death. I'm thinking you're right, to want to clear this thing for him. And I have to be honest with you, looking at this from a strictly selfish point of view, I'm thinking it's going to be that much harder for you and me to move forward with our own relationship while there's still this long, dangling thread in your life."

He hesitated, expecting her to break in, but she remained silent, so he went on.

"So, maybe just one look, to see if, I don't know, maybe something will jump out at us. Then, maybe, you and I . . . well, then maybe we can see where we are . . . where we both want this thing to go . . ."

Evan was pacing along a berm at the edge of the clearing where the latest body had been found. "I know the Bureau's best has been on this, so I guess it sounds presumptuous for me to even suggest it—"

"I don't think it's presumptuous at all," Annie said softly.

"You don't?"

"No. You're a great investigator. And there's always the chance that a fresh eye might see something everyone else has missed. But are you sure you want to spend your time on this?"

"I'm sure that I want this to work between us. I'm sure that the only way that's going to happen is for you to feel that you've done everything you can to do right by Dylan's memory. The way I see it, as long as Dylan's murderer is out there, you're always going to be looking for him. Not that I blame you. I understand why it's important. But it just seems to me that in order for you to move on with your life, you need to know that everything that could be done has been done."

"That's very insightful."

"And you thought you were the only one in this relationship with a little psychology know-how," he joked, knowing there was a vast difference between his three undergrad psych courses and her doctorate. "There's no guarantee that this case will ever be solved. But I think it's worth one more look."

"Thank you." Her voice caught. "Dylan deserves to have his killer brought to justice. I know Aidan and Connor and a bunch of his cousins have looked at the case, but not one of them was able to uncover anything new. So chances are, nothing will change. But one more look—sure, it's worth the time. I'll be in the office tomorrow. I'll see what I can get my hands on."

"Can you send me a copy of whatever you find?"

"I'd rather bring it up this weekend."

"Even better."

"But you're swamped with your case. I'd better send copies of the reports overnight. That way, when we finally do get together, you'll have had time to read them through. Maybe something will pop out at you."

"Sounds like a plan."

"Evan, I can't thank you enough. For understanding. For putting your own feelings aside—I know this has to be hard for you."

"Not nearly as hard as the thought of losing you."

"You wouldn't have lost me over this. My loving you is separate from wanting what's right for Dylan."

"I know that, but I also understand that you'll never be completely happy as long as you feel he's not at rest, Annie. I know your Irish soul."

"It's his Irish soul that worries me. I just need to know it's found peace."

"We're going to do our best."

"One thing you need to know . . ."

"What's that?"

"I am happy with you; I've been happy with you. And I do love you. Without reservation. Regardless of the outcome, I will never forget that you offered to do this, with the case you're already working on. I don't know any other man who would be as sensitive as you are to this whole thing with Dylan."

The crime-scene technicians had finished processing the scene and signaled that they were waiting for him.

"Annie, I have to go. You get those reports and send them up; I'll find the time to look them over. Then we'll talk . . ."

Dan Crimmons, the Prattsville chief of police, was walking up the hill toward him. Evan knew he'd have a million questions about the crime scenes in Lyndon and the other parts of the county where bodies had been found. In the distance, he could see the lights from the cars parked along the road. Newspaper, magazine, and TV reporters and their cameramen were gathering again.

Evan switched off his phone and walked down the hill to meet Crimmons, thinking that his instincts had served him well. Annie wouldn't be completely at peace until Dylan was. He would give it his best effort.

It hadn't been false modesty on his part to say that he felt a bit presumptuous, taking on something that the Bureau's finest had already looked into. Dylan's brothers and cousins were all known to be top-notch agents. What were the chances he'd succeed where they had all failed? If it helped Annie to know that they'd done their best, and that helped her to move on, what did they have to lose?

Nothing at all, he reassured himself as he walked

down the hill, his hand extended in greeting to the chief.

"Chief Crimmons, I see the sharks are right on the scent. How many officers do you think you can spare to keep the press from getting anywhere near the crime scene . . . ?"

Annie scooped the folder into her arms and strolled casually back to her office. It wasn't that she was doing anything wrong—she did sign out the file—but she was just a little reluctant to advertise the fact that she was looking over the records relative to Dylan's death yet again. People might think she was obsessed.

She read through the now-familiar reports, looking for something, anything, that might catch her eye. But there was nothing out of the ordinary. She'd read through the accounts of the agents who were present that night, including Aidan, who had been badly wounded and at one point, early on, wasn't expected to make it. Thank God he did, Annie thought. Losing Dylan had been hard enough. Aidan had been her friend long before he'd become her brother-in-law.

The alarm on her watch reminded her that she had a lecture to deliver to a group of agents-in-training at two. She closed the file and pushed it to one side of her desk, then grabbed her purse from the back of her chair.

"Hey, Annie, how's it going?" Brendan Shields poked his head in through the doorway.

"Great, Brendan, thanks. I was just on my way to—"

"Was that a great wedding or what? And Mara was just the most beautiful bride. Dylan would have been pleased to see his little brother married to your little sister. Funny, isn't it, the way that worked out?"

"I guess it worked out the way it was supposed to."

"Nice guy, that detective you were with, by the way. A couple of the guys said they'd worked a few cases with him up in Pennsylvania, said he was top-notch."

"Evan Crosby. He's good, yes. I've worked with him, too."

"Well, good luck with him, if that's the way it's going for you and him. God knows you're due for something good, Annie."

"Thank you, Brendan. That's really very nice of you."

"Hey, is that the file on the McNamara case?" He looked beyond her to her desk. "I just stopped down at the records room and Angie told me she'd signed it out to you yesterday."

"The McNamara file is in the trunk of my car. That"—she nodded toward her desk—"is Dylan's file."

Brendan raised an eyebrow.

"Evan and I were talking the other day, and we thought we'd give it one more look-see." She shrugged as if the idea had little merit. "We just thought maybe . . ."

"Maybe this time something might jump out at you?"

"I guess. I know it's a long shot."

"You know we've all looked at that file so many times it's a miracle we haven't worn the ink right off the pages."

"I know. I guess we just thought maybe fresh eyes . . ."

"Hey, sure, why not? Can't hurt. God knows we weren't able to come up with anything. Good luck with it."

"I've got to run," she told him, "but if you walk out with me, I can give you the McNamara file right now."

"Great. You have everything you need here?" He turned off the light, then followed her into the hall. "By the way, you don't happen to know where my cousin Connor is, do you?"

"Über-agent Shields? No." She laughed. "No one ever knows where Connor is, Brendan. You know that. He comes in, gets his secret assignment, and leaves before anyone even knows he's been in the building."

"Yeah. The ultimate secret-agent man. No one was happier than Connor when the Bureau expanded its operations after 9/11. I think he was the first from the Bureau to apply. He just eats up that covert stuff. My sister, Mia, made the comment the other night at the wedding that maybe he should have joined the CIA."

"Very funny. Did you try his cell phone?"

"No. Grady was looking for him this morning; I was just wondering if you knew if he was still in town."

"Sorry. I haven't seen or heard from him since Friday night. But if by some chance I do, I'll let him know to call Grady."

"Good enough. Well, you're going to have to push the speed limit to get down to Quantico on time as it is, so let's hope this is one of the days when the elevator actually works." He poked the down arrow.

"I'll be fine, as long as the traffic doesn't back up somewhere along the way." She watched the elevator lights descend slowly from the upper floors. "Or the elevator doesn't pass us by."

The elevator pinged as the doors slid open, then pinged again as they closed. It took less than forty-five seconds to reach the lobby. Annie, who detested elevators, counted off every one.

They passed through the lobby to the parking garage, where Annie had parked three cars in from the stairwell.

"You were here early," Brendan noted.

"I had to be. I'd left the notes for my lecture in my office. Don't ask me where my head was."

She unlocked the trunk of her car and reached in for the file she'd been studying in the hopes of coming up with a profile for the killer who'd been terrorizing a small town in Idaho.

"Any thoughts on this one?" Brendan asked as he tucked the file under his arm.

"He's young and he's angry. Probably was in the service, my guess, right out of high school. I'd put my money on an early discharge, not necessarily honorable. He has definite issues with women." She slammed the trunk lid. "I can send you an e-mail with a copy of my full evaluation when I get home tonight. My notes are all there."

"Great. Appreciate it." Brendan kissed her on the cheek. "You take care, Annie. And listen, if it's what you want, I hope that all works out with . . ."

"Evan."

"Sorry. His name slipped my mind, honest to God. That wasn't intended as an insult."

She smiled as she got into the car. Brendan and his sister, Mia, were probably the only members of the Shields family for whom that might be true. Andrew and Grady had made no effort to disguise their disapproval of Annie showing up at a Shields wedding with another man.

"Call me if you have any questions after you get my memo," she told him as she started her car.

"Will do." He stepped back from the car as she pulled from the parking spot. Annie waved as she headed toward the exit.

The highway ahead was clogged as a result of an unfortunate combination of volume and a three-car accident. Annie debated taking an alternate route, one that would take her through several small towns and would cost her at least forty minutes in time. She weighed the known delay against the uncertainty of the tie-up on the highway, and opted for back roads.

It was turning out to be a wonderful, sunny day. At times like this, she wished she'd chosen the convertible over the sedan she'd recently bought, but she opened the sunroof, rolled down the windows, and slipped Enya into the CD player. The sun on the top of her head soothed, as did the music. She felt herself relaxing for the first time in days.

Well, it had been an unusual week.

First, there'd been the wedding, and all that it entailed. It wasn't every day your sister got married.

Annie thought back to Mara's first wedding, to Jules Douglas.

"I never did like that pompous ass," Annie muttered, recalling how her first reaction to Jules had been right on the money. "Slick little bastard."

But Mara had fallen for him, and nothing Annie could say had opened her sister's eyes. In the end, Annie recognized as fact, when someone is hell-bent on making a mistake, sometimes you just have to stand back and let them.

And what a mistake it had been. From early on in their marriage, Jules had betrayed his wife with an endless string of his college students who'd fallen for him in the same way Mara had. By the time Mara had discovered his affair with a fellow faculty member, their daughter was five years old. Mara asked for and was granted a divorce. The day after it was finalized,

Jules took Julianne and disappeared for seven long, agonizing years.

Well, he wouldn't get that chance again. Even with his plea bargain to testify against Reverend Prescott, they were going to keep his sorry ass behind bars until he was so old he wouldn't even remember his name.

Any of them, she thought dryly, recalling that Jules had taken several aliases while on the run.

She stopped at a red light and watched a young woman casually push a stroller across the street. Life in these small towns . . . Annie smiled to herself. Everyone takes their time.

And why not? We spend too much time hurrying along, not noticing our surroundings, not—

The light had turned green, and the driver of the pickup behind her apparently wasn't of a small-town mind. This was a reality she understood. She pulled away from the light and wondered if the accident on the interstate had been cleared away yet. She turned on the radio and scanned for a news station.

Her finger paused on the station where Bono sang about "one love." Dylan had been a huge U2 fan and had loved that song. Hearing it never failed to bring back the memory of a drive they'd once made to the Outer Banks, when he'd played the CD over and over so many times she finally threatened to toss it out the window as they crossed the Wright Memorial Bridge.

Thoughts of Dylan led inevitably to thoughts of Evan.

Initially, Annie had been surprised at Evan's reaction to Dylan's seeming presence at the wedding. After all, it was Dylan's brother who was getting married, and the first gathering of the clan after Dylan's death—except for his funeral. It was bound to be emotional. But after looking back on the night, on the way events had unfolded, she had to admit that things might have gone a bit far. Not might, she told herself. Did. Thomas Shields simply could not move past his pain. When she'd realized that Evan had left, she had secretly suspected that the Shieldses' focus on their fallen brother could possibly have had something to do with it.

But she'd been genuinely surprised at Evan's suggestion that they take one last look at Dylan's death. While she refused to delude herself into thinking that they'd solve the case, the fact that Evan understood, that he made the gesture, endeared him to her even more. She hadn't been exaggerating when she'd told him that finding him, realizing that she could find love again, had stunned her. She'd not even considered looking, assuming that she'd spend the rest of her life alone. She had pretty much made her peace with that. No one, she'd figured, had the right to expect that kind of total love, total devotion, more than once in a lifetime. It had shocked her to learn it could happen—and that it had happened to her.

She was so deep in thought that she missed the call on her cell phone. She picked it up and looked at the screen. Connor. Speak of the devil. She hit the automatic-dial number and he answered on the first ring.

"Hey, sorry. I missed your call by about one ring," she told him. "Where are you?"

"Now, you know that if I told you, we'd have to kill you."

She smiled at the overused quip, which, in his case, could be true.

"Did you talk to Grady? I saw Brendan this morning. He said Grady was trying to reach you."

"We spoke. He just wanted to know if I'd be around this week."

"Are you?"

"No. I won't be around for a while."

"Okay, I won't even ask."

"Thank you."

"So what's up?"

"I just wanted to congratulate you and Mara on the wedding. You did a great job putting it together. Everything was just terrific, Annie."

"Thanks, Connor. I never realized how much work a simple wedding could be. But we did manage to pull it off. Everyone seemed to have a good time."

"Well, that's another thing that I wanted to talk to you about. I think I need to apologize on behalf of all the Shieldses for having maybe misdirected some of the focus."

"Meaning?"

"You're sweet, Annie, but I know you know what

I'm talking about. Too much Dylan, too little Aidan. We owe him an apology, too."

"I doubt he felt slighted."

"Knowing Aidan, no, I'm sure he didn't. But looking back over the night, one thing seemed to lead to another . . ."

"It's okay, Connor."

"I just feel a little embarrassed about it."

"Connor Shields, international man of mystery, sheepish? Puh-leeze."

He laughed.

"Anyway, it's done. Don't give it another thought."

"Must have made things uncomfortable for the new guy."

Ah, she thought. *That's what this is really about.*

"Evan was fine with it."

"That why he left early?"

"He's a homicide detective, Connor. He got a call . . ."

"Oh. Okay. Just wanted to make sure we didn't somehow mess that up for you."

"Not at all. As a matter of fact, he's made an incredibly generous offer."

"What's that?"

"He thinks we should take another look at the circumstances surrounding Dylan's death."

A long silence followed. Finally, Connor said, "Why would he do that?"

"He understands that something inside me will be

unsettled as long as Dylan's killer has gotten away with his murder."

"And he thinks he's going to be the one to solve it? Is he aware that it's been investigated more than once? That we've all looked into it?"

"He knows all that, Connor. And he's not going into this thinking he's going to show anyone up, or that he's going to take one look at the file and say, 'Aha! I know who the killer is!' I think it's his way of showing me that he respects Dylan's memory and wants to give it his best shot."

Another silence.

"He must be quite a guy, this homicide detective of yours."

"He is, Connor."

"Then tell him if he needs anything, if he has any questions, to talk to me."

"I'll do that. Thanks."

"Listen, I have to run. You take care, Annie, and remember, if you need anything . . ."

"I will. It was great talking to you, great seeing you on Friday." Her emotions unexpectedly got the better of her and she felt her throat tighten. "You take care, Connor, wherever you are, whatever it is you're doing. You take care of yourself."

"Will do. See you, Annie . . ."

She dropped the phone into her purse and bit her bottom lip. She couldn't help but worry about him. She always did. For men like Connor Shields, there was no telling where or when—or from whom—the danger might come.

A finger of cold crawled up her neck, and she shivered, then shook it off. Connor had faced a thousand dangers during the ten years he'd been with the Bureau. Surely he'd emerge from whatever obscure corner of the world he was now in, unscathed as always. She wondered what it was that made him thrive on the danger, that kept him accepting the most perilous assignments.

That well's too deep for me, she told herself as she passed a tractor trailer when the road expanded from two lanes to four. Leaving Connor's psyche for another day, she slipped a cassette into the dash to play back a taped session of a lecture she'd given to the last group of agents-in-training to refresh her memory. She had less than an hour before she was to speak, and needed to focus now on her speech.

Annie tucked away all thoughts of Connor and Dylan and even of Evan. She had work to do.

_____CHAPTER_____
FIVE

LUTHER BLUE CHECKED HIS ROLEX AND DECIDED
that it was none too early to make a call. If he was up,
everyone should be up.

He dialed and waited.

"Shields."

"I know who I called, thank you," Luther said
dryly.

"What's up?"

"You tell me."

"Tell you what?"

"Tell me what I want to hear."

"It's too early to play games, man."

"Tell me if I'm going to run into your cousin Connor when I arrive at headquarters this morning."

"No. No, you definitely will not run into Connor."

"So you are telling me you took care of the problem?"

The pause was just a beat or two too long.

"You didn't do it, did you?" Luther tried to keep
his temper under control.

"I honest to God haven't had an opportunity."

"A good agent doesn't wait for opportunities. He makes them."

"Look, he was around this weekend, but the entire family was there. My dad, his dad, my brothers, my sister. He was never alone. There was just no chance to—"

"This is just more of the same to me, Shields. I'm really tired of hearing it. As far as I'm concerned, you created this problem, one, by bumbling into him in that alley down in Santa Estela—what, two fucking years ago? And two, by not taking care of him right then and there." The anger began to build. "You're telling me in two fucking years, there wasn't one time you could have taken him out?"

Silence.

"Shields?"

"I heard you, man, I—"

"You're just so much bullshit, you know that? Do I need to remind you who works for who here?"

"No. No reminder necessary."

"Then tell me how you're so certain I won't be coming face-to-face with him any time soon?"

"He's out of the country."

"Where?"

"No one knows, except maybe the guy he reports directly to, and the Director."

"So how do you know he won't be around?"

"I talked to him yesterday. He said he'll be gone for at least three, probably closer to four, weeks."

"Did he say anything about that deal in Santa Estela?"

Another pause.

"Shields?"

"Not recently."

"What the fuck does that mean?"

"He asked about it when I saw him the first time, maybe a month, two months after that night. The night he saw you. I told him it had been taken care of. That everyone had been arrested and the authorities were ID'ing all the kids to send them home. He was concerned about that."

"He never followed up?"

"Why would he?"

"Oh, maybe if he saw me walking through the office, it might shake his memory."

"I told you. You're not going to run into him. He's gone for probably a month."

"You don't seem to understand my situation here, Shields. I am at a real disadvantage. I don't know what this guy looks like. I could be standing next to him in an elevator, or passing him in the hall, and he could be remembering me, and I won't even know it. You have any idea of how vulnerable that makes me?"

"He's never seen you at HQ, he'd have said something to me, but—"

"I'm tired of looking over my shoulder, you understand me? I've spent the last two years looking over my shoulder, and I'm goddamn tired of it. Every new assignment here in the States, I'm holding my breath, wondering who I'm going to be working with, who I'm going to run into. Well, I've been reassigned back here for a while. I do not want to have to be concerned about this again." Luther took a deep breath, tried to calm himself. He knew that when he got really upset, his voice had a tendency to grow shrill. He hated when that happened. "When he gets back here, I want him taken out. No *if*s, *and*s, or *but*s, you hear me? No excuses. Take care of him. I'm done with this shit, Shields."

"Okay, I hear you."

Luther checked the date on his watch. August 9.

"I want him gone within a week of his stepping foot off the plane, hear?"

"I heard you."

"Hear this." In spite of his best effort to maintain control, Luther could feel the anger, the need for control, rising in him rapidly. "By the fifteenth of September, one way or another, there *will* be one less Shields on the federal payroll, and frankly, at this point, I don't care which of you it is."

He hung up before the agent could respond.

Dumb son of a bitch. It's that old, blood-is-thicker-than-water crap. Connor Shields was lucky he was out of reach right now. For two cents, Luther would take care of him himself. If he knew where he was, and what he looked like.

Luther had connections everywhere. Unfortunately, he didn't know where Connor was. He'd just have to be patient and wait for Connor to come to him.

Patience was not one of Luther's virtues.

He sipped at his coffee, then put the cup down slowly and forced himself to concentrate on the breathing exercises they taught him in anger-management class. Sometimes it helped, sometimes it didn't.

Today it did. When the waitress returned to ask him if he'd like another cup, he smiled and declined like a gentleman.

A gentleman who, at midnight tonight, would receive a fresh shipment from a very small, very poor Central American country where the chief export was its children, and its import was the money sent back by the workers who had fled illegally to the United States to work as laborers.

Luther took out the wish list he'd compiled from his roster of usual clients and studied it carefully.

Four of the older girls, between the ages of ten and twelve, were to go directly to a lovely Tudor-style house in a northern New Jersey suburb. At this most unlikely-looking brothel, they would replace four girls who were being sent to a house outside of Philadelphia, where they would be traded for four girls who would move on to D.C.

"Keep 'em moving, keep 'em confused," he told the owners of the houses. "And keep the product fresh. Make sure there's always something new. That's the way to build up that repeat business."

And when the girls reached their midteens, worn out in mind, spirit, and body?

"You just dispose of them. You can't send them back to their families." He'd given this speech to all of his customers at one time or another. "Look, you got a cop or two on your payroll, right? Of course you do. Now, if I were you, when the girls just don't have it anymore, when they start losing that fight, I'd give 'em to the cops, a little reward for their loyalty. When they're done with the girls, they can take care of them. Trust me, no one knows how to get away with murder better than a cop."

He drained the coffee in the cup and left a ten on the table with the bill for his breakfast. Once outside in the swelter of an early August Virginia morning, he paused and took a deep cleansing breath, just as he'd been instructed to do.

To have a good day, keep the anger at bay.

It had become his mantra. Not that it always worked, but today, it was good enough to take the edge off. He got into his car and prepared for his meeting.

Then it was off with the Rolex, on with the Timex.

Damn, but he loved that gold watch with the diamonds, loved the feel of it on his wrist, loved the way it looked, so classy, so expensive. With a sigh, he dropped it into its box and placed it in his briefcase.

He had yet to meet the FBI agent who could afford a watch like that. The watch, the house in Myrtle Beach, the condo in Manhattan, the apartments in

Paris and London—all real estate in his mother's name, of course—the new Jaguar . . . who could live like that on what the government paid?

He wondered idly how his good friend Agent Shields spent his share of the money they'd made since he'd recruited him three years ago. He hoped Shields was as smart about it as he himself had been. Maybe he should have a chat soon, find out where it was stashed. In the unfortunate event that something should happen to his good buddy, shouldn't someone know where to find the cash?

After all, in their line of work—legitimate as well as illegal—an untimely accident could occur at any time.

And as far as Luther was concerned, Connor Shields was headed for an accident, as soon as he'd taken care of one little loose end.

Maybe sooner.

_____ CHAPTER _____
SIX

ANNIE SAT CROSS-LEGGED ON THE FLOOR OF HER apartment, the contents of the thick file stacked around her in piles. Police reports here, photos of the crime scene there, autopsy report and photos on the edge of the coffee table.

In her hand she held the master list of the contents of the file. She'd read through the reports of Dylan's death many times, but this time she thought she'd put them in the same order in which they appeared on the list. It would be easier for Evan, who'd be taking his first look at the records this weekend. It would go a lot faster if he could just follow along and check off each report as he read it. Unfortunately, the file had been taken apart and read by so many people over the past two years, nothing was where she'd expected it to be.

The photos were easy to put in order. They were numbered in chronological order. The witness statements were a little more challenging. It seemed that few of them had been returned to their rightful place.

No time like the present, she told herself as she proceeded to search the file for the first report on the list. She found it near the bottom of the stack. She checked it off, then went on to the next. Three hours later, she had most of the reports where they should be. There were three, however, she'd not been able to find.

One was a report attributed to Connor Shields. She frowned, trying to recall if she'd previously seen a report from Connor in the file. She didn't think she had. And why would there have been a report from Connor? Hadn't he been out of the country at the time of Dylan's death?

If he hadn't been there, hadn't been involved, what could he possibly have contributed to the investigation?

She was tempted to call and ask him, then thought better of it. Who knew where he was, or with whom? Better to send an e-mail that he could read at his leisure.

She opened her laptop and typed her message.

TO: CShields00721
From: AMMccall00913
RE: Report
Hey, Connor—Just a quick question. Brought Dylan's
file home tonight, it's all out of order (too many
hands in this pot over the past couple of years)—
quite the mess. Started trying to organize, using
the master list as a guide. Found all but three
items in file, including a report that was
attributed to you. Could I ask you about the nature

of your report? Do you remember? Did this reflect
directly on the op, or did this deal with
identifying Dylan at the M.E.'s office, maybe? Am
confused, since I was not aware you had been
involved in this op in any way.

   Just curious—would like to tidy up the file, as
well as try to find some closure. I guess we all
would like that.

   Annie

She turned her attention back to the file and its
master list, which continued to guide her in her quest
to put the file in perfect order before sharing its contents with Evan. Some minutes later, she heard the
ping that announced in-coming e-mail. She leaned
over the computer to see who the correspondence
was from and was surprised to see that Connor had
responded so quickly.

To: AMMccall00913
From: CShields00721
Re: Yours
Hey, Annie—You're sure that report isn't stuck
inside another folder or something in the file?
Definitely turned it in. Didn't contribute a whole
hell of a lot to the investigation. They just
wanted me to confirm that I had been pulled from the
op at the last minute and that Dylan substituted
for me and why—how that whole thing had been set

up. All before-the-fact stuff. Nothing that shed
any light on the events later that night.
    Anything I can help you with, any other
questions, I'm here.
    Connor

Annie read the e-mail, then reread that one line
over and over. *They just wanted me to confirm that I
had been pulled from the op at the last minute, and
that Dylan substituted for me and why—how that
whole thing had been set up. All before-the-fact
stuff . . .*

Annie stared at the screen. Connor had originally
been part of this operation? Dylan had been sent at
the last minute as a substitute for Connor? Why had
she not heard this before?

Or had she? In the dense fog of confusion and pain
she'd been trapped in for weeks after Dylan's death,
had someone mentioned this?

Maybe.

She doubted it, but then again, there was much
from that time she couldn't remember. She was hard-
pressed to remember Dylan's funeral, had little recol-
lection of the viewing, and none whatsoever of the
graveside services, though certainly she'd been there.
Maybe someone had mentioned that Connor originally had been slated for this assignment, and the information had been lost in the midst of her grief. She
couldn't honestly say she hadn't been told. On the
other hand, she couldn't say she had.

She drummed her fingers on the side of her laptop, trying to determine the importance of this new information.

She dialed Evan's number and was grateful that he picked up on the second ring. She told him about the e-mail from Connor, then said, "I'm trying to decide how—or if—this changes things."

"I guess the only way to answer that is to know what else Connor had been involved in back then."

"You mean, if he'd been involved in something someone might have wanted to kill him for?" She laughed roughly. "That's every assignment Connor's ever been on."

"Look, why not just ask him if there was anything going on back then that sticks in his memory."

"Even if there was, he wouldn't be able to tell me."

"Maybe not, but maybe it's something he can look into himself. You won't know if you don't ask."

"True. Maybe I'll just e-mail him . . ." She opened her laptop and debated on how best to put forth the question.

"Good idea. Bring it all with you this weekend and we'll toss it around a little more."

"How's your case going?"

"Not well." His voice dropped with something more than disappointment. "In the past week, we've had three victims. I was going to call and ask for your opinion on this. Have you ever known a serial killer to target different types the way this guy is? I mean, two distinctly different types of victims? This guy is going back and forth between the pampered and privileged to girls who haven't even been reported missing a week after we've found their bodies. It just doesn't make sense to me."

"It is odd. And no, to answer your question, I've never heard of a case like this one." She pondered the facts he'd given her. "Maybe I should take a look at the files while I'm up there this weekend. Can you get me copies of all of them? It will give me something to do while you look over Dylan's file."

"You show me yours, I'll show you mine?"

"Something like that." Annie smiled.

He laughed.

"We're going to be all right, aren't we." It wasn't a question.

"We *are* all right," he told her.

He appeared to be about to say something else, but his thoughts were interrupted by a click on the line.

"Hold up, Annie, I have a call coming in." He put her on hold.

Moments later, he was back.

"I have to go," he said, and she knew by the tone of his voice he was wanted at a crime scene.

"I'll see you Friday night, then," Annie told him. "I'll be flying up, then I'll rent a car at the airport."

"You sure you don't want me to pick you up?"

"You might be tied up. I'll just go to your place, and you'll get there when you get there."

"I'll see you then," he said as he hung up. "I love you, Annie."

"I love you too, Evan."

Later that night, Annie opened her laptop and checked her e-mail. Amid several from the office, there was one from Connor.

To: AMMccall00913
From: CShields00721
Re: Missing Reports
Forgot to ask—what were the other missing reports?

Annie went in to the living room and opened the file, searching for the note she'd made, then returned to her laptop to respond.

To: CShields00721
From: AMMccall00913
Re: Missing Reports
One was written by SA Melissa Lowery. The other is a diagram of the crime scene drawn by SA Lou Raymond.

Connor's reply was almost instantaneous.

To: AMMccall00913
From: CShields00721
Re: Missing Reports
Special Agent Raymond killed in car ax almost two

years ago. Heard Missy Lowery quit the Bureau but don't remember when.

Annie stared at the e-mail as it appeared on the screen, and a little chill sneaked up her spine.

Don't look for something that isn't there, she reminded herself. *People die in car accidents every day. Agents quit the Bureau every day.*

She began to type.

To: CShields00721
From: AMMccall00913
Re: Missing Reports
Thanks for the info. BTW, I noticed there's no reflection in the file that you had been set for this assignment originally—other apparently than the report you wrote, which is missing. Seems odd to me. Just out of curiosity, was this widely known? That you were on this op? And called off at last minute?

———

To: AMMccall00913
From: CShields00721
Re: Missing Reports
It was no secret that Aidan and I were running this—don't know who knew that Dylan stepped in for me when I got called out. What are you thinking? That I was intended target?

———

To: CShields00721
From: AMMccall00913

Re: Missing Reports
Well, it did cross my mind. Can you think of
anything you might have been working on back then
that could have made you unpopular in the wrong
places?

———

To: AMMccall00913
From: CShields00721
Re: Missing Reports
You're kidding, right?

———

To: CShields00721
From: AMMccall00913
Re: Missing Reports
That's what I thought you'd say. Would you let me
know if anything comes to mind, maybe something . . .
odd or strange that happened that made you think
twice? Sorry if I sound off-the-wall. I just don't
recall having heard that you were slated for that
night. Strange no one else mentioned it.

She hit *send,* then waited. And waited. But there
was no further reply from Connor that night. Nor
was there e-mail from him waiting for her in the
morning.

She'd touched a nerve, no doubt, and felt a stab of
regret. If Connor started to question if the bullets that
killed his brother had been intended for him, he'd
have one hell of a time forgiving himself.

Then again, knowing Connor, there'd be no question that he'd put his own personal feelings aside to search for the truth.

Annie turned off her computer, content with that knowledge, for now. If the truth had been buried with Dylan, there was no one more likely to help her ferret it out than Connor.

CHAPTER
SEVEN

ANNIE STEPPED OUT OF HER OFFICE AND BEGAN THE long walk to the elevator, made longer this afternoon by the heavy files she juggled in both arms. One had come just that morning from a police department in Michigan that had requested a profile on a killer who was targeting homeless men. The other was Dylan's.

She turned the corner and stopped in her tracks. Thirty feet down the hall, near the conference room, a group of men in dark suits were gathered. All tall, dark haired, well built.

All Shieldses.

Andrew, Brendan, Grady, and Aidan.

From the back, they were nearly identical. Oh, some were a bit taller—Aidan and Grady were a few inches shorter than the other two—but even someone who knew them all as well as she did could have a tough time telling them apart from the back.

From this angle, any one of them could have been Dylan.

She had no idea how long she'd stood there, staring, before Aidan turned and saw her.

"Hey!" he called to her, his mouth curving into a wide smile. "My favorite sister-in-law! I was just on my way to see if you were in your office when I ran into this motley crew."

The group walked toward her, and her stomach knotted. They were all so damned alike. Brendan and Aidan even walked the same way.

"Good to see you, Aidan." She turned her cheek for him to plant a kiss. "I just left voice mail for Mara. I wanted her to know I'd be out of town for a few days."

"Business or pleasure?" Grady peered around his brothers to see her better.

"A little of both. I'm going to Lyndon, Pennsylvania, to see Evan, but he's in the middle of a case he wants me to look over."

She stole a quick peek at her watch.

"I have to get going or I'll miss my plane. See you all later. Aidan, tell Mara to call me when she's free."

The men stepped aside and allowed Annie to pass. She waited for the elevator, anxiously tapping her foot. She should have left at least a half hour ago.

Maybe the plane will be late, she found herself hoping.

"Annie, hold the elevator."

She caught the door with her foot and held it open for Andrew.

"Thanks, Annie." He entered the car and hit the

button for the lobby. "You are going to the lobby, right?"

She nodded and shifted the files.

"Here, give me one of those." Andrew took the nearest file from her arms.

"Thanks. I was just starting to think I might lose that one."

He glanced at the label.

"I heard about this case. Catherine Cook was just sent out on it. What's the count up to now, seven homeless guys?"

"Eight, as of this morning." She watched the light follow the floor numbers, then stepped back when the elevator stopped at the third floor and the doors opened.

Two women in summer business suits smiled absently as they entered the elevator. No one spoke until they arrived at the lobby.

"Which level is your car on?" Andrew asked Annie.

"I'm right outside the door."

"You must be a real early riser, to have gotten a spot at the door."

"Early enough." She smiled and reached for the file.

"I'll walk you out."

He followed her across the lobby, then held the door to the parking lot open for her.

"Give me the other file," he said when they got to

her car and she began to search her bag for her keys. "I'll hold them while you open the car."

"This is Dylan's file," Andrew said softly after glancing at the label.

"Yes." She unlocked the door and tossed her bag onto the passenger seat.

"How many times have you read through this?" he asked.

"Lots. You?"

"Lost count." He looked past her, toward the exit. "Every time I think, I wish I had been there. Maybe I could have done something . . ."

"There was nothing anyone could have done. Aidan was there, and he couldn't save him."

Andrew merely shook his head.

"Andrew, when was the last time you looked at this file?"

"A couple of weeks ago," he admitted. "We were all sitting around at Aidan's bachelor party, talking about how much we missed Dylan, and I just felt—I don't know, compelled, somehow, to take another look. I guess I always somehow hope this time it will end differently." He shrugged. "Of course it never does."

"Do you happen to remember seeing a report from an agent named Melissa Lowery?"

"Not really. I remember her, though. Didn't she leave the Bureau a while ago?"

"Not long after Dylan died. She was on the backup team that night."

"Maybe she had a tough time dealing with it." He cleared his throat. "She wouldn't have been the only one."

"Any idea where she is now?"

"No. I didn't really know her. I only know her to say hi."

Annie opened the back door, then turned to take the files from Andrew. She placed the files on the backseat, then got into her car and started the ignition.

"By the way, Andrew, did you know an agent named Lou Raymond?"

"Yeah. What a waste. He died in a car crash out near I-95 a couple of years ago."

"That's the one."

"He was on one of the exit ramps coming off 95 into Maryland. Three or four in the morning. Word was he apparently fell asleep or something and the car hit the guardrail, then went out of control and flipped over. At least, that's the story that was going around at the time. Best I recall, there were no witnesses."

"No other cars involved?"

"Not as far as I know. It was called in by a tractor-trailer driver who came across the scene at some point after it happened." He cocked his head to one side. "Did you know him?"

"No. I just saw his name in the file—Dylan's file—and was curious, that's all. The master-file list notes that Raymond had sketched the crime scene, but there's no sketch in the file."

"You mean the sketch that shows where everyone was at the time of the shooting?"

"I'm not sure what it was. I haven't been able to find it. Likewise a report written by Melissa Lowery."

"I worked maybe two or three cases with Lou when I first got out of training. He always drew things out, made it part of his report. He'd show where everyone was stationed, parked, standing, whatever. Put his whole account in pictures. It was pretty interesting, actually." Andrew appeared to think for a minute. "I don't remember ever seeing sketches that Lou drew in this file. Not ever. And like I said, I've gone through it a couple of times. Can't say I remember a report from Lowery, either, but that doesn't mean it wasn't there. At some point, they must have fallen out."

"Must have." She put the car in gear. "Thanks for carrying the files for me."

"Anytime." He stepped back to allow her to back out of the parking space. "Tell what's-his-name I said hello."

"It's Evan," she told him. "His name is Evan . . ."

"Sorry." He shrugged, much as his brother had a few days earlier, and waved to her as she drove off.

"So, you think this guy is targeting homeless guys because he thinks he's on some kind of a mission to clean up the streets?" Evan sat on the sofa, his bare feet propped on the coffee table.

"I think he has a vigilante mentality. Look, check out this letter he sent to the local papers." Annie found the newspaper and read, " 'The city belongs to the people who pay the taxes that pay the police and the firemen and the city workers. I'm a street cleaner, just like them.' "

"Ugly." He frowned. "Who thinks like that?"

"Some misguided soul in Denton, Ohio." She yawned and closed the file cover. "How about your case, you ready to talk about it now?"

"I don't know what else to tell you that you haven't already read for yourself. I'm finding it confusing as hell."

"It is confusing, but I still think you're looking for two different people, Evan."

"The killer is doing exactly the same things, in exactly the same manner. Rape the girl, slash the throat. Dump the body. Steal the shoes. The murders are identical."

"Except for one very important difference. The victims. And you know what I always say." She poked him in the ribs with her pen.

"Yeah, yeah. Know the victims, know the killer."

"Are you humoring me?"

"Nope. That's what you always say. And you're usually right; at least, in my experience with you, that's held true. I just don't see how it could be two different killers. Especially since we haven't released any of the details about the crimes. I just wish we had something—hair samples, DNA, something—that we could use to confirm one way or the other. We've kept the MO, the signature, all of the important things, under wraps. And as far as I know, there haven't been any leaks."

"Well, someone is talking. The second killer has to be someone close to the investigation."

"You realize what you're saying?" He bristled. "The only people close to the investigation are the cops working the case. I've known all these guys forever, since I joined the force in Lyndon. I've worked with every one of them at one time or another, either as a county detective or as a Lyndon cop. I can't believe that any of these guys would kill a kid."

"Someone's killing them, Evan. And you of all people should know that killers don't look like killers. They look like the rest of us."

"I can't argue with that, but I just don't see any of these guys killing little girls. I couldn't even narrow the list down to a few likely suspects, Annie."

"It'll be the person you least expect. It always is," she said almost absently as she made notes on the yellow legal pad.

"So, you almost finished with your analysis?"

"Almost." She nodded. "I won't be too much longer. I want to get this e-mailed to the chief of police tonight."

He sat up and began to lay the photos of the murdered girls side by side across the table.

"Those are your vics?" She looked up from her notes.

He nodded and continued setting out the pictures in order of the girls' deaths.

Annie put her notes aside and sat next to him, studying the photos.

"It's not the same guy, sweetie," she said softly.

"Annie . . ."

"Look at these girls in their school uniforms, at the way they project such innocence. Now look at them through his eyes, at the way he's left them, defiled. He's ruined them. He's taken something clean and pure and ravaged it. He's stolen from them. He has tremendous power over them now. He's definitely feeling very proud, very smug. He's stolen something precious, and no one can stop him. No one is *powerful* enough to stop him."

"You think this is mostly about power for him?"

"It is only about power. My guess is he works a low-level job where he's in contact with people whom he perceives as socially and economically superior to him."

"We all come in contact with people like that."

"This is daily, this is close contact on a daily basis. He resents that he's placed in a position of inferiority, of subservience, when he knows he's morally and intellectually superior to all of them. That he's forced to work for them, that his livelihood is dependent on people he thinks are less than he. That they can't see his brilliance marks them all as fools. This is how he retaliates. He's showing *them* who has the power. He's showing them who's really in charge."

"And you don't see that here?" Evan tapped on the photos of the last three victims.

"Not at all. Where are the symbols of purity, of innocence? He's tried to make them look the same as the others, I think in an effort to fool the police. To make you think this is all the work of the same man. So far, he's succeeding."

"You feel that strongly about this?"

"There is no question in my mind." She studied his face. "I'm sensing a lot of resistance here, Evan. Why so reluctant?"

"If I take this in to the office, I have to be able to convince the chief of detectives that there are two killers, not one, out there targeting young girls. Yet I have no DNA, no trace, nothing, to distinguish the crimes."

"Want me to write a memo or something outlining why?"

"Sort of like a note from my mother to give to my teacher?"

"You're the one who's pressing here."

"Maybe a memo would help," he conceded. "And keep in mind that right now there is no link. We're still waiting for the lab results from the first two vics."

"What's taking so long?" She closed the file and set it on the table near the photos.

"It's a small lab, only a few techs. They're doing their best, but this is not the only open case in the county right now."

"Why not send what you have to the Bureau's lab?"

"What's the timetable there?"

"Depends on who's asking." Annie grinned.

"Suppose you asked . . ."

"We'd have the results in a week, maybe better."

"And if I asked?"

"What year is it now?"

"So how do we get you involved?"

"I write that memo, you give it to your chief, tell him we can get the evidence expedited if only he asks. I can take it from there."

"You have friends at the lab?"

"You betcha."

"What's your take on this possible second killer? You're pretty specific about the first one; how do you peg this other killer that no one sees but you?"

"I'm still working on that." She stood and stretched, then took his hand and pulled him to his feet. "I thought maybe I'd sleep on it."

"Excellent idea. I think I'll sleep on it, too." He tugged her toward the steps leading up. "I'm thinking maybe between the two of us, we should be able to come up with something . . ."

_____CHAPTER_____
EIGHT

EVAN SAT ON THE EDGE OF THE DESK IN THE MEDICAL examiner's office, reading through the autopsy report of Caitlin McGill and last night's unnamed victim, and waited for the M.E. to finish washing up.

"So the throats were definitely slashed with different blades?"

"Definitely." The county M.E., Agnes Jenkins, washed her hands at the sink in the far corner of her office. "Not even close. The knife used on the schoolgirls was thin and finely sharpened. The knife used on the unidentified girls was thicker, duller. Different width."

"What do you think of two different killers?"

She reached for a roll of paper towels to dry her hands.

"I think it's highly likely. As a matter of fact, I'd bet on it. The schoolgirls—let's call them the group-one victims, just for the purpose of this conversation—had been, for the most part, still in possession of their hymens before the attacks. Not so the unidentified girls—the group-two vics, if you will. Internal examination showed that these girls were no novices."

"Prostitutes?"

"That, or they were real party girls." She frowned. "They were pretty young, though. Hard to tell for certain; their teeth weren't well cared for and two of them showed evidence of old healed fractures. And all three of them were small, physically. I'd guess from poor nutrition at some time in their life, most likely early childhood."

"Semen?"

"Not in or on any of them. Both guys wrapped up first." She rolled up the paper towel and tossed it into a nearby trash can. "It will be interesting to see what we get back from the lab, don't you think?"

"I've asked the chief to okay a transfer to the FBI lab, just to speed up the process. Our county lab is way behind and just isn't willing to expedite this case over any others in the pipeline."

"That would be Jeffrey Coogan." She named the head of the lab and made a face. "He's not much of a team player. You'll never get him to put one case aside to work on another. He's so goddamned anal. Everything in strict order."

"He's not happy about giving up the samples, but the chief leaned on him good and hard. I suspect the D.A. might have made a call as well."

"Sometimes you just have to talk tough with the assholes, Crosby." She grinned. "Anything else I can do for you?"

"You could get me a copy of the autopsy report on our latest victim."

"As soon as Mary Ellen out there finishes transcribing my tape, it's yours. I'll have her call you and you can stop back and pick it up."

"Thanks. I appreciate it."

"And you'll get me a copy of the lab results as soon as the FBI gets them to you?"

"Absolutely." He hopped off the desk and started to the door.

"Sounds like a deal." She smiled and turned to answer her ringing phone. "Oh. There was one more thing. Our unidentified girls all had tattoos on their left hips."

"Tattoos?"

"Little stars. Somewhat crudely made, but they were definitely stars. Three tiny stars, right below the waist at the top of the hip on the left side. What do you make of that?"

"Stars?" Annie asked.

"Right. I'm faxing you a photo right now. Can you see if it matches up with anything in the Bureau files? I tried to scan it into our computer, but once again, the computer is giving me the finger. Some glitch in the firewall, they're telling me."

"Go ahead and fax it down, let me take a look."

"It should be there any minute." Evan paused, then said, "Dr. Jenkins agrees that we're dealing with more than one killer."

He reiterated the gist of his conversation with the medical examiner.

"Prostitutes? Fourteen-, fifteen-year-old prostitutes?" She thought for a minute, then said, "Well, that would make sense, wouldn't it? Maybe they were tattooed by whoever is putting them out. Then again, they could be gang members. That's just as likely, don't you think? Maybe the stars identify them as a member of a specific gang. Or maybe they mark them as the property of a gang."

"It's worth looking into, but I have to tell you that I haven't heard of anything like that around here. I'll check with Philly, Trenton, Scranton, Camden, Newark, New York—maybe someone will have seen this before."

"If they were prostitutes, it would explain why you haven't received missing persons reports. If it's a gang thing, though, you might still have parents involved somewhere. The girls would most likely live at home. If that's the case, someone should be looking for these girls, Evan. Still no calls?"

"None. And we've told the dispatchers from every community to call us the minute anyone inquires about any one of these kids, but there's been nothing. I'll put out inquiries up and down the East Coast, though. See if someone, somewhere, is looking for them."

"I think the tattoos might help us track them." She bit at a cuticle, something she almost never did. "I just can't help but think that somewhere, someone is crying their eyes out over these girls. Someone has to have missed them. These kids have names, they have families somewhere."

"Well, maybe one of us will get lucky and we'll find out where that somewhere is."

"Let me make a call or two and get back to you."

Annie was searching her desk drawer for the office directory even as she hung up. She found the number she was looking for, dialed, then waited.

"Fletcher."

"My favorite computer geek." She sighed dramatically.

"My favorite profiler." Will Fletcher laughed. "How's it going, Annie?"

"Good. You?"

"Terrific. Great wedding, by the way."

"You and Miranda seemed to be having a good time." She paused, then added, "Especially Miranda."

"Hey, my girl does love to party. Never met a band she couldn't dance to."

"And dance, she did."

They both laughed, then Will said, "But you didn't call to talk about Miranda's happy feet."

"Actually, I was hoping you could give me a hand with something."

"This have anything to do with you and Evan looking into Dylan's death?"

"How'd you know about that?" she asked. "Oh. I almost forgot. The word is that Will Fletcher knows everything. Word is that you have mysterious sources."

"Not so mysterious. I saw Brendan yesterday. He mentioned it."

"Evan and I are taking a look at the circumstances surrounding Dylan's death, but this has nothing to do with that."

"Doesn't matter. I'm happy to help, either way."

"Actually, this has to do with a case Evan is working back in Pennsylvania."

"Those young girls that have been murdered?"

"If you know that, you probably know that they have three victims that are similar but unrelated."

"I heard a rumor, but no details. Tell me."

She did.

"So you're looking to identify the tattoo."

"For starters, yes. I can fax you a picture of them." She reached over and studied the faxed image again.

"When do you need an answer?"

"As soon as you have one."

"Let me get to work on it and get back to you. I assume if I get a hit, you want all available information?"

"Absolutely."

"I'll see what I can do."

"Thanks, Will. Give me your fax number."

She wrote it down, then programmed the number into the machine next to her desk.

"It's on its way."

"I'll be waiting for it."

How did anyone ever get anything done without all

of this modern technology? she wondered as she fed the picture into the machine.

Well, they got it done, it just took a lot longer.

Evan's fax fed through the machine and the buzz assured her the operation was completed. If anyone could trace that tattoo, it was Will Fletcher, whose skills were legendary in the Bureau. She had full confidence that if the tattoo had been entered into the system, Will would find it. She mentally moved on to the next task on her list of things to do.

Find Melissa Lowery.

____CHAPTER____
NINE

Chris Malone, chief detective, Avon County, was staring out the window, a sheet of paper in his hand, when Evan knocked on the doorframe. Malone turned to look over his shoulder.

"Come on in, Crosby."

"What's up?" Evan entered the office and leaned over the back of a leather wing chair.

"Same thing that's been up. The D.A. has the entire county on his back over this killer who's running around, snatching the daughters of some of our leading citizens off the street, and we're all being toasted in the press."

"Yeah, the parking lot is full of news vans. I had to park down on Fourth Street again this morning."

"Well, get used to it. None of them are leaving until this is over. Did you see this morning's paper?"

He walked to his desk and held up the front page of the county's tabloid. LOCAL LAW ENFORCEMENT STYMIED. HOW MANY MORE VICTIMS WILL THE KILLER CLAIM?

He turned the page and opened it to the lead story

on page three and read the screaming headline. " 'Will Your Daughter Be Next?' "

Malone tossed the paper onto his desk in disgust.

"And up until this morning, we didn't have one fucking clue."

"What happened this morning?" Evan asked.

"This." Malone handed him the sheet of paper he'd been holding. Evan studied it for a full minute before reacting.

DEAR CHIEF OF DETECTIVES MALONE,
I SAW YOU ON THE NEWS TONIGHT. YOU SAID THAT
YOU FOUND THREE MORE VICTIMS OF THIS GUY
WHO IS KILLING GIRLS IN AVON COUNTY. WELL,
THAT WOULD BE ME. AND I AM TELLING YOU THAT
I DID NOT KILL THOSE OTHER GIRLS, THE ONES
YOU FOUND IN THE WOODS. THAT IS SOMEONE
ELSE'S WORK, IT IS NOT MINE. STOP SAYING I
KILLED THEM ALL. I KNOW WHO MY GIRLS WERE
AND WHERE I LEFT THEM. THESE OTHER GIRLS, I
DON'T KNOW WHO THEY ARE OR WHO KILLED
THEM. IT WAS NOT ME.

AND ANOTHER THING. WHAT DO I HAVE TO DO
TO GET A SPECIAL NAME FROM YOU GUYS? YOU
KNOW, LIKE THE BOSTON STRANGLER, OR THE
GREEN RIVER KILLER. I THINK I HAVE EARNED A
SPECIAL NAME. I LIKE THE SCHOOLGIRL SLAYER. I
THOUGHT SOMEONE AS SMART AS YOU WOULD
THINK UP A NAME. SINCE YOU DID NOT, I HAD TO
MAKE UP MY OWN. I THINK IT IS A GOOD ONE. I

HOPE YOU LIKE IT. YOU'LL BE USING IT OVER AND
OVER. JUST NOT FOR THESE OTHER GIRLS. WHY
WOULD I WANT TO KILL A BUNCH OF NAMELESS
NOBODIES? HOW COULD YOU BE SO STUPID TO
THINK THOSE OTHER GIRLS WOULD INTEREST ME?
   SIGNED,
   THE SCHOOLGIRL SLAYER

"You think this is legit?" Evan asked.

"What do you think?"

"He seems pretty indignant that we would assume that the other vics were his. Like somehow he's above them." Evan read from the letter. "This whole last part, about those other girls being nobodies . . . he clearly thinks they weren't worth his time."

He handed the letter back to Malone. "As if one girl's life was more important than another's."

"He's certainly implying that."

"I spoke with Dr. Jenkins a little while ago, right after she finished the autopsy on our last unidentified vic," Evan told him. "She says the weapon used to kill the schoolgirls is not the same weapon used to kill our as-yet-unidentified girls. She thinks that the physical signs point to a high level of sexual activity on the part of the girls who still haven't been reported missing, no such activity on the part of the others."

"So she's seeing two distinct types of victims, two different killers."

Evan nodded.

"I also took the liberty to discuss the case with one of the FBI's profilers, Dr. McCall, and she—"

"The same Dr. McCall who accompanied you to the D.A.'s fund-raiser last month?"

"Ah, yes." Evan had forgotten that Malone had met Annie at a party to raise money for the district attorney's reelection campaign. "Right."

"What was her take on all this?"

"She feels pretty strongly that there are two different killers. She's working up a report for us."

Malone pointed to the letter, which was still in Evan's hand. "Think she'd be able to look at that and give us her thoughts? Any chance we could meet with her? If nothing else, we can tell the press we've brought in the FBI."

"I can ask her. You may have to go through the Bureau, and they'll probably want to send some of their own agents to work the case."

"I've already resigned myself to bringing them in. It's a tough call, since there are so many police departments involved. On the one hand, it looks like we've got every PD in the county on this, and this guy is still dancing around us. Doesn't look good, you know what I mean? Looks like we have no confidence in our local people." Malone reflected on this for a moment, then added, "On the other hand, if we're being outsmarted at every turn by this guy, and we don't ask for help, we look like stubborn fools. At this point, I feel we need all the help we can get. I hate to say it, but without a suspect, without any leads—

hell, we don't even know where he's killing these girls. We're just finding them where he leaves them."

"I'll call Annie and see when she's available." Evan couldn't help but be pleased at the prospect of working with Annie again, even if it was only for a consult. He hadn't been able to see his way clear from this case to figure out when they could spend time together. The thought of even one night with her was a gift, despite the tragic circumstances.

"One more thing. Jenkins noted that each of the three unidentified victims had three stars tattooed on her left hip."

Malone's head snapped up.

"Gang members?"

"Maybe. Maybe a pimp, branding his property."

"Any history on these tattoos?"

"I didn't recognize them and couldn't find anyone who did. I already faxed the photos of the tattoos to the FBI. Apparently, there's someone on staff who's really an ace at tracking down stuff like this. Annie says if it's in the system, they'll find it."

"Good move. And you already sent the samples from the lab down there as well?"

"I did, as soon as the lab director agreed to release them. Thanks for stepping in there."

"Coogan can be a hard-ass. Sometimes you just have to remind him who's in charge. In this case, it would be the county D.A. He had no problem getting Coogan to see things his way."

"Whatever it took. I'll just be happy to see a little

solid evidence. It's frustrating to gather all those samples, all that potential evidence, then have to wait weeks to see what's what," Evan admitted.

"In this case, a few weeks could mean the difference between life and death for another young girl. Or two. The killer has definitely put us on notice. He's not finished."

"What are you going to do with the letter?" Evan pointed to the paper in his hand.

"I've already sent the original to a handwriting analyst at the FBI—you're not the only one with contacts, you know."

"How do you propose to respond?"

"Well, I was hoping Dr. McCall might have some thoughts on that."

"I'm sure she will. But in the meantime—"

"In the meantime, I've sent letters to every school in the county, advising parents and school officials that until this guy is caught, no one's daughter is safe. Your kid goes no place alone, checks in with the parents, and reports any suspicious activity. Anything, from anyone. And if she's not home when she's supposed to be, the first call the parents make is to their local police department."

"Tough talk."

"Can't be tough enough. This guy has killed five young girls—all daughters of well-off, influential county residents, so that just adds to the colossal heat we're taking. This last girl was the daughter of the next-door neighbor of one of the town supervisors in Broeder."

"I heard about that." Evan nodded. "My sister's fiancé is the chief of police down there."

"Right. Sean Mercer. He's got the local politicians and a passel of reporters crawling up his butt over this, so of course he's crawling up mine. Not that I blame him, but it isn't as if we aren't trying to track this guy. We just don't have much to go on."

"How much are you going to make public?" Evan asked. "Are you going to let it be known there are two killers? Are you going to release the letter to the press?"

"Not yet. Right now, I don't want to change the status quo. I'd really like to wait to see what Dr. McCall has to say. Maybe she'll have some insight into whether silence or publicity is to our best advantage. I don't want to throw something out there only to have it bite us in the ass later on. Let's get the best advice we can before we act. For now, just proceed as you were. Keep the letter under your hat, for now. And let's sit on this two-killer thing until after I've spoken with Dr. McCall." Malone drew a hand through the thinning hair on top of his head. "The one thing I do want is every department in this county on alert. I know everyone's been on this, Crosby; don't jump on me. But I want every available man on the street."

"Chief, it's impossible to cover all these private

schools. They're in this county, they're over in Landro County. There's no way we can cover all these kids."

"No, but we can cover them when they get back to our jurisdiction. So far, he hasn't hit any town in Landro County. He's confined his work here, in Avon. That could mean something, maybe not. Who the hell knows what this guy is thinking, what sets him off, what makes him go after one girl and not another? For now, the best we can do is to warn parents to keep their eyes on their kids and make them understand the danger, that to a certain degree they are going to have to be responsible for themselves and for their friends."

"Let's hope the lab results are back soon and give us something. Right now we have nothing."

"And he knows it. Bastard knows that right now he has us chasing our own tails, and he's enjoying it," Malone told Evan. "Let's see what we can do to ruin his fun before he kills again."

At Annie's suggestion, Malone made his request for FBI assistance directly to John Mancini, who headed up a special unit within the Bureau to handle sensitive cases. John personally reviewed the files, which had been messengered to him overnight, before assigning three of his top agents to the job.

"Shouldn't take you more than a day or so," he said to Annie while authorizing her to provide an analysis of the killer's psychological profile to the chief of detectives in Avon County. "What's on your calendar right now?"

"The Ohio case. A case out in Michigan. Something that came in last night from Oregon; I'm taking that with me to read on the plane. I have a meeting in Seattle next Tuesday. Otherwise, I'm okay."

"Great. See if you can shed some light on this case." John pushed his chair back from his desk, his habitual nonverbal notice that the meeting had concluded.

Annie stood and gathered her bag and her briefcase, noting that John's job was clearly taking its toll.

"You okay, John?"

"As okay as I've ever been, I guess."

"Genna okay?" she asked, referring to John's wife of two years.

"She's fine." His eyes narrowed. "What's with the interrogation?"

"You just look a little tired, that's all."

He laughed. "When have I not been tired?"

"You just look a little more worn out than you normally do."

"It's just the job, Annie. But I appreciate your concern."

"Maybe you should be the one going to Pennsylvania and out of here for a few days."

"Well, actually, I'll be doing just that. Genna's got that cabin out on that lake up in the northeastern corner of the state, you know. We're supposed to go for a week, starting on Tuesday."

"Do it. Make it your priority. Don't let anything come between you and that time off, John. Seriously. I can't remember the last time I called this office and you were on vacation." Her voice softened. "You need the time, John."

"You been talking to my wife?"

"Just looking out for you, pal."

"I appreciate the sentiment," John told her. "You keep in touch, and have a safe trip."

"You, too."

She left John's office and headed straight for her own on the seventh floor. She was gathering up files she'd left on her desk when Brendan Shields appeared in her doorway.

"Hey. Where's the fire?" he asked.

"Oh, I'm on my way to Pennsylvania to look into that serial killer they have on the loose, and I need to take some of these notes with me." Where was the file she'd started with her own notes on Dylan's case? She checked her briefcase and found she'd already tucked it away.

"I heard Mancini's sending a couple of agents up there," he said. "I heard Miranda Cahill, Mike Hoffman, and Kevin Muller were going."

"Oh, great. I love working with all of them. I should check with Miranda and see when she's leaving. Maybe we can fly up together."

"She's in Maine right now. I think she's heading down there tomorrow."

"Word travels fast around here."

Brendan shrugged. "I had lunch with Will a while ago. Miranda called him while we were eating."

"I can't believe how incestuous this place is. And how quickly news travels." She laughed and added one more file to her briefcase. "Gotta run."

Brendan backed into the hall to allow her to pass.

"See you when I get back." She stepped around him and started down the hall, then stopped and turned around. "By the way, do you know an agent named Melissa Lowery?"

"Name sounds familiar, but I can't place her. Why?"

"She was on the scene the night Dylan died, but her report is missing from the file."

"You sure?"

"Positive."

"It probably dropped out at some point, or got stuck to something else and misfiled. Happens all the time."

"Anyway, I was just wondering what was in the report, if she might remember what she'd written, but no one seems to know where she is."

"I can ask around, see if anyone knows."

"Thanks, Brendan." She smiled and resumed her quick trot to the elevator, calling to the woman who was just about to enter the car, "Hey, could you hold that for me, please . . . ?"

CHAPTER TEN

ANNE MARIE SAT ON THE BLACK LEATHER SOFA IN the office of the Avon County district attorney and read through the letter she'd been handed almost immediately upon entering the room.

"This is what we're dealing with, Dr. McCall," the District Attorney, Art Sheridan, told her. "We think this is, in fact, from the killer, but we want your opinion. On the author of the letter as well as on the contents."

Annie took her time reading, then read it through a second time.

"I agree this is from your killer. There's so much going on here . . . ," she told the men who had gathered in the office and appeared to be waiting for some revelation from her. "But this isn't like a psychic reading. I need a little time to think this through. But I can tell you up front, I do believe it to be genuine. He fancies himself as very intelligent, very much in control of this situation; he's very cocky about having you all on the ropes, and is quite proud of that. Yet, at the same time, he's telling you a great deal about himself."

"Such as . . . ?" Sheridan asked hopefully.

"This is not a very young man. I'm thinking he's in his late twenties, perhaps his early thirties. He's not well educated, but he believes he's quite smart and is annoyed that everyone doesn't recognize his brilliance. He's in a low-level job—I think he has been for years, which is why I think he's in his thirties—a job that makes him subservient, and he hates that feeling. He knows he's better than everyone else, so he's smug, even as he's humiliated by the menial tasks his job requires of him." She looked up at Sheridan. "I wrote a preliminary profile for Detective Crosby. This was all in that memo."

"Anyone have that memo?" Sheridan looked around the room.

"I have it." Malone passed it to Sheridan, who glanced at it, then asked, "How come I didn't get this?"

"I, ah, sent you a copy," Malone told him. "It might still be in your interoffice mail."

"In any case"—Sheridan gestured to Annie—"continue, Dr. McCall."

"You're looking for someone who does menial work for a lot of people who are much better off financially than he is, or who comes into contact with such people on a regular basis. He resents what they have, doesn't understand why he hasn't been able to make as much or to have the kind of life that they have. His resentment is deep-seated and has been building inside him for a long time. He thinks he's as worthy as they—more so, actually—but they don't recognize this. They probably don't see him at all. So he's forcing them to look at him, to stand in awe of him, by taking something precious from them, something they value greatly, to prove to them how much control he has over their lives. He's stealing their daughters, defiling them, taking their lives. And flaunting what he's done." She looked from one man to the other. "He will not stop. He will keep on going for as long as he can."

"Are you saying this is socially motivated, that this is a class thing . . . ?"

"If you want to use those terms, Chief Malone, but this goes so much deeper than that. Look here, in his letter. He's incensed that you would think that he would have bothered with these other victims, these nameless girls. He's infuriated that someone is trying to copy what he's done, but even angrier that this copycat killer has targeted girls that *he* feels are so beneath him. It's bad enough that someone is copying his style, but to have the deaths of these girls who he feels are inferior and therefore so unworthy of his attention—well, he's just not going to take that. Uh-uh. He wants you to make sure the public knows his standards are much higher than this copycat. And he wants this copycat caught."

She held up the letter.

"See here, what he's telling you. 'Why would I

want to kill a bunch of nameless nobodies? How could you be so stupid to think those other girls would interest me?' "

"He's going after girls whose families are well-known," Malone murmured.

"We already knew that," Sheridan reminded him brusquely.

"But now we know why. That's his game. If I understand Dr. McCall correctly, this is his way of shoving it to people he feels look down on him."

"Not only in the sense of retaliation, but in showing them that ultimately, he can control them, not the other way around, that he can impact their lives in ways they'd never have imagined," Annie told them. "Look for someone who's worked a menial job for a long time, ten years or better, in a place where he'd come into daily contact with the victims' families. A country club, golf course, restaurant, a pool company, landscaping company . . . some business that would attract the well-to-do or the influential from the community."

"Green Briar Country Club. It's the only country club in the county. Only golf course, as well," Malone offered.

"See if the victims' families were members," Sheridan told him.

Malone reached for the telephone, made a call, then hung up. "I've got someone on that. We should have a list of members within the hour. I also requested that contact be made this morning with the parents to find out who they used for landscaping, if they have a pool or handyman—all the possibilities Dr. McCall just talked about. We'll see if we get any matches."

He turned to Annie.

"Any chance we can pick your brain on this second killer while we have you here? You have any thoughts on him?"

"I think it's all staging," Annie said. "He's tried to make his victims look as much like the others as he could. He's copying the other killer's style because he wants to go unnoticed. He wants these girls dead, but isn't making a statement, the way the first killer is. I'd be willing to bet the shoes he took from his victims were tossed into the trash. Unlike our first killer, who is keeping them in a special place and treating them like treasures. These other killings were more like executions than murders that involved any passion or fulfilled any need or fantasy of the killer."

"Why would someone want to execute a fourteen-year-old girl?" Malone murmured.

"Because she knows something that the killer doesn't want anyone else to know, or has seen something he didn't want anyone to see," Annie suggested. "Or because she's in his way. Possibly she's served a purpose and isn't needed anymore. She's disposable, for whatever reason, and so he disposed of her. Having a serial killer in the area preying on young girls was simply a matter of convenience for him. He figured he'd just piggyback onto that, make his kills look the same. And at first glance, they do."

Malone swore under his breath.

"Yes." Annie nodded. "My thoughts exactly."

"Dr. McCall, there are details about the killings that were not released to the public. That still haven't been released to the public."

"Like the fact that the girls' throats were slashed and their shoes were taken?"

"Yes."

"Well, as I said to Detective Crosby, either someone connected with the investigation is leaking information . . ." She paused.

"Or someone connected with the investigation is the killer," Sheridan finished the thought.

He and Malone stared at each other. Finally, Malone broke the silence.

"I can't even begin to imagine a suspect from that pool. We've got the entire Lyndon police force, we've got county detectives. We've got Broeder police, we've got Chapman PD, the D.A.'s office. How the hell do you narrow that down?"

"Someone is going to have to." Annie looked from one man to the other. "Identifying the girls—knowing who they are, what brought them together with their killer—will help lead you to him. I have someone at the Bureau trying to identify the identical tattoos these girls had. Right now, that's all we have to go on. Within twenty-four hours, we should have reports back from our lab on the trace from both groups of victims. Hopefully, we'll have something that will lead us in the right direction. Until then, do what you can with what you have."

"First order of business is getting our hands on the membership list from Green Briar," Malone noted.

"Which is more direction than we had an hour ago," Sheridan reminded him. "Let's see where that takes us . . ."

"What a treat this is." Annie glanced around the handsome dining room at the restaurant, which overlooked the small man-made lake nestled in the heart of the beautifully manicured golf course.

Evan nodded. "Lots of dark wood, lots of flowers. It's a pretty classy place."

"Well, the room is lovely, and the view spectacular, but I was referring to the fact that you and I are actually having dinner together in the middle of the week."

"And even more surprising, it isn't cold pizza out of the fridge at two in the morning." He took a sip of wine. "It is pretty nice, isn't it."

She laughed. "You are a master of understatement."

He refilled her glass and set the bottle off to one side of the table.

"What a coincidence that you chose the Green Briar Country Club for dinner tonight." She lowered her voice. "Don't think you're fooling me. I know you're dying to go into the kitchen and start interrogating the busboys."

"All in good time." He smiled at the waitress who served their salads.

"You wouldn't."

"If I had a better idea who I was looking for, sure. We just haven't narrowed things down enough yet. But sure. If I knew for certain our guy worked here, I'd be in there in a heartbeat." He grinned. "Of course I'd wait until after dessert."

"But you have confirmed that all of the victims' families were members here."

"Yes, but we also confirmed that they all bought their pools from Kava's and three out of five bought their groceries at Marshall's and had them delivered." He pushed the croutons aside on his Caesar salad. "And we're still trying to figure out how many of these families had their yard work done by the same landscaper and used the same handyman."

"He's there, though, Evan. I can feel him." Her voice dropped even lower. "You're going to find him in one of those places, and you're going to find him soon."

"You sound awfully sure of yourself."

"I am sure of myself. Sometimes I'm not so sure. Sometimes I give it my best guess, and sometimes I'm right, but I've been wrong, too. This time, I know I'm right."

"Well, then, I think we should drink to a speedy resolution." Evan refilled his glass.

Annie touched the rim of her glass to his, then took a sip.

"Here's what bothers me, though," she told him. "You will get this guy, and you will get him soon. The other one—the one who killed the girls with the tattoos—he's a different duck altogether. He's going to be hard to find. Tracking him down is going to take your best skills. Your best use of the available science."

"You really think he's a cop?"

"I think he's most likely a cop or someone close to one of the investigating departments." She tapped her fingers on the stem of her glass. "You might want to ask Sheridan to bring this investigation strictly into the county, have only your people handle it from here on out."

"Less chance of a cover-up if it's a cop." He nodded. "Of course, that means I'll be stepping on a lot of toes."

"But there'll be a greater chance for justice for those three girls. For them and their families."

"That's the bottom line, isn't it? Finding out who these girls are and helping to bring closure to their families." He took another sip of wine and added, "Someone needs to pay for what he did to them."

"If we can identify the significance of the tattoos, there's a good chance we'll be able to determine where these girls came from. Then maybe we can figure out who they are and how they got from there to here."

"It should only be so easy."

"Easy? Not on your life." She tilted her glass in his direction. "But I promise you, the payback will be huge. When you look into the eyes of the parents of these girls and tell them the man who did this to their daughters has been captured and will be punished, that their daughters can rest in peace, you will know it was worth every hour you spent, every bad lead that you followed, every toe you stepped on along the way."

"I can't argue with you. I'll speak with Malone in the morning, see if he agrees, see if he wants to talk to Sheridan himself or if he's okay with me taking the lead here."

"What are the chances he'll toss this to the Bureau as part and parcel of the other investigation?"

"I'd be real surprised. I think he's going to keep this totally separate, and frankly, I think he should. For one thing, we all believe the killings are not related. For another, he'll want to assure the more prominent citizens that the deaths of their daughters merit the attention of the FBI. These other girls, maybe not. Which is okay with me. I want to handle this case myself."

"What will you do if Sheridan doesn't want to bring that investigation into the county?" she asked. "What are the chances he'll want to permit the local departments, the locals where the bodies were found, to work the individual cases?"

"If I know Sheridan, he's going to weigh this very

carefully from a political angle. If he thinks there's a chance his office can track this guy down and make a collar, he'll jump at it. If he thinks it's a long shot, he'll put me off until he thinks we have something."

"Then we'll have to get him something." She leaned back in her seat to permit the waitress to serve their entrées. "And we'll start with the tattoos. As soon as we get an ID on them, you'll have something to take to him. In the meantime, you have all the resources of the FBI at your disposal. Use them."

"Sheridan hates the FBI, you know."

"I know." She grinned. "But it's going to make him look really good if he can hold a press conference and assure the county movers and shakers that he's brought in the best the feds have to offer to take this killer down." She pounded her fist lightly on the table for emphasis.

Evan laughed at her attempt to mimic the D.A.

"That's all good for tomorrow's agenda, but no more shoptalk. Tonight is ours, and I want to enjoy every minute of it with my girl."

"Well then, let's eat up and head home early." She smiled and toyed with her fork. "The night, as they say, is still very, very young . . ."

CHAPTER
ELEVEN

"Dr. McCall, I'm surprised to hear from you so soon." Art Sheridan had grabbed the phone as soon as he heard who was on the other end of the line. "Should I be encouraged?"

"A little optimism is always good," Annie replied. "And in this case, warranted. I have the lab results from the Bureau. I'd like to go over them with you. When would be a good time?"

"How soon can you get here?" He sat up straight in his chair, hopefully anticipating a break in this god-bloody-awful case. Praying for one.

"Fifteen, twenty minutes."

"You're still in town, then. Terrific. I'll be waiting. Okay if we have Chief Malone and Detectives Crosby and Weller in on this?"

"Certainly, whomever you feel you need. You might want to include the three agents the Bureau sent up as well," she replied. "I'll see you soon."

The D.A. buzzed for his secretary without bothering to hang up the phone. "Lois, I need Malone,

Crosby, and Weller here in fifteen minutes. No excuses."

He stood and went to the window to look out. Those damned news vans were everywhere. Outside the courthouse, in the parking lots, down the side streets. He knew a press conference was overdue, but he had nothing, not one bone to toss to the reporters who badgered his every move once he stepped out of the safety of his office. They followed him home, had even followed him to his son's softball game last night. He knew he owed them, but wasn't about to speak until he had something real, something legit. He'd seen too many D.A.s make asses out of themselves on television by calling conferences when they had nothing to talk about but yesterday's news. He wasn't going that route. Never let it be said that Arthur M. Sheridan wasn't smart enough to learn from the mistakes of others. When he called the press in, he'd have something solid. End of story.

Still, he was hoping that day was close at hand. He was up for reelection in November and was looking forward to blowing out the competition, a man he'd gone to law school with and had never liked.

"Sanctimonious ass," he muttered to himself. The mere thought of his rival always brought out the worst in him. Now, *he* would be just the type to call a premature press conference just to get his pretty face on national TV one more time. Well, Sheridan wasn't going to play that game.

The D.A. just hoped that whatever the FBI had was

something he could use, and use now. The pressure was mounting daily. Even his wife had gotten into the act, since their children attended the same private school as one of the victims.

"Honestly, Art, I'm afraid to show my face at Northgate. Everyone wants to know what you're going to do about this monster who killed the Fuhrmann girl. Everyone's scared."

"Everyone should be scared," he'd told her at the time. Christ, like we're dragging our feet here . . .

"What's going on?" Chris Malone stuck his head through the doorway.

"Come on in. Where are Crosby and Weller?"

"Crosby's on his way in, Weller is right behind me."

As if on cue, Jacqueline Weller tapped on the door, then entered without waiting for an invitation. She was tall, plain, humorless, and a decent detective with lofty ambitions. She'd been at the job three years longer than Evan and had earned the respect of everyone in the county. Those who knew such things whispered her name as a possible successor for Sheridan once he moved up the ladder.

"Jackie, take a seat." Sheridan motioned to the five matched chairs that had been arranged in a semicircle around his desk. "We're going to be joined by Detective Crosby and the profiler the FBI sent us. Apparently, she's received the results from their lab and is eager to share with us. I'm hoping she's going to be bringing us good news."

"I suspect she'd merely fax it if she didn't have something solid," Malone observed. "She doesn't seem to be the type to waste her time."

"May I come in?" Annie rapped on the door much as Jackie Weller had done.

"Dr. McCall." Sheridan walked from behind his desk to greet her. "I can't tell you how happy I am to have you back here so soon. I'm hoping you have something good to share with us."

"I think I do."

"Have you met Detective Weller?" The D.A. smiled. Next to the petite profiler, who was always meticulously dressed, Weller looked like an unkempt Amazon. Sheridan wondered if Crosby knew just how lucky he was.

"I have. How are you, Detective?" Annie offered her hand.

"I'm hoping I'll be better once we hear what you have to say."

"Were you able to get in touch with Agents Cahill, Hoffman, and Muller?" Annie asked pointedly.

"Ah, no. I thought, since time was so short, I'd let Detective Weller here pass along whatever information you might have."

"I see," Annie said.

"Ah, here's Detective Crosby." Malone tilted his head in the direction of the door, where Evan stood.

"Come on in, Evan. We're just about ready to start. Take a seat there"—Sheridan pointed to the remain-

ing unoccupied chair—"and let's see what Dr. McCall
has for us."

"I think you might want to copy these so everyone
has their own." Annie held up the folder containing
the lab reports.

Malone left his seat and reached for the folder.

"I'll take care of it," he told her, and left the room.

"Just so you know"—Sheridan addressed Annie—
"I'm treating these murders as two separate cases.
We're going to work on the assumption that we do in
fact have two different killers. Detective Weller is
going to be in charge of the Schoolgirl Slayer killings;
Detective Crosby will lead the investigation of the
unidentified victims. As far as the public is concerned,
however, this is one case. Maybe if this second killer
thinks he has us fooled, he'll get careless."

He turned to Evan.

"Just remember this was your idea, when Jackie
solves the big case and gets all the publicity." Sheridan's idea of a joke.

"Jackie brings that guy in, she is more than welcome to the publicity." Evan turned to her as Malone
came back into the room. "Hey, this case could make
you a star."

"Right," she said without smiling. "And the book
deal could make me rich."

Before anyone could comment on that, Malone
started passing out the lab reports.

"Dr. McCall, if you'd like to start . . . ," Sheridan
said.

"Just a few things of note," Annie told them. "First of all, we have recovered several areas of trace evidence. On all your victims, Detective Weller, the lab found traces of maroon carpet fibers. The fibers were matched to carpeting used by several auto manufacturers—specifically Ford and GMC—between 1992 and 1999."

"Any particular models?" Weller asked.

"No. They used this pretty much across the board. But we're checking to determine if this color carpet was used exclusively with any exterior colors. We'll narrow it down as much as we can. In the meantime, there is more . . ." Annie turned to the next page in the pack. "On these same victims, the lab found snippets of grass."

"Grass?"

"Grass, Chief Malone. Green grass. Which fits quite nicely with our theory that the killer is a laborer. I understand you've narrowed the field down a bit, Detective Crosby?"

"We've determined that three businesses were common to all of the victims. Green Briar Country Club, Sweet Summer Pools, and Davison's Lawn and Garden. All employ workers who would come into contact with mowed grass."

"Wait a minute, I thought this was my case," Detective Weller said crisply, the only animation she'd shown since she arrived.

"It is, as of this morning," Evan responded pleasantly. "I went through all of the businesses and services the victims might have had in common last night. I found that some were used by two or three of the victims' families, but only these three were utilized by all of them."

Jackie Weller turned to Annie.

"Anything else that pertains to my case?"

"Actually, I think the rest of the report is pretty much self-explanatory. Most of the remaining trace I'd like to address right now concerns the three unidentified girls."

"If I might be excused, then?" Weller looked at the D.A. "I'll need to talk to the agents who came up yesterday, fill them in."

"Of course. Go right ahead." Sheridan nodded. "Just keep in touch. We'll want to know the minute you think you have a viable suspect."

"Will do." Detective Weller grabbed her bag, said her good-byes, and left the room in a blur.

"Now, what else do you have for us?" The D.A. turned his attention back to Annie. "You said you have information pertaining to the other girls?"

"Hair from three different men and a dog."

"Three men and a dog?" Malone leaned forward slightly to look at her, his brows raised.

"Right. Pubic hair from two of the men, head hair only from three. Dog hair from an as-yet-unidentified breed. The lab is still working on that."

"So three guys are involved; only two had sex with the girls?"

"Looks that way. The hair we found on all three

victims is the same. Same three men. Same two pubic hairs."

"So what's this other guy doing, watching?" Malone frowned. "With his dog?"

"Don't know. But the third man has been close enough to the vics to leave a little bit of himself with each of them," Annie told him.

"Any other trace? Carpet fibers like the others?" Sheridan wanted to know.

"No carpet, no fabric fibers of any kind. I'm wondering if he wrapped them in plastic before he transported them from where they were killed to the place where they were left."

"Maybe that's the third guy. Maybe he just moved the bodies."

"You said the lab was still working on the dog hair. Can they even determine the breed of dog?" Malone asked.

"It will take a little longer to get a match, but yes, they can. Of course, it may well be that the girls came in contact with the dog someplace else. No one's saying a dog was on the scene. The dog could have belonged to the girls. The evidence just tells us that at some point, all three of these girls came in contact with the same dog, or with something that had dog hair on it."

"Three guys—one of whom may or may not have a dog—two of whom rape and murder these three girls, while another guy only handles the bodies, maybe only to move them?" Malone rubbed the back of his neck. "Anyone else think that's odd?"

"There is one other thing," Annie told him. "All three of these girls had dirt under their fingernails and in the tiny creases of their feet. Dirt with the same composition. We're checking to see if the dirt samples check out with the areas where the bodies were found, but I'm betting they don't. We already know that the girls were killed elsewhere and dumped where they were found. There's no evidence of struggle, nowhere near the amount of blood there'd have been if their throats had been cut right there at the drop site. So they must have been taken someplace, someplace where they were raped and murdered, then moved to these other areas where they were found."

"Someplace where they would be easily found. Posed, like the other girls, their shoes missing." Sheridan noted.

"That little detail is key," Evan reminded them. "Since no one knows about the shoes . . ."

The statement hung there between them.

"Okay, let's accept the fact that someone near to the investigation is involved in this." Sheridan finally broke the silence. "From here on out, no information about these unidentified girls gets released to anyone, unless I personally approve it. Let's keep a lid on all of it, from the fact that it's a different killer to the very real possibility that someone in or close to law enforcement could be the killer."

"Honest to God, Art, don't you think that's a

stretch? I can't believe any one of these cops—," Malone began, and the D.A. stopped him.

"I can't believe it, either, Chris, but the fact remains that someone is leaking information, and we're going to have to deal with that." He turned to Evan. "Give this the best you've got, Detective. Find whoever killed these girls. And if it's a cop, God help him. I personally will nail him to the wall."

"I'll hold him down." Malone nodded.

"Well then, since we're all in agreement on that point, let me just add that I'm still waiting to hear about the tattoos," Annie told them. "I think if we can match them to other similar tattoos, we'll be on our way to identifying the girls."

"How much longer do you think before you have something?" Sheridan asked.

"I can't estimate how long it will take," Annie said. "I'll check in later today with my office to see if anything has turned up."

"One thing," Evan spoke up. "About the tattoos. I'd like to keep that from the press, too. Actually, I'd like to keep that from everyone who is not in this room."

"I agree." Sheridan nodded without hesitation. "There are four of us here; how many people working on this at the FBI?"

"One," Annie replied.

"And the M.E. knows about them," Evan reminded him.

"That makes six people," Sheridan said. "If this

gets out, it will only be because one of us six let it out."

"You think it's that important to keep it under wraps?" Malone asked.

"I think it could prove to be. I think the less we talk publicly about this second killer, the better off we'll all be." The D.A. stood, signaling the meeting had come to an end. "Let him think he's fooled us."

"Anything else? Dr. McCall? Anything else to add?" he asked.

"I think we covered it all today." Annie stood also and gathered her notes from the end of the desk. "You have my card if you need to get in touch with me. My cell phone number is there. You can also get to me through one of the agents assigned to the other case. Agent Cahill can always find me."

"We'll look forward to hearing whatever you find out about those tattoos." Sheridan opened the door for her, and she stepped into the hall. "I assume you'll give the information to Detective Crosby."

"As soon as I have something to give him."

Annie and Evan walked to the stairwell together, careful not to walk too closely to each other.

Once they were outside the building, she asked, "Where are you headed now?"

"I thought I'd take a ride out to visit the places where my three girls were left."

"May I go with you?"

"Sure. May not be much to see, but sure."

"I can call Will from the car. I wanted to check in with him, just in case he's got something to tell me."

"I want so badly to solve this one, Annie," he told her as they walked down to Fourth Street, where he'd parked his car. "Jackie can have the big-profile case, she can have the publicity and all the glory. I'll be more than happy if I can find out who these girls were and what happened to them."

"What about the book deal?" she teased.

"She can even have the book deal." He smiled. "Someone has to make it right for these kids. I'd like it to be me."

"And the possibility that a cop is involved has nothing to do with your wanting this case all to yourself."

"It won't be all to myself. I'll have help if I ask for it. But yeah, if a cop's involved, I want to bring him in."

They turned the corner on Fourth and crossed the street to Evan's car, which he unlocked with the remote. He opened Annie's door for her, pausing to nuzzle the side of her face.

"You smell good," he whispered.

"Now, Detective," she said sternly. "What would District Attorney Sheridan have to say about such a public display of affection?"

"He wishes he were me, don't kid yourself." He kissed her neck.

"Save it." She smiled as she slid into the front passenger seat. "I'll be here at least until tomorrow."

"Yippee." He slammed the car door and walked around to the driver's side. By the time he opened the door and got behind the wheel, she was holding the phone to her ear.

"Hey, Will, it's Annie. Got anything for me on those tattoos yet?"

Evan started up the engine, but she put a hand on his arm, silently asking him to wait. He turned off the engine.

"Can you send me all this via fax to . . . Evan, what's the number of the new fax machine at your house?"

He told her and she repeated the number for Will.

She listened to Will for a few minutes longer, then said, "Would you repeat that?"

She scribbled quickly on a piece of paper she found in her purse.

"And you're sure?" She hesitated, then said, "I wish I could remember why that sounds so familiar. I guess it'll come to me. Give me a call if you find anything else. And thanks, Will. This is great. I owe you. Yeah, another one . . ."

"He's identified the tattoos?"

"He found several other similar victims in Chicago. Three girls, all Hispanic. Cause of death was different from yours, though. These girls all died from gunshots to the head. All from the same gun."

"More executions."

"That's what I thought, too, when he first said it. I'm wondering if these girls of yours would have been shot had there not been a serial killer in the same general geographic area. Making the kills look the same could have been simply a way to camouflage the hits."

"What did he have to say about the tattoos?"

"This is really interesting. These girls in Chicago all had those little stars in the same place, top of the hip, left side. None of them had any identification, but one of them had some kind of dried bean seeds in a small vial on a cord around her neck."

"Dried bean seeds?" Evan frowned.

"Right. The cop handling the investigation found that these beans apparently are grown in Central America."

"Could he be more specific?"

"He mentioned a small country called Santa Estela as a possible source."

"Never heard of it."

"I have. And it took me a minute, but I just remembered where I heard the name."

"You going to share that with me?"

"Connor was there, a few years ago. I remember overhearing him and Dylan talking about it."

"Maybe he has a contact there who could help us to identify the tattoo."

"I'll ask him. I'll e-mail him tonight." She leaned back against the seat. "We can go now."

"Thank you." He turned the key in the ignition.

"Sorry. I didn't mean to be rude. I'm just thinking."

"You're thinking that if the kids from Chicago

were from Santa Estela, maybe these girls—my girls—
are, too."

She nodded. "And wondering why they're here,
how they got here."

"Want to skip the tour of the crime scenes for
today and go straight to my place so you can use your
computer?"

"Do you mind?"

"Not at all. I'm itching to find something concrete
on this case."

"Will is going to fax over everything he has, including the name and phone number of the cop in
Chicago who worked this case."

"I can't wait to talk to him."

"I had a feeling you'd say that."

Once they were back at the townhouse, Evan went
directly to the fax machine and Annie to her laptop.
She turned it on, and typed her message.

```
TO: CShields00721
From: AMMccall00913
Re: Santa Estela
Connor, strange development on a case here in PA.
Tattoos on the vics found to be identical to those
found on three vics in Chicago. Young girls, one of
whom appears to have a connection traced back to
Central America, possibly Santa Estela. Do I recall
correctly that you had spent some time there? Any
contacts remain?
   A
```

She hit *send* and waited, but the immediate response she'd hoped for didn't come. Maybe tonight, maybe tomorrow.

In the meantime, she wanted to see the fax Will had sent Evan. Maybe the Chicago cop had found answers to the very questions Evan was now asking. Maybe he could give them a lead. Maybe this was the thread that, once pulled, would help Evan to send the girls home.

CHAPTER TWELVE

"WHAT'S ON YOUR AGENDA FOR TODAY?" EVAN ASKED Annie over breakfast early on Monday morning.

"First thing I want to do is try Will again." She sat across from him at the small table next to the only window in his narrow kitchen.

"Checking to see if he found out anything else about the tattoos?"

"No, he'll contact me as soon as he has something on that. I want to ask him about Melissa Lowery." She sipped at her coffee. "Have I mentioned her to you before? She's a former agent who was on the scene the night Dylan was shot. She wrote an account of the events of that night, but the report isn't in the file."

"I think you did mention her. Did you ask around the Bureau?"

"No one seems to know where she went after she left. Which is odd in itself, since she was with the Bureau for seven years. She must have had friends."

"I guess you didn't ask the right people. Someone

knows where she is. Did you check with HR? Wouldn't they have a forwarding address?"

"Privacy issues. They don't give out anyone's home address."

"So how would Will be able to find her?"

Annie laughed. "No one really knows how Will finds out anything. He just has a knack with computers and uncanny instincts. If anyone can track her down, it will be him."

She rested her elbow on the windowsill and gazed out.

"You need a little help finishing that deck?"

"Maybe. Depends on who's volunteering."

"I could work on it with you next weekend, if you get the boards that go across the frame." Her left index finger tapped on the window glass.

"Decking."

"What?"

"Those boards that go across the frame are called decking." He downed the last of his coffee and stood. "If you really want to, we can work outside next weekend. If it rains, we can work inside." He leaned down to kiss her neck.

She smiled and reached up her hand to touch his face.

"Either way, we win."

"Either way," he agreed.

"What's that I see going on out there by the fence?" She tapped on the glass again. "Looks as if someone has been digging."

"I started to dig up that garden bed for your roses, but I didn't get around to finishing it."

"Maybe we could put that on the list for next weekend, too."

"Hmm. Build the deck. Plant the garden." He grinned as he walked to the sink to rinse out his cup. "Sounds like what the married guys in the office call a 'honey-do' weekend."

"It'll be good for both of us to spend some time outside, do a little manual labor. I'm up for it."

"I'll make a point next week to pick up the rest of the material for the deck. We'll start early on Saturday and just work through until it's finished. Or until one of us falls over."

"That would have to be you. I'm in great shape." She tilted her head to one side. "Is that my phone ringing or yours?"

"Mine. And it's upstairs on the dresser." He bolted from the room and took the steps to the second floor two at a time.

Annie cleared the table and stacked the breakfast dishes in the dishwasher. As small as Evan's townhouse was, she loved it. It was cozy and homey. With just a little paint on the cabinets, maybe lose that old wallpaper and add some textured paint to the walls, put in a new tile floor, the kitchen could be absolutely charming. She smiled to herself, knowing that such a kitchen would exist only in her mind. Evan would never think to do it on his own, and she'd never suggest it to him. It was, after all, his house.

She went to the back door and looked out onto the small yard. The deck would take up almost all of the space, but there was still room for those roses. She opened the door and stepped out, careful to avoid the box of nails and scraps of wood he'd left on the porch, and walked to the back of the yard where she'd planted the peonies. They hadn't bloomed this year, might not bloom for a few more years. She'd heard they were temperamental and didn't like being moved. She was thinking about making a stop at the local nursery to look for something that might bloom now when she heard the back door slam.

"That was Sheridan," Evan told her as he made his way across the yard to where she stood. "I have to go."

"Please don't tell me they found another girl . . ."

"No. But they did get another letter from the killer. Apparently, he's really pissed."

"Sheridan or the killer?"

"The killer. He'd expected Sheridan to let the media know that he was not responsible for the deaths of the three unidentified girls. He wants everyone to know there's a copycat killer out there, and he wants the media to start referring to him as the Schoolgirl Slayer. He thought Malone was going to take care of these issues for him after he'd written that letter, but as you know, we thought we'd sit on that for a few days."

"What's he done?"

"He wrote a second letter. Only he sent this one to

Fox News. They aired it about ten minutes ago, right at the top of the seven a.m. show." He gave her a long kiss on the mouth.

"I miss you so much when you're not here, Annie."

"I miss you when I'm not here, too." She leaned her forehead against his.

"Sooner or later, we're going to have to talk about that."

"I know." She nodded. "It's getting a little crazy, all this back-and-forth."

"If I didn't have this case, I'd be able to come to you."

"You can't not be here when something like this is going on. You have to be here."

"Still . . ."

"It's not something we're going to resolve right now, Evan. We'll talk about it. Maybe next weekend."

"Okay. Gotta go." He kissed her again before heading toward the door. "I'll catch up with you later."

"What's Sheridan going to do?"

"Damage control, he says. Whatever the hell that is at this point." He waved and went through the garage as a shortcut to his car, which was parked out front.

Annie walked back inside, locked the door, and went upstairs to gather her things. Back downstairs in twenty minutes with her bag and laptop, she decided to check her e-mail before leaving. She set up the computer on Evan's desk in his study and turned it on. There were e-mails from the office—including one from John asking her to meet with him later that afternoon about the Michigan cases—but nothing from Connor. She turned off the laptop and slipped it into its case, then called the airport to see if there was an earlier flight she could catch back to Virginia. There was one, at 12:45. She booked herself on it and called the office to let John know she'd be there.

She hung up just as her watch beeped the hour. It was nine o'clock. If Will was running true to form today, he'd already been at his desk for several hours. She dialed his cell phone, just in case he'd had a late start and was still in transit or in the field.

"Hey, Annie. Did Evan get my fax?" Will answered, having recognized Annie's number on the caller ID.

"He did. He's going to follow up with the investigating officer from Chicago this morning. Thanks so much. That might prove to be the information he needs to crack that case."

"I hope it helps." He paused, then asked, "What else is on your mind this morning?"

"You know me all too well." She sighed, a long deliberately dramatic sigh, and he laughed.

"You just don't make social calls, Annie. None of us do. Way too busy. So tell, what's on your mind?"

"Melissa Lowery."

"What about her?"

"You know her?"

"I did know her. Not well, but I knew her."

"Everyone says that." She frowned. "Everyone seems to know who she was, but I can't seem to find anyone who really knew her. And no one seems to know why she left the Bureau or where she went."

"Who needs to know?"

"I do. I need to speak with her." Annie explained about the missing report from Dylan's file. "I want to ask her if she remembers what she'd observed that night, if she remembers what she wrote."

"I'm trying to remember if I know anyone who was friends with her." He was silent for a moment. "I saw her in the lounge once or twice with Mia; maybe she knows something."

"Mia Shields?"

"Yes. Give her a call. In the meantime, do you want me to see if I can find an address for Melissa?"

"Would you mind?"

"Not at all. I live for these little intrigues. Let me see what I can do. I'll call you when I have something."

Annie smiled. Not *if,* but *when.*

"Great," she said. "I'll give Mia a call now. You wouldn't happen to have a number for her, would you?"

"Sure. She's in the directory." Will read the number off to Annie.

"Great. I love you, Will."

"Of course you do. Just don't tell Cahill. She has a nasty temper."

Annie laughed and hung up. Miranda Cahill, their fellow agent and Will's live-in love, was as well-known for her even disposition and good humor as she was for her statuesque beauty and her smart-aleck mouth.

Mia Shields answered her phone on the third ring.

"Mia, it's Annie." Annie greeted her and made small talk for a few moments, then said, "I'm trying to track down an agent who left the Bureau about two years ago. Someone said they thought you were a friend of hers."

"Who's that?"

"Melissa Lowery."

"Oh, Melissa. Sure, I knew her."

"Do you know where she is now?"

"No clue. I didn't know her all that well, I just knew her because of Grady."

"Grady?"

"He went out with her a couple of times, then when he stopped calling her, she'd corner me and want to know what was up with him, was he seeing someone else, that sort of thing."

"Grady dated Melissa Lowery?" Annie digested this. "Funny, when I asked your other brothers about her, they claimed not to know her."

"They may not have. I don't think they dated for all that long. If neither Brendan nor Andy was around at the time, they may not have been aware Grady'd taken her out. It was never a serious thing, not that I know of anyway, just a few dates. At least, that was my impression."

"You think Grady knows where I can contact her?"

"You can ask him. I think he's in his office. Want me to transfer you?"

"That would be great, thanks."

"Annie, did she do something . . . ?"

"Oh, no, no. I just wanted to ask her about a report she wrote a few years ago, that's all."

"Oh, okay. She didn't seem like the type to be involved in anything shady."

"I'm sure she wasn't."

"I'll transfer you now. Take care, Annie. I hope to see you soon."

"Me, too. Thanks, Mia."

Annie listened to Grady's phone ring and ring. Finally, his voice mail picked up and she left a message for him to call her about Melissa Lowery. She was on her way to her car when her phone rang.

"Annie, hi." Grady sounded rushed, as if he was hurrying off someplace. "What's this about Melissa Lowery?"

"I wanted to talk to her, but no one seems to know where she is."

"What makes you think I'd know?"

"Mia mentioned you used to date her."

"I wouldn't say I used to date her. We grabbed a movie together a time or two, had dinner once or twice, no big deal." There was a long silence on the phone. "Why do you need to talk to her?"

"Because, as you know, Evan and I were looking over Dylan's file, and there are several items missing, one of which is a report written by Melissa."

"Oh, it probably slipped out of the file or got misplaced."

"That's what one of your brothers said."

"Well, it happens . . . By the time a file is retired, who knows how many times it's been read through. Things fall out and get tucked back into the wrong file by accident."

"This isn't a retired file, Grady."

"Sorry, Annie. Look, I don't mean to make light of this. It's just a fact of life that papers fall out of files. It happens all the time."

"I guess." She set her bag on the ground next to her rental car while she unlocked the driver's door. "So you don't know where Melissa went after she left Virginia?"

"No, sorry, I don't."

"Any idea where she's from, where her family might be?"

"No, it never came up in conversation."

"You wouldn't happen to know anyone who might know where Melissa is now, would you?"

"No, sorry. We didn't keep in touch, and I didn't go out with her long enough to find out who her friends were. Sorry."

"Yeah, me, too. Thanks, Grady." Annie disconnected the call and tossed her purse onto the front passenger seat. The conversation with Grady had left her dissatisfied. It wasn't that she thought he was lying as much as she felt he'd brushed over certain things. Who dated someone and didn't ask where they were from? Wasn't that part of that whole small-talk thing, like where you went to college? When you're just getting to know someone, wasn't that just basic?

She tucked the overnight bag behind the driver's seat along with the case holding her laptop. Her phone rang again just as she turned the key in the ignition.

"Annie, it's Evan. Would you have time to stop in at Sheridan's office before you head out?"

"Not really. My flight leaves in two hours. What's up?"

"All hell's breaking loose around here. Our killer apparently was very busy last night. Writing letters, including one to the local paper," he hastened to add. "Which is preferable to some of his other nocturnal activities. Sheridan is calling a press conference at noon and was hoping to have you there."

"For what purpose?"

"Between you and me, I think he just wanted to parade his bevy of FBI personnel so that county residents could see that all the big guns are out on this one."

"If he wants me to look over another letter from the killer, I'm happy to do that. He can fax it to my office. But I don't have time to take part in a dog and pony show today. John wants to meet with me later this afternoon, and since he's going to be out of the office all of next week, I can't put him off. There are things he wants to talk about before he leaves tomorrow."

"Hey, no apologies necessary. I agree with you. I'll tell him your plane took off already, I couldn't reach you. No big deal. Frankly, I'd like to take a bye on this myself."

"He wants you there, too? Even though you're not working the case anymore?"

"He wants everyone there. But as soon as he's done talking, I'm outta there. I called the cop in Chicago, and I'm still waiting to hear from him. That's my priority today." He paused. "I don't suppose you heard from Connor?"

"No, but that's not unusual. He'll get to me when he can. I'll let you know as soon as I hear from him." She stole a look at the clock on the dashboard, then turned the key in the ignition. "I need to get going."

"I'll give you a call tonight."

"Maybe we'll have news to exchange by then." She thought of the conversation she'd just had with Grady. "Oh, speaking of news. Guess who used to date Melissa Lowery?"

"Art Sheridan."

She laughed as she pulled away from the curb. "Grady Shields."

"You're kidding?"

"Nope. Of course, he tells me it was just a casual thing, just a few movies and dinners."

"Does he know where she is now?"

"No. He claims to not even know where she's from."

"You say that as if you don't believe him."

"I thought there was something slightly evasive in his responses. I mean, how do you go out with some-one and not know where they're from? That's the type of thing you ask when you first meet someone. But maybe that's me. And maybe he just felt it was none of my business who he dated. And of course, it isn't."

"Well, maybe Will can come up with something."

"I'm counting on it." She made a left at the light and headed for the highway. "I have to go. I'm mov-ing into heavy traffic. I'll talk to you tonight."

Annie dropped the phone into her lap and set it to voice mail, then eased onto the four-lane highway that would take her to the airport.

She sped along, reflecting back on the morning's events. The Schoolgirl Slayer had revealed more of his hand by sending yet another letter, which she was eager to read. Evan had a solid contact in his case, and she was a step closer to Melissa Lowery. All in all, it had already been quite a day.

She hoped that the officer in Chicago would have something that would shed light on the deaths of the three young girls—his girls, as Evan had started refer-ring to them. She knew he'd work this case until he solved it, and she loved him for that, for caring about three nameless girls who seemed to go unnoticed in death. What they had been in life had yet to be determined.

There would be no glory for him in the resolution of that case, unlike the case of the Schoolgirl Slayer, which would undoubtedly land Sheridan, Malone, and Weller on CNN and *Good Morning America*. It was more than likely that Sheridan wouldn't even bother to call an all-out media conference once Evan found their killer. Since they were lumping these deaths in with the others—at least for now—there'd be no band playing for Evan, no recognition of his dedication and hard work.

Unless, of course, there was a cop involved. That would be news.

Spoken like a true cynic, she thought wryly.

As far as her own search was concerned, Will would come through for her, of that she was certain. God only knew where that trail would lead, or what she'd find, once she finally found Melissa.

_____CHAPTER_____
THIRTEEN

IT WAS ALMOST 6:00 P.M. WHEN ANNIE CLOSED THE door of John Mancini's office behind her. She was stiff from sitting, earlier on the plane on her way back from Philadelphia, later in the day for the two-hour meeting that had just broken up. She rolled her shoulders while she walked to her own office, then stood next to her desk as she listened to her voice mail. When she'd heard all the messages, she smiled, snapped off the light, and took the elevator to the floor below.

"I just got your message." She stood at the doorway to Will Fletcher's office. "I'm glad I caught you before you left. You have something for me?"

"I was just getting ready to close up shop. I wasn't sure if you were in the building. Someone said they'd seen you earlier." Will leaned back in his chair. "Come on in, and I'll—"

"Will . . . oh, hi, Annie, I didn't know you were here." Brendan Shields stood in the doorway. "We're all heading over to Pike's. It's my brother Andrew's birthday. You should come, too, Annie."

"That's the best offer I've had all week, since my

girl is still in Pennsylvania and I've got nothing better to do." Will stood and stretched. "I was just getting ready to leave anyway. How 'bout it, Annie? Come with us to Pike's?"

"I think I'll pass. I've been away all week and have to leave town again tomorrow. I have a lot of work to catch up on and a presentation to prepare. But thanks, Brendan. Next time."

"I'll hold you to that." Brendan looked back at Will. "You ready now?"

"I was just packing up. You can go on. I'll meet you there."

"I don't mind waiting," Brendan told him.

"If you're sure . . ." Will piled some papers into his briefcase, hesitated momentarily, then folded one and handed it to Annie.

"Before I forget, here are the directions to that restaurant you and I talked about," he said.

"Thanks." She stuck the paper in her pocket without looking at it.

"Which restaurant is that?" Brendan asked.

"Oh, a crab place on the other side of the bay. In Rock Hall. It's a favorite of Miranda's and mine," Will told him.

"Hey, I'm always up for crabs," Brendan said. "What's the name of it?"

"I'll tell you about it while we're walking to Pike's. We are walking, right?"

"Sure, why not? It's just a few blocks." Brendan waited at the door for Will, then held it open for

Annie before closing it. "Sure you don't want to come down for a quick beer and a burger?"

"I'm sure, but thanks."

"Catch you next time, then." Brendan paused, then asked, "Say, you still unofficially working on Dylan's case?"

"The file's still open, so yes. I'm still taking a look at it."

"Find anything we missed?"

"No. Nothing yet." She smiled pleasantly in spite of the fact that Brendan's attitude seemed annoyingly patronizing. "But then again, I haven't had much time. It's been a busy week. I promise I'll let you know if we learn something new."

"Were you able to find that agent you were looking for? What's her name . . ."

"Melissa Lowery."

"Yeah, her. You find her yet? Has her report turned up?" He stuck his hands in his pocket and struck a casual pose.

"No." She glanced at Will, but as he gave no indication of having any knowledge of Melissa's whereabouts, she followed his lead. For whatever reason, he didn't seem inclined to share whatever information he'd found.

"I'll keep asking around. Maybe she's been in touch with someone. I can let you know."

"Thanks, Brendan. I'd appreciate it."

Annie fingered the piece of paper in her pocket. "And thanks again, Will, for the directions."

"Anytime, Annie." He slapped a friendly hand gently on her back. "Anytime . . ."

Annie walked with the two men to the elevator, her patience put to the test while the car stopped three times on the way to the lobby. She wanted nothing more than to open the folded sheet of paper and see what Will had found for her, but was forced to wait until she'd said good-bye to her coworkers. Once in her car, she opened the paper and read eagerly.

Grinning, she refolded the paper and stuck it in the top of her purse. She'd known Will wouldn't let her down.

Melissa Lowery was living in West Priest, Montana, as Mariana Gray. Will hadn't found a phone number, but he'd found an address.

The minute Annie arrived at her apartment, she checked the travel website for flight connections from Seattle, where she'd be at a conference from Tuesday afternoon through Wednesday night, to the airport closest to West Priest.

"Looks like that would be Great Falls," she murmured as she studied the flight schedules.

The Wednesday-night flight wouldn't get her in until late, and she'd still have to find a place to stay. But if she booked the 6:00 a.m. flight on Thursday, she'd be in Great Falls by 12:30. She could rent a car and be in West Priest—thirty-five miles according to a map she located through Google—by three. West Priest didn't appear to be a very big town. Surely someone there would know Melissa.

A few clicks of the keyboard later, she'd booked the flight to Great Falls, a room at the closest motel for Thursday night, just in case, and a flight to Philly on Friday morning. Satisfied with her arrangements, she checked her e-mail before logging off the computer, hoping for some word from Connor, but there was nothing.

She showered and dried her hair and wrapped herself in her favorite robe, then went into her small bedroom she used as an office. She sat on the edge of the desk to listen to her phone messages.

"Annie, it's Will. I didn't want to say anything about Melissa in front of Brendan—no particular reason except that I figure if she's taken such pains to disappear—and believe me, it wasn't easy finding her—well, she must have a reason. Makes you wonder what she's hiding, doesn't it? Or from whom?" Will took a deep breath. "Anyway, you missed a hell of a party. All the Shieldses were out in force—except Connor, of course—though it started breaking up earlier than I'd have expected. Andrew apparently has a late date, and Grady has already downed his limit and has gone home, so that leaves me with Brendan, Mia, and Chloe Snyder, you remember her? Well, keep in touch, hear? Have a safe trip to the West Coast, and good luck connecting with Melissa. Let me know what you find."

The line went dead and she erased the message. The next was Evan. "Annie, give me a call when you get in."

One hang-up, and another message from Evan.

She dialed his number and counted the rings. On the fourth, right before the answering machine picked up, he answered.

"How was your meeting?" he asked.

"Long. How was the press conference?"

"Pretty much what we expected. Did you have time to look over the letter from the killer to Fox News?"

"I don't have a copy."

"I faxed it to you."

"Oh." She crossed the room and took several sheets from her machine's in-tray. "There are a couple of faxes here . . . wait . . . yes, it's here. Want me to look at it now?"

"If you have a minute. But hurry up, I have news I'm itching to share."

"The fax can wait, then. Did you hear something from Chicago?"

"I thought you'd never ask." She could hear the smile in his voice. "This cop—he's a detective now, Don Manley—has been looking into the case for months. He said he has several files he thinks I should take a look at."

"Are you going to meet with him?"

"I'm flying out first thing tomorrow morning. He said he didn't want to discuss it on the phone, but if I came out there, he'd tell me everything he knows."

"Sounds intriguing."

"I am so antsy to talk to this guy, Annie. It sounded as if he's got some really hot information."

"Sheridan's okay with you going out of town for a day or so in the middle of the investigation?"

"Sheridan's attention right now is on Jackie Weller's case."

"How's that going?"

"They've interviewed everyone at the country club and the pool company; no luck there. Apparently, there was some mix-up in scheduling with the owner of the landscaping company, but I understand they're on for first thing tomorrow morning to talk to his crews."

"I'm starting to feel they've pushed the limits on this, Evan. This guy's gone what, over a week without another body turning up? He's got to be due. He's got to be jonesing for a kill right about now. If they don't get him within the next twenty-four hours, they're going to have another dead body on their hands."

"Unfortunately, I think you might be right."

"What information did they release to the press?"

"Only that they had traces of carpet fibers, years, makes, models of possible vehicles. Nothing about the grass clippings, though."

"Good. That's how they'll nail him, you know."

"You FBI types think you know it all, don't you?"

She knew he was teasing but felt compelled to defend herself anyway.

"Hey, you study behavior, sometimes patterns emerge. Sometimes you read the patterns correctly, sometimes you don't. It's part science, part art. Neither is exact. You just do your best to read the signs and hope you're interpreting them correctly."

"Annie, I was joking."

"I know." She sighed. "I guess I'm just giving you the speech I wanted to give Sheridan the other day."

"Why didn't you?"

"I guess because ultimately, he's your boss."

"Don't ever let that stop you. I'm a big boy."

"Okay, then, how about I felt it would have been unprofessional and borderline rude to correct him in front of the others."

"That's much more acceptable."

"I have news, too." She curled up in the chair and pulled her legs up under her. "Will found Melissa Lowery."

"He really is good, isn't he?" Without waiting for an answer, he asked, "Where is she?"

"Montana, living under the name Mariana Gray. I'm going to fly there on Thursday morning. I'm praying she'll talk to me, and that she remembers what she put in that report. If I'm really lucky, maybe she'll have kept a copy." Annie bit her bottom lip. "That's assuming she'll talk to me."

"Why wouldn't she?"

"I don't know. She's gone to such lengths to conceal herself out there, even changed her name. That's pretty extreme."

"Maybe she just got stressed out with the whole routine, you know? It wouldn't be the first time someone opted out of law enforcement and just tried to start their life over. And you know, she could have gotten married, which would account for the name change."

"That would explain the last-name change, but not the first."

"You think she's hiding from something?"

"Or someone. Yes, it's possible. She might just slam the door in my face once I tell her who I am."

"Assuming that she does speak with you, do you think there's anything in that report that will tell you something you don't already know?"

"Probably not," she admitted, "but it bothers me, that her report disappeared, then she disappeared. Then the other agent whose report is missing, Lou Raymond, is killed in a freak car accident. It's making me uneasy, the more I think about it. It just seems . . . weirdly coincidental."

"And anyone who knows you, knows you don't believe in coincidences."

"Have you ever met an FBI agent who did?"

"Now that you mention it, I guess I haven't."

He was silent for a moment, and she could almost see him, one elbow leaning on the desk in his office, the other resting on the arm of the chair. He'd have his shoes off and his shirt unbuttoned to the third button and his shirttails out. The familiarity of the image brought a smile to her face.

"So what are you going to do now?" she asked.

"Right now, I'm going to bed and praying to God the phone doesn't ring so that I can get one good night's sleep this week. Then, at the crack of dawn, I'm going to go into the office and copy the file on my girls, make an extra set of photos and lab reports to take to Chicago. I want to give Detective Manley a copy of everything I have on this guy. I'm hoping between the two of us . . ."

"You're hoping to find what you need."

"Exactly. I want to find whatever it is we need to catch this bastard. Bastards, I should say. There are obviously several at work here."

"In the long run, that should make it easier to solve. The more of them there are, the more likely it is that one of them will screw up eventually."

"One could only hope." He yawned. "Sorry, babe."

"No apologies necessary. Get some sleep, Evan. I'll be turning in, too, in a few minutes."

"Wish you were here, Annie."

"So do I." She stifled a yawn of her own. "But I'll be there by Friday afternoon, Friday night at the latest. We should have a lot to talk about while we're working on that deck."

"Well, here's hoping we both find the answers we're looking for. You in Montana, me in Chicago . . ."

Annie hung up the phone and looked for her glasses so she could read the fax. The letter was exactly what she'd been led to expect.

DEAR FOX NEWS PEOPLE:

I THINK YOU NEED TO TALK TO D.A. SHERIDAN IN AVON COUNTY AND ASK HIM WHY HE DIDN'T TELL

YOU ABOUT THE LETTER I SENT TO HIM EARLIER IN
THE WEEK. I TOLD HIM THAT I DID NOT KILL
THOSE OTHER THREE GIRLS—YOU KNOW ABOUT
THOSE THREE GIRLS, RIGHT? THE ONES NO ONE
KNOWS WHO THEY ARE? I DID NOT KILL THEM AND
DO NOT LIKE THAT EVERYONE IS SAYING I DID.
THERE IS A COPYCAT KILLER IN AVON COUNTY AND
NO ONE IS LOOKING FOR HIM. THE GIRLS HE KILLS
ARE NOT LIKE MY GIRLS. ANY IDIOT COULD TELL
YOU THAT.

ALSO, I TOLD D.A. SHERIDAN THAT I WANTED TO
BE REFERRED TO AS THE SCHOOLGIRL SLAYER. DID
HE TELL YOU THAT?

I DIDN'T THINK SO. SINCE HE DIDN'T TELL YOU
ANYTHING, I AM FORCED TO TELL YOU MYSELF. I
THINK HE THINKS HE IS PLAYING A GAME WITH ME.
HE SHOULD KNOW THAT THIS IS NOT A GAME.

I THINK YOU ARE SMARTER THAN HE IS AND
WILL CALL ME BY MY NEW NAME.

THANK YOU. THE SCHOOLGIRL SLAYER

More posturing, more of the same demand for attention. Interesting that he hadn't mentioned any new
kills, though, and had made no threats.

Annie read through the letter again.

He had to know that the police were closing in on
him. Maybe that's why he was not being too cocky. He
was just setting the record straight, as he saw it, and
trying to take full advantage of his fifteen minutes.

"Your days as a free man are coming to an end,

buddy," she murmured as she folded the fax and tossed it onto her desk.

In the morning, she'd call Sheridan and discuss the case with him, give him the benefit of her thoughts on the matter. Don't react publicly. Don't do anything, because he'll be in custody within twenty-four hours. That was the reaction of both her gut and her intellect, but Sheridan would do whatever he felt was in his best interest. Only he knew what that was.

Annie locked up her house and turned off the lights. She got into bed and searched for the remote control for the TV on the stand opposite her bed. She found it under her pillow and tried to remember when she might have put it there. She watched the news until she fell asleep.

She slept later than she'd intended the next morning, and when she awoke, the television was still on. She turned up the volume while she washed her face in the bathroom steps away from her bed, and had just started to brush her teeth when she caught scraps of dialogue. She stuck her head around the corner, her toothbrush still in her mouth, in time to see a handcuffed man being helped into a police car.

". . . who, according to detectives here in Avon County is the self-proclaimed Schoolgirl Slayer, apprehended early this morning by county detectives . . ."

The camera zoomed in for a close-up of a man with thinning brown hair and glasses, wearing a polo shirt with some kind of logo on it. Annie got as close to the screen as she could, but still couldn't make out the writing.

When the phone rang, she knew it would be Evan.

"Do you ever get tired of being right?" he asked.

"This one wasn't so tough. I figured once you narrowed the field, he'd be easy to spot."

"Can you guess who spotted him?"

"Cahill."

He swore softly under his breath and she laughed out loud.

"Miranda has a lot of experience. This is far from being her first serial-killer case. They sent her because she has an uncanny knack for seeing things that other people miss," she said. "Are you going to tell me who and how, or do I have to hang up and get the details from the TV?"

"His name is Albert Vandergris. He is, just as you had predicted, thirty-five years old and he works for the landscaper who did the lawns for all the victims' families. Has worked for them, cutting lawns, for twelve years."

"Sounds good so far," she told him, "but it wasn't a prediction."

"Right. Anyway, Jackie called the owner of the landscaping company yesterday, set it up to talk to his employees before they started for work around seven this morning. All the crews report in by six, get the day's assignments, pick up the trucks and their equipment. So Jackie shows up with the three from the FBI and a few other detectives, and the owner explained to his crews what was going on. He had all the guys waiting there in the barn and starts calling the men up, one by one, to speak with Jackie. And while she's talking to workers, Cahill wanders out of the barn and around the back. Who do you think she finds trying to slip out the back door?"

"Albert."

"You're really good at this, aren't you?"

"Yes, I am. So Miranda nabs him and brings him in?"

"Not until she and Albert had a little chat."

"And she managed to get him to confess."

"Yeah, she did." Evan's voice held a touch of awe. "She told him she'd read the letter he'd written to the news station and pointed out the grammatical errors."

"And he got his back up and began to argue with her?"

"How do you know all this? You already talk to her this morning?"

"No. But she did this once before, in Indiana. Almost the exact same scenario." Annie laughed again. "But let me guess, Jackie is going for the credit here?"

"I'm betting there will be a press conference by noon this morning, complete with a carefully worded statement, prepared and read by the district attorney, praising the work of the county detectives, especially lead detective Weller, and thanking the FBI for their cooperation. I'm almost sorry I won't be here for it."

"That little weasel."

"Yeah, well, at least they got one killer off the street."

"Which leaves your case. Is Sheridan going to make the announcement that Albert is not the killer of these girls?"

"I don't know what he's going to do. I'm hoping he doesn't. I'm hoping whoever is involved with this thinks he's gotten away with it."

"I agree. Keep him guessing. Even though Vandergris has already said he hasn't killed those girls, I think it's best to keep everyone guessing on that point. I wouldn't address it until I had to."

"Yeah, maybe the killer—killers—will do something stupid. And it's not as if anyone seems to care much, one way or another, about my girls. Their deaths haven't gotten too much attention these past few weeks. All the focus has been on the other girls, the kids from the nice families and the good neighborhoods."

"Unfortunately, you know that makes better press. And like it or not, this was a story that had strong emotional appeal and a certain amount of built-in sensationalism. But the lack of focus on your vics may work to your advantage."

"Well, either way, I imagine the D.A. will find a way to keep Vandergris in the foreground for a few more weeks so he can wring every potential future vote out of it."

"Cynic."

"Oh yeah. My middle name."

"Well, with luck, Detective Manley will be able to give you some insights that could help lead you in the right direction."

"I'm afraid that might be too much to hope for." Someone spoke in the background, and Evan covered the phone with his hand. When he came back on the line, he said, "Gotta run. They're calling my flight. See if you can catch some of the press conference this morning."

While she finished packing for her trip, Annie surfed the channels hoping to find coverage of the conference, but apparently it was being carried only locally at the time. Perhaps later in the day, one of the networks would broadcast it, but she was likely to miss it.

Already running late, Annie turned off the TV and closed her suitcase. The Schoolgirl Slayer was in custody, her interest in him on the wane. Her attention was focused now on those who still escaped detection, those who, somewhere, were waiting to strike again.

___CHAPTER___
FOURTEEN

EVAN SAT ON A METAL FOLDING CHAIR IN THE cramped windowless room that Detective Donald Manley called his office, and read through the reports that had been copied for him.

Manley, a tall gaunt man with long fingers and a long sharp nose, went about his business of making calls on a battered-looking phone from a desk that appeared to have been abused at the hands of many. Occasionally, Evan would ask a question or two between Manley's calls, but other than that, there had been little conversation between the two men.

Each was following his own agenda. Manley's focus was on tracking down a witness to a shooting the night before. Evan's was on following the story Manley had laid out for him.

According to the file, eight months earlier, the bodies of three young girls, each killed by a single bullet to the back of the head, had been found in Bonsall Park in the city. For a while, it appeared the case—the press had dubbed it the Bonsall Park Murders— would be retired to the cold-case room, since there

were no witnesses and no suspects. But through net-
working and scanning the Internet, Manley had located other cases that had a similar feel to them. So
far, after having made endless phone calls, he'd found
that victims in two other cities—Boston and New
Orleans—had little stars tattooed on the upper part
of their left hips. Boston's two, Chicago's three, and
New Orleans's four accounted for nine young girls
with tattooed stars. Evan's three made it an even
dozen.

"Why do you suppose it took New Orleans so long
to put this together?" Evan asked when Manley had
ended his phone conversation.

"Only two of the bodies were found in the city. The
others were found in two other parishes and appeared to be unconnected. It wasn't until a curious
detective in New Orleans noticed the tattoos that he
started looking for cases where the vics were similarly
marked."

"How did you find him?"

"I went state by state on the computer, looking for
young girls who'd been killed execution style. These
cases stood out." Manley rubbed a hand across the
stubble on his chin, a telltale sign he'd been on the job
since early that morning.

"Then there's a possibility there could be more,"
Evan said softly.

"Sure." Manley nodded wearily. "We can only
track what's been entered. We both know that there
are departments that aren't up to snuff when it comes

to using computers. Some of the smaller departments don't have personnel who can spend time entering the data. Others just aren't comfortable with the technology, don't ask me why."

Manley removed his glasses and rubbed his eyes slowly.

"Come on." He stood and stretched. "Let's take a ride."

Evan drove his rental car because the air-conditioning in Manley's department-issued vehicle hadn't worked for the past two summers and he hadn't gotten around to getting it fixed. The day had been hot and humid, and the sun had several hours to go before it set. Following Manley's directions, Evan wended his way through busy city streets, then pulled into a broad parking lot when they reached their destination. Somehow, Evan had known they'd end up here. It was exactly where he'd have taken Manley if their positions were reversed.

They got out of the car without speaking, and Evan followed his host along a winding path that led to a stream that tumbled over a rocky bottom.

"Man-made." Manley pointed to the stream as they crossed over it on a wooden footbridge. "They brought the rocks in, stocked it with fish and other water creatures. Those trees along the banks? All brought in by some big-time landscaper from back east. Designs city parks. The city spent a fortune to make the place look as natural as possible."

They continued along the path until they reached a

fountain that sat in the center of the convergence of four paths.

"They were all found there, in the fountain. Draped over the wall, facedown in the water." Manley walked closer, pointing as he spoke. "My victim number one right here. Number two, eight, ten feet to the right. And over here, my vic number three." His jaw clenched almost imperceptibly. "She didn't look like she was older than thirteen, fourteen."

"Which one of them was wearing the seeds around her neck?"

"Little number three. That's the only clue I had, going into this. Those bean seeds. It was curiosity that led me to send them over to the university to have them analyzed. I never dreamed they would prove to be the lead that could eventually help us to find her killers."

He turned to look Evan in the eye.

"And I will find them. It may take a while longer, but I will find them. I like to think she brought those seeds with her so she'd always have a part of her home with her. It would be fitting, don't you think, if those seeds are the connection that helps us to find that home so we can take her back?"

"Have you thought of circulating her picture and those of the others, through the press down in Santa Estela?" Evan asked.

"I did send the girls' photos down to the police in Cortés City, the capital. I got an acknowledgment by way of a phone call." Manley kicked at the side of the fountain. "The Cortés police informed me that many kids from those poor countries—such as Santa Estela—go missing every day. Some of them are from villages well beyond the city limits. We'd have to get very, very lucky to get an ID on any of these kids, he tells me. Chances are, anyone who'd recognize them doesn't read the papers. He says some of those villages are pretty damned remote."

"In other words, don't waste his time."

"Pretty much, yeah, that was the impression I got. He said that it was likely, if the girls were from one of those remote towns, the families have stopped looking for them already."

"Thinking, what, that the kids are runaways to the city? That they've been eaten by alligators or whatever swims in the rivers down there? Where do they think their daughters have gone?"

"Kidnapped by the slavers. A huge percentage of the kids that go missing are sold into slavery. In some cases, the parents, or other family members, have sold the kids to the middlemen, the ones who obtain the kids through whatever means—kidnapping if not outright purchase—who then deal with the slavers. The traffic in slaves—particularly children—is a big business in some countries right now. Some child-advocacy groups are saying as many as two million children could be involved worldwide. Others are more conservative, but still . . ."

"Yeah. One is too many. How does a parent think his or her kid was caught up in this and not make any effort to find her? Wouldn't you be moving heaven and earth to bring her back if she were your kid?"

"Or he. As many young boys as girls are sold into slavery. There's a huge market for little boys, especially overseas, which is where a lot of these kids end up."

"So you think our girls were sold to slavers in Santa Estela and brought to this country . . ."

Manley nodded. "And branded with those little stars so there's no mistaking whose property they are. Then they're sent up here, to the U.S., by boat, by car, by truck. Sometimes they're literally walked across the border. A buddy of mine in immigration told me that anywhere from fifteen to twenty thousand are smuggled into this country every year." Manley paused, then added, "Most of them are just out-and-out kidnapped, but so many others come voluntarily, under false pretenses."

"Promised jobs that will pay enough that they can send money back to support their families at home. I read something about that recently."

"Right, except they have to pay off their transportation expenses first. These bastards charge them thousands of dollars to get to this country, then make them work off the fees in the brothels. Of course, they're rarely released, even after their supposed debt is paid off. Very few ever go to the authorities because they're afraid they'll be killed or their families back home will be killed. For the most part, they don't trust authority because the authorities all along the way have turned a blind eye and have let these terrible things happen to them because they're on the take. Sometimes, the kids have been told that their families were the ones who sold them in the first place, so they figure they have nothing to return to." He smiled wryly. "In a lot of cases, they're right."

"You figure that's the case with these girls?"

"I hate to even venture a guess with these kids. On the one hand, I know that Santa Estela and the surrounding countries are really poor. Some of the big banana plantations have been sold and the monopoly has driven wages down, so we're talking about real hardships here. Poverty that you and I can't really comprehend, so there's a good chance a family member turned the girl over for some cash. On the other hand, kidnapping is so rampant in Mexico and South and Central America, your guess is as good as mine as to how these kids got here."

Manley stood for a few long quiet minutes, deep in thought, in front of the spot where the body of the youngest victim had been found.

"This little girl had cocaine in her system. Sometimes, when a girl's uncooperative, they force her to take drugs, get her addicted. Cocaine, crystal meth, whatever it takes. That way, they can control her, through her addiction. She isn't likely to try to leave as long as she's dependent on her captors for her drugs." He averted his eyes, absently scuffing one shoe in the dirt at the base of the fountain where the girl's body had lain. "I like to think that this one fought hard; that's why they had to drug her. Because she wouldn't give up the fight."

"You know there have to be federal agencies involved here. Have you contacted Immigration, the FBI, the CIA . . . ?"

"All of the above. I've spoken to every one of them, and they tell me they're working on it, but that tells me nothing at all." He swore under his breath. "More accurately, it tells me there's a massive cluster fuck going on over this. They're all so damned territorial, you know? No matter what they say, no one wants to share. That's never going to change, no matter what they tell us. Which means that except in maybe an individual case here and there, no one is talking to anyone else. And of course, that just opens the door for more of the same."

Manley shook his head slowly.

"Frankly, I don't see where it's ever going to end."

Manley turned abruptly and walked back toward the parking lot. Evan followed, a thousand times more depressed than he had been when he'd arrived in Chicago early that morning. He found Manley waiting at the car when he found his way back to the parking lot.

"So what do you do about this?" Evan held the keys to the car in his right hand, but made no move to unlock the door.

"I don't think that anything can be done, frankly. I think it's way too big."

"Then why did you call me out here if you're convinced you'll never solve the case?"

"I didn't say I didn't think I could solve this case. Sooner or later, someone will have information to trade. I've got the word out; someone will step up to the plate when they're getting hauled off for possession with intent to deliver and their back is against the wall. It may take me a while, Detective Crosby, but I have every intention of solving my case. If it's the last thing I do on this earth, I will find the sons of bitches who murdered these kids. But the overall thing, this traffic business, that's something else. But my girls . . . I want to take care of my girls."

"That's how I feel," Evan told him. "I want to solve this for their sakes."

"I know." Manley met his eyes across the roof of the car. "That's why I wanted you to come out here."

"Sorry?" Evan asked.

"I needed to know there was someone else who really cared about what happened to these kids. That someone else is willing to keep on this, even after everyone else is convinced that it was a waste of time."

"No one's told me it's a waste of time, Detective Manley," Evan said as he unlocked the car doors.

"Someone will." Manley swung the passenger door open. "Sooner or later, someone will . . ."

_____CHAPTER_____
FIFTEEN

ANNIE TOPPED OFF THE TANK OF THE RENTED FORD Taurus sedan at the station advertised as the last gas for 167 miles. She had started out from the airport with a full tank, but wasn't sure how far she'd have to drive to find Melissa Lowery and figured that "Last Gas" sign must have been put there for a reason.

Mariana Gray, she corrected herself. She'd have to assume that Melissa was known around West Priest as Mariana Gray.

The last road sign told her that Priest lay twenty-four miles up the road, but Annie had driven in the west before and had found that sometimes the mileages weren't exactly accurate. It appeared from the map she'd picked up at the airport that West Priest lay just a few miles beyond Priest. She should be able to make the drive in well under an hour.

She was pleased to find herself arriving at Priest a mere forty minutes later. She went straight to the post office, where she was given directions that would take her three miles outside of town on Old Fort Road.

When she reached West Priest, the postmistress assured her, she'd know it.

The road between the two towns consisted of two skinny lanes of flat gravel with no shoulder on either side. The scenery, however, made it worth the caution one was forced to take in maneuvering the roadway. In the distance rose the East Front of the Continental Divide, with its scraggy plateaus and rolling grassy hills. Annie stopped once, pulling off onto the edge of the hard-earthed field to photograph the landscape. She would want to share its beauty with Evan, and knew words alone could not do it justice.

The tiny town of West Priest grew on both sides of the highway, two blocks in either direction from the intersection with Main Street, which, as its name implied, was the primary thoroughfare, with one bank and three churches. A post office shared a white clapboard building with an insurance agent and a flower shop. Next door a sign advertised guns and ammunition, and across the street was a general store with a "Help Wanted" sign in the window.

Annie parked in front of the post office and, as she'd done in Priest, asked directions from the sixty-something man behind the counter.

"I'm looking for Big Creek Road," Annie told the postal clerk.

"South or North?" the man asked.

"I don't know." Annie frowned and searched her pockets for the paper upon which Will had written Melissa's address. "It only says Big Creek Road."

"Who you looking for?"

"Mel—" She corrected herself: "Mariana Gray."

"She's out on East Big Creek."

"I thought you said South or North." Annie frowned again. "How could it be East, too?"

"Different creek." He returned to whatever it was he'd been doing when she came in. To Annie, it looked as if he'd been counting stamps.

"Could I get directions?"

"Not from me." He shook his head. "We're not allowed to give out anyone's address."

"You're not giving me the address," Annie said patiently. "I have the address. You only have to tell me how to get there."

"I don't think we're supposed to do that. You could probably get directions from Sullivan's, though. Someone there will know."

"Sullivan's?"

"Little restaurant around the corner. Only restaurant in town."

"Thanks."

Sullivan's was, as promised, just around the corner. Set in a little building made of ugly rough stone, it had a tinny bell that rang when the door was opened and a chalkboard right inside listing the day's specials. Annie took a table and ordered the soup of the day—black bean—and a small salad. The waitress appeared to be assessing her—hair to clothes to jewelry—even as she took the order.

"By the way, the man at the post office told me you

might know how I could get to Mariana Gray's place," Annie said when the waitress returned with her salad, an uninspired pile of lettuce adorned with three ragged slices of cucumber and some anemic-looking tomatoes.

"You a friend of hers?"

"Friend of a friend. I know she's on Big Creek Road, but I don't know the address."

"Out there, there are no addresses, not like we have here in town."

"How do I know which house is hers?"

The waitress continued her silent evaluation, and apparently decided Annie looked harmless enough.

"To get to Mariana's place, you just go straight back there at the intersection, then go right at the bridge, then straight for about four, five miles. Mariana's is the house you come to on the left side of the road."

"Thanks."

"Welcome. You ready for your soup?"

Annie nodded, and checked her voice mail for messages while she waited for the soup to arrive. She hoped it would prove to be tastier than the salad had been.

It was excellent, a rich spicy broth filled with dark beans, tomatoes, small pieces of beef, and topped with a dollop of sour cream. After three days of hotel food, Annie savored every spoonful.

She bought a Diet Coke in a to-go container and a brownie to take with her in the car. On the way out of town, she passed the motel where she'd made reservations for that night. She debated whether or not to stop, then decided against it. She was anxious to meet Melissa, curious to see what the woman remembered and what light, if any, she could shed on Dylan's death.

Melissa Lowery's mailbox stood at the end of a wide driveway that cut through a dusty front lawn and bore the name GRAY in blue letters that looked hand-painted. Wavy green vines bearing yellow flowers wrapped around the white metal box. A double garage sat off to the left by itself, and Annie walked over to peek through the windows. A dark blue Ford Explorer was parked inside next to a John Deere riding mower and a workbench upon which rested some garden tools. A hoe stood next to the bench, and a collection of various shovels leaned against the side wall. Behind the garage was a barn that appeared to have seen better days, and a small empty paddock. Across the back of the property ran a dense hedgerow, and Annie wondered as she walked back to the house if it marked the back boundary. If so, depending on how far to either side the property stretched, this would give Melissa several acres.

The house itself had once been painted yellow, but over the years had faded to a pale dull ivory. There were no plants around the foundation, but a pot of dark pink begonias stood on the bottom step of the concrete porch that led to the front door. Annie looked for a doorbell, but there was none, so she knocked instead. When there was no response, she knocked again, louder.

Leaning her ear to the door, she listened for sounds of life. All she could hear was a faint sort of humming. It took a moment before the sound registered with her. She stepped back from the door, then peered into the nearest window. Inside, the glass was covered with flies.

"Oh God, no . . ."

She reached for her phone and dialed 911.

The sheriff arrived in less than ten minutes. It wasn't every day he got a phone call from someone identifying themselves as an FBI agent who was standing on the front porch of a house that appeared to be filled with blowflies. They both knew what that most likely meant.

"I take it you didn't go inside," Sheriff Al Brody said as he got out of his car.

"No. If there's a body in there, as I suspect there might be, it could be a crime scene."

"Do you mind showing me some identification?" he asked.

Annie dug in her purse and pulled out her badge as he reached for the doorknob. "You must suspect it, too, or you wouldn't have gotten out here so quickly."

"Let's just say I was intrigued." He glanced at her credentials, appeared satisfied, then turned the knob.

The door did not open. "Let me run around back, see if something's open back there . . ."

A minute or two later, Brody opened the front door from the inside, holding a hand over his mouth.

"Do you have something to cover my shoes with? Paper boots, maybe?" she asked.

"Not with me. You sure you want to come in? This ain't pretty," he told Annie, and blocked her entry into the house.

"It never is." She stepped inside, careful to watch where she walked lest she step on evidence.

"Well, I guess this won't be the first time you've seen a body after the maggots have gotten to it." Brody moved to the left to permit her to pass.

"Not by a long shot."

"She's in there, between the living room and the dining room." He followed her, his hand still covering his nose and mouth. "At least, I'm assuming it's a she, going by all that hair. It can be tough to tell sometimes. I've known men with long hair, but none who wore pretty little flower barrettes. You know whose place this is?"

"She was going by the name Mariana Gray." Annie knelt a foot from the body and studied it carefully, looking past the writhing mass that was the second generation of maggots and focusing on searching for an obvious cause of death.

"Going by?"

"Her real name is Melissa Lowery. She's a former FBI agent. At least, I'm assuming that's who she is.

You're going to need to confirm that." Annie looked up at him. "What do you think, two weeks, give or take?"

"Judging by the condition of the body, yeah, I'd say she's been dead around two weeks."

The body was dressed in jeans and a red sweatshirt worn over a white cotton turtleneck. A thin gold bracelet circled what was left of her right wrist, and about her neck hung a small bezel-set diamond on a gold chain. On the third finger of her left hand was a wide gold ring. As the sheriff had noted, her long brown hair was held up on one side in a barrette fashioned out of a yellow silk flower.

"Driver's license says Mariana Gray." Brody stood in the doorway holding a tan leather wallet.

"There's no sign of blood," Annie murmured to herself as much as to the sheriff. "No sign of trauma to the head that I can see, but with all the insect activity, it's going to take an autopsy to determine cause of death."

She looked up at Brody and asked, "How's your M.E.?"

"He's good. He's real good." He reached in his pocket for his phone. "And I guess now's as good a time as any to bring him in. I'll be right back, Dr. McCall. I'm going to have to step outside for some better reception. I need to call in the troops."

Alone with what was left of the woman she assumed was Melissa Lowery, Annie tried to ignore what part her inquiries into the woman's where-abouts might have played in her death.

We don't know if she was murdered, Annie silently protested against the first twinges of guilt. *She could have been ill, she could have had . . .*

What? Annie asked herself. *What could she have had that might have caused her to die at the same time as I was looking for her? How coincidental could it be?*

Annie just hadn't seen enough true coincidences in her life to start believing in them now.

She stood and began to take note of her surroundings. The house was small but neat and well kept, the walls freshly painted, the furniture relatively new. She walked from one room to the next and found the entire house had a just-decorated feel to it. However long Melissa had been in Montana, she'd only just recently started to feather her nest.

A few family photos stood in a line across the mantel over the living-room fireplace. The same young, dark-haired woman appeared in several of them, and Annie thought that might be Melissa. In one photo, she appeared with a younger woman and an older man, a large black dog on the ground in front of them. In another, there was just her and the dog. In a third, she sat on a large outcropping of rock, with two other young women, all of whom bore a strong resemblance. Sisters, maybe, Annie thought. The older man might be the dad.

Annie went into the living room and straight to the

dark green leather bag that had spilled from a chair onto the floor. She looked over the contents—makeup case, cell phone, a small address book, several keys on a brass chain from which a large letter *M* dangled. Her fingers itched to pick up the address book and the phone, but she hesitated, not wanting to add her prints to the surface or to smudge those already there.

"You wouldn't happen to have a pair of rubber gloves I could borrow, would you?" she asked Sheriff Brody when he came back into the house.

"I might have, in the trunk. I can check," he said, but made no attempt to go back outside to his car.

"Was there something you wanted to ask me, Sheriff Brody?" Annie stood and folded her arms across her chest.

"I'm wondering what your interest is here. What brought you here. What business you had with Ms. Gray. She wasn't a friend of yours, judging by your reaction." His eyes narrowed. "You've had no visible emotional reaction to seeing her body, the way you would if you knew the deceased. So it's got me wondering why you're here."

"Agent Lowery was involved in an operation that took place a few years back. Recently, some questions about the operation itself have come up, and in reviewing the file, it was discovered that the report she wrote is missing. I needed to ask her a few questions about what was in the report."

He nodded slowly, as if mulling over the information.

"It just occurred to someone in the FBI that her report was missing? After a couple of years?"

"I don't know when the report went missing."

"And you came all the way out here to ask her about it?"

"Yes."

"Why didn't you just call her?"

"I had a presentation to give in Seattle this week, so I thought I'd make a stopover and speak with her in person."

He went silent again, thinking it through.

"Still seems like a long way to come, when a phone call would have gotten you the same information."

He paused, as if waiting for her comment. When none was forthcoming, he said, "Unless for some reason you thought she wouldn't speak to you."

"There's a good chance she may not have," Annie told him.

"What are you basing that on?"

"She's gone to great lengths to change her identity. You don't go to all that trouble unless you don't want to be found."

"Maybe she was being stalked. Maybe she just needed some peace and quiet." He leaned back against the doorjamb. "I grew up back east. Can't say I'd blame anyone who felt like they needed to escape."

He folded his arms across his chest and appeared to be waiting for her to say something more.

"Look, I don't know why this woman came out

here or why she changed her name. I don't know for certain that she was hiding out here, but I feel very strongly she was trying to get as far from someone or something as she could. I'd be real interested in knowing who that person was." Annie turned to look over her shoulder at the corpse that lay fifteen feet behind her. "It has to make you wonder, doesn't it? What brought her here under a phony name? Why she'd leave a career with the FBI and just disappear?"

"I'm sure she wasn't the first FBI agent who decided to quit."

"True. But many former agents leave the Bureau and join local law enforcement agencies. Private security, that sort of thing. Any idea what she was doing for a living?"

"No idea." He shook his head. "Maybe someone in town will know, maybe one of the neighbors."

The sound of car doors slamming drew their attention to the driveway, where several sheriff's vehicles and a beat-up black sedan had parked, their occupants filing up the walkway to the house.

"Looks like the gang's all here," Brody observed. "Let me get you those gloves, Dr. McCall, so we can put you to work along with everyone else. I could see you're interested in the contents of that purse there. Let's see what's what . . ."

The first thing Annie did was start to check the numbers of the last calls that had been made to Melissa's cell phone, but one of the sheriff's deputies made a point of looking for that item, so she had to hand it over. While doing so, she tucked the address book under her leg as she knelt on the floor next to the spilled purse. When the deputy walked outside to start calling back the numbers, she took the small red book and stepped around the M.E. to walk into the kitchen. There she opened the back door and sat on the top porch step to skim through the pages.

For some reason, Melissa seemed to prefer listing some of her contacts not by name but by initials. Annie went page by page, studying the entries, but none were recognizable. Until she came to the *S*s.

G.S.—followed by a number Annie did not recognize.

Grady Shields?

She tapped the book against the palm of one hand. Could be an old phone book. Could be a number Melissa hadn't called in a long time. Annie took her cell phone out of her pocket and checked the number she had for Grady. It wasn't the same as the one in Melissa's book. Annie dialed the number and listened to it ring.

"Hello?" A familiar male voice answered.

"Grady?"

"Yeah, who's this?"

"It's Annie."

He hesitated, then asked, "How did you get this number?"

"I found it in Melissa Lowery's phone book."

"What are you doing with Melissa's phone book?"

"Looking for someone who might have had a reason to kill her."

The silence that followed was so long and so complete, Annie thought Grady had hung up.

"Melissa . . . ?" he whispered, his voice little more than a rasp.

"She's dead, Grady."

"But . . ." Another silence, then finally, a click.

"Grady?" Annie asked, though she knew he was no longer on the line. She disconnected the call and slid the phone back into her jacket pocket.

"You find anything interesting in that book?" Sheriff Brody asked from the top of the steps.

"Not really," she said, handing it to him.

"Well, we got two of the neighbors out front, just drove by and saw all the cars, so they stopped in. I'm just about to go on out and talk to them, thought you might want to come out with me."

"I would. Thank you."

Brody came down the steps and walked toward the corner of the house.

"Too much going on in there," he told her. "I want to stay out of everyone's way as much as I can."

"So we figure she's been dead approximately two weeks." Annie fell into step beside him.

"Yeah, that's what we figured." He nodded.

"And no one missed her in all that time?"

"From what I gathered, from the folks out front, she didn't work. Went into town for food and supplies every two weeks or so. Stopped at the library to pick up a couple of books while she was there, maybe had lunch at Sullivan's. Other than that, it seems like she kept to herself."

"Well, let's see if the neighbors remember if she's had any company lately . . ."

The neighbors did.

In particular, Mrs. Owens, a widow in her midseventies who lived half a mile up on the other side of the road, distinctly recalled having seen a tall, good-looking dark-haired man with the deceased on several occasions.

"Recently?" Annie asked.

"Last time, maybe a month ago. Maybe a little less."

"Within the last two weeks?"

"Not him, but there was a car parked here week before last."

"How do you know it wasn't him?"

"He always came at the end of the week, stayed till Sunday or sometimes Monday morning. This was in the middle of the week, and the car was only here for the one day."

"Do you remember what day of the week it was?"

"It was a Tuesday."

"Are you sure, Mrs. Owens?" Brody spoke up for the first time since Annie had engaged the woman in conversation.

"I'm positive. I was on my way into town to the dentist. Dr. Jacobs. He's only in West Priest on Tuesday's. Rest of the week, he's in Priest or over in Tall Trees."

"This tall, dark-haired man . . . ," Annie began.

"Good-looking. Don't leave out the good-looking part."

"How often did you see him? Twice a month? Once? Every two months . . . ?"

"Maybe once a month, sometimes twice, close as I remember."

"Do you think you'd recognize him if you saw him again?"

"Oh yes. He really was a looker."

"Thanks, Mrs. Owens. If you remember anything else, you just give me a call, hear?"

"Will do." Mrs. Owens nodded but made no effort to leave. "What do you suppose happened to her? You got any suspects?"

"Now, now, don't go talking about suspects. We don't even know what she died from. Could be natural causes. Let's not go jumping to conclusions, Mrs. Owens. That's how rumors get started."

"Well, you know I'm not one to gossip," she said to the sheriff and to Annie.

"That's good, then. We don't need any speculation going around town until we know for certain what happened here. And we might not know that for a few more days. Gotta give the medical examiner some time to do his thing."

Mrs. Owens nodded her understanding and turned to leave.

"You don't suppose someone killed her deliberately, do you, Sheriff?"

"Mrs. Owens, I thought we just agreed we would not be speculating," Brody said sternly.

"Just wondering." The older woman resumed her walk to her car. "She was such a lovely thing, so sweet. Always waved when you went past."

"Mrs. Owens," Annie called to her. "Would you happen to know where Mariana worked? What she did for a living?"

"Oh, she didn't work. I think she had some sort of family money or something, some inheritance, maybe it was." Mrs. Owens opened her car door. "But she sure didn't work. Up all hours of the night; I used to see lights on down here all the time. I said something to her once, about her staying up late and was she reading or watching TV, and she said most nights she didn't sleep well, that she slept better during the day. Which I thought was strange, you know. The way she said it, made me think that she was afraid to sleep at night, like she was safer sleeping during the day."

"Why do you say that?" Annie asked.

"Just a feeling I had. She had that house lit up like a Christmas tree all night, every night, and the one night I stopped by to drop off some mail that got put in my box by mistake, it took her like a full minute to unlock all the locks."

Annie and the sheriff looked at each other.

"Did you notice a lot of locks?" Annie asked the sheriff.

"No, but let's go take a look . . ."

An inspection of the inside of the front door proved there to be a dead bolt, a slider, and a regular bolt.

"The only lock that was on when we first got here was the slider," Brody told Annie. "I unlocked that to open the door for you. I guess I missed the others because they were unlocked, and because I was so busy at the time covering my nose and mouth and dodging the swarming flies."

"Let's check the back door," Annie suggested.

There were three locks on the back door as well. Locks on the windows. A dead bolt on the basement.

"Sheriff, what's the crime rate out here?"

"Zilch. I can't remember the last robbery. Murders? None in the three years I've been sheriff. We had a few hunting accidents, and last year an old man died of a heart attack up the road, a little higher up in the hills. But crime rate? I gotta say we don't have one."

"Then why would she have all these locks?" Annie bent closer to inspect them. "Fairly new, too, all except the slider. The dead bolts were installed more recently. Certainly within the past year or so."

"Well, we've only got one place in town that sells locks. Larsen's Hardware. They sell, they install."

"Maybe someone should drive down there and talk to them."

"Just as easy to call Hank Larsen on the phone, have him come on up here and identify the locks as his."

"Maybe he'll remember chatting with her. Maybe she told him what she was trying to lock out."

"Maybe. It's a good place to start," Sheriff Brody agreed, but made no move toward the house.

"Were you going to call him today?" Annie asked.

"I thought I'd wait until the body was moved out, Dr. McCall. Not everyone can walk past a partially decomposed body and appear not to notice."

"I notice, Sheriff Brody." Annie started back into the house.

"Dr. McCall," Brody called to her as she stepped over the threshold. "May I ask who you called earlier?"

"Excuse me?"

"You went out the back a little while ago with that little phone book of the deceased's. Looked to me like you called one of the numbers."

"I called a fellow agent who was an old friend of Ms. Lowery's."

"That friend of a friend you mentioned earlier."

"Yes."

"That friend have a name?"

"Grady Shields." She hated having to give up his name, not knowing what Grady's involvement with Melissa might have been, but she couldn't lie, either. "Special Agent Grady Shields."

"And his relationship with Ms. Lowery—or Ms. Gray—was what, do you know?"

"Former coworker. Friend."

"That number for Agent Shields, it's in the address book?"

"Yes. Was there something else, Sheriff?"

"Not right now."

She closed the door and went back inside, hoping for a moment with the medical examiner. While she waited for him to finish preparing the body for transport, she stepped out onto the back porch to make one more phone call.

"Evan, I'm afraid there's been a change in plans . . ."

CHAPTER SIXTEEN

CONNOR LEANED ON THE IRON RAILING THAT ENclosed the balcony overlooking the Atlantic coast of Morocco and watched the gulls circle overhead. An occasional protesting scream pierced the tranquillity of the morning as a coveted morsel of fish was snatched from one beak by another. The sky was as blue as he'd ever seen it, and the breeze as gentle as a caress. Coming on the heels of the past few weeks spent in a Middle Eastern desert, the peaceful morning was a balm to his soul.

There was a rap on the door, and he answered it without hesitation.

"Your breakfast." The dark-eyed woman carried a rectangular tray in both hands and headed straight for the balcony. "You should eat here, in the sun. It will relax you."

"Magda, you're more like my mother than my mother was."

"Someone has to watch out for you," she said without smiling. "It might as well be me."

She placed the tray on the small glass table and removed the napkin to reveal a plate of warm croissants, figs, a thinly sliced pear, and a small mound of white cheese.

"Sit and eat. I'll be right back with your coffee."

"You're way too good to me," he said as he sat at the table.

"I certainly am." Magda went through the double doors into the room and disappeared into the hall. When she returned, she brought a second tray, upon which stood a tall carafe and two cups. She poured coffee into both cups, placed one before Connor, then sat opposite him at the table.

"Nice of you to join me." He offered her the croissants, but she waved him off.

"I eat early, at dawn. You know that. I need an early start if I'm to take care of you and the rest of my guests in the manner in which I've made you accustomed."

"There is no finer hotel in Essaouira. It's the reason I've come to love this city. The reason I spend any available free time right here." He tilted his cup in her direction before taking a sip. "And besides, there's no better coffee anywhere in Morocco."

Satisfied, Magda leaned back in the chair and raised her face to the sun, her eyes closed.

"There's a new guest who checked in two days ago. An American woman. She's an archaeologist, she says, on holiday."

"So?"

"So you should make her acquaintance. She's very pretty. Blond. Soft-looking. She doesn't go out much."

"So maybe she's tired. Maybe she sleeps a lot."

"Maybe she's lonely. Maybe she'd appreciate a little companionship from a fellow countryman."

"Why are you always trying to set me up?"

"Because you live like a mercenary."

"I'm not a mercenary."

"I know what you are. But you still need a nice girl in your life."

"I have a nice girl in my life. I have you."

"I'm old enough to be your mother, and if you ever looked at me that way, Cyril would slit your throat." She smiled, but her eyes remained closed.

"Your husband should be jealous of you. You're one in a million, Magda."

"I know." She tucked an errant strand of graying hair into the bun at the back of her neck.

"Magda, if I wanted to make a phone call"—he placed his cup on the table to refill it—"there would be a secure line?"

"Of course. All of my lines are secure." She lifted her head and opened her eyes. "I check them myself every day, just like you showed me. Do you think I forget such things?"

"I was just wondering if you were still in the habit."

"You need not worry. This is a small hotel, most of our business is repeat. Same people, over and over. Many of them, like you, require that extra measure of security." She drained the coffee from her cup and rose. "For you, there will always be security here. Whatever you need. We don't forget, Cyril and I."

She patted Connor fondly on the arm and walked past him.

"The American woman takes tea in the courtyard every afternoon at four," she said without breaking stride. "Today she'll be seated at one of the tables for two, in the corner near the palms."

Magda closed the door behind her.

Two gulls were battling on the top of the courtyard wall, and Connor watched idly as he finished his meal and thought over the e-mail he'd gotten from Annie. It had been dated the previous week, but he'd only just received it last night, after checking in to his room and turning on his computer for the first time in days. He'd known there'd be no electricity where he'd been headed, so he'd left the laptop locked in a safe deep in the basement of the hotel. He'd had no qualms about leaving it there. Magda and Cyril would guard it with their lives.

There was something to be said about having someone in this part of the world in your debt, he acknowledged, though that had never entered his mind the day he dove off the prow of a fast-moving pleasure boat to rescue a young boy who'd fallen over the side. Without a life jacket, the panicked child would have quickly drowned. The boy's horrified parents had watched helplessly from the dock as the tall dark-haired stranger reached their son and carried him back to the boat, whose captain had circled back around and cut the engine, the other passengers calling encouragement. From that day, the best room in Villa André had always been available to Connor. He knew that he could always count on the most comfortable accommodations, the best food, the best service—and some motherly fussing—from Magda.

He leaned back in the chair, his face to the sun much as Magda's had been, and went back over Annie's message in his mind. He hadn't thought about Santa Estela in months.

He moved the tray out of the way and set up the laptop in its place. He booted up and scanned his incoming mail before opening the saved e-mail from Annie.

Connor, strange development on a case Evan is handling in PA. Tattoos on the vics found to be identical to those found on three vics in Chicago. Young girls, one of whom appears to have a connection traced back to Central America, possibly Santa Estela. Do I recall correctly that you had spent some time there? Any contacts remain? Am looking for source and/or significance of the tattoo.

He drummed his fingers on the table, thinking back to that night in the alley in Santa Estela, of the truck filled with terrified children. Any connection between dead young girls in two cities and Santa Estela was way too coincidental. He'd thought that business had been shut down two years ago. His cousin had personally worked on that and had assured him the trafficking of children had been dealt with.

He brought the phone from the room onto the balcony and plugged it in, then dialed the familiar number. When the answering machine picked up, he said, "Hey, it's Connor. Hope all you guys are doing well. Just wanted to ask you a quick question. About Santa Estela and that report I asked you about a few years back, you remember? Do me a favor and take another look at that situation, would you? I'll check back in with you in another day or two, hope you have something to tell me."

Connor started to hang up, then said, "And hey, if you see my brother, tell him I said hey, all right? Your brothers, too. Take care, cuz . . ."

He disconnected the call and stood up to stretch. From the balcony he could see into the courtyard, where, right at that moment, a woman in a gauzy white dress had stopped to put a large hat atop her head. Before her hair had disappeared under the hat, he'd noticed it was blond, cut short in a choppy style, as if done without artistry or skill. She was tanned, almost as tanned as he was, and even from a distance, he could see she was very well put together.

The American Magda had told him about?

Tea in the courtyard at four might be interesting after all. He watched her disappear through the courtyard gates and hesitate, as if unsure of her direction.

He was tempted to join her, to offer her a tour of the marketplace, but he had a meeting in twenty minutes with a man who had information Connor's superiors were eager to obtain.

He turned off the laptop, located his sunglasses, and locked the door behind him, the memory of the events of a dark night in Santa Estela and all thoughts of the pretty blond American put aside for a while.

_____CHAPTER_____
SEVENTEEN

ANNIE LAY SPOONED BESIDE EVAN, HER EYES OPEN IN the dark, watching the rain splat against the bedroom windows. She'd arrived late the night before and had deferred any discussion by climbing into bed next to him and keeping him otherwise engaged for nearly an hour.

She knew him well enough to know that he knew she was not asleep. When she felt him pull the sheet up over her bare arm, she knew that sooner or later, the concerned questions would begin.

She didn't have to wait long.

"So, you want to talk about it?" he asked softly.

"I thought maybe you might want to tell me about Chicago."

"Ladies first."

"Melissa had a number in her phone book listed to a G.S. I called it. Grady answered."

"That was the only number in the book?"

"No."

"Why'd you pick that one to call?"

"Because of the obvious—the initials. I knew

Grady had dated Melissa, but when I asked him about her, I got the feeling he wasn't being truthful. Something told me it wasn't as casual a relationship as he tried to pass it off. No matter how casual a relationship is, there are certain things you have a tendency to talk about when you first meet someone, and for him to claim to know nothing about her, nothing about her background, it just didn't ring true. So when I saw those initials with a Virginia area code, I thought I'd dial it and just see what happened."

"Did you tell him Melissa was dead?"

"Yes."

"And . . . ?"

"And he hung up on me. He sounded genuinely stunned. Stunned, and upset."

"Which plays back to him having more of a relationship with Melissa than he'd wanted you to know."

"But why? Why would he lie about that?"

"Why was she hiding in Montana?" he asked. "I think if you answer one of those questions, you'll have the answer to both."

"I guess the only one who knows is Grady. And the only way to find out is to confront him."

"Have you heard yet from the M.E. in Montana as to cause of death?"

"I'm still waiting. I expect they should know by today. God, I'm hoping it was natural causes."

"What difference would it make?"

"The difference between her dying a natural death or one that I possibly led someone to—"

"Whoa. Hold up there." He sat up partially and turned her to face him. "Where is this coming from?"

"It's coming from the fact that Melissa seemed to be living quite happily in Montana until I started looking for her."

"Annie, please don't tell me you think you are in any way responsible for her dying."

"If she was murdered, yes, I have to question why now. The thought that somehow I could have brought this on her is making me physically sick."

"You can't be serious?" One look at her face assured him she was. "Okay, let's take a look at this, shall we? Let's assume for a moment that Melissa was murdered. You found her, Annie. What makes you think that someone else couldn't have found her, too? Someone who maybe started looking for her long before you did."

"I've been looking for her for a few weeks. My search and her probable date of death are suspiciously close, Evan."

"That is supposition on your part."

"No, that is fact. Shortly after I started asking about her, she died."

"Who knew you were looking for her?"

"Just about everyone in the Bureau. I asked so many people, and some of them probably asked some other people . . . Evan, if I hadn't been so adamant about finding her, she might still be alive."

"I think that's a long shot, Annie. I think it's way too soon to start beating yourself up over something that may not even be true. Let's put it aside until we find out what caused her death. It could have been any one of a number of things. Before you blame yourself, let's get the facts."

She lay silent for a long time, then turned in his arms and said, "All right, then, it's your turn. Tell me what you found in Chicago."

"This detective, Don Manley, is quite a guy. You know he's devoted the past eight months of his life to finding the killers of these girls? He's totally committed to this case, even though it's been shelved. No leads at all."

"How likely is it that he'll find a lead now? Realistically?"

"He says he has a lot of feelers out. He thinks that sooner or later, someone will have some information to deal. He's willing to wait."

"How does this help you in your case?"

He lay silent for a moment, as if he hadn't considered the question before.

"It helps me to know that there's someone else out there who isn't giving up. It helps me to know that when the day comes that Manley gets his lead, he'll pass on whatever he learns to me."

"In the meantime . . . ?"

"In the meantime, for me, it's back to the evidence. Avon County isn't Chicago, and I don't have the network that Manley has. If I'm going to find our killer, it will have to be through the evidence."

"Unfortunately, there isn't much of that, as I recall. Or did something turn up while I was away?"

"Nothing new," he admitted. "And you're right, there isn't a lot to go on."

"You had some dirt," she murmured. "Did a full analysis come back on that?"

"Not that I've seen."

"I can follow up on that for you, have our lab break it down as far as it can go. Maybe that could lead somewhere."

"Oh, and the dog hair. Let's not forget about the dog hair."

"Do I detect some sarcasm there?"

"I keep thinking the lab report will come back with a match to a golden retriever. 'Cause there are so few of them around, it would be real easy to track the owner."

"Hey, you've been in this game long enough to know that you don't discount anything."

"Yeah, I know. It's just a little frustrating. The Schoolgirl Slayer is in custody. Seemed awfully easy to solve that case."

"Not to the parents of the girls who died."

"True enough. Oh, hell, I think I'm antsy after meeting with Manley and wanting so badly to make this right for these girls, to find out who they were and take them home. You look at what's happened to these kids—sold or kidnapped or lied to in order to get them under control, sent to work in broth-els. Forced into prostitution before they're even in their teens. Then tossed aside for whatever reason—executed." Evan made no attempt to disguise his anger and disgust. "And let's not lose sight of the fact that as long as he's still out there, other girls could be at risk."

"You're thinking there are more girls in the area?"

"Why not?" She could hear his wheels turning. "Let's assume for a minute that there was in fact a working brothel in the area. A brothel with only three girls? Not likely." He shook his head. "So there would be others . . . but would they all be from Santa Estela?"

"How do you find out?"

Annie felt his body tense slightly and smiled to her-self, recognizing that he was onto something and, in minutes, would be out of bed and getting dressed, in anticipation of going wherever the thought would lead.

"A few years ago, the D.A. started this program where whenever they picked up a woman for prosti-tution, they picked up the john and printed his name in the paper. It caused a lot of grief for a lot of guys. After the third arrest, you not only got your name in the paper, you got jail time. Light time, but time all the same. Imagine being some big executive type, or some big lawyer down in Philly, having to take a month off to do time. The program sort of fell to the wayside after a while. Not a lot of guys actually served any time."

"So, you're thinking if you had a list of the men with two arrests, you could check in with them, see if any of them knew or heard about some young foreign girls in a house."

"Right." He had slowly disengaged himself from her and was sitting on the edge of the bed.

"And they would speak with you now because . . ." She began to mentally count the seconds before he stood and started looking for the clothes he'd earlier discarded.

"Because maybe if they thought the program was being reactivated, they might appreciate a heads-up before such a sweep—and a possible third arrest— might take place."

. . . twenty-two, twenty-three, twenty-four . . .

"Twenty-five," she announced.

"What?" he asked as he retrieved his jeans from the floor.

"It only took you twenty-five seconds between the time you sat and the time you stood. You beat your own best time of thirty-seven by a mile."

"You really think you have me pegged, don't you?" He laughed softly.

"Absolutely, I do. I can see right through you."

"Like what you see?" He pulled a T-shirt over his head and started to tuck it into his jeans.

"I love what I see."

He hesitated, then asked, "Annie, are you sure you don't mind if I just look a few things up—"

She cut him off. "Of course not." There was no point in making him explain. She knew his heart, and knew that he'd do what he had to do. Just as she would. "It's an excellent idea. You need to follow up on it."

"It may lead nowhere."

"Or it may lead to your killer." She sat up and wrapped the sheet around her.

"Will you be here when I get back?"

"Actually, I probably will not. I need to talk to Grady, and I don't think a phone call is the way to do that."

"Want me to go with you? It's Saturday. I could drive down with you later this afternoon, we could go see Grady, then I can drive back tomorrow night."

"I would love to have you come home with me. But I think I'll get more out of Grady if I'm alone. I don't think he'll tell me anything if you're there."

"Okay." He leaned over to kiss her. "But I can still drive down later today, if you want."

"Why don't you wait and see how many names you come up with, and see how many are willing to talk to you. If I know you, you'll be up to your neck in this for the rest of the day."

"God, I hope I can get a break." He looked under the chair for his shoes, then remembered he'd left them downstairs. "I need something solid on this."

"So go for it."

"You're sure you don't mind?" He hovered over her, studying her face.

"Go." She glanced at the clock on the nightstand. It was 4:30 in the morning. "Actually, I think I'll get up now, too. The earlier I get back to Virginia, the sooner I'll be able to sit down with Grady and see if I can get some of the truth about his relationship with Melissa."

"Good luck, babe." Evan kissed her one last time. "Maybe I'll see you later tonight . . ."

"And maybe I'll wake up tomorrow and be my longed-for height of five-eight," she murmured as he went down the steps. "Neither is likely, but one can always hope . . ."

Annie stood in the vestibule of the building that housed Grady's condo, along with five others, all of which had mailboxes lined up along the wall to the left of the front door. Junk mail overflowed from the black box bearing a label that read, *G. Shields, 2B.*

Interesting he hasn't picked up his mail in a few days, she thought as she rang the bell for his unit, but his car is in the parking lot. She went outside and looked up at his apartment. There were air conditioners in two of the three front windows, and she could hear their faint humming. She went back into the vestibule and rang the doorbell again. She rang it over and over, until finally, she got a response.

"What." It wasn't so much a question as an expression of exasperation.

"It's Annie, Grady."

"Not now, Annie."

"I'm not leaving until I talk to you."

"You're talking to me now."

"Let me come up, Grady. We need to talk about Melissa."

"I did not kill her. And I don't know who did. What else do you need to know?"

"Do you really want me to go into that right here, right now, where anyone could come along and—"

He buzzed her through the locked front door, and she crossed the lobby to the stairwell that rose directly in front of her. She climbed the steps and found Grady waiting for her in the doorway of his apartment. From his appearance, she guessed that the mail had been piling up in the box because he hadn't left the apartment in several days. It had certainly been that long since he'd shaved.

He stepped aside and motioned for her to come in, then closed the door behind her.

"So tell me what it is you're looking for, then you can go and I can get back to the business of getting myself good and drunk." He walked into the living room, and she followed.

"Looks like you've made some progress there." She noted the empty bottles of wine that formed a circle on top of the coffee table. "Odd choice, though. Most men drink themselves into a stupor on beer or hard liquor. Merlot doesn't seem to fit."

"What is it you want?" He flopped onto the sofa but did not offer her a seat.

She pushed some newspapers onto the floor and sat anyway.

"Why were you so secretive about your relationship with Melissa Lowery?"

He appeared to be trying to formulate a response.

"Come on, Grady, just say it."

He still searched for words.

"All right, let's try this approach. Why did Melissa change her name and move to Montana?"

"Free country." He picked up the nearest bottle and checked its contents. Finding it empty, he moved on to the next one and refilled his glass.

"Cut the bullshit," she said softly. "We both know she was afraid of something. Or someone. Was it you?"

"Me?" The question took him off guard. "God, no."

"What was your relationship with her?"

"She was . . . my best girl." His eyes filled with tears. "She was . . . my wife."

"Your . . . ?"

He nodded slowly. "We were married in Reno eight months ago."

"Why all the secrecy? Why was she hiding, Grady?"

He exhaled slowly, a long breath fraught with pain.

"Someone scared her."

"Who?"

"Now, don't you think if I knew that, I'd have dealt with it?" He lifted his head and met her eyes, and she understood exactly how he would have dealt.

"She gave you no information, she never told you why—"

"Yeah. That much I know. She was on a job, she saw someone who shouldn't have been there, and included his name in her report."

"Who wasn't she supposed to have seen?"

"I don't know. *She* didn't even know who it was. All I know is that after she wrote the report, someone contacted her by phone and told her she was to forget that she had been there, forget who else she'd seen there, and to destroy any copies of her notes. He left a bag with a lot of cash—a *whole* lot of cash—on her doorstep and suggested she resign from the Bureau and take the first train out of Dodge."

"Or . . . ?"

"Or he'd kill her."

"Why didn't she go to someone at the Bureau?"

"Who would do what, Annie? Protect her from someone she couldn't even identify? Someone who obviously *works* for the Bureau?" He got up and ran a hand through his dark hair. "Believe me, we went through all of this. Whoever was threatening her works for the Bureau. He's supposed to be one of the good guys. He could have been anyone. How do you even begin to figure out who you can trust?"

"Well, what about the job she'd been on, start with

that. Look at the people who were there, figure out—"
She stopped short, staring at him. "Grady . . ."

"Annie, please don't even ask."

"Tell me it wasn't the job where Dylan was killed."

He was agitated and drunk. He swayed when he stood, then sat slowly back down.

"And that's why Melissa's report was missing, because someone took it deliberately and made sure she wouldn't replicate it?"

"Yes."

Annie digested the information.

"I'm sorry, Annie. I'm really sorry."

She waved away his apology, past that now. "Why," she asked, "didn't he just kill her?"

"I don't know." He took a long swallow of wine, this one straight from the bottle. "I've asked myself that same question a dozen times. Why didn't he just kill her."

He wiped tears from his face with the hem of his shirt.

"I guess the question really is, why did he kill her now?"

"I have a call in to the sheriff in Montana. As soon as I've heard about cause of death, I'll let you know."

He cleared his throat. "Appreciate it."

"In the meantime, why not put the wine away? Take a shower, get something to eat. Get some sleep."

"Merlot was the only thing she ever drank." He held up the bottle and studied the label as if it held some weighty truth.

"Grady, I am so sorry about Melissa. I don't know what to say." She swallowed hard. "I'm more sorry than I can say, if my looking for her, for her report, was the catalyst—"

"Don't, Annie. There's no point . . ." He shrugged helplessly.

"Still . . ."

"Just . . . don't, okay?" He looked away.

"I'll call as soon as I hear anything." It was the only thing she could think to say.

"Okay."

She wanted to go to him and put her arms around him, but she knew that nothing would comfort him. Instead, she walked to the door to let herself out. She opened the door to leave, then turned and asked, "Did anyone know that you and Melissa were married?"

"Only my brothers."

"You didn't tell your sister?"

"Nah." He smiled weakly. "You know Mia, she talks to everyone. But my brothers, well . . . you know how they are. They're both so closemouthed, you never know what's going on with either of them."

____CHAPTER____
EIGHTEEN

EVAN TOOK A SIP OF COFFEE AND GRIMACED TO FIND it had gone cold during the course of his telephone conversation with john number twenty-seven on the list of seventy-four he'd gotten from the D.A.'s files when he arrived at the courthouse at 5:30 that morning. To say the guard at the front door had been surprised to see anyone at that hour—least of all on a Saturday—would have been an understatement.

"Early day, Detective?" The man had yawned as he unlocked the front door.

"Yeah." Evan shifted the cardboard carrier holding the three large cups of coffee he'd picked up at the local convenience store. As he passed through the metal detector, he handed one Styrofoam cup to the guard. "Thought you could use a wake-up this morning, too."

"Thank you, Detective Crosby. Nice of you to think of me."

"Nice of you to let me in." Evan smiled and walked the dimly lit hall to the stairwell, and took the steps down to the basement, where the county detectives and some of the assistant district attorneys were housed.

The hallway was darker here, and it had taken him several tries before he managed to open the main office door. He locked it behind him and walked through the common area, lit only by an "Exit" sign on either side, and went directly to his small office at the end of the hall. He'd placed the coffee on one side of the desk and turned on his computer. He searched the files until he found what he was looking for, opened one of the coffees, and sipped at it while he scanned the screen, occasionally making notes on a yellow legal pad he'd pulled from the bottom drawer. By the time his list was complete, the sun had come up and enough of the morning had passed that he could begin making his calls without risk of having anyone complain that it was too early.

By noon, he'd called almost one third of the names on his list and had spoken with twelve. The others had either not answered or were no longer at the number he had on record. Out of the twelve, only five were willing to speak with him about their prior arrests. He'd left telephone messages for several others but was not optimistic that many—if any—of his calls would be returned.

Of the five he'd spoken with, none of them admitted to knowing anything about any young Hispanic girls working in an area house in which they might be held against their will.

"I wouldn't go for none of that, man, none of that

young stuff," one of the johns had told him. "That's disgusting, man . . ."

"There are a couple of Hispanic chicks working the corner at Seventh and Warwick," another had offered when pressed, "but they ain't no kids."

"I don't usually ask to see ID, you know what I mean?" another had snorted.

Evan rubbed his eyes and stood to stretch. His legs felt cramped and his shoulders stiff, and he thought a walk outside, even just around the courthouse, might be refreshing. He opened his door and noticed lights on in several of the other offices. He'd been so engrossed in his research that he hadn't heard anyone else come in.

He stopped at Cal Henry's door to chat for a moment, but left when Cal's girlfriend called. Their verbal feuds were legendary, and Evan had witnessed more than enough of them in the past. He waved to Cal and continued on his way outside.

"You take care, Detective," the guard at the door called to him, barely looking up.

"I'm just running out for a minute. I'll be back."

Evan stepped into the sun and shielded his eyes from the glare. He took a deep breath, and deciding he was as much in need of food as of exercise, he walked two blocks to Main Street, where he picked up lunch from the deli on the corner. He returned to the courthouse and took a seat on one of the benches on the front lawn and proceeded to eat his ham and cheese on rye while mentally replaying the conversations he'd had that morning, hoping to find some in-advertent comment that might lead him to something concrete.

Reluctantly, he had to admit he hadn't missed anything the first time around. There'd been no slip of the tongue, nothing he could use as an excuse to call any of the men back to confirm. He rolled up his lunch trash in the bag it had come in and started toward the trash can when he heard someone calling his name.

"Hey, Joe," he called back to his former partner, who was walking up the sidewalk with a large brown file folder under his arm.

"Evan. Good to see you." Joe Sullivan met Evan in the middle of the sidewalk.

"What brings you in on a Saturday?"

Joe held up the file.

"I just got a call at home from Shelley Stern telling me this case is going to trial on Monday and she needed whatever materials I had that she didn't have." He shook his head. "How am I supposed to know what she has?"

"I'm going back in, want me to drop it off for you?"

"Nah, I'm going to need to talk to her anyway."

Evan tossed his trash in the direction of the open can and missed.

"I see moving up to county detective hasn't done anything to improve your aim," Sullivan noted.

"It'll take more than a new job to do that. What's new in Lyndon?"

"Not much. Things have quieted down a lot since the slayer was brought in. Nice job Jackie did with that case, wasn't it?"

"Nice job that *Jackie* did?" Evan scoffed.

"What's that supposed to mean?"

"It means Jackie had a lot of help from the FBI."

"That's not the way I heard it."

Evan shook his head in disgust and waved to the guard, who was already on his way to unlock the door.

The two men went through the procedure to enter the building, then walked together down to the D.A.'s office. Joe stopped off at Shelley Stern's office—the third door on the left—and Evan continued on to his office. Fifteen minutes later, he looked up to find Joe in the doorway.

"So you working all day or what?"

"Most of it. I'd hoped to finish up early enough to make a trip down to Annie's for the rest of the weekend, but I guess that's not going to happen."

"What are you working on?" Joe asked. "That the other killer case?"

"What other killer case?" Evan looked up from the file.

"Word around is that the Slayer didn't pop those last three girls, the Hispanic ones." Joe came in and plopped himself in the seat near the door.

"Where'd you hear that?"

"Just around. Don't remember where, exactly."

"Good thing it wasn't supposed to have been kept under wraps or anything," Evan muttered.

"So if you're not going to see the old lady, want to meet up later for a few beers and a burger down at Taps? I'm meeting a couple of the guys at six."

"Rosemary is letting you out alone on a Saturday night?"

"She's off with her sister this weekend. She and Joey. They'll be gone through tomorrow afternoon."

"How's he doing, your son?"

"He had a better year in school this year." Joe nodded. "He had a rough time for a while. You know, he's small for his age, isn't real good at sports. It's tough for a boy like that. We finally did find something he liked doing, though, so he's doing better."

Evan was about to ask what that thing was when his cell phone rang. He checked the number and found it to be one of the men for whom he'd previously left a message.

"Sorry, Joe, I've got to take this."

"Hey, no problem. Stop down at Taps later, if you can. We'll all be there. It would be great if you could join us. Like old times. If not, we'll get together sometime soon."

"Sounds like a plan. Thanks."

Joe waved and left the office as Evan answered his call.

"Yeah, Manny, thanks for calling me back. I appreciate it. Listen, about that incident a few years back . . .

yeah, that one. Hey, I hate to bring that up, but there's a rumor going around the D.A.'s office that they're thinking about bringing back that three-strikes-and-jail-time thing again, and I just wanted to see if you were keeping clean . . ."

It was almost eight by the time Evan finished the last of his calls. He was starving and for a moment considered Joe's offer. Then he looked at the pages of notes he'd made, all the information he wanted to enter into the computer before Monday came around, and decided he'd do takeout on the way home instead. He'd enjoy a night out with his old friends and coworkers, he acknowledged as he packed up a few files to take home. They had a good bunch of guys down there in the Lyndon Police Department, and there were times when he missed working with them, missed the companionship and the familiarity of having the same partner every day.

Well, maybe he'd have time for a beer or two. He turned off the overhead light on his way out of the office and dialed Joe's cell phone as he walked up the steps. When there was no answer after six rings, Evan disconnected the call without leaving voice mail. Tonight he was tired and had a lot of reading to do, none of it light, he told himself as he waved good night to the guard, so it was just as well he hadn't been able to hook up with Joe. He'd catch up with the guys later in the week.

Maybe by then, Joe would have remembered where he'd heard about the second killer. The one whose existence wasn't supposed to have been discussed outside the D.A.'s office.

He wondered who'd been talking, and how the information had made its way to the Lyndon PD.

He stopped for pizza on the way home and ate standing up at the kitchen counter while he listened to his voice mail. Then he locked up the house and took his files to his second-floor office, where he read until he passed out. Sunday morning he showered, shaved, and started all over again, making calls and taking notes, crossing names off one list and adding them to another.

At four in the afternoon, he looked out the back window at the dirt patch that was Annie's garden and hoped that by this time next week, they'd be together, working on it. He put the thought aside and went back to his phone calls. He worked until midnight, then closed up shop and went to bed.

At four o'clock Monday morning, the phone rang, and he answered it groggily.

"Crosby? Sargeant Crocker, Broeder Police Department. Got someone here who wants to talk to you."

There was a soft rustle as the phone was passed from one person to another.

"Hey, Detective, Perry Jelinik; remember me?"

"Sure." Evan pulled himself up onto one elbow and tried to stifle a yawn. "I busted you for possession two years ago."

"And four years before that."

"You get picked up more recently by someone else, Jelinik?"

"Yeah, actually, I was." There was a pause. "I was wondering if you could help me out with that. Talk to the arresting officer or the D.A. for me or something."

"Why would I do that?"

"Well, I hear you're looking for an address . . ."

___CHAPTER___
NINETEEN

AFTER TWO SOLID DAYS OF REVIEWING POLICE RE-
ports to prepare a profile for a D.A. in Florida, Annie
was almost happy to be going back into the office
again. She felt as if she'd been in solitary confinement
since she arrived home on Saturday morning. She was
trying to recall when she had ever welcomed a Monday quite as much when she heard her fax beeping to
signal that something was being sent to her machine.

She went into her office and leaned over the desk to
pull the sheet of paper from the incoming tray and
was surprised to see a copy of Melissa Lowery's autopsy report.

Annie scanned it quickly, skipping over the sections
she deemed inconsequential to cause of death ("... the
liver has been removed and upon examination is found
to weigh ...") and going straight to the chase.

Cause of death: Exsanguination due to gunshot
wound to the chest.

Melissa had been shot and left to bleed to death.

Not something Annie was looking forward to sharing with Grady.

She was still wondering how to handle that when the phone rang.

"Dr. McCall?"

"Yes."

"Sheriff Brody."

"Oh, Sheriff. I was just about to call you to thank you for faxing the autopsy report on Melissa Lowery."

"Told you I would do so. Glad I caught you on your home phone. Your cell phone wasn't picking up."

She searched her purse and found the cell at the bottom. She'd turned it off the night before after she spoke with Evan because the battery was running down, the charger was in the car, and she hadn't felt like going out in the rain to get it.

"So now that we know for certain she did not die a natural death," he was saying, "you have any thoughts on that?"

"Not just yet."

"I was just wondering if maybe your reason for coming all the way out here to see her might have something to do with her being murdered."

"Sheriff, with all due respect, at this time I cannot discuss the reason for my visit." Annie bit her bottom lip, wishing she'd been able to talk to John before she had to have this conversation with Sheriff Brody. "I'm not trying to be evasive, and I apologize if it sounds as if I am, but my visit had to do with an FBI investigation, and I really can't discuss that with anyone at this time. Please keep in mind that my position with the Bureau is primarily as a profiler. I try to stay out of the bureaucratic aspects. I can give you the name of the special agent in charge to whom I report, if you'd like to give him a call."

"I'd appreciate that." Brody didn't sound at all surprised to hear that he wouldn't be getting information from Annie.

She gave him John Mancini's office number, knowing John would be out of the office for another few days. Having called John on Saturday to bring him up to date on Grady Shields' involvement with Melissa, and Melissa's involvement in Dylan's case, Annie knew John would want to avoid Sheriff Brody for as long as possible.

"Just a few other questions for you, Dr. McCall."

"I'll answer what I can, Sheriff."

"Any thoughts on why an unemployed former FBI agent might have a few hundred thousand dollars stashed away?" Before she could respond, he added, "Ms. Lowery had a savings account with a little over six hundred thousand dollars in it."

"Wow."

"That was pretty much my reaction. Lot of money just sitting there, can't help but wonder where it came from. And this is after some substantial outlays of cash. Seems Ms. Lowery paid cash for that spread she was living on, only eleven acres, not much out here, but still . . ." He cleared his throat. "Paid cash for that new SUV, cash for a bunch of new furniture. Any idea how she could have done all that?"

"No. None." Annie hated lying, but now wasn't the time to tell Brody about the nameless someone who had given Melissa what Grady had described as a lot of cash in exchange for her resignation from the Bureau and her disappearance. "Maybe she had some family money."

"Her father was a bus driver and her mother retired with a twenty-five-year pin from the local school district. They have no idea where the money came from."

"I'm sorry, Sheriff, I just can't help you."

"You wouldn't have any thoughts on who this gentleman friend might have been?"

"No, sorry. Did you ask her parents if they knew who she was involved with?"

"They said they thought she had someone special in her life, but she didn't talk about it. You think that's strange, not to talk to your mother about your boyfriend?"

"Since my mother died before I was old enough to have boyfriends, I wouldn't know."

"Sorry about that, Dr. McCall."

"And a lot of women just don't discuss their personal lives, especially if it's not a serious relationship, you know?"

"Maybe." He sighed heavily. Annie could tell he was frustrated, that he knew she had information that could help him, but he'd apparently dealt with the Bureau in the past. He didn't push, and that made her feel that perhaps he'd pushed before and gotten nowhere.

"Oh, one more thing," he said. "I spoke with the locksmith in town. He said Mariana Gray had come in one day about seven months ago and asked for all new locks, doors and windows. He thought it was unusual at the time—nobody out here locks up like that, there just has never been a cause for it in the past. That could change, in light of this murder. Anyway, the locksmith said he went out to her house, and she had him double-dead-bolt all the doors and put locks on every one of the windows. Said he never saw anyone so worried about her house being broken into."

"Well, she did live around D.C. for several years. We have our share of crime out east, you know. Maybe her place here was broken into, maybe she'd been the victim of a crime in the past and it made her skittish."

"Or maybe she was afraid of someone." He cleared his throat again. "Guess she was right about that, eh?"

"It does look that way, doesn't it?" she replied, momentarily distracted by the call-waiting signal. She walked to the phone base to check the caller ID. It was an overseas number she didn't recognize. Connor?

"Well, I guess I'll give your agent Mancini a call,

see if he'll throw me a bone or two and give me a few leads."

"If he has any, I'm sure he'll be more than happy—"

"Please, Dr. McCall. I've been down this road with the FBI before. We both know that you know what's at the bottom of this. I just hope that if you find Melissa Lowery's killer, you'll at the very least let me know so that we can stop wasting our time looking for him—or her—out here."

"Sheriff Brody, you have my word. If we find the killer, you will be the first to know."

" 'Preciate that, Dr. McCall. Hope it's soon. We've got some nervous people out here." He hung up without waiting for any further comment.

Annie immediately placed a call to John, but had to leave voice mail detailing her conversation with Brody. She was relieved that he was away for a few more days. At least he had a legitimate excuse for ducking the sheriff.

Annie started to return the phone to the cradle when she remembered the call that had been coming through while she was speaking with Sheriff Brody. She sat on the end of her desk and listened to the message.

"Hey, Annie, it's Connor. Sorry I missed you, but I wanted to get back to you about Santa Estela. When you get into the office, ask John to give you clearance to look over a report that would have been written, oh, I guess around the end of 2002, maybe early 2003. It concerns our successful efforts to shut down

some traffic. I tried to get in touch with one of the
agents involved, but I haven't heard back. I'm guessing he's in the field or undercover somewhere and
hasn't gotten the message. I don't know who was in
charge of this at a supervisory level, or who else was
involved, but it must have been a fairly big op. If you
see the report, you'll know who the agent is, and you
can probably get the green light to talk to him directly. But until you're cleared, I can't give you any
other information. All I can say at this point is that
there is a report, and it should contain names and
places. Read the report—you'll know where to go
from there. Sorry I missed you. Get back to me if you
have any other questions. See ya."

Annie listened to the message two or three times
before hanging up the phone.

There was a report. The Bureau had a report.
Names, places . . . contacts. Maybe they'd even be able
to locate the families of the girls who'd been killed.
She practically danced into her room to finish getting
dressed. She couldn't wait to tell Evan, couldn't wait
to see the report.

She put in another call to John, but there was no
answer. She pulled on a pair of linen pants and
slipped her feet into flat shoes, searched her dresser
for earrings, a bracelet, all the while thinking of how
wonderful it would be if she could find the evidence
that could lead to the resolution of these killings.

She went back into her office, picked up the autopsy report on Melissa Lowery, and tucked it into

her briefcase. She tried both John and Evan one more time, but wasn't able to reach either one of them. No matter, she told herself. She'd get through to both of them before the day was over.

Buoyed by the turn of events, she turned off the light and headed off to work.

CHAPTER
TWENTY

"SHE WAS MY BROTHER'S WIFE, LUTHER."

"She was a loose end. Another of your loose ends," Luther said calmly.

"She wouldn't have gone back on the deal."

"You don't know that. And with Annie McCall right on her heels, there was too big a risk. She knows how to work a witness. I don't think Melissa would have had a chance."

"Melissa didn't even know I was involved. I was really careful. She had no clue as to which name on her report was the one that wasn't supposed to be there."

"All she had to do was give Annie the names of the agents she remembered seeing that night—and we know she would have remembered having seen you—and sooner or later, McCall would have been able to put it together."

"There were a lot of agents there that night."

"Only one of whom wasn't assigned to the op." Luther spoke as if explaining something tedious to a child. "And let's not even bother to talk about the fact that you were *family*, Shields, and never mentioned to anyone in your *family* that you were there that night? You think that wouldn't seem odd to anyone?"

His comment was met with silence.

"I saw the report, Shields," Luther continued. "She saw you with the rifle case."

"About fifteen people were carrying rifle cases, Luther."

"Only one of them was noted coming out of the building. A building that no one had been assigned to enter."

"I explained that to her. I told her I'd gone upstairs after hearing the shots fired. I told her I was looking for the shooter. She believed me."

"She might have, but someone less trusting, someone trying to put the pieces together—someone like Annie McCall—might not be so quick to accept your explanation."

"Melissa wouldn't have told Annie anything."

"Look, this whole thing has been stupid on your part since day one. It was stupid to even try to deal with her. You should have just pushed her in front of a train or something."

"We could have moved her, we could have—"

"Enough, all right? It's done. I did what you should have done in the first place."

"Luther . . ."

"Yeah, yeah, I know. Your brother was in love with her. I heard it before. I never should have let you handle that yourself. You just let your emotions get in your way. You're pretty much useless to me at this point."

Another silence.

"But you can still redeem yourself. I'm going to give you one chance—but only one."

"Connor." The name was said with a sigh.

"Forget about Connor. I'll deal with him myself. You've already proven that you cannot be trusted when it comes to your own family."

"Are you kidding? Didn't we just talk about Dylan?"

"That was two years ago, you killed the wrong man, and you came close to being caught." Luther laughed out loud. "Besides, what have you done for me lately?"

"Not funny, Luther."

"I wasn't trying to be."

"What is it you want me to do?"

"As I said, Dr. McCall is getting a little too close."

"You want me to kill Annie?"

"I want you to help me set it up. Just get her to the right place at the right time, and I'll take care of the rest."

"You know what, Luther? I'm out. You can keep the money from the last shipment, you can keep the contacts. I want out."

"You just can't walk away from this, Shields. You owe me."

"I don't owe you jackshit, Luther. I did my job all along. I handled the security in Santa Estela, I handled the cops down there. I did everything you needed me to do. But I'm done."

"This one last thing, and we'll call it even."

"I can't help you kill Annie."

"It's her, or it's you, Shields. You make the call."

The pause on the other end of the phone had been laughably brief.

"What do you want me to do?"

He'd listened to Luther's plan, and his stomach had turned. He'd known Annie for years, they'd been friends. They'd worked together, socialized. How in the name of God could he let this happen?

And yet Luther had made the consequences very clear.

He crossed the room and gazed out the window, wondering how his life had gotten so crazy.

Oh, he knew the answer; there was no big mystery there. Back in the beginning, it had all seemed so easy. He was just the lookout, back then. That's all. It was just an easy way to make some extra cash. Enough for a new car—nothing flashy, of course. No one in the Shields clan went for the flash. Expensive cars, expensive jewelry, designer clothes—none of that was understood. He'd never have been able to explain a Mercedes, not even one of the smaller ones. In his family, work was honorable. You worked for the sake of the work itself, not for the rewards.

And that had been his downfall, going for the rewards.

The irony of it was that he'd barely spent any of it. The single largest purchase had been to buy Melissa's silence. He knew he'd gone overboard there, had given her way too much, but he figured she'd given up a lot. Her job, her home, and, he'd thought at the time, her relationship with Grady. He'd felt obligated to give her more than enough to help her start and maintain a new life. It had never occurred to him that Grady would miss her, would find her. Would fall in love with her.

Would marry her.

All he'd really wanted was to keep her quiet, to keep her in the background.

And, he admitted now, to keep her off Luther's radar.

He was sweating profusely and pacing like a caged animal.

He went into the bathroom and stripped, dropping his clothes thoughtlessly on the floor. He turned the shower on high and stepped in, letting the hot water beat against him until his skin was red. Even then, he didn't want to leave the steamy shelter.

It all went back to that moment when Luther had asked him to do a little side job for him—to serve as a watch while Luther conducted a little business. There, in Central America, everyone, it seemed, was on the take. It hadn't seemed like such a big deal.

Then he'd run into Connor in the alley in Santa Estela.

His life had been all downhill from there.

He'd murdered his own cousin, for Christ's sake. Worse, he'd murdered the *wrong* cousin.

Killing Connor would have been one thing. They'd all grown up in his shadow, and since Connor was older than the rest of them, he never really felt he'd known him at all. But Dylan . . . oh, they'd had their differences growing up, sure, but shit, he hadn't wanted him dead.

When he saw what had happened in the aftermath, how the family had crumbled, how his own old man had sobbed uncontrollably, well, it had made him sob, too. He cried as he served as one of Dylan's pall-bearers, cried through the funeral mass, and wept like a child as the coffin was lowered into the ground. Every detail of that entire day had been etched into his brain so deeply that even now, two years later, he could recount every minute.

He woke up many nights shaking, having relived the entire thing. At those times, only his own cow-ardice had kept him from shoving his Glock down his throat and pulling the trigger.

He hadn't dared tell Luther that Connor was now asking about the report. The report that didn't exist, about an op that never took place. If he knew any-thing at all about Connor, it was that he was tena-cious. He wouldn't let go of this until he got what he wanted.

He stayed in the shower until he couldn't stand the sound of beating water any longer. He got out and used a towel to wipe the steam off the mirror. He stood and stared at his reflection, and realized he barely recognized himself anymore.

He forced himself to shake it all off, to get control of himself. He couldn't think about Melissa anymore, couldn't think about Annie. He put both women from his mind, wiped their names from the slate as if neither existed. They were no longer of consequence.

He dried and went into the bedroom to dress. He glanced at the clock on the bedside table and realized most of the afternoon was gone. He picked up the pace and dressed as quickly as he could. He hated to be late, especially today, when he was expected at Grady's, where he'd offer his condolences to his grieving brother.

CHAPTER
TWENTY-ONE

OUTSIDE THE BROEDER POLICE STATION, IT WAS A typical early August morning in eastern Pennsylvania, with temperatures and humidity in the eighties and rising. Inside, the faulty air-conditioning system pumped a steady warm breeze into the small room. Evan stood behind the glass for several minutes, wiping the sweat from the back of his neck and watching what was happening on the other side to get a feel for the way things were going with Perry Jelinik. Apparently, they were going okay.

Jelinik sat in a high-backed plastic chair in the Broeder PD interrogation room, his hands folded on the tabletop, his head down. Every once in a while, he'd look up at the clock, but he pointedly avoided making eye contact with the Broeder detective who was leaning against the wall, his arms folded, a look of disgust on his face.

Evan rapped on the door with his knuckles, then let himself in.

"Detective Carr, good to see you," he said as he stepped into the room.

Carr nodded without smiling. He clearly was not happy with the way things were playing out.

"So what's going on here?" Evan asked Carr.

"Here we have Perry Jelinik, who we picked up at three this morning selling coke out of the back of his station wagon," Carr said without expression.

"Who was he trying to sell to?"

"Detective Olensky."

"Not smart, Perry." Evan shook his head. "Not smart at all."

Perry wisely said nothing.

"So, where's your lawyer?" Evan asked.

"I only got one call," Jelinik told him, "and that was to you."

"Really? I'm flattered." Evan sat on the edge of the table.

"I figured you were a better bet. Last time, my lawyer didn't do such a great job keeping me out of jail."

"Maybe it's time to get another lawyer."

"Maybe it's time for you and me to talk." Jelinik addressed Evan, then turned to look pointedly at Detective Carr.

Carr raised both hands in front of him, as a gesture of surrender, and walked backward to the door.

"He's all yours," he told Evan as he left the room. "Chief Mercer said to let you do your thing."

"You and Mercer must be tight," Jelinik said.

"We know each other." Evan wasn't about to share the news that his sister, Amanda, and Sean Mercer had recently become engaged. "Lucky for you he believes in professional courtesy."

"Yeah. Lucky for me."

"So let's cut to the chase, Jelinik. What do you have—or think you have—that's good enough to serve as a Get Out of Jail Free card?"

Jelinik lowered his voice. "I got an address. The one you're looking for. That whorehouse in Carleton."

Evan stared at him without reaction. Carleton was a small middle-class town a few miles away, and might have been one of the last places Evan would have looked.

"Maybe it's old news."

Jelinik just smirked and said, "Do we have a deal?"

"What exactly do you want?"

"I want out of here."

"No can do, Perry." Evan shook his head. "You're looking at a mandatory sentence."

"We both know you got pull with the D.A." Perry sat back in his chair and folded his arms over his chest, his smile replaced with thinly disguised impatience.

"No one has that much pull, Perry." Evan slid off the side of the table and started toward the door. "I could maybe help get your sentence reduced, but I can't make it go away."

"How much?" Jelinik asked as Evan opened the door to leave.

"Depends on how good the information is and what kind of mood the D.A. is in when I talk to him."

"The information is good." Jelinik was less cocky now, but still confident.

Evan turned and gestured for Jelinik to continue.

"You're gonna do the best you can for me, you promise? You give me your word?"

"I give you my word, I will do the best I can for you."

"The house is on Lone Duck Road, just past where it goes into a Y with Franklin, you know where I mean? There's that small lake there, the one with all the geese around it?"

"I know it, sure." Every kid who'd grown up in Avon County had, at one time or another, swum in that lake in the summer or skated on it in the winter. Evan had almost drowned in that lake as an eight-year-old when he fell through the ice. He knew it well.

"About a quarter mile down the road, past the lake, on the opposite side, is a driveway. It's one of those half-circle things, goes in on one side, comes out on the other."

"That's it?"

"That's it." Jelinik nodded.

"And you know this because . . . ?"

"Because I was there, man." He paused, then shook his head. "No, no, not for that. Those girls out there don't even speak English. Well, no more than they have to, to do their jobs, if you get my drift. At least, that's what I heard. I was only there to tow a car; this was back when I was working for Stock's, you know the repair place? I drove their tow truck."

"Whose car needed to be towed?"

"The lady who was in charge, I guess she was. Older lady, maybe fifty or so. Short dark red hair, kind of on the skinny side."

"What was her name, you remember?"

"Dotty something. I didn't need to know her name, I only needed to tow her car. Calvin might know, though. He owns the shop."

"You still work there?" Evan glanced in the mirror but was unsure if anyone was there on the other side, listening.

"No, man, I got canned about six months ago."

"How long ago was it that you towed this woman's car?"

"About that long. I didn't work there for long, maybe a couple of weeks, that's all."

Evan took a sip of his coffee, then made a face.

"Shit, it's cold. How's the coffee here, Perry?"

"Not too bad. It's still early, so it hasn't had time to solidify in the bottom of the pot."

"I'm going to see if I can get a refill. You okay there?"

"I'd rather have a soda. It's hotter'n shit in here."

"I'll be right back." Evan ducked out into the hall.

"You see Carr?" he asked the officer at the door.

"He's in there." The officer pointed to the next door.

"You get that, Carr?" Evan went into the room. Through the mirrored wall he could see Jelinik staring up at the ceiling, one knee bouncing nervously.

"Got it. House right past the lake."

"Would you call Chief Benson over in Carleton

and ask him to send someone out to Stock's Auto Repair and see if they can get a name and address for this woman? We're going to need the exact address for the warrant, and we're going to need to check the tax records to find out who owns the property. My guess is that it doesn't belong to the woman who's running it."

"I'm on my way." Carr left the room without glancing at Evan.

Must have been something I said, Evan thought, catching the door that Carr had allowed to swing back. He went into the break room, dumped the coffee in the sink, and dug in his pocket for change. He dropped the coins into the soda machine and hit the Pepsi button, then repeated the process. After both cans had dropped, he returned to the interrogation room.

He set the cans on the table and Jelinik took his, clutching the can with both hands as if to cool them.

"So, let's go back to the house where you picked up the car that day. You said the girls there don't speak English. How'd you know that?"

"Oh, Stock's kid told me. He goes out there once in a while, spends a little time, drops a little cash."

"Which one of Stock's kids?"

"Chuck, the oldest one. He's about twenty-five or so."

"He work at the shop?"

"Him? Nah, he wouldn't work there. He went to college, he's some kind of insurance guy. He just stops in to see his old man once in a while, and this one time, he was talking about this place."

"What else did he say about the girls, other than that they don't speak English? He say what language they spoke?"

"Spanish." Jelinik nodded readily. "Said he took Spanish in school, so he had no problem talking to 'em."

"He say anything else about the girls?"

"Just that some of them were young. Like, real young."

"You know anyone else who might have frequented that house?"

"No. But Chuck might."

"I'll be sure to ask him. Thanks, Perry. You've been very helpful."

"Wait a minute. You're just going to leave me here? I thought we had a deal . . . ," Jelinik began to whine.

"I told you I would speak with Chief Mercer and with the D.A. I made no promises other than that I would do my best to get the best deal I could for you. I won't go back on my word." Evan walked toward the door. "But we both know that under the circumstances, there's no way you can just walk out of here right now. Give me a little time to talk to some people, see what I can do. But in the meantime, you're a guest here in Broeder, and there's nothing I can do about that, so I suggest you make yourself comfortable. Take a nap, Perry. Watch a little daytime TV."

"Can't blame a guy for trying," Jelinik muttered as Evan closed the door behind him.

Once he'd entered the hall, Evan's stride lengthened and he headed for the lobby, his cell phone in his hand.

"Beth, Evan Crosby. I need to talk to Sheridan . . . no, no, I'll hold . . ."

By noon, Evan had the name of the person to whom the property on Lone Duck Road was registered, though he doubted that he'd be face-to-face with Lawrence Bridger anytime soon. A warrant for the search of the premises was obtained, but by the time the county detectives, along with several officers from the Carleton police force, arrived, the house was empty.

"They can't be gone for more than a day," Evan observed. "The Sunday paper and the one from today are the only ones on the front porch. *Damn.*"

He kicked the newel post.

"I can't believe we got this close . . ."

"What do you suppose tipped them off?" asked Bob Benson, Carleton's chief of police.

"Who the hell knows?" Evan grumbled. "Guess we need to get the crime-scene techs out here. Let's go over the place, basement to attic. Fingerprints, fluids, whatever we can find."

"You want to call in the county people?" Benson suggested. "They're faster and there are more of them."

Evan called Sheridan for the fifth time that day and

told him what they'd found—an empty house—and asked that he send out the best techs he had on staff.

"I want Carlin Schroeder and Mark Schultz," Evan told him.

"You got 'em," Sheridan replied without hesitation. "And I'll call Jeffrey Coogan down there in the lab and let him know this gets priority or I'm going to recommend a career change for him. Let's get every iota of evidence from that house. Let's find these bastards and nail them."

"Amen." Evan paused, then added, "I have to tell you I'm feeling real uneasy about the timing."

"You mean the fact that they folded their tents just when you're starting to ask questions on the street . . . ?"

"Yeah."

"Who knew you were asking?"

"Every john in the county who'd been busted more than once over the past two years."

"So someone tipped off someone over the past few days."

"Jesus, I just started making my calls on Saturday. How could anyone have moved that fast?"

Bob Benson walked around the side of the house, waving to Evan excitedly.

"Looks like Benson's men found something," Evan said as he walked toward the back of the property.

"Go check it out. Just keep me in the loop, Crosby," Sheridan told him. "I'll get the techs you asked for and send them out ASAP. In the meantime, we'll keep looking for Lawrence Bridger and any other properties he might own, and I'll have someone track down Chuck Stock and see what he can tell us about the place."

"Thanks. I'll be in touch." Evan closed the phone and slipped it into his pocket.

"What have you got?" he called to Benson.

"There's a small shed out back; the door's padlocked; but we got it open," Benson told him. "Lucky for us, someone had the presence of mind to include 'any and all outbuildings' on the warrant. Anyway, there's a mess in there. My officers thought it was paint at first, but it sure looks like blood. All over the walls, the floor . . . even on the ceiling."

Two officers stood silently outside the wooden shed that was set at the very back edge of the property, where it backed up to dense woods. They stepped aside as Evan and their chief approached, and held the door open for the two men to enter.

The shed was no more than twelve feet wide and fifteen feet long. Rusted garden tools lay in a forgotten heap against a back wall. There was a metal folding chair near the door, and dirty blankets were piled in the middle of the floor. One small window on each wall was covered with dark paper, and in the August heat, the room was claustrophobically still. Benson waved away a yellow jacket and pointed to the wall.

"Check out the spatter," he said to Evan. "Odd patterns, don't you think?"

Evan knelt near the door and studied the way the blood had hit the back wall.

"Lot of blood to have come from one person," he noted. "The D.A. is sending the county CSI team over, including our two best techs. Let's see what they find. First, let's get a confirmation from them that this is, in fact, blood."

Ordinarily, Evan wasn't one to speculate, but his gut told him whose blood they would find mingled in the harsh abstract work that adorned the dark walls of the shed. The thought of what had happened to those young girls—his girls—in this room made his hands shake with rage.

His phone rang, and he was grateful for the excuse to back out of the airless enclosure. He stood under a half-dead maple in the backyard and listened to the news. When the call was complete, he hung up and motioned to Chief Benson.

"The D.A.'s office has located another house registered to Lawrence Bridger."

"Nearby?"

"Between here and Reading."

"That one vacant, too?"

"No." Evan smiled for the first time since he'd arrived on the scene. "No, that one is a busy place, apparently. The sheriff has had it under surveillance for several hours. Whoever lives there has had a lot of visitors this afternoon. All of them men."

"Well, fancy that."

Still smiling, Evan headed toward his car.

"Hey, Detective, aren't you going to wait for the lab people?" Benson called after him.

"Nope. I don't need to be standing around watching them swab the stains and dust for prints. It's going to take them hours—maybe days—to process this place. You give me a call if anything comes up, but for now, I need to be down in Oakmont. The sheriff is waiting on a warrant, and I want to be there when it arrives. I intend to be the first person to speak with the lady of the house . . ."

"Dorothea Rush." Evan looked from the woman to her driver's license and back again. "That your real name?"

She nodded sullenly.

"I want my lawyer."

"There's the phone." He pointed to it. "But you haven't been arrested yet; you're aware of that, right?"

She nodded again, this time warily.

"Then why did they bring me down here to the police station?" she asked.

"We just need to ask you a few questions. Look, Dotty . . . is that what people call you, Dotty?"

"My friends do." She stared at him straight on.

"Well, maybe by the time this is over, you'll consider me a friend."

She scowled, and he amended his statement to, "Okay, maybe not a friend, but I may be in a position to help you."

"Help me how?" That got her attention.

"Look, we know you don't own that house, we know you don't bring the girls in, we know your only role is in running the day-to-day. Keep the riffraff out, keep the girls clean, that sort of thing, am I right?"

"Sure." She nodded without meeting his eyes. "That's pretty much it."

"So you have to know that you're not the person we want. We want the person who owns the house."

"I don't even know who that is."

"You live in a house, but don't know who owns it?"

She shook her head. "I never met him."

"What do you do with the"—Evan searched for the word—"proceeds?"

"Someone comes by on Mondays and Thursdays. I hand over what we took in since the last pickup. On Mondays, he pays me. On Thursdays, he pays the house."

"Pays the house . . . ?"

"Expenses for the girls. Doctor's visits, prescriptions, that sort of thing."

"How often do the girls see a doctor?"

"Only if they're sick."

"When was the last time someone was sick enough to call a doctor?"

She shrugged. "I don't remember."

"Who does the food shopping?"

"I do. Online. I order through a website once a week, the stuff is delivered to the house."

"You pay with cash?"

"Credit card."

"Credit card?" Evan frowned. "Yours?"

"No, Orlando's."

"Who's Orlando?"

"He's the one who picks up the money."

"His name is on the card?"

Dotty nodded.

"Where's the card now?"

She opened her handbag, took out her wallet, and handed over the card.

"Orlando Ortiz. This his real name?" Evan studied the card.

"How would I know?"

"Good point." Evan tapped the card against the palm of his hand. "I'll be right back."

He disappeared into the hall, where he met Dan Conroy, one of the county assistant D.A.s. He handed over the card without a word, and Conroy, grinning from ear to ear, took it happily.

"Let's see where this little gem leads us. You'll be the first to know," Conroy promised Evan.

"Okay, so, does Orlando Ortiz own this house, you think?" Evan asked Dotty when he returned to the room.

"I don't know. Honest to God, I don't know where he lives or who he works for, if that's his real name or not. For all I know, his real name is John Smith."

"Who hired you?"

"Orlando."

"How did that happen? You saw an ad in the classifieds for a madam and thought you'd apply?"

"He came to me. I used to work someplace else. He offered me a job, said someone was starting up a new house, they wanted someone with experience to run it. Said I'd be paid well if I ran a tight ship and I asked no questions. I figured what the hell."

"When did they move you out of the house in Carleton?"

"Sunday." Her eyes flickered nervously.

"How'd that come about? You lose your lease?"

"He—Orlando—came by early in the morning and told me that everyone was moving out in the afternoon. They were sending trucks and they'd be taking us to another house."

"You didn't think that was odd?"

"I thought maybe the house was sold. I was paid to not ask questions. I didn't ask."

"Did you ask questions when those three young girls disappeared about a month ago?"

"They didn't disappear. They were moved."

"Moved? Moved where?"

"I don't know." She shrugged again, a flip of her shoulders, but the movement appeared overly casual.

"Because you don't ask questions."

"Right."

"Even when you see their pictures on the front page of your morning newspaper, after they turned up dead?"

She opened her mouth, but no words came out. Her face flushed crimson, and she averted her eyes.

Evan turned to leave, then stopped near the door and turned back. "Who watches out for you?"

"What do you mean?"

"Who's your security?"

She studied her nails for a long time, and Evan knew she was trying to decide which side in the drama that was about to play out would most benefit her. Finally, she said, "There were a couple of cops who came by at night. I don't know their names, and I don't know what police department they were from, so don't ask me. I don't know. But it was just the two of them, every time."

"They were in uniform?"

"No."

"How do you know they were cops?"

"Orlando told me."

"What else did he tell you about them?"

"Only that the boss bought them to keep the peace and to protect his interests."

"Would you recognize them? These cops?"

"Maybe. Maybe not . . ." She met his gaze head-on.

Evan knew the look: *Depends. What's in it for me?*

Disgusted, he left the room, determined to find the rogue cops, with or without Dotty's help.

". . . SO WE PUT TOGETHER AN ALBUM WITH PHOTOS
of every cop in the county, and she just looks at them
all and goes, 'I don't know, I don't think so . . .' "

Annie could hear the exasperation in Evan's voice.

"Honest to God, Annie, to get this close and to
have to play this kind of game . . ."

"She's not going to give you a thing she doesn't
have to give up. Not now, anyway. She's going to hold
on to every card she can get her hands on, save them
'til she needs them."

"Maybe we should turn the heat up on her, give her
a reason to start talking."

"It couldn't hurt. She can only give you more at
this time, right? She can't give you less."

"True. She gave us some information, but nothing
that would implicate anyone other than this guy she
calls Orlando."

"And that may or may not be his real name."

"Exactly." He exhaled loudly.

"Well, here's something that should cheer you up.

It looks like I have a lead on the kiddie trade coming out of Santa Estela."

"What?"

"I got a call from Connor—voice mail, actually. He said the Bureau was involved in some op down there to shut it all down, about two years ago. There's apparently a report in the office. Unfortunately, I have to wait for John to get back from his vacation tomorrow to get my hands on the report, but I'm hoping it will give us something you can use."

"God, that's phenomenal! I can hardly believe it. But why do you have to wait for John?"

"It must have been highly classified. I don't have clearance to pull the case, but John will, I'm sure. That's why I called you, to tell you that you might have another thread to pull soon."

"That would be terrific. This case has been like a black hole from day one. Honestly, this job is such a pain in the ass sometimes."

"Hey, you know what John said. Anytime you're ready to make a career move, come see him."

"That would simplify things, wouldn't it?" His voice softened.

"Not if it's not what you want to do. That would only create other problems."

"But we could spend a lot more time together. This catch-as-catch-can is wearing me down, Annie. I want to be with you."

"I know exactly what you mean, my love. I get

worn down, too, you know. And I want to be with you, too."

"So what's the solution? You're there, with a job you love; I'm here with a job I love. In spite of what I say sometimes, I love what I do."

"We could both move to Baltimore and commute to our respective offices."

"Hey, swell idea. Why didn't I think of that?" He tried to make light of the situation, but his retort came out flat, and he made no more attempts at humor. Instead, he said, "I'm just better when I'm with you. None of it—none of this shit—is as bad if I can come home to you."

"I know. Me, too. We'll work it out, Evan. We'll think of something."

"Damn it. Hold on, Annie, I have another call coming in . . ."

Annie walked to the front window and looked out over the small grassy section in front of her building. The sun had yet to set, but the day was already beginning to fade. She stepped out onto her small balcony and leaned on the railing to watch the sky turn colors. The geranium she'd bought early in the summer sat dried in its pot, the soil petrified, the plant almost mummified. She couldn't remember the last time she'd watered it, or what she'd been thinking when she bought it. As much as she loved flowers, she always let them die. Too much work, too much time spent away from here.

"That was the lab," Evan said as he came back on

the line. "Preliminary reports show that the blood in the shed matches my girls' blood types. Of course we'll need to match the DNA, but I know that's where they were killed. I knew it the second I stepped inside. It was as though—" He stopped, knowing he'd been about to say something that would sound irrational, then decided he didn't care. "It was as if they had led me there, as if they opened that door and went inside with me. As if they wanted me to see what had happened to them there, like they were standing behind me, pointing around the room. They showed me where and how they died." He hesitated, then asked, "Does that sound crazy?"

"Not to me," she assured him. "Now all you need is for them to tell you who."

"Sooner or later, they will. I told you before that I really believe the answer is already there, in the evidence. It's like a big puzzle. I just haven't found the right way to fit the pieces together. But when I do . . ."

"When you do, you'll have the key to the whole thing, from here to Santa Estela. I'm hoping I can help you with that. I was so excited this morning, after I got Connor's message. I couldn't wait to get into the office. Then of course I got there and realized that I had to wait for John. But this is going to come together soon. I can feel it."

"God, I hope you're right. If we can find this guy, this Orlando, maybe he'll lead us to the next rung on the ladder."

"How about the girls who were in the house? Were they able to tell you anything?"

"They're all with social services right now. I won't be able to talk to them until the morning, but I don't expect them to know who's running the operation. At least they should be able to tell us who they are and how they got here. We can take them back to their homes, get a lead on the kidnappers in their part of the world. The Bureau report should help us with that. It might take a while, but we can close down this little cottage industry. Maybe not permanently, and maybe only this little piece of it, but it's something."

"And then maybe you can find out who the murdered girls were."

"I'm hoping so. Right now, we don't know if these girls were from the same villages or even from the same country. But you're right. Maybe soon we'll be able to start tracing backward to find their homes."

"That should make you feel a lot better."

"I'll feel better when I've got their killer—killers—in prison, awaiting trial."

She started to say something, then heard the click on her phone.

"That's your call waiting, Annie. Go ahead and take it. I'm going to try to get a little sleep tonight, get an early start in the morning."

"Are you sure? I can let the call go into voice mail . . ."

"Go on and take it. I'll talk to you tomorrow. Love you."

"Love you, too." She paused, then clicked off his call to pick up the incoming. "Anne Marie McCall."

"Annie? It's Brendan."

"Hey, Brendan, what's up?"

"You still looking for a copy of those reports, the ones that have been missing from Dylan's file?"

"Of course. Why do you ask?"

"Well, I'm not sure, but I might have found them."

"Are you serious?" Her heart leaped in her chest. "Where? When?"

"Well, like I said, I'm not positive these are what you're looking for, but they might be. I found them this afternoon, stuck in a file. A shooting out in Oakland the same day that Dylan was shot. I guess at some point the reports might have fallen out, and maybe someone just looked at the date and filed them in the first file that popped up with that incident date on it. Anyway, I meant to bring them home, but I left them in my briefcase, and wouldn't you know, I left that locked in my office. I thought maybe I'd drop copies off tonight, but I have a tire going flat . . ."

"I'll come for you. I can be there in fifteen minutes." Annie didn't wait for a response. She hung up the phone and grabbed her bag, marveling at her good luck that day. *I should have bought lottery tickets today. First, I get a call from Connor with a tip that could lead to something on Evan's case, and now this. If my luck holds, maybe I'll get into the office and find that John is back and I can get my hands on that Santa Estela case.*

She all but whistled all the way to Brendan's house, a neat little bungalow set back on a narrow lot on a pretty street halfway between her apartment and the office. She parked in the drive and turned off the ignition, then followed the brick walk to the front door.

She rang the bell and waited for him to answer. When he did not, she rang it again, then a third time.

"Strange," she muttered aloud. "He knew I was on my way . . ."

Annie pushed against the half-open door and called Brendan's name. She stepped inside and called again. He stepped out of the kitchen, his cell phone to his ear. He waved to Annie to give him a minute, then walked toward the back of the house. At one point, he raised his voice, but quickly lowered it. When he came back into the living room, his phone had already disappeared into the pocket of his jacket. He smiled at Annie and apologized for not having let her in.

"Sorry. I was on the phone."

"Hey, it happens. Are you ready to go?"

"Yeah, just one second."

Brendan left the room for a minute, then came back in, tucking something into his belt.

"Don't trust my driving, eh?" she asked playfully.

"What?" He frowned.

"The Glock." As her duties were primarily those of a profiler, Annie rarely carried a weapon, but she knew that many of the other agents could not step outside their homes without one. She rarely thought anything of it.

"Oh. I just . . ." He stood in the middle of the room, and for the first time since she arrived, she took a good look around. There were piles of newspapers, magazines, and mail on the floor around the sofa. An empty pizza box and several empty beer bottles stood on the coffee table.

"Brendan, is everything all right?" She turned to him.

"Sure. Fine. Why do you ask?"

"Whenever Dylan had something on his mind, he forgot to pick up after himself. I was just wondering if it was a family trait." She tried to make a joke out of it, but she knew it fell flat and had sounded more like criticism than observation. "Sorry, I don't mean to sound like your mother."

"Oh, that." He waved off the mess. "I started cleaning up earlier, didn't get to finish. I've just been so busy lately, running from one job to the next, it seems—"

"Hey, I understand. We all have weeks like that." She jingled her car keys. "Shall we go?"

He stared at her for a moment, then said, "Yeah, let's do it."

Brendan followed her out the front door and down the steps. They had just started down the walk when a man in a dark suit stepped out from behind a car parked in front of the house and called out.

"Brendan! Let her go!"

"Wha . . . ?" Brendan grabbed Annie by the arm and held her protectively.

"Put the gun down, Brendan, and let her walk to me."

Brendan stood stock-still.

"It's no good, Brendan. Let her go!" The man was shouting as he came slowly up the walk, his gun drawn.

"Brendan . . ." Annie tried to twist away from him, but his grip on her right arm tightened. When she turned, she saw the gun in his hand. "Brendan, for God's sake . . ."

"Luther, you bastard." Brendan raised the gun, but before he could get a shot off, the man on the sidewalk fired twice, striking him in the chest.

Brendan crumbled to the ground, the gun still in his hand, and Annie screamed.

"Dr. McCall, are you all right?" the man asked anxiously.

He removed his glasses, and Annie recognized her savior.

"Luther," she gasped. "What the hell . . . ?"

"Just tell me you're all right, that he didn't hurt you."

"No, no. But I don't understand . . ."

Luther Blue knelt down next to Brendan's body and sought a pulse. "He's dead."

"Oh my God . . . Brendan . . ." Annie's knees began to shake.

"Come on, here, sit." Luther led her gently to the

steps and helped her to sit, even as he was calling for backup on his cell phone.

Annie began to sob. "I don't understand . . ."

"I'm sorry, I'm so sorry, but he had his gun up to your back, and I was afraid he was going to kill you . . ."

"No, no, he and I were going in to the office, he found reports I've been looking for, about Dylan's death, he left them locked in his desk—"

"Dr. McCall, Brendan didn't have these reports. I do. Believe me when I tell you, he wasn't going to turn them over to you or to anyone else."

"What are you talking about?"

"I'm talking about the fact that I believe the report implicates Brendan in Dylan's death."

"I don't believe it."

"I'm sorry, but I'm afraid it's the truth." He took an envelope out of his jacket pocket and handed it to her as the first of the unmarked cars pulled up in front of the house. "Brendan Shields shot and killed his cousin and fellow agent Dylan Shields. The proof is in that envelope. And if I hadn't arrived when I did, I'm afraid he would have killed you as well . . ."

"Isn't John here yet?" A shaken Annie met Will Fletcher in the office lobby. She'd called him because, with John out of town, Will was the acting supervisory agent in charge.

"Yeah, I called him the minute I heard. He should be back anytime now." Will put his arm around her.

"What do you want to do? Do you want to go upstairs and wait in the office, do you want to get something to eat while we wait for John? What do you
want, Annie?"

"Maybe we can just get something cold to drink."

"When did you last eat?"

"Lunch, I think."

"It's almost midnight. Let's walk across the street
and grab a sandwich or some soup or something. You
look real shaky."

"I *am* real shaky."

"Did you give a statement to anyone yet?"

"Not a formal one. They're waiting for John."

They stepped outside into a muggy D.C. night. Will
took her arm to steady her and they walked across
the street to the all-night deli on the corner.

"Did you call Evan?"

"Yes." She nodded. "He wanted to drive down
tonight, but I told him to wait. He's right on the brink
of cracking a case he's been working on for weeks,
and I don't want him to distract himself from that.
I'm okay, I wasn't hurt."

Will held the door for her and walked into the deli
behind her. It was cool and quiet inside, and they
went up to the counter to place their orders, then
took a booth.

"So, you want to tell me what happened tonight?"
Will asked.

"I'm still not sure I understand." Annie rested her
elbows on the cool porcelain tabletop.

"Start from the beginning, maybe we can piece it together."

"Well, it started with Brendan calling me earlier tonight. He said he found the reports that were missing from Dylan's file, that he'd left them in the office. He said he was going back to pick them up, but he had a tire that was losing air, so I told him I'd come over and get him." She stopped to take a sip from the glass of water the counter waitress had brought her. "When I got there, he was on the phone. He didn't even hear me ring the bell, so I went inside. I could see him back in the kitchen area, and when he saw me he waved, you know, like 'I'll be with you in a minute.' He got off the phone, and we started out of the house. We got as far as the top of the sidewalk when Luther showed up, started to yell at Brendan to drop the gun and let me go, and something about, it was all over, not to hurt me . . ." She rubbed at her eyes. "The next thing I knew, Luther was shooting at Brendan and Brendan fell . . ."

"Had you seen a gun in Brendan's hand?" Will asked quietly.

"Not outside, but then again, I wouldn't have. He was behind me. I knew that he had one with him, though. I saw him put it in his belt."

"He needed a gun to go to the office?" Will frowned.

"A lot of agents don't go anywhere without their Glocks; you know that, Will."

"True enough." Will stirred a packet of sugar into

his iced tea. "Had you felt threatened, did you know that Brendan had pulled the gun?"

"I had no clue." She shook her head vehemently. "I had no idea there was anything wrong until Luther showed up and started shouting at Brendan."

"You said Luther was yelling at Brendan to drop the gun, to not hurt you, to let you go . . ."

"Right."

"Did Brendan yell anything back at Luther?"

"It all happened so fast, I don't . . ." She rubbed her index finger across her chin, a gesture he'd seen her use when she was deep in thought. "He called him a bastard. 'Luther, you bastard.' That's the only thing I remember hearing him say."

"That's an odd thing to say, don't you think? Under those circumstances?" Will frowned.

"I don't know. He might have said something else. I was just so stunned, so startled, I was having a hard time figuring out what was going on. Everything happened so fast, Will . . ."

His phone rang, and he took it from his pocket.

"Fletcher." He listened for a moment, then said, "I'm with her right now. Sure. No problem."

He folded over the phone and returned it to his pocket.

"That was John. He's on his way in from the airport."

"Does he want me to meet him at his office?"

"No. He wants me to take you home and make

sure you get some sleep. He'll give us a call in the morning."

She frowned. "You'd think he'd want to talk to me."

"He does. In the morning. Right now, he wants to talk to Luther Blue."

CHAPTER TWENTY-THREE

LUTHER SAT CALMLY IN THE SMALL LEATHER SIDE chair that faced John Mancini's desk and waited for the interrogation to begin. He'd been there for almost two hours awaiting John's arrival, in the company of Special Agent Harold Kimble, a man Luther considered to be stupid and without imagination. He might actually enjoy this.

"Okay, Agent Blue," Mancini was saying as he eased himself into his own well-worn leather chair. "It's been a long night for all of us, so let's get to the point. What the hell happened?"

"I shot Agent Shields," Luther told him. "I killed him."

"We know that part, Luther," John said, his face and voice both weary. "Let's talk about why."

"He was going to kill Dr. McCall."

"Why would he want to do that?" John frowned.

"I'm thinking it was because she was—"

"You're thinking? You don't know?" Kimble rose half out of his seat.

"Sit down, Harold." John motioned him back into his chair. "Let him finish."

"I think it was because she'd been asking about the reports that were missing from the Bureau file of the investigation into Dylan Shields's death."

"Why would that have been a concern to Agent Shields? He and Dylan were cousins."

"I believe it was because the reports would show that Agent Shields—Brendan—fired the shots that killed Dylan."

"Agent Blue, you understand the seriousness of this accusation?"

"Sir, I understand full well. That's why when I found the reports—"

"You found the reports?" Mancini's eyebrows rose in tandem. "All three of them?"

"Yes, sir, Agent Lowery's report, Agent Raymond's report, and a memo from Agent Shields. Connor Shields. I found them by accident. I was looking through the McCullum file, and I found the reports in an envelope stuck in the back of the file. I immediately realized these were the missing reports—"

"How did you know about that? How did you know they were missing?"

"Sir"—Luther smiled benignly—"everyone in the unit knew about the missing reports. Dr. McCall had, at one time, asked just about everyone about them, especially the report written by Agent Lowery."

"Had she asked you?"

"No, not directly, but I heard about it from several

people. And then, with Agent Lowery having been found dead so recently, I thought I'd read over her report and see what the big deal was."

"The big deal?"

"There was a buzz going around the office that there was something in her report that might have been the reason she'd been killed. So I thought if maybe I looked over the report, something might jump out at me."

"And did something?"

"Not at first. I had to go back to the old file—the original file. It took me a few hours, but I figured it out."

Mancini gestured for him to continue. It was all Luther could do to keep from grinning like a fool. He had the man eating out of his hand.

"The file contained the customary list of FBI personnel assigned to the op. It's stapled in the front of the file. So that's where I started. With the players. I heard that's what Dr. McCall had done, so I did the same. I read through the file, read all the reports, to put the entire op into perspective. Then I read the other three reports again, in context. That's when I realized several things." He paused for effect. Mancini and Kimble were hanging on every word. He let them hang for as long as he could. "Agent Lowery's report mentioned seeing Agent Brendan Shields leaving the building identified as Building A on the diagram."

He looked from one to the other, then asked, "May I show you?"

"Please do."

"If we could get the file in here? I left it on my desk, with the original reports." Luther smiled weakly at John. "I made a copy of the three reports, but I gave them to Dr. McCall."

"Why?"

"Because she'd been looking for them."

"When did you give her these reports?"

"Tonight. After I . . . after the . . . after the shooting at Agent Shields's."

"You took them with you?"

"Yes. I wanted to confront him about why—"

Mancini held up a hand to stop him. "We're getting ahead of ourselves."

"I can run down and get the file, if you like."

"Please . . ."

Luther hustled down the hall to his office, buoyed by his own enjoyment of the situation. He was relishing the spotlight, loving the script he'd written for himself. It was, he thought, quite simply brilliant. By the end of the night, he'd be hailed as a hero. He could hardly wait to get to the part where he'd explain how he'd saved Annie McCall's life.

He returned with the file and opened it on Mancini's desk.

"Okay, here's the list of personnel, in front, then the list of documents in the file. I think everyone agrees that all the documents were here except for Agent Lowery's report, a memo from Agent Shields—that would be Connor Shields—and a sketch of the scene from Agent Lou Raymond." He looked up first at Mancini, then at Kimble, and said meaningfully, "Interesting, don't you think, that both Agents Lowery and Raymond died suspiciously? She, murdered just last week, and he, a one-car accident on a dark stretch of highway?"

"How do you know Lowery was murdered?"

"Sir, everyone in this unit knows she was murdered."

"And you found all three of those items in the McCullum file yesterday? Doesn't that strike you as odd?" John leaned back in his chair, and Luther could feel his eyes bore through him.

"Yes, of course it does." Luther nodded calmly. "I was thinking, if someone had gone to the pains to remove the reports in the first place, why didn't they just destroy them? It makes no sense to hide them in another file, where they could be found, but who knows what this person was thinking? Maybe he'd just stuck them in there to get rid of them when someone else came in the room, and meant to go back to get them . . . I don't know. I wasn't the one who put them in there in the first place. I only found them."

He flipped open the cover of the file and took out the three documents under discussion. He handed them in turn to Mancini. "Here's the sketch Lou Raymond made of the scene, showing where everyone was at the time of the shooting. Here's the report from Melissa Lowery, and the memo to the file from Connor Shields."

He gave John a minute to look over the documents, then said, "You'll notice Brendan Shields is not listed on the personnel list, and his name does not appear on the diagram Lou made showing where everyone was standing. But Lowery notes that she saw Brendan exiting the building—the building from which the shots were fired that killed Dylan Shields and badly injured his brother Aidan—right after she and the others arrived on the scene." He leaned over the desk to point to a section on the back of the report. "As you can see, Brendan was noted carrying a high-powered rifle in one hand and a rifle case in the other. Lowery's report notes he told her that he'd gone into the building to see if he could apprehend the shooter, but found the building empty of all except Bureau personnel at that time."

John studied the sketch.

"Here you see who all went into the building; Lou places them all right here." Luther pointed to the sketch showing six stick figures representing each of the agents who had gone into the building after Dylan had been shot. "Brendan is not represented on the sketch."

"So we have one report indicating that Brendan was on the scene, in the building, with a high-powered rifle—despite the fact that his name does not appear on the list of assigned personnel. And we have a sketch by a fellow agent that doesn't place him on the team that went into the building, yet he was seen coming out right around the time that some of the other agents arrived on the scene." John rubbed his chin thoughtfully. "It is incriminating."

"And, sir, you have the report from Connor Shields there." Luther pointed to it.

"The significance of that is . . ." John skimmed the report. "Of course. I remember. Connor was supposed to have been on this op with Aidan. At the last minute, we pulled him off to send him to . . ." He hesitated. "We needed him someplace else that night. We sent Dylan in as a substitute because he and Connor look so much alike that even—"

He stopped in midsentence, took off his glasses, and rubbed his eyes.

"They looked so much alike, even someone in their own family couldn't tell them apart in the dark." Luther finished the sentence.

"You seem to be implying that Brendan thought he was killing Connor," John said thoughtfully.

"I think the evidence could be interpreted that way."

"Why would Brendan want to kill Connor?"

"I guess you would have to ask Connor that, sir."

"I guess I will." John nodded. "In the meantime, let's get back to what happened tonight."

"Yes, sir. I went to Brendan Shields's home with the copies I'd made of the reports."

"Was he expecting you?"

"Well, I'd called him earlier in the afternoon, and—"

"Did you tell him what you'd found?"

"Not in so many words, but I may have implied it. I probably did." Luther appeared contrite for a moment. "In retrospect, I should have kept my mouth shut about that."

"What time was that?"

"Late afternoon, early evening. Maybe around six or so."

John gestured for him to continue.

"Anyway, I called him again, just a few minutes before I arrived. I'd been to his house once before, but wasn't sure of where to turn off Capital Road. He told me he was just leaving, and that now wasn't a good time for me to come by. He tried to brush me off, but since I was almost there—"

"Did he give you directions then?"

"No . . ."

"You said you weren't sure where you were going. How did you find the house?"

"A lucky guess, I suppose."

"Lucky for Dr. McCall." Kimble nodded.

"Yes. Well, I pulled up in front of the house, and I saw Agent Shields exiting the front door with Dr. McCall. He had her by the arm, and it looked as if he was steering her along. I got out of the car and called to him. He turned slightly, and that's when I saw he had his gun in his right hand."

"Where was the gun pointed?"

"Square at Dr. McCall's back."

"So you did what?"

"I called to him to drop the gun, to let her go. But

he sort of pulled her in front of him as he came down the sidewalk. By this time, he had the gun raised and pointed in my direction, and he appeared to be about to fire, so I fired first. There were civilians in the area, the woman next door had started out of her house and went back in—"

"How many shots did you fire?"

"Two."

"How many shots did Agent Shields fire?"

"None, sir. I shot him before he could fire."

"And both of your shots struck Agent Shields."

"Yes, sir." Luther lowered his voice and tried to appear sorrowful. He gave it his all. "Sir, I can't begin to tell you how sorry I am that this happened. I've known Agent Shields for years—God, we worked together—I couldn't believe what I was seeing in that file. I wanted to talk to him about it, I thought there must be another explanation. That's why I went there. I wanted him to tell me there was another reason why he'd been in that building before the rest of the team went in, why he was there at all, since he hadn't been part of that team." Luther looked up at his boss and said sadly, "I'd tried, but I couldn't think of one."

"Why do you suppose Dr. McCall was there?"

"I have no idea, sir. I guess you'll have to talk to her about that."

"Oh, I'll definitely do that."

"Just out of curiosity, why had you pulled the McCullum file?" John asked.

"Oh. Well, I was looking for the name of a CI that we used in that case. I have another case in Detroit and I could use a little inside information."

"Did you find it?"

"Yes, thanks. I already put in a call."

"Good. In the meantime, we owe you a huge thank-you. It appears you may very well have saved Dr. McCall's life. Of course we need your gun and your badge until the investigation is complete . . ."

Luther nodded solemnly.

". . . and the Director is going to want to talk to you first thing in the morning. He and the Shields brothers—that's the last generation, Thomas and Frank—go way back. This is going to be very hard on everyone; I'm sure you understand that. But God only knows what might have happened to Annie if you hadn't been there to save her."

"I only did what any of us would have done, sir."

John nodded and stood up, a clear sign that the interview was over.

Luther was half out the door when John called to him. "I'm going to ask you not to discuss this with anyone for the time being. We have the local police to deal with. We're going to try to keep this out of the press as much as possible. I don't have to tell you what a PR nightmare this is going to be. And then there's the Shields family. As I'm sure you know, they've given more than their share to the Bureau. Brendan's father is going to be heartbroken over this whole thing. We need to be sensitive and respectful of their situation. And it goes without saying that I have your word you will not be leaving the area."

For a moment, John Mancini appeared to be about to cry.

Luther left the office feeling better than he had in a long, long time.

Were it not for the fact that it would surely have drawn suspicion, he'd have been skipping down the hall and whistling a happy tune. He'd gotten rid of one horrendous thorn in his side and made himself look like a hero at the same time. Oh, sure, his original plan had been to get rid of Annie, too, but then that woman next door had come out and blown that.

What the hell, at least he'd come out of it looking good. And it was actually better for him in the long run, he rationalized as he walked to the elevator. Annie could corroborate his version of what happened, and no one would ever question Anne Marie McCall.

All in all, it had been a very good day.

____CHAPTER____
TWENTY-FOUR

CONNOR SAT IN THE DARKENED ROOM, SWIRLING THE amber liquid around in his glass until it spun like a whirlpool. If there ever was a time in his life when he wanted oblivion, it was now.

He'd been en route from his weeklong rest in Essaouira to his latest assignment when he'd gotten the call from John Mancini on his cell.

"Call me from a secure line. Now."

It had taken Connor another hour to return to the Villa André and make the call. He'd spent every minute since wishing he had not.

His cousin Brendan was dead, shot by a fellow agent who'd seen Brendan with a gun pointed at Annie McCall's back.

At first he'd been tempted to laugh out loud. How crazy was that scenario? Brendan holding a gun on Annie? Was he kidding?

Then came the bombshell.

From all the evidence, it appeared that Brendan had been the one who shot and killed Connor's own brother Dylan.

For Connor, the world had tilted and was now spinning off its axis. None of this could be true. Brendan couldn't have killed Dylan, Connor had told John. Brendan hadn't even been there that night.

"Actually, he was. His presence was mentioned on a report. A report he may have killed to have kept secret."

And then John had told him about Melissa Lowery's report, and her disappearance, and her death . . . and her marriage to Grady.

No way would Brendan have killed the woman his brother loved, Connor had insisted. This is all insanity.

"Connor. If he killed Dylan, what would have stopped him from killing a woman he barely knew?"

"What are you doing to determine whether or not he did in fact kill Dylan?"

"We've confiscated the weapons from his house. We're going to start running ballistics tests this morning."

Then came the kicker.

"Connor," John said, "can you think of any reason why Brendan would have wanted you dead?"

"Me? You think he was coming after me next?"

"No. The theory is that you might have been the original target."

"That's just crazy."

"Think for a minute, would you? I know this is all coming as a shock, but put your emotions aside and think. Is there any reason Brendan would have wanted you dead? Anything you had over on him, or anything that you knew that could hurt him, anything questionable about his actions, anything strange that struck you as odd or out of the ordinary. Anything he seemed secretive or evasive about?"

"Santa Estela." The words left Connor's lips before he'd even thought of them.

"What about it?"

"A couple of years back, I was there right before the elections . . ."

"I remember."

"On the night I was to leave, I was on my way down to the dock for the boat that was to pick me up, and I took a shortcut through an alley that ran between some abandoned warehouses. There was a deal going down; I watched from the alley. Six, seven men, a truck filled with kids. One of me. I was trying to figure out what to do when I ran into Brendan."

"You ran into Brendan in the alley?" John had been clearly surprised.

"He walked in one end while I was at the other. Almost didn't recognize him at first, it was dark, and let's face it, the last person you expect to run into under those circumstances is a member of your own family."

"What was he doing there?"

"He told me he was on the op that was just about to close down the kiddie traffic."

"What op?"

"The operation to shut down the traffic in children

coming out of Santa Estela. He told me not to worry about the kids in the truck because he was part of the team that was shutting it down that night. When I asked him about it later, he blew me off as if it wasn't important, but an op like that could have had international repercussions and I . . ."

"Connor, there was no team in Santa Estela that had been sent in to work on the child-slave trade."

"He must have been working for another unit then, because he told me—"

"Listen to me. He was working for me. He's always worked for me, and only for me. There was no op. He was there to keep an eye on the rebels, to keep the political situation stable."

"John, you're wrong. They closed it down that night, he told me they did. There's a whole file on this, he wrote a report—"

"Did you see it? Did he show you the report?"

"Well, no, but he told me—"

"Connor, we're talking about the man who may have killed your brother. Why are you defending him?"

"I can't believe any of this. The Brendan I knew—"

"Just how well did you know him?"

Connor had paused to take a deep breath.

"If any of what you're telling me is true, I'd have to say I didn't know him at all."

There'd been talk after that of a memorial service to be held the following week.

"You might want to think about coming home for it, Connor."

"I don't have to think about it. I won't be there."

"I can arrange for you to come home."

"That bastard." Anger had started to take over. "The bastard. How could he have pulled the trigger on Dylan?"

"Well, like I said, he might not have realized he was shooting Dylan. It was dark, you were supposed to be there with Aidan that night. I don't think Dylan was the target."

"You think he wanted to kill me because I'd seen him in Santa Estela? You think he was part of that, selling truckloads of children? There's no way he would have been involved in something like that, John."

"Think it through. Why else would he have been there? We know there was no op to shut it down, so if he wasn't shutting it down—and we know he lied to you about that—he must have been part of it. It had to occur to him that sooner or later, you would ask about that, and there was the danger that you'd figure out what was going on."

"You really think he was involved in the trafficking?"

"I think he had to have been. And he had to know that sooner or later, you would be asking about how that all went down."

"I did," Connor had said softly.

"What?"

"I did ask. A week or so ago. I left a message on his answering machine, asking him what happened."

"Why? What made you think of it?"

"Annie was asking me about Santa Estela. She knew I'd been there, and her new guy, that detective from Pennsylvania, had a murder vic who might have had ties to Santa Estela." He had stopped to recall exactly what Annie had said. "I think it was more than one vic, young girls, and there was a question about some tattoos."

"Did you tell Brendan that Annie had been asking?"

Connor closed his eyes, trying to remember what he'd said on the message. "Honest to God, John, I don't remember if I did or not."

There was silence while each digested what had been said.

"Is there a chance that Brendan wanted to kill Annie because I told him she was asking questions? Jesus, John, I don't know."

Before he hung up, Connor had asked, "How's my dad doing? Have you spoken to my uncle Frank?"

"I spoke with your brother. Maybe you should give him a call. There was some talk about who would be the pallbearers."

"Well, they can count me out. No fucking way." The anger resurfaced. "Son of a bitch murdered my brother, I'm going to carry his casket? How could Aidan even consider it?"

"I don't think Aidan is thinking about honoring the

dead as much as he's thinking about honoring the living."

Connor had let that sink in. Regardless of what Brendan might have done, his father—Connor's uncle Frank—would be devastated at the loss of his son. To lose a son under these circumstances would be humiliating for a man—a family—who had served the Bureau long and well.

"Call Aidan, Connor," John had said. "And if you change your mind about coming home, just let me know. I'll clear it."

"Don't expect to hear from me."

Connor had hung up and had gone to the balcony to look out over the water, his eyes stinging with tears. He'd had a hell of a time processing the information he'd received. His cousin had wanted to kill him, but shot and killed his brother instead. Then he himself was shot and killed while apparently planning on killing Annie.

What the hell had happened to his world?

He thought of Brendan as a young boy, almost a decade younger than Connor. He'd been the quiet one, the one who always held to the background. There'd been a time when he and Dylan had been adversaries of sorts, but that had long since passed. No, he couldn't believe that Brendan could have fired that shot. Brendan, who had sobbed as he'd carried Dylan's coffin down the steps of St. Bernadette's Church; Brendan, who had comforted Connor's father as well as his own.

Connor had started drinking after the conversation with John, and hadn't stopped. Unfortunately, the whiskey hadn't made him drunk, hard as he'd tried to silence the voices in his head.

He had called Aidan and berated him for even considering bearing Brendan's coffin.

"It's not for him, Connor," Aidan had said. "It's for Uncle Frank. And for Dad. You remember how Dad leaned on Uncle Frank through Dylan's—"

"Yeah, I remember." Connor had cut him off. "But this is different. This is the bastard who killed Dylan. Of course he thought he was shooting me."

"That's what's bothering you, isn't it?" Aidan had said. "You're feeling guilty because Dylan took the shots that may have been for you."

Connor had tried to respond, but couldn't get words out.

"Con, no one is ever going to blame you for not dying that night. Jesus, Con."

When Connor still did not reply, Aidan had said, "Look, come home and be with us through this. Dad needs you, Uncle Frank needs you. Mia, Andrew . . . shit, Con, I need you."

"Sorry, little brother. You do what you want. But I'll have no part in it."

"If you change your mind—"

"I won't change my mind. Give everyone my love, though."

And with that, Connor had hung up.

There were lights from the boats that still came and

went in the small harbor, even at this late hour. Connor stood by the rail, watching, wishing he was on one of them.

Maybe tomorrow, he told himself. Maybe tomorrow he'd take a boat out. Maybe he'd just keep it going until it ran out of gas. And then, maybe he'd just slide overboard and let the water take him where it would.

He went back into his room, picked up the phone, and called downstairs for another bottle.

CHAPTER
TWENTY-FIVE

"HOW ABOUT IF I JUST MEET YOU AT THE CEME-
tery?" Evan rolled down the window of the rental car
he'd picked up at the airport and cursed himself for
not checking the air-conditioning before he'd gotten
onto I-95. Now he was stuck in a massive traffic jam,
the temperature had risen into the high eighties already, and the fan was blowing warm.

"That's fine, Evan," Annie told him. "The church
is going to be packed to capacity, if the number of
cars already in the lot is any indication."

"I'm surprised that so many people came out for
him, a disgraced FBI agent."

"It's for his family. His dad has ties that go back fifty
years. He and Dylan's dad were very highly regarded in
the law enforcement community. Yes, there's certainly
a lot of embarrassment, but at the same time, there's
been a lot of support. I'm really not surprised that so
many people are here to pay their respects to Frank.
And to Andrew, and Mia. And the others."

"Are Connor and Aidan there?"

"Aidan was at the viewing last night. Connor apparently is having a real hard time of it, according to Mara. She said Aidan was just devastated by what's happened, and the fact that Connor refuses to come home and support the family is really bothering him."

"She's been there all week?"

"Of course. She's Aidan's wife. She'll stand by them."

"Even though Brendan was going to kill you?"

"In spite of it."

"I think you're pretty remarkable, to go to the viewing and the funeral of the man who tried to take your life. Not to mention the fact that he murdered Dylan."

"I'm too close to the family to not go, Evan. We talked about this. If you don't want to come to the services, you shouldn't feel you have to."

"I want to be there with you." He craned his neck to look out the window at the traffic that still hadn't moved. "However, at this rate, I'll be lucky if I'm out of here by noon."

"Well, since the service here is going to start in about ten minutes, why not just plan on meeting me at the cemetery?" She was walking now. Evan could hear the click of her heels, the change in her breathing. "You have the directions?"

"Yeah. Assuming I ever get off 95 to use them. I'll catch up with you at the cemetery."

"Okay. Look, I'm going into the church. I'll see you later."

Evan ended the call and tossed the phone onto the

front seat, then leaned heavily against the door. The car in front of him moved forward by about a foot, and all the other cars inched up behind one another hopefully.

There was nothing worse than a traffic jam on a major highway on a hot, steamy, humid August morning. Evan felt along the floor for the water bottle that had earlier rolled from the passenger seat and took a long drink once he'd successfully snagged it. The cars began to move, slowly at first, then a little steadier. With all the car windows down, there was a slight bit of breeze. He was debating whether to get off at the next exit and try to find the church, or simply go ahead to the cemetery, as he and Annie had discussed, when the car in front of him came to a halt, and the others stopped behind it. Traffic stalled once again, making the decision for him. He turned up the radio and searched for last night's baseball scores.

Luther stood alongside his car and watched the faithful flock to the tent that had been erected next to the gaping hole in the earth that would serve as Brendan Shields's last earthly home. Luther hadn't gone to the church with the others from his unit that morning—he felt that would have been too much for the family; his presence would have been more noticeable there. But here, under the open sky, where all of the family and those closest to the dearly departed had gathered together under the tent, he could hug the back of the crowd and disappear into it. He wasn't sure how anyone would feel about having the man who was responsible for the gathering mingling among the mourners, and thought his best bet would be to stay out of sight as much as possible.

But that was fine, as far as Luther was concerned. He'd rather be in a position where he could observe the goings-on. Once everyone arrived and the coffin was in place and the preliminaries dealt with, he'd stroll through the headstones off to his left and find an inconspicuous place for himself amid the crowd that spilled from the rear of the tent.

From his vantage point, he watched the procession of long black limos slowly approach, watched the bereaved family—a huge mass of black hats and black suits—walk together across the grassy expanse. The pallbearers gathered at the back of the hearse to carry the coffin, which the priest followed in the company of Frank Shields and his brother, Thomas, and their children.

Luther knew each of them by name, had worked with several of them over the years. He felt nothing for any of them, not even the beautiful Mia, who, once upon a time, had been the focus of many of Luther's fondest dreams.

Other cars eased along the drive, looking for places to park and hoping to find a spot under a tree where there might be some bit of shade. It took a full twenty-five minutes for all the cars to empty and the mourners to make their way to the gathering place. From a slight rise back near a line of trees, a lone bagpiper began to play "Amazing Grace," and even Luther was touched by the poignancy of the moment.

A fitting tribute to one who had fallen from grace, Luther was thinking as he closed the car door and started across the grass, well behind the tent and the overflow of friends and family. Once he reached his destination, he was careful to pick a spot at the very back, where no one he knew stood.

At least, he thought he had.

Then the woman in front of him turned around, and he was face-to-face with Anne Marie McCall.

She smiled, her big blue eyes brimming with tears, and patted his arm, a gesture meant to comfort him, he assumed, to show that she understood why he felt he had to be here. He smiled gently in return, as if silently communicating his thanks.

As if I would have missed this. As if I'd be anywhere else today. Brendan Shields had been a stone around his neck—had been for the past year or so—and had brought all this on himself. He'd screwed up just about everything he'd been asked to do.

It was beyond Luther to understand why any of these people mourned his loss.

Connor scanned the crowd, searching for his father and brother under the tent, but was having a hard time placing them. Finally, he located his dad in the middle of the first row of seats, between his cousin Mia and his brother Aidan. He'd catch up with them later. He knew they'd be happy to see him.

He regretted that he hadn't arrived early enough to be there with them now, that he hadn't been there for the past week to share the pain and the grief—and yes, the shame—with the family, especially his uncle Frank. It embarrassed him every time he realized it had taken him way too long to understand the importance of his presence here, both to himself and to his family. He hoped they would forgive him for his shortsightedness.

The crowd was huge, much larger than he would have expected, and he was wondering if the others in the family had been equally surprised at the numbers. He made his way to the back of the tent, where friends and coworkers spilled onto the grass twenty or thirty deep, and was moved by the show of support for his uncle and his cousins. He took a place in the very last row.

He nodded a silent greeting to several people from the Bureau as the priest began to pray, his words echoing through the small speakers on either side of the tent. Connor stood with his hands together, his head bowed, a sign of reverence he'd learned as a small boy in a large Catholic family. The priest finished the prayer, and the piper began to play again, a tune Connor didn't recognize. He gazed around the mourners in the crowd in front of him and thought he recognized Annie, though in that hat, he couldn't be certain it was her. She turned and saw him, then smiled and winked. As she turned back toward the front, a man behind her glanced back at him. Connor caught his gaze, and held it.

A shock went through him as he realized where he'd seen that face before.

In the headlights of a truck, in the shadow of abandoned warehouses, in Santa Estela . . .

The man continued to stare at Connor, at first almost quizzically, then, as if in recognition. He smiled broadly, stepped forward, and whispered something in Annie's ear before moving to the far side of the crowd with her, one hand on her arm, the other hidden inside his jacket.

Connor moved along with them, keeping thirty feet behind, as they stepped from under the tent and made their way around the headstones and monuments. He heard footfalls behind him and spun around, his gun drawn.

Evan Crosby was moving fast to catch up. They greeted each other silently, and Evan motioned that he'd be following from the tree line. Connor nodded in agreement, and both men took off across the gently rolling terrain in pursuit of Annie and her abductor, the identity of whom was a mystery to both Connor and Evan.

The cemetery ended at a high black iron fence capped with tall spikes. It was too high to vault over, and impossible to climb. Connor approached cautiously, his gun in plain sight, slowing his step.

"So. We meet," the man holding Annie called to him. "I've heard a lot about you, Connor Shields."

"You have me at a disadvantage," Connor replied. "I know *what* you are, but not *who* you are."

"Allow me. Luther Blue." He pronounced the name defiantly.

"Luther Blue? But you're the one who . . ." Confusion crossed Connor's face for just a second.

"The one who shot Brendan, yes. Yes, I am."

"I was going to say, the one who saved Annie." He kept his eyes on Luther, willing himself not to glance at Evan, who approached Luther slowly from behind, as quiet and deliberate as a cat stalking a mouse.

Luther Blue laughed. "So the story goes."

"What do you mean, so the story goes?" *Keep him talking,* Connor told himself. *Give Evan time to get himself into position.*

Luther grinned.

"Brendan didn't have his gun drawn, did he?"

"Well, he drew on me."

"But not on Annie." Connor met her eyes, and silently begged her to be silent, to be still, not to give Luther any reason to react. But she was a pro. She'd know what to do.

"It's immaterial." Luther shrugged. "He was planning on killing her, not there and then, but yes, it had already been decided. However, after that was set up, it occurred to me that I could kill two birds with one stone—you're going to have to forgive that lousy pun—and still come off looking like a hero. You have to give me credit, it was pretty damned slick."

"About as slick as the back of your head is going to

be if you so much as blink." Evan stood behind Luther, the barrel of his gun flush against Luther's skull.

"I can still take her out with one shot," Luther said calmly, as if they were discussing where to have lunch.

"You'll be dead before your finger twitches."

"Shall we see?" Luther remained cocky, even as he began to pale.

Evan pushed the barrel into Luther's head.

"What do you think, Shields? Who's your money going on?" Evan asked.

Luther's eyes shifted back to Connor, who had not moved from his spot twenty feet away.

"My money's always been on you, pal," Connor said.

"Nice." Luther smiled, careful not to move his head. "I think you two must be best buds."

"I'll tell you what I think," Evan said. "I think you have two choices here. I think you drop the gun and take your chances with a jury, or I put a bullet through your brain right now."

"What do you think, Agent Blue?" Connor spoke softly, evenly. "A minute ago, you were bragging about how slick you are. Think you're slick enough to outwit a jury? Slick enough to make a deal? I'll bet you know plenty about the kiddie slave trade, plenty the government would love to hear. Who knows, you could trade a little of this for a little of that."

"Or," Evan repeated, "I could put a bullet through your brain right now."

The air was thick and the sun almost directly overhead. The four stood stock-still for a full minute. Three were holding their breaths; the fourth was weighing his options.

Finally—*clunk*.

The Glock hit the ground, and Luther released his hold on Annie, who stepped away from him and into Connor's arms. Connor knew she must be aching to go to Evan, but the scene had yet to play out.

Luther held up both hands in a gesture of surrender.

"Crosby, you've got cuffs?" Connor asked as he walked toward them.

"No." Evan shook his head. "You're going to have to take him in, anyway. I don't have jurisdiction here."

"Now he tells me," Luther muttered.

Connor stood in front of Luther, the gun in his hand pointed straight at Luther's chest.

"I want to know one thing. Did you kill my brother?"

"Saint Dylan?" Luther asked. "No. No, that was Brendan."

"Do you know why?" Connor stepped closer.

"Because he thought Dylan was you." Luther smiled and pointed in the direction of the road. "Shall we go?"

"Why did he want to kill me?"

"Because of what you'd seen in Santa Estela. He was afraid you'd ask too many questions."

"What about Santa Estela?" Evan frowned.

"Our friend here was running a kiddie shuttle out of the country, sold them off to—where, Luther?" Connor asked.

"To whoever offered the most money, of course."

Evan stopped and stared at Luther's back. The man continued to walk as if he didn't have a care in the world.

"Who did you sell to in Pennsylvania?" Evan asked. He called to Connor, "Stop for a minute."

He caught up with Connor and Luther and grabbed Luther by the lapels. "Who did you sell to on the East Coast?"

"I didn't do the selling, Agent . . ." Luther paused. "I didn't catch your name."

"Who did the selling, Blue? Who did you give the kids to?" Evan persisted.

"They were brought to me by a contact in Santa Estela. I moved them out of the country. Where they went to once they left Santa Estela, I have no idea."

"Who paid you?" Evan was almost in his face.

"I don't think we're going to continue this conversation any longer." Luther turned to Connor. "If you're taking me in, take me in. Let's not waste any more time. It's hot out here . . ."

They walked between the rows of graves, an odd little parade of four. Luther first in line, Connor directly behind, his gun drawn. Still calm, Annie walked hand in hand with Evan, keeping the pace. They were within thirty feet of the tent when Connor put his hand on Luther, bringing him to a halt.

"Annie, find John Mancini. I don't want to go into the crowd with a gun drawn," Connor said.

Evan walked around in front of Luther, his hand on the gun inside his waistband.

"Just in case you're thinking about taking off into the crowd," Evan told him, "there's nothing that would make me happier than putting a bullet in you."

Annie returned in minutes, John and several other agents in tow. John walked silently around Luther, as if inspecting him.

Finally, he said, simply and without emotion, "Take him in."

Connor handed Luther over to several of his colleagues, one of whom cuffed him and started to lead him away.

"Luther," John called out, and Luther turned.

"There was no CI in the McCullum case."

"What?"

"There was no confidential informant used in the McCullum case."

"You stay up all night last night, looking for that?" Luther asked.

"Didn't have to," John told him. "I was the special agent in charge. And it was Memphis, by the way, not Detroit . . ."

_____CHAPTER_____
TWENTY-SIX

FOUR NIGHTS LATER, EVAN LEANED AN ELBOW ON THE bar at Taps and looked around, still dazed by all the attention he had received after his role in bringing in Luther Blue had been announced by the FBI in a statement crediting him with the apprehension of one of the major players in the international traffic in child slavery.

"Way to show up the feds." Todd Holiday slapped him on the back for at least the fourth time. "Unbelievable, man. You made us all proud."

"Hey, I heard the FBI wants to hire you; that true?" Joe Sullivan sidled up behind him.

Evan shrugged. "Hey, you know, rumors are flying around about everything this week."

It was true—John Mancini had offered Evan an assist in getting into an accelerated program—but Evan didn't feel like getting into any of that right then and there. Tonight was Disco Night at Taps, and with the Bee Gees playing, Tom singing along in a weak falsetto, and all his old friends there with him, Evan pushed all thoughts of his next career move from his mind. He waved to Sean Mercer, the police chief from Broeder, who was weaving through the crowd with Evan's sister, Amanda.

"Hey, hero-man." Amanda hugged her older brother. "I saw you on the news last night. The local stations are really playing you up big-time, aren't they?"

"There's so much focus on the arrests of the crew who was running those brothels in the county, it's a good thing. Not the publicity for me, but shining the spotlight on this trafficking in children . . ."

"I couldn't believe this was happening, right there in Carleton." Amanda frowned. "Everyone I've spoken with has reacted the same way. No one believes it could happen here."

"It's happening in a lot of places. It's good that the story's out there. People should be aware that this is going on in their own backyards; it's way more common than even I ever imagined. And I'm a cop."

Sean motioned to the bartender, who promptly set up three beers. He handed one to Amanda and one to Evan, who waved it off and pointed to a place on the bar where six or seven beers were already lined up.

"If I drink every beer that's been bought for me tonight, I'll have to crawl home. I've already had three, not counting this one. I think I'll just nurse the one I have for a while."

"I'm really proud of you, Evan," Amanda whispered.

"Thank you. But it doesn't take much heroism to save the woman you love when someone is holding a gun to her head."

"Where is said woman you love?" Amanda looked around the crowded bar.

"She's still in Virginia. She'll be here on Friday, though. We have big plans for the weekend."

"A romantic weekend away? Cape May? New York?" Amanda asked.

"West Broeder. The backyard. Just me, Annie, and a couple of rosebushes." He grinned. "I already bought 'em. They're lined up along the back fence, just waiting to be planted."

"Way to plan a getaway," Sean deadpanned.

"Hey, that's what my girl wants, that's what she gets."

"Crosby, the boss is here. He's looking for you." Johnny Schenk slapped him on the back. "He wants to kiss your butt a little. I say let him."

Evan laughed and stepped around his sister to greet Chris Malone, who, still in his dark suit and dark tie, looked out of place in the smoky, loud neighborhood bar. He was a sport to stop in, Evan acknowledged as he accepted the congratulations and words of praise Malone had offered.

An hour later, his ears ringing from too many repetitions of "I Love the Nightlife" and Blondie's "Heart of Glass," Evan slumped into a booth opposite Joe and leaned against the hard wooden back. They had a basket of chips and a bowl of peanuts between them, and a couple of beers. Just like a hundred other nights they'd shared in this booth, in this bar, after their shift together as detectives in the Broeder Police

Department. Those were the good old days, Evan was thinking as he grabbed a handful of peanuts.

"Getting too old for this kind of partying, Sullivan," Evan told Joe.

"Hey, I know what you mean. Nights when I'm not working, I'm asleep by now." He glanced at his watch. "I should probably get going soon. Rosemary and Joey are leaving early in the morning, and all the commotion always wakes me up."

"All what commotion?"

"Oh, you know, getting everything out into the car, the dog starts barking . . . though I have to say, they're getting better at it. It doesn't take 'em as long to get on the road as it did when they first started."

"Started what? I'm confused. What are they doing?"

"Didn't I tell you? We've been looking for something for Joey to get into, something he could do, so on a whim back in November, we took him to this dog show down near Philly, the big one, at the big expo center. Honest to God, Evan, you never saw so damned many dogs in your life. And all of them just groomed so nice, better than a lot of the guys in here tonight, I gotta tell ya."

Joe took a sip of his beer.

"Anyway, this show is what they call benched, which means that the dogs are all up on these tables for most of the day, and you can walk back there, see them, ask questions, and learn about the different breeds. It was interesting, I gotta admit, but Joey, he was just beside himself. They have these kids, they call them junior handlers, who compete in the rings with their dogs. He started talking to a couple of them, got interested, and next thing we know, he's asking if he can do it, too. How do you like that? We spent years shuttling him to soccer, baseball, football—all that stuff he hated and didn't do well at. And here he gets all psyched up about showing dogs."

"So what did you do? How does a kid get started in that?"

"While we were there, he talked to someone in one of the local kennel clubs, who took a shine to him. This woman, she's a breeder out near Reading, she invited him over, taught him the ropes, worked with him all winter. She's a terrific lady; she and Rosie have gotten to be good friends. Anyway, she offers to let Joey show one of her dogs in one of these junior handling competitions back in the spring. He doesn't win, but he does okay. Next thing I know, it's every weekend." Joe rested his arms on the table and laughed. "It's a pain in the ass, vacuuming all that damned dog hair out of the back of the car—I had to buy Rosie one of those big SUVs to carry around the dog and the equipment, you wouldn't believe all the crap you have to cart around—but it's been worth it. The kid is happier than I've ever seen him. Doing better in school, too. It's like a miracle has occurred."

Evan felt a twitch start somewhere low in his gut, the twitch that was the equivalent of a light going on or a distant bell starting to ring. He stared at his beer, not wanting to analyze the twitch, or look into the light, or hear the bell.

"So did you buy him a dog?" Evan didn't want to look at Joe, didn't want to let his imagination take him further than he wanted to go.

"Naw, didn't have to. The breeder has an older dog she lets him show. Dog stays in our house, sleeps in his bed. This big, hairy thing. Clumber spaniel, you ever seen one of them? Rare, this breeder is the only one in this part of the state. Great dog, though, gentle as a lamb. Loves Joey, Joey loves him. It's been great for the kid."

"That's great, Joe, that you found something for your son to enjoy." Evan couldn't even raise his eyes to look at Joe. If he was wrong . . .

Evan prayed he was wrong.

He'd known Joe for fifteen years. He'd danced at his wedding, he'd held his son in his arms at the hospital on the day he was born. For years, he'd watched Joe's back, and Joe had watched his.

"Yeah, it's been real good for him." Joe nodded and popped a few more peanuts into his mouth.

"Hey, I'm going to hit the men's room," Evan told him. The gnawing at his insides was unbearable. "Don't go anywhere. I'll be right back. I might ask you for a ride home. I'm feeling a little woozy after all those beers. I'm not used to drinking so much anymore."

"I hear you, buddy." Joe nodded again. "I'll be here."

Evan walked to the back of the bar and down the short hall that led to the restrooms.

It could be coincidence, he told himself with every step. It probably doesn't mean a thing, and I'm blowing this whole conversation out of proportion because I want so badly to solve the case. The thought of Joe being involved was ludicrous, wasn't it?

Evan could think of only one way to find out.

At the very end of the hall was a door that opened to the parking lot. Evan pushed the door open and stepped outside; at the same time he was taking his phone out of his pocket and speed-dialing Annie's home phone.

"Annie," he said when she picked up, "did the full lab reports ever come back on the trace from my girls?"

"I miss you, too, sweetie," she said, yawning, her voice groggy from sleep.

"Sorry, babe, I'm in a hurry"—he tried to disguise his impatience—"and this is important."

"The trace from the FBI lab on the girls?" she asked.

"Yes. You were going to have them run a full analysis on some dog hairs that were found on the bodies."

"Oh. The dog hairs. Yeah." She yawned again. "I saw that."

"Annie, it's important. Where's the report now, do you know?"

"Probably in my briefcase. What is it you needed to know at one thirty in the morning?"

"I need to know what kind of dog the hair came from. I hate to ask you to get out of bed to look for the report, but I really need to know."

"That's all you need? The breed of dog the hair was from?"

"Yes. And I need it now. So could you please go get the report and look it up?"

"I don't need to, I remember. It was a dog I never heard of, and I actually called the lab back to double-check because I thought maybe there was a typo or something," she told him. "It was hair from a Clumber spaniel. You ever hear of that breed?"

"Yeah. Unfortunately, I just did. Thanks, babe. I'll call you in the morning."

Evan went back into the bar and slid into his seat. Joe was on his cell, explaining to his wife that he might be a little late.

He looked up when Evan sat and told him, "Rosie said to tell you hi, and that she's proud of you."

"Thanks, Rosie." Evan's throat was tight, and he wondered how in the name of God he was going to be able to do what he was about to do.

He stared at his beer while Joe completed his call, then, when he'd hung up and put the phone back into his jacket pocket, Evan asked quietly, "Why'd you do it, Joe?"

"Why'd I do what?" Joe frowned.

"The girls. Why'd you get involved in that whole thing?"

Joe's face froze for several long minutes, then he said, "What girls are you talking about, Evan?"

"Joe, for the love of God, don't." Evan closed his eyes, squeezed them tightly shut. He couldn't bear to look at his former partner, even as he accused him. "Don't even try to talk around it, okay? I know you were part of it. I need to know what part, and I need to know who else."

"Jesus, Evan, how could you even think I'd . . ." Joe tried to stand, but Evan's arm shot out and grabbed him by the throat.

"Talk to me, Joe. Talk to me now."

"I got nothing to say. Let go of me."

Evan tightened his grip.

"You raped and murdered three little girls, Joe. You—"

"No, no." Joe went white and shook his head vehemently. "No, I didn't have a hand in none of that. I would never . . . no, God no, I never touched those girls, Evan. You have to believe me."

"How did the hair from a Clumber spaniel get on their bodies, Joe? You just told me how rare the breed is, how there's only one breeder in this part of the state." Evan's voice rose to a near shout. "How did the dog hair get on their bodies?"

The music had been lowered as the crowd had thinned, and those standing close to the booth turned, wide-eyed, as even-tempered Evan Crosby pulled his former partner out of his seat and slammed him against the bar.

"How did the dog hair get on their bodies?" Evan repeated.

"I didn't kill them, I swear to you." Joe was beginning to shake. "I only moved them."

"Moved them from where to where?" Evan demanded.

"From the place where they were . . . from where I was told to pick them up, to where I left them."

"Jesus God, Joe, how could you?"

The two men began to struggle, and the startled bystanders intervened to subdue Evan and to surround Joe with questioning eyes.

"I didn't kill them, I didn't rape them. I never harmed those girls," Joe said, looking from one man to the next, wanting them to understand that his role had been limited to taking care of the girls after the fact. "I tried to help them, see? I left them where they'd be found right away, I made them look like that other guy had done them, so they'd get some press, maybe someone would recognize them and they'd go back to their families. I tried to do the best I could for them . . ."

He turned to Evan, tears running down his face.

"I tried to do the best I could so they'd be found, so they wouldn't be lying out in the rain. I couldn't stand to think of them lying out in the rain, all alone like that . . ."

CHAPTER
TWENTY-SEVEN

"HERE. CATCH." ANNIE STOOD ON THE BACK STEPS of Evan's townhouse and tossed him a bottle of water.

"Thanks," he said, catching it in one hand. "The sun is brutal today."

She looked up and squinted. "I don't think this is a good time to be planting roses. We're better off waiting until later in the day, when the sun drops down a little. I read someplace that you're not supposed to plant in the heat of the day."

"Hey, that works for me." He jammed his shovel into the overturned dirt in the flower bed they'd spent the morning preparing and wiped his brow with the hem of his T-shirt. "I'd just as soon wait until it gets a little cooler."

"We can still finish getting the bed ready, dig the holes, put in that stuff you bought that's supposed to be good for the roots."

"Or we could wait until later and do everything when it cools off." He grinned hopefully.

"I say we dig now, plant later." She walked to the side of the yard, where four rosebushes stood, still in their black pots, in the shade. "The poor rosebushes have already been waiting an extra week to be planted. It's a miracle they're still alive."

"They look awfully comfortable there, in the shade. Are you sure we should move them?" Evan opened the water and took a long drink.

"It's going to be overcast tomorrow morning, then rain for the rest of the weekend. Planting them tonight will be perfect."

He took another drink, then replaced the plastic cap and set the bottle on the fence, between pickets, where it tottered unsteadily.

"I am worried, though, about them drying out while we're in Santa Estela." Annie frowned.

"Maybe I can get Amanda to stop out a few times during the week to water them."

"Good idea." Annie pulled her hair back behind her ears and looked for the container of root food she'd left near the fence.

"How do you think that's going to go, meeting the girls' parents?" she asked.

"I hope it goes okay, at least with two of the families." He leaned on the handle of the shovel. "The police suspect that the third girl, the one who still hasn't been identified, was probably sold by her family in the first place. They aren't likely to come back now and claim the body."

"Maybe by the time we get down there, they will have." She pulled on her gardening gloves and tossed a handful of granules into the first hole Evan had dug.

"I still can't get over John pulling all those strings, getting the locals down there to start showing the girls' pictures around until they located the families. Arranging for the bodies to be transported back to Santa Estela, and for us to accompany them . . ."

"John understands how important it is for you to take them home, sweetie. And if you want to look beyond that, I think it's important for the new government down there to assure the people that every effort is being made to find their lost children and to bring them home. It's a brilliant PR move on the part of the new president of Santa Estela, and a goodwill gesture on the part of our government."

"For whatever reason, I'm grateful. And I'm really happy that they're sending Don Manley as well. He's so grateful for the chance to go, to take his vics back. It was good of John to suggest it. If it weren't for Don's girl, and the little vial of bean seeds around her neck, we never would have been able to put this all together."

"That's what happens when everyone pools their info. Things get done." She smiled and added, "I'm really looking forward to the trip. I just know this will be something I'll always remember."

"Yeah, real romantic vacation." Evan stopped digging and looked at her almost apologetically. "Ten days in a hot, steamy, third-world country whose most lucrative export is its kids. With luck, maybe we'll even get some mosquito netting for our tent.

Maybe the piranhas will be migrating and we'll be able to get in a swim."

"It'll be the best vacation either of us ever had, you wait and see." She wrapped her arms around his waist. "We'll still be talking about this when we're old and gray. You will always have the memory of having returned those children to their families, to be buried with love and respect. I'm proud of you, that you cared enough to take that on when no one else seemed to give a damn about them."

"John said something like that when he offered me the job."

"Are you still thinking about that?"

"No. Right now, I'm thinking about planting a garden with my best girl, and taking a trip with her through a snake-infested jungle. I'll think about the job offer when we get back."

"Fair enough." She gave him a tap on the butt before getting back to work, measuring another spoonful of fertilizer and dumping it into the next hole.

"Two more," she told him, pointing to the rest of the plot, where holes had not as yet been dug.

"Here?" he asked, the shovel poised to dig, and she nodded.

"Hey," he said, "while I dig these last two holes, why don't you plant those geraniums in that big planter at the end of the deck?"

"Wouldn't you rather wait until you finish the deck?" She frowned. "If I plant this up now, you'll have to carry it up onto the deck, and it's going to be heavy."

"No big deal." He shrugged. "Just go on and plant the flowers, we'll worry about moving it later."

"Okay, if you say so."

Annie carried the pot of geraniums and ivy to the large planter Evan had left at the foot of the deck, and poured in a bag of potting soil. Next she pulled the plants from their pots and started to transplant the ivy. When she started on the geraniums, he heard her exclaim, "Oh."

She looked at him from across the small yard.

"There's a little box in the bottom of the geranium pot."

"Is there, now?" He stuck the shovel into the dirt and started walking toward her. "Well, maybe you should open it."

She shook the small dark blue box from the pot and opened it.

"Evan," she said softly, meeting his eyes as he walked toward her. "Evan."

"What do you think, Annie?" he asked. "Think it's time to make it legal?"

She nodded.

"Well then, let's see if it fits." He took her hand, then took the ring from the box and slid it onto her finger. "What do you think? Does it fit all right?"

"It fits perfectly." She had not taken her eyes from his face.

"Do you like it?"

"I love it."

"You haven't even looked at it."

She looked at her hand, at the simple gold band with the round diamond and nodded. "It's perfect. I love it."

"So, I guess this means yes?"

"This means yes."

He gathered her in his arms and kissed her.

"Will this get me out of digging for the rest of the afternoon?"

"Probably not"—she laughed—"but it might get you a bonus at the end of the day."

"I like the sound of that." He kissed her again, then said, more seriously, "I'm thinking a Christmas wedding might be really nice, you know? All those red flowers they always put in the church—"

"Oh! Bad timing on my part. Sorry, guys."

Annie and Evan looked up to see Grady Shields walking down the drive that ran behind the house.

"Hey, Grady," Annie called to him. "This is a surprise."

"Yeah, well, I just wanted to drop by to see you before I left. I wanted to thank you and Evan for what you did to bring that bastard Luther Blue in." He turned to Evan. "The only thing I'm sorry about is that you didn't blow his head off when you had the chance. He's still trying to make deals, you know that? Still offering to give up other members of the kidnapping and trafficking ring in exchange for a reduced sentence."

"Maybe the feds will offer him something on the kidnapping, but he'll still have to face murder charges in Montana," Annie assured him. "I spoke with Sheriff Brody a few days ago. I had promised I'd call if we found Melissa's killer. He understands the situation very well, but he's willing to wait his turn to prosecute Luther for Melissa's death. He won't be getting away with it, Grady. It may take a while, but he will stand trial in Montana."

"That's the first good news I've had since this started," Grady said. "Maybe I'll still be out there when that day comes."

"You're going to Montana?" Annie asked.

"Melissa left the property to me. At first I thought I couldn't live in the house where she died. Then I started remembering all the good times we had there, and I was thinking maybe it would help her spirit to rest if I went back for a while. Maybe it would help my spirit, as well, to be with her." He shrugged. "I can't think of anyplace else to go right now."

"Are you taking a leave, then?"

"I talked to John yesterday; he told me to go. He'll take care of the paperwork for me, send me what I need to sign. Told me just to keep in touch, let him know when I want to come back."

"I hope you do, Grady," Annie told him sincerely. "I'll miss you."

"I'll miss you, too." He gave her a quick hug, then offered his hand to Evan. "Take care of her, Crosby."

Evan merely nodded.

Grady took a few steps backward, then let himself out of the gate. He walked to the end of the drive, then turned once to wave before disappearing behind the corner house.

"He looks terrible," Annie said.

"He's lost the woman he loved. I'd look terrible, too, if anything happened to you. It just reminds me to cherish each day, to never take it for granted." He paused, then said, "If I take the job John offered, the main reason would be so that we could be together every night, instead of this crazy commuting back and forth."

"You're not going to think about it until we come back from Santa Estela, remember?" Annie reminded him. "I think you should stick to that. Besides, there are other things we need to talk about, as far as the trip is concerned."

"Like how to tell the parents what happened to their daughters." Evan grew sober again. "How to tell them why they had to die."

"Maybe it will give them some solace to know that they never accepted the horrible things that had been done to them, that they'd been unwilling participants. And that they died because they would not stop fighting, they would not cooperate, isn't that what Joe Sullivan told the D.A.? That these girls were killed as an example to the others?"

"Bastard. I still can't get over him getting involved in something like this. I can't reconcile the Joe Sullivan I knew all these years with the man who participated in any way in prostituting young girls . . ." Evan shook his head. "And for the worst of reasons."

"It's not the first time a man sold his soul for money, and it won't be the last." She put her arms around him. "Just be grateful you were able to put a stop to it."

"This was just the tip of the iceberg, Annie. You know that."

"But at least that tip was cut off," she told him.

He appeared to be about to say something when his phone rang.

"Crosby," he answered, listened for a few minutes, then said, "Give me fifteen minutes."

He snapped the phone shut and turned to Annie. "That was Malone. They found two bodies in a boarded-up house down on Longwood. A couple of transients, it looks like, and I—"

"Go. I'll be here when you get back."

"Annie, I'm sorry."

"Don't be. Go."

"I guess I should run upstairs and get cleaned up, get out of these dusty clothes." He looked around the yard, at the half-dug bed and the plants sitting here and there. "I hate to leave you with this mess."

"Don't give it another thought. I'll finish up out here."

"Are you sure? I'll probably be gone for at least the rest of the afternoon."

"It's okay. Go on and do what you do." She kissed

him and turned him in the direction of the house. "I'll be here when you get home . . ."

She watched him take the steps two at a time, knowing that his mind was already on the crime scene and what he would find there. It was what he did, and who he was.

Annie wouldn't have had him any other way.

Read on for a taste of
Mariah Stewart's latest book

FINAL TRUTH

available in hardcover
from Ballantine Books.

LESTER RAY BARNES WAS A MAN OF MANY ADDICtions.

Nicotine, alcohol. Sex, drugs, rock and roll. Underage girls. Gambling. There were others, acquired over the years, but right now, it was the latter that was sending that old familiar hum of excitement buzzing through his brain to remind him just how good he'd once been at playing the odds.

It had started when he'd overheard Dan, the night shift guard, chatting up Armas, the guy in the next cell.

"So, Armas," Lester Ray had heard Dan say, "guess you're gonna be looking to have your DNA retested, huh?"

"Whachu talking about?" Armas had mumbled in his lazy, offhand way.

"Heard Cappy—the lifer down on D?—had his done over, month or so ago. Tests came back different this time."

Lester Ray could picture the smirk on Dan's face.

"What different?" Armas's voice moved closer to Lester Ray's cell now as he got off his cot to approach the guard. "Whachu mean different? What Cappy done?"

"What Cappy *done* is get himself a Get Out of Jail Free card." Dan paused—for effect, Lester Ray figured—then dropped the bomb. "This new test said it couldn't tell for sure if he did rape that woman."

"How come it couldn't tell?" Armas asked.

"They're saying the guy who owned the lab, he was messing up the samples. Like, maybe he tested the wrong stuff or something, and didn't testify right. I didn't get the whole story. All I know is, he wasn't doing right and now they're saying there is no way of knowing for sure if it been Cappy or not."

There was silence on the cell block as the news was absorbed and processed.

"How can that happen?" Lester Ray heard himself ask as he, too, gravitated to the end of his cell.

"Beats me. That's just what I heard." Dan stood in the center of the hallway as if on center stage. "And I must have heard right, since Cappy's lawyer filed some kind of appeal with the court and it was heard this morning. Cappy's going home."

"Just like that?" Lester Ray's brows knit together as he tried to comprehend it. "Just like that, they're letting him go?"

"Judge said they couldn't hold him any longer. Gotta let him go since there was no way o' knowing if the test had been right. So, he'll be out of here as soon as he finishes signing them papers upstairs." Dan shuffled on down the hall, eager, no doubt, to spread the word beyond death row. "Don't that just beat all?"

"How'd he get them to do another DNA test?" Lester Ray called after him. "How'd they know to ask?"

"Somebody told on the lab guy, told about how there was some problem with the way he was testing stuff. Then he'd come in and testify at people's trials and didn't say right, something like that. Messed up lots of peoples' stuff. And somebody told a lawyer, Cappy's lawyer, and he went to the judge. Everyone downstairs is talking about it. And Cappy ain't the only one." Dan laughed dryly. "Me, I think Cappy's lawyer just played the odds. I'm thinking he figured, hey, some of the results were bad, maybe Cappy's were, too."

The guard paused, then half-turned in the direction of Lester Ray's cell.

"Hey, you're the gambler, right? The hustler? You feeling lucky, Lester Ray?" Dan laughed again and continued on down the hall, talking all the way to the door. "Maybe talk 'em into giving you another test, maybe beat that date you got with the needle, Lester Ray. Warden's got your name on the calendar with a big red circle around it. Middle of June sometime, right? Be here before you know it."

Ignoring the taunt, Lester Ray called louder. "What

lab was this, where this happened? You hear which one?"

"Fremont, I think it was," Dan said as he passed through the doorway. "Pretty sure it was the lab up in Fremont."

Lester Ray sat down on his worn thin mattress, his forearms resting on his knees, and replayed the entire conversation with Armas and the guard over and over in his head.

Fremont, Dan had said.

Hadn't his own DNA been tested in the Fremont lab?

"Lester Ray?" Armas whispered. "How you figure this? You think this could be true?"

"Dan said it was."

"But Cappy say he done that woman. He *tole* us he done her, remember? Said he messed her up real bad."

"I remember."

"How could a test say he didn't, if he say he did?"

"I don't know." Lester Ray lay back on his mattress, his brows knitting together as he pondered that very thing.

First thing tomorrow, he was going to check into this. Call that lawyer the court appointed to represent him for his appeals. Find out what this lab thing was all about. If it was the same lab . . . if there was a chance, any chance at all . . .

Shit, he thought as he closed his eyes, maybe there

was a way to beat his sentence, after all. He contemplated the odds.

The way things stood right now, his odds were a billion to one, definitely not in his favor. But if he could get them to retest him, too, the odds rose to fifty-fifty. Dead even. Didn't take a genius to decide whether or not to toss those dice.

Lester Ray mentally ticked off the number of times he'd bet the house—and won—on worse odds than these. Well, it was time to roll 'em one more time. God knew the stakes had never been higher.

Once a gambler, always a gambler. Lester Ray smiled to himself in the dim cell.

He lay awake long into the night thinking about how he'd spend his time, once he was out.

On Thursday afternoon, three days after hearing about the DNA debacle at the Fremont lab, Lester Ray sat across from Roland Booth, the attorney who'd been appointed by the Florida court system to walk him through his death row appeals.

"So what do you know about this DNA stuff?" Lester Ray folded his arms on the narrow table that stood between him and Booth, and turned his intense stare on the lawyer. "What are you hearing?"

Booth looked at him blankly, his expression a definite *huh?*

"Guy in here got out this week because of something being wrong with his tests." Lester Ray's calm whisper belied the urge to wrap the lawyer's tie around his neck and pull it as tight as he could. What the hell kind of a lawyer hadn't heard about the major fuckup in the Fremont lab? Every inmate on every block in here knew about it. What kind of clown was Booth that he didn't know?

"The lab in Fremont." Lester Ray was practically growling, wondering, not for the first time, what the state of Florida had been thinking when they gave Booth a license to practice law. "They're saying, the guy in the lab got the results all screwed up, then lied on the stand to cover it up, and some guys are getting out because of it. Don't you know what's going on around here?"

"Of course, I'm on top of it."

Lester Ray didn't bother to try to hide the smirk.

"So that means you have a plan?"

Booth nodded, his lips pursed, as always giving the appearance of listening carefully, though Lester Ray often wondered if he was maybe doing something else in his head, like making up a shopping list or thinking about what movie he was going to see that weekend.

The attorney's hands, pale and large—farm-boy hands, Lester Ray thought—lay perfectly still atop the file that sat unopened on the table between them. His face was equally pale, with little sign of having been touched by the sun—odd for one who lived in the Sunshine State. He wore thick glasses with round tan frames that looked almost feminine. He always wore the same seersucker suit and dark blue tie.

"You do know that Fremont was the lab that did my DNA testing, right?"

"Of course. I know that."

Right.

"I want my DNA tested again. I want it done now."

"I'll certainly look into this for you, Lester Ray." Roland Booth told him solemnly. "But you understand, of course, that even if it is the same lab that tested your DNA, and even if the lab tech under investigation was the same one who testified at your trial, and even if we can prove there were some irregularities, there have probably been dozens of appeals filed already. This could be backed up for a long time."

"I don't give a shit about them." Lester Ray leaned forward, his pale eyes flat and cold. "And I don't have a long time. I'm on death row here. I have barely two months left and I don't give a crap about anyone but me, you understand? You're my lawyer. You're supposed to be working on my appeals. That means you work for me, right? I'm the client."

He was almost in Booth's face, as close to the lawyer as he'd ever been.

"I want that DNA test done over. ASAP. You find a way to make it happen, and make it happen fast. They're not going to put me down like some sick dog without a fight, you hear?"

"I hear you, Lester Ray." Roland Booth had tried to maintain his cool, but it was clear to Lester Ray that he'd rattled the attorney when he'd gotten too close.

Lester Ray made a mental note of that fact.

"I'll see what the criteria are for retesting, see if there are grounds to have your test results reviewed." Booth looked as if he was about to break into a sweat.

"Reviewed, retested, re-evaluated—whatever it is they're doing, I want mine done too."

"I'll see what I can do, but I can't promise anything. Like I said, others have most likely filed already."

"How many of them are on death row, Booth? How many of them are going to be strapped to a table and injected with some shit that's gonna stop their heart?"

"I'm not sure, Lester Ray, but like I said, I'll—"

"I don't think we're communicating very well here, Booth. As my lawyer, you have a moral obligation to do whatever it takes to protect my best interests. The way I see it, my best interests are in staying alive and getting out of here. Now, you tell me what we have to do to get my name moved to the top of that list."

"I can request that, since the date has been set for your execution, your petition for review be given priority consideration, but there's no guarantee . . ."

"What else?" Lester Ray asked impatiently.

"That's about it, I don't know if the courts—"

"Then find out, for Christ's sake. If you don't know, find out. And fast." Lester Ray shook his head in disgust. "Maybe we need to go to the governor. What's the best way to get his attention?"

"I don't know, Lester Ray." Booth looked at him with growing irritation. "Maybe you should look for some celebrity to take up your cause."

"You mean, someone famous?" Lester Ray's eyes narrowed. "You mean, find some famous person and get them to talk me up?"

"Pretty much, but hey, I was only—"

"How do I do that?" Lester Ray ignored Booth's attempts to explain. He'd already figured out that Booth's suggestion had been made sarcastically. Lester Ray, however, saw the potential. "How do I get someone to go to bat for me?"

"I don't know. I guess you need publicity about your case. Then you need to convince him or her of your innocence. Then, I suppose, you—"

"That's it?" Lester Ray stared at the scratched tabletop as if the answer would be found somewhere in the midst of the random marks.

"Look, Lester Ray, it isn't going to be easy to get—"

"I don't give a shit about *easy*. You think it's *easy*, sitting here, every day and every night, thinking about what's gonna happen to me come the middle of June?" Lester Ray was about to explode. "Way I see it, it's your job to make sure it doesn't happen. So you go on TV, and you talk about how I'm innocent and I only have a couple more months and how the state of Florida has to let me have this chance to prove I'm innocent."

Lester Ray stared directly into Booth's eyes.

"You should be able to do that, piece of cake."

"Well, first I have to petition for the retesting. Then, I guess it would help to get someone to give me some print."

"Print?"

"Get a reporter to write the story, hope it gets picked up by the AP, get public opinion on our side." Booth's fat fingers stroked his chin.

"It's not going to be easy. The D.A. is going to fight this every step of the way. You know he believes you killed not only that Preston woman, but I heard he was looking at you for a couple of others, too. He's not going to stand by and let you walk without raising holy hell."

"Let him." Lester Ray snorted. "Look, all they had was this DNA test, right? The lab guy testified at my trial that the DNA in that girl matched mine. They had no eye witnesses, no one to put me anywhere near that girl that night. They had no other evidence, Booth."

Roland Booth sat quietly, his face a mask of concentration.

"They had the neighbor who was out walking his dog," Booth reminded him. "She testified that she saw you outside Carolyn Preston's apartment."

"She said she saw a man who looked like me—medium height and build, brown hair, and wearing a khaki jacket." Lester Ray's smile was slow and sly.

"How many men in central Florida do you suppose match that description?"

Booth nodded almost imperceptibly.

"Maybe. Maybe," he said. "I can try Harvey Crane from the *Journal*. Maybe he'll run with this. Maybe . . . if I can convince him . . ."

"That's your job, Booth." Lester Ray sat back against the chair and studied the younger man's face.

"I'll see what I can do."

"You'll give it your best shot?"

"Of course."

"Cross your heart and hope to die?" Lester Ray unexpectedly leaned across the table again, causing Booth to startle.

"Right." Booth broke eye contact, pushed his chair back from the table, and began to stuff the folder into his black leather briefcase. He stood abruptly and signaled to the guard at the door that he was finished and ready to leave.

Lester Ray stood as well. "So I'll hear from you when?"

"As soon as I know something."

"Next week. I want out of here, Booth."

"Everyone wants out of here, Lester Ray." Booth left the room without a backward glance.

"Yeah, well, for some of us, it's a matter of life and death."

Lester Ray paused, giving thought to what he'd just said.

"Life and death," he repeated softly. "Mine . . ."

"Come with me, Tracy. I need to hold you in my arms."

Adam held out his hand to her. "Tracy," he murmured as the smooth beat of a gentle love song filled the air.

"Adam, I can't," she whispered.

"Yes, darling, you can. The music's slow, and I'll be with you."

Tracy looked up into his eyes, wanting to take his hand, but afraid.

Suddenly, completely trusting, she did as he asked. He led her through the crowd to the dance floor; once there, he waited a moment while she gathered her courage, then opened his arms. With a soft sigh of relief she stepped into them.

It was awkward at first, but soon Tracy moved closer, until she was nestled in Adam's arms. Neither knew that the band played the song twice, nor that those around them watched in silent pleasure.

As the final notes of the song faded away, they wandered arm in arm through the nearby trees and stopped by a brook that sparkled in the moonlight. Adam drew her close to him, and his fingers tilted her head so he could look into her eyes. As though in slow motion, he bent to kiss her, parting her lips in the caress of a lover. Tracy met his need with the fire he had kindled, and gave herself up to enchantment . . .

WHAT ARE *LOVESWEPT* ROMANCES?

They are stories of true romance and touching emotion. We believe those two very important ingredients are constants in our highly sensual and very believable stories in the *LOVESWEPT* line. Our goal is to give you, the reader, stories of consistently high quality that may sometimes make you laugh, sometimes make you cry, but are always fresh and creative and contain many delightful surprises within their pages.

Most romance fans read an enormous number of books. Those they truly love, they keep. Others may be traded with friends and soon forgotten. We hope that each *LOVESWEPT* romance will be a treasure—a "keeper." We will always try to publish

LOVE STORIES YOU'LL NEVER FORGET
BY AUTHORS YOU'LL ALWAYS REMEMBER

The Editors

LOVESWEPT® • 84

BJ James
A Stranger Called Adam

BANTAM BOOKS
TORONTO · NEW YORK · LONDON · SYDNEY · AUCKLAND

A STRANGER CALLED ADAM

A Bantam Book / March 1985

ISBN 0-553-21693-7

Published simultaneously in the United States and Canada

PRINTED IN THE UNITED STATES OF AMERICA

OH   0 9 8 7 6 5 4 3 2 1

For Kathy,
who believes a friend is for keeps

One

_____

"Lost!"

"A child is lost."

"Where?"

"On Shadow."

"Oh, God!"

"Will she come?"

"She must. She and her devil dog."

Like wildfire on a dry summer morning the whispered words spread. Fearful eyes turned, one after another, to the towering monolith whose peak pierced the clouds. Like a miscalculation of God it rose boldly, an angry spear, far above the other softly rounded and tree-strewn mountains. Its roughhewn face hid zigzagging paths that lost themselves in deep, secret caves and mysterious swamps. There were no fields of grassy clover scattered over ridges like a broken necklace of bright green pearls. The dense evergreens that clung tenaciously, their insidious roots penetrating and cracking the unwelcoming granite, grew twisted and gnarled. Stunted and black green, they were as ugly as their hostile host.

In dark reminder and true to its name, as the morning sun rose in the sky, it cast its shadow over the village and the valley that nestled at its base. Then time moved slowly and sound was hushed. Birds ceased their singing; the buzz of insects dwindled. The early rising mountain folk slowed their pace, taking stock of the day, until the sun won free and bathed them in unfettered brilliance.

The people who inhabited the valley of Shadow were compelled to spend a part of each day in a passionate love-hate tryst with the monster that hovered over their rooftops. Yet, beneath it all, they were fiercely proud that this was their mountain.

As with all misfits, the mountain drew the thrill-seekers and the curious. Legends were rife. Not one villager was without his tale of the dark mountain. Many were myth; many were fact.

Adam Grayson had come with pen and camera to record the mountain and its legends. It was his daughter who was lost. She was tiny, and blond, just six years old, and her name was Summer.

"How in the hell could you be so irresponsible?" Adam Grayson whirled in his pacing and stared with piercing eyes at the cowering young teenager. His chest rose and fell in angry agitation, and the hand he raked through his disheveled silver hair was unsteady. "You were to do only one thing—watch Summer."

"But I wasn't gone very long. Summer wanted a drink of water and I went inside to get it. It truly took only a minute. Mr. Grayson." The trembling girl stared down at her hands that were endlessly twisting and knotting a lacy white handkerchief. Her southern drawl dropped to an even softer murmur as she repeated, "It was only for a minute."

"Do you expect me to believe that? Am I suppose to think that in the length of time it took you to pour a glass of water, a six-year-old child could vanish?" Several times his hands opened then clenched into tight, impotent fists.

"It's true, it's true. I swear it." Tears that had gathered in her eyes spilled down her pale cheeks as her painfully thin shoulders shook with heaving, strangling sobs. "She was alone hardly any time at all. I just—Oh, no!"

"What is it?" In the agonized silence her stricken eyes met Adam Grayson's clear gray ones.

"The phone did ring. It was your sister. She asked how Summer was and I said fine. And all the time she was . . . sh-she . . ." A mournful wail, desperately stifled, cut off her words. The knuckles twisting in and out of the mutilated handkerchief were white with strain.

There was a perceptible relenting of Adam's stiff posture, as he sat down and drew the sobbing girl into his arms. He soothed her with gentle hands and crooned words of assurance to her, though his own face was the bleak, wintry hue of despair.

"Shh. Hush, Melinda. I know you didn't mean this to happen. Shh, don't cry. I'm sorry I attacked you. It was only because I was so worried. Hush now, hush. We'll find her." It was a comforting litany for the girl where there could be none for the man. He held her, offering silent apology for his harsh words. He knew in his heart that Melinda was no more to blame than he.

At the first ring of the telephone he was on his feet, snatching the receiver from its cradle. The sharp bark that was both greeting and demand came from an aching, constricted throat.

"Yes?"

"Chief Halloran here, Mr. Grayson."

"Have you found her?"

"No, sir, but we think we might know where she is."

"Then for God's sake, man, tell me so I can go get her."

"It's not that simple, Mr. Grayson." Something about the terse sentence triggered an even greater alarm in Adam. In a cold wave of bitter premonition he fearfully clutched the receiver like a life line and waited for the inevitable. "We think she's wandered on the mountain," Halloran said.

"Shadow?"

"Yes, sir." There was a long pause, then he added inadequately, "I'm sorry."

"What do we do?" The bitter taste of his own blood filled Adam's mouth as he bit down hard on his lip. He struggled to remain calm, fighting the surge of paralyzing fear that could swiftly become unthinking panic.

"I've already called the search teams. They're gathering supplies and equipment. We should be ready to move within the hour, and we've sent a message to Tracy Walker. If anyone can find your daughter, it will be Tracy and Wolfe."

"Tracy Walker?" Even in Adam's dazed mind the name stirred a memory that nearly surfaced, then skittered away to be buried under an avalanche of anxiety and worry.

"Tracy and Wolfe know that mountain like nobody else. I doubt there's a path or a stream they haven't explored over the years."

"Where is he? How long will it take him to get here?"

"Her."

"What?" Again a memory nagged at the raw edges of his mind, nebulous and unformed, but there all the same.

"Tracy Walker is a woman, and Wolfe is her dog. Together they're the best damn trackers in the country. If there's anything lucky about this situation, it's that we have them."

"How long before they get here?" Adam repeated.

"Can't say for sure. Jack Peters has gone over to her cabin at the far side of the valley now. Depends on whether or not she's there and how long he has to wait for her."

"What do we do in the meantime? We can't just stand around. Damn it, man, my daughter's up on that monster." A note of hysteria, foreign to his nature, had begun to creep into his voice.

"We'll be gathering at the base of the mountain at ten-thirty, about an hour from now. That gives the search parties over eight full hours of daylight." Halloran paused, searching for words of comfort, but there were few. "We'll do our best to find her."

"I know you will." Adam's shoulders slumped wearily. His last words had been an apology of sorts for his curtness, but they went unheard. The buzzing of an empty line signaled that Halloran had hung up. Adam stared out the window at the brooding spire of the mountain, hearing in his mind the trill of his daughter's delightful laughter. The very real sound of a smothered sob drew him back from the haunted land of his thoughts.

Replacing the receiver, he turned to the dejected girl who was huddled on the sofa. She was really no more than a child herself. Perhaps the care of a six-year-old had been too much for the teenager. But she and her mother had been so sure, and it had been for only two days.

"Melinda," he said with a return of his characteristic gentleness, "why don't you go on home now? There's nothing more you can do here."

"Oh, no. Please let me stay. I have to know that Summer's been found. That she's all right."

"No, go home. The word's sure to be out, and your mother will be worried. I'll let you know as soon as we have her back." He injected a confidence he did not feel. Now that his initial blind rage had calmed, he knew he had been unfair to heap the blame on her frail shoulders. "Go along now, your mother will be frantic."

"Yes, sir." She rose fluidly, with a hint of the grace that would be hers in the future. At the open doorway she stopped and turned back. "I forgot! I forgot to tell you what your sister said. She's all through with her doctor's appointment and she'll be here tomorrow."

"Thank you, Melinda." He turned unseeing eyes away from the waiting girl. When he said no more she quietly opened the screen door and stepped onto the porch.

"Damn!" The word exploded from Adam as he

slammed his hand against the wall. The irony of it was too much. "Why couldn't you have come today, Liza? Then Summer wouldn't be lost and wandering on a great, hulking mountain."

"I think it's safe to assume that she's still on the lower side. There's no way she could be too far up; it's just been a bit over two hours." Chief Halloran was standing in the middle of a group of men, each dressed in heavy clothing and boots to withstand the vicious brambles and vines of the dense undergrowth they would be searching through. "If it weren't for these damn caves and the swamp, we could probably find her easily."

"I don't think she would go into a cave," a deep voice called.

"And I wouldn't have thought she would go up the mountain," Halloran snapped, and fixed the protestor with a stern stare. "We will check the caves."

The murmur of the gathering crowd rose and fell, a pulsating sea of sound. First one grew quiet and then another, until total silence preceded the tall silver-haired man who made his way to the group around Halloran.

"If she's in those caves we'll never—" The speaker stopped, saying no more when he realized that it was Adam Grayson who stood at his side.

"What about the caves?" Adam said quietly.

Halloran flicked a concerned look at the composed face before him. Such calm was unnatural. He had enough to worry about with the little girl. If the father lost control, he'd have his hands full. A keen assessment of the pale gray eyes showed no lurking hysteria. Matching stare for stare, each took the measure of the other.

They were of a size, and in a fractional flicker of recognition each understood that they were of a kind. Halloran realized that Adam Graywon would approach a given situation much as he himself would, coolly and controlled, with shattered emotions masked. He decided to be brutally truthful, to give Adam the unvarnished facts. It was what he would prefer.

"What about the caves?" Adam prompted when he saw Halloran's decision had been made.

"This side of the mountain is riddled with honeycomb caverns. Some have been explored and charted, some haven't. There are some that go deep into the heart of the mountain." Their eyes met, Halloran's holding a warning.

"And Summer could be lost in one of the caverns?" At Halloran's nod Adam closed his eyes for a second, hiding the resurgent fear in them. Shaking it aside, he asked the question that had to be asked. "Are they large enough that she could lose her way and not be able to find the entrance?"

"Some of them." Halloran put no softening frills on the truth. He knew Adam would not need them.

"Then we'll be lucky to find her." Summer's place in his heart was a raw, ragged ache.

"You've forgotten, Mr. Grayson. We have something on our side. We have Tracy. She knows those caves, and Wolfe can find your daughter's trail when no other dog could." Halloran's hand on Adam's shoulder was kind, offering what little encouragement he could.

"Jed, could I speak to you a minute?" The small spare man had just joined the group. He drew the chief out of earshot and spoke animatedly, gesturing wildly. Jed Halloran shook his head sadly, his gaze never leaving Adam's face as he listened. Then with slow, reluctant steps he returned to the waiting group.

"What's wrong?" Adam sensed a tension, a prescience of dread.

"Tracy says she can't come."

"What!"

"I don't understand it; she's never refused before." Jed

shoved his hands deep into his pockets, angry at his own helplessness.

"Where is she? I'll convince her. Surely she can't refuse to help a little girl."

"No." Halloran's restraining hand on Adam's arm halted his headlong rush through the crowd. "If she says she won't come, nothing you can do or say will change it."

"But why?" Adam looked bewilderedly at the tall dark man who had become his link with sanity in the last hour. "Why wouldn't she come?"

"Who knows?" Jed shrugged. "Usually she's very agreeable and more than willing to help. She works well with us, but no one really knows what's behind those black eyes of hers."

The sound of a heavy motor followed by the screech of brakes and the slamming of many doors interrupted their quiet consultation. More than twenty men and women emerged from two vans and began to set up the paraphernalia of a mobile television newscast. In only minutes cameras were trained on the crowd and the mountain. The newscaster spoke into his microphone in funereal tones.

"We are here, ladies and gentlemen," the reporter said into his microphone, speaking rapidly and dramatically, "at the base of the mountain. Rescue teams are preparing to move out at any moment. There is an air of fear running through the crowd as they stare up at the silent mountain. On the faces of those about me I read terror. Has Shadow claimed another?"

"Carpenter!" In two quick strides Jed was at the speaker's side. He planted himself firmly before him, deliberately using his superior size to intimidate. "Stop that drivel! You can film all you want as long as you stay out of the way. But I won't have you frightening the people with that supernatural claptrap. If I hear one more word of it, or if one member of your crew gets in our way, I'll smash you and your cameras. Is that clear?"

"You can't do that," the smaller man blurted out.

"Watch me." Jed turned back to the rescue teams, dismissing the self-important man with not so much as a shrug. With a quick, appraising eye he checked the readiness of the teams. When all seemed to be in order, and with a curt nod to Adam, he addressed the waiting men. "All right, each of you knows what you're to do. We have a lot of daylight left. Let's make the most of it, and good luck."

"Wait!" a high, shrill voice called from the crowd. "Look, it's Tracy."

As one, the group turned to follow the direction of the boy's thin, gesturing arm. To the west a small cloud of dust moved constantly nearer. A battered jeep jolted over the rough road of the flat valley floor. In hovering quiet all waited.

Adam Grayson watched, his rage rising, for soon he would face the woman who had refused to help in the search for his child.

It seemed an eternity before the aged, dented vehicle reached the crowd, which parted to let it pass. The unblinking eye of the television camera followed her as she braked to a halt a short distance away from everyone. With no flicker of greeting, she pulled a heavy pack from the back of the jeep, then unfolded her five-foot-six frame from beneath the wheel. With a flip of her long dark hair she turned to face Jed Halloran.

Adam realized then that she was older than she first appeared. This Tracy Walker was not a young girl. Her body was slender and strong-limbed. Her hair was swept back into a single braid, its silver-black sheen a marked contrast to the streak of stark white that began at her left temple to interlace with the dark strands. No smile curved her lips. Her solemn face was perfectly symmetrical, with highly arched brows, strong cheekbones, and shadowed hollows that were a photographer's dream. Obsidian eyes stared through a heavy fringe of lashes, equally as dark. Only the slashing scar that began at her forehead and curved downward to meet and blend with the white of her hair marred the smooth texture of her skin. The incongruous first beginnings of laughlines at her eyes softened the too perfect face. Tracy was nearly thirty, and looked every bit of it.

Silently, with only a gesture, she signaled for the dog sitting in the passenger seat to join her. He was coal-black with only tips of silver at his chest to relieve the inky shine of his coat. With the prowling movements of a stalking animal, he eased from the seat and moved to her side.

He was more massive than large. The breadth of his chest recalled an ancestry of beasts of the wilderness. As Tracy walked to join them, he trotted by her, pacing his step with her stride. Silver eyes blazed beneath his canine brow, telling the world he was tame because he chose to be. Wolfe was well named.

"Well, Tracy." Jed stepped forward to meet her. "You changed your mind."

"Yes." No inflection shaded the single word, but it was enough. The husky contralto triggered instant and total recall in the harried mind of Adam Grayson.

As he stared at the calm, self-assured woman before him, he remembered a fresh young actress who had talent, beauty, and had been a rich man's plaything. He had photographed her many times, in many places and many poses. Then at the height of her success, tragedy, death, and scandal had struck and she had disappeared.

Now, nearly ten years later, she stood before him, little changed but for the laughlines, the scar, and the streak of white hair. Adam could not reconcile himself to the fact that she alone held the life of his daughter in her hands.

"Tracy." Jed, by word and nod, drew her into the waiting circle. "This is Adam Grayson. It's his daughter who's lost on the mountain."

"Mr. Grayson." She nodded curtly but no recognition

stirred in her eyes. She turned back to Jed. "What are your plans? Have you divided into sectors?"

Soon both were immersed in talk of schedules, sectors, procedure, and assignments. Tracy listened attentively, offering few comments until Jed addressed her specifically.

"Where will you begin?"

"With the first of the caves, then work my way up."

"The first is unstable and dangerous," Jed muttered harshly, leaving unsaid a dreaded thought.

"Yes. It's all the more reason to get started." She, too, did not speak of the dangers of a cave-in and what it might do to the small child.

"Then you are ready?"

"You all go on. I'd like to speak to Mr. Grayson for a minute. Wolfe and I will be working alone, so I need not start with you." Jed nodded his agreement and with his men moved toward the mountain. Tracy watched as they scattered in the different directions each team was to take. She stared for long quiet moments at the towering mountain, then pivoted gracefully and turned her back on its dark presence. With another subtle motion of her hand she signaled that the dog should remain, and took the few short steps needed to bring her face to face with Adam.

The sun beating down on her gave a golden glow to her dusky skin and lighted her hair with a blue-black iridescence. She was astonishingly lovely. Bile rose in Adam's throat as painful memories assaulted him. Memories of a young dark Tracy intermingled with those of a young blond starlet, equally as talented, equally as lovely, and lost to him forever.

The futile sense of loss, fed by a helpless, hidden panic, turned to resentment. He resented, irrationally, that she was here and well, and that at this moment she was the most important person in his life. The simmering, unreasoning rage spilled over as he virtually attacked her, hating her for being so vibrantly alive.

"So, the prima donna decided to come down from her mountain after all." His snarl took her by surprise, but she did not show it.

Tracy's only response was the lifting of one eyebrow. The other winged brow did not move, but the scar seemed to pull and tauten. Many women might have hidden the angry welt with a sweep of hair, but not Tracy. She accepted it as an inescapable part of herself, and she had learned long ago from a man of great wisdom not to fight what she could not change. It was in this spirit she accepted Adam's anger. She had dealt with frantic people before and understood that worry assumed many forms. For this reason she was tolerant and ignored his attack.

"Was it the lure of the cameras that enticed you here?" he continued, "Do you want to see your face splashed over the screen again? Even older and scarred, it's still a pretty face." Cold rage glittered in his eyes as he raked her with a contemptuous look, despising her beauty even as he acclaimed it.

"I came to help find your child, Mr. Grayson," she answered calmly, standing in a relaxed posture, refusing to give him the fight he was so obviously seeking.

"Of course you did, but not until after the TV cameras and the newsmen arrived. It's been ten long years and you still need the mindless adulation, don't you?" As the bitter, accusing words were spoken, something in the back of his mind recalled Adam to sanity, warning him that he shouldn't be acting this way. Like her or not, he needed this woman. She could easily turn away and go back to her side of the valley, destroying his best hope of finding his child. His thoughts must have been reflected on his anxious face, for the woman before him smiled in quiet understanding.

"I came to help and for no other reason, I assure you, Mr. Grayson. I would prefer that the cameras and the crew were not here." She shrugged lightly, relegating this, too, to that realm beyond her control and accepting it. "But it would seem the news media is an irrevocable part of our lives. I can't trouble myself with them. Your child is my first and only priority."

Something in her tone and her stance told Adam that she meant it. Sincerity and concern were in her eyes, and he realized that he had misjudged her. Weary from the mind-battering tension and uncertainty, his shoulders slumped. He ran his hand over hot, burning eyes, then clenched it into a tight fist to stop its shaking.

"I will find her. Wolfe and I haven't failed yet." Impulsively she touched his arm in a gesture of comfort. She did not add that though they had never failed, they had at times been too late. Always protective of others, she felt a curious and even stronger need to shield this bitter stranger from the horrors that might be.

For the first time, Tracy really looked at the man before her. He was half a foot taller than she, broad of shoulder and narrow-hipped. His shaggy gray hair was shot through with black and was lustrously thick. Wintry-gray eyes stared bleakly at her from a craggy, ashen face. Deep creases lined his mouth but could not destroy its sensual shape. He had about him that closed-in look of a man who had been struck one more mortal blow yet still survived. He hurt, and it was all the more painful because he would not allow himself to show it. Tracy's heart ached for him, and she tightened her hand on his sleeve.

It was easy to forgive him his insults. She had seen and heard it all before. There was even a pattern she had come to expect. The stronger and more capable the man, the more unreasoning and irritable he became when faced with a rare instance of helplessness. Adam Grayson was most definitely a strong and capable man who was unaccustomed to not being in command.

It was not his insults that puzzled her, for she felt that perhaps because of her initial reluctance to come she deserved them. It was their direction that dumbfounded her. Few people remembered her sojourn into acting, and those who did never gave tongue to the memories. It had been a lifetime ago, another time, another place, another person. She had risen quickly, brilliant and unique. Then, in the face of personal tragedy, had withdrawn to be easily and quickly forgotten by a fickle public. She had returned to her beloved mountains to heal, to relearn simple skills, and to resume the life that had been her first love.

None here spoke of her past, and few beyond the insular mountains associated this Tracy Walker with the glamour of Hollywood. None but a stranger whose tension translated through her fingertips an exquisite awareness. She wanted to stroke the deeply etched lines from his brow and bring the brightness back to his sad eyes. She would find his daughter, and pray that it wouldn't be too late.

"What's her name?" Tracy moved her hand down his arm, letting her fingers rest above his clenched fist. It did not occur to her how rare this was, for she seldom touched people.

"Summer." His voice was a rusty sound laced through with the steel of desperate control. "Her name is Summer, after her mother."

"Is Summer close to her mother?"

"Her mother's dead, Miss Walker. She died two years ago."

Again his expression closed. The slight softening she had sensed earlier had gone. Tracy cursed herself silently, aware that she had added more pain to the nearly unbearable burden this man was already carrying. Not a stranger to loving and losing, she recognized that emptiness in the far depths of his eyes. She saw it deepen and darken at the mention of his wife. The loss of this child would be all the greater if the father had invested a double portion of love, that of the mother as well as the child.

"Would you tell me a bit about Summer?"

"She's little, and she's lost. By now she's probably scared out of her wits. What else do you need to know?" he snapped, helpless irritation resurfacing.

"Yes, she is," Tracy said calmly. "It's because she's scared that I want to know something about her. I want to be able to talk to her about familiar things so she won't be frightened of me."

"Why?" A blunt, demanding question.

"Frightened children sometimes hide from strangers in strange places, Mr. Grayson."

"Oh, God. Do you mean she might run away from help?"

"It's been known to happen," she answered softly. As would Jed Halloran, Tracy knew instinctively that Adam would prefer the truth, straight and to the point.

"Yessiree," an old, quavering voice interjected. "I mind the time we looked fer the Talbot boy. Knowed he was about. Found his sign. It was a week fore we got 'im."

"Hush up yore mouth, Ezra Price." A tiny sprite of a woman, gnarled and wrinkled, dressed in a faded print dress and apron, glared up at the thin, cadaverous man. Satisfied that he was properly hushed when he shoved his hands deep into his overall pockets and rocked uneasily back and forth on his heels, she said encouragingly to Adam, "The Talbot boy was afore Tracy come back to the mountains. Her and Wolfe would of made quick work of finding that fool young'un."

Though Adam flinched, he ignored this muttered exchange. Only the harsh hiss of his ragged breathing signaled that he had heard it. He had forgotten the crowd that stood quietly, expectantly, waiting about him. From the moment Tracy had arrived he had concentrated exclusively on her. Despite his hateful sarcasm she had become his anchor. Even now his eyes devoured her, as if wanting to absorb her skills, making them his for his daughter's sake.

"Will you tell me about her?" Tracy repeated, insisting gently as much to distract him as in need to know. She took her hand away from his, aware that a man such as he would not appreciate her knowing how violently he was trembling.

He took a long, harsh breath, then, as if a dam had burst, began to speak. One fact tumbled out after another. Listening intently, Tracy learned that the child was small for her age, but never shy; that she loved to be sung to sleep, but not since her mother died; that she loved the stars and the moon, but hated dark, cloudy nights; that she loved dolls, but her favorite toy was an aged teddy bear.

That she was all he had left of a woman he had loved very much, Tracy thought.

"She doesn't play with Bear anymore," Adam went on. "He's too old and fragile, but he sleeps on her pillow every night." The thought of his little girl, lost and afraid and without her best friend, cast an even chalkier pallor to his face. The skin seemed to pull so tautly, the bones of his finely chiseled jaw grew more prominent and harsher.

"If you will get Bear for me, I'll take him to her." She looked with compassion into his empty steel-gray eyes, hoping she wasn't making an impossible promise. No! She willed herself not to doubt. The child would be found alive and well; she would make it so.

"I have him in the car. I thought if . . . when they found her, she might need him." For the first time his control seemed in danger of breaking. "I'll get him for you."

Turning swiftly, he made his way to the car parked nearby. From the seat he lifted a tattered, faded stuffed teddy bear that had been well loved. One eye was missing; an ear had been chewed until it resembled a cauliflower. A wisp of stuffing protruded from a tiny split in his lumpy belly. One glance and Tracy knew that this

was the security the child would need. She took it from
Adam gently, holding it much as a little girl would.

"I'll take good care of him and see that Summer has
him as soon as possible," she said in a husky voice.

As she moved to her pack to make her last preparations, Adam made a lightning-quick decision. "I'm
going with you."

"No."

"Damm it, Tracy. That's my child out there. I can't just
sit here doing nothing." The break had come. If he had
not been so strong, it would have come long before.

"No." Tracy was adamant. She understood how he
felt, but his place was here. "You know you need to be
here when they bring her out. If you're with me, what
will she think? She's going to want her father. You have
to be here for her."

"You're the one who will find her," he said confidently.
"If I'm with you, she'll have her father that much
sooner."

"You can't go." Tracy shook her head. She couldn't
allow him to see what she might find. "I always work
alone. You would just be in the way."

"I'm no fool," he snapped. "I wouldn't hinder you."

"You aren't dressed for Shadow."

"I'm dressed as you are." He impatiently swept her
slender body with an assessing glance. She wore a heavy
cotton shirt tucked snugly into even heavier jeans. A
wide belt with a sheathed knife hanging from it circled
her small waist. The legs of the jeans were encased by
knee-high boots that were laced with leather cords.

"No, Mr. Grayson, you aren't." Tracy turned away,
gathering up her pack and her coat. Even in the heat of
summer, nights on the mountain would be cold. Moving
quickly, before he could ask any more questions, she
signaled for Wolfe, and the two of them headed for the
dense underbrush at the foot of the mountain. If he
asked, she would tell him the truth, but if she could

avoid that one question, perhaps he could keep a small portion of his terror at bay.

Adam watched her stride away. Her long legs covered the ground easily. The huge dog trotted by her side. At the forest's edge she turned, waved once, then disappeared into the trees.

"I should have gone with her," Adam muttered under his breath.

"Now, Mr. Grayson, Tracy was right. You ain't dressed right for the mountain," Ezra said in his reedy voice, startling Adam. He had again forgotten the waiting crowds and the cameras.

"I have on jeans like all the others."

"You ain't got no boots, Mr. Grayson," Ezra said laconically.

"Boots?" Adam's tired mind was barely functioning as he looked down at his tennis shoes. "What does that matter?"

"Rattlesnakes."

"Rattlesnakes! Oh, my God."

"Yessiree, I mind that time we kilt one over on Piney Ridge that was seven foot if he was a inch, and big around as a man's arm. That feller had eighteen rattles. Old Billy Simms has that rattle now. He—"

"Ezra, hush up." Again the tiny woman glared up at him as he warmed to his story. "Is yore tongue loose at both ends? Land sakes, you'd scare a body to death with yore wild tales. Just don't you pay him no never mind, Mr. Grayson. Tracy'll find yore little purty, and bring her back to you safe as a bug in a rug."

Rattlesnakes! Adam had sensed that Tracy had avoided telling him something. Rattlesnakes! He stared up at the sun; it had hardly moved at all. He wished this nightmare of a day would end, but was afraid that night would come before Summer was found. It promised to be a hard day no matter what. He looked again toward the trees where Tracy had disappeared.

"Please find her, Tracy," he murmured, not thinking

how incongruous it was to trust so implicitly where only minutes ago he had literally hated. "Please."

Adam's face was desolate as he watched and waited. He was not aware of the comforting hand little Sarah Price placed on his arm.

Two

The sun continued its trek across the cerulean sky, burning away the last of August's morning mists. Its white-hot rays bore down relentlessly, threatening unusual and sweltering temperatures.

"Mr. Grayson," someone said, and Adam accepted the cup of cool water that was thrust into his hand. He drank sparingly, barely assuaging his thirst, his anxious eyes never leaving the mountain. Was Summer thirsty? Was there a spring or a creek she could drink from? Looking in contempt at the cup in his hand, he crushed it, unaware of the blood that mingled with the water that spilled over his fingers and the broken plastic. His gaze returned to the mountain, looking for a sign that wasn't there.

"It shore is hot, ain't it?" Ezra Price squatted by Adam. "Might be a good sign. Them snakes won't crawl in this heat. Instid, they'll lie up in the shade till cool of day."

"Land sakes, Ezra, be still!"

"Now, Sary, I jest wanted to make him feel better." Ezra turned from his wife back to Adam. "Ain't wimmen the beatinest? Marry a little mite of a gal then find out she's all mouth. Talks alla time. Big eater too."

Adam heard the words in the dim recesses of his

mind. Perhaps later, when he was no longer in the grips of this numbing fear, he would appreciate the awkward efforts as a kindness. Then he would chuckle at the absurdity of this loquacious man considering his tiny, nearly silent wife a talker. Perhaps. But not just now. Now he was consumed by the gut-twisting worry that grew with each passing tick of the clock.

As the day continued, other than the TV crew and Melinda, who hovered at the fringes, the only constants were Ezra and Sarah. Sarah had appointed herself Adam's personal guardian. She saw to it that food was brought, offered, and when it was refused by a slight shake of his head, unobstrusively taken away.

Quietly and efficiently she rode herd, guarding her well-meaning husband's tongue and keeping the prying newsmen with their "infernal contraptions" away. None dared cross this miniature myrmidon whose bright green eyes snapped and shone from among the wrinkles and folds left by age and a life of hardships.

As the twilight faded and the first of the night creatures began their song, the rescue teams came slowly in from the mountain. One by one, spent and weary, they walked past Adam. None spoke, but several patted him on the shoulder, despairing shakes of their heads meeting his hopeful gaze. Jed Halloran was last to emerge from the dense underbrush. Adam knew at a glance that he had fared no better.

"Not a trace." Jed stopped before Adam, his face harsh and grim in the purple darkness. "We'll start at first light tomorrow."

"Tracy?"

"None of us saw her. She should be in any minu—" Three shots rang out, echoing through the valley, bounding off the adjoining hills, then sounding again. "She's found her!"

"Thank God!" Unthinking, Adam rushed toward the sound. Jed's hand at his arm stopped him. Clawing at the powerful hold, Adam snarled, "Let me go, damn you. Summer will need me."

"No! Adam, listen to me. We don't know where she is. We can't go up there in the dark; it would be suicide."

"But I heard the shots. They came from the right," Adam protested with a wave of his hand.

"Maybe they did, maybe they didn't. The echo here can play tricks on you. Three shots means Summer's all right. Trust Tracy. She'll bring her out in the morning when it's safer."

Adam recognized the wisdom of his words. He knew Shadow's reputation as treacherous and unforgiving. This time it was giving up its hostage, wrested from it by Tracy. But not until morning. Adam must wait; there was little else he could do.

On Shadow, in the sheltering hollow of a shallow cave, a campfire burned. Flame licked greedily at the dry wood, its light and warmth welcome to the three who sat before it.

Sitting cross-legged, Tracy held a small child in her lap. With her curls and smooth, translucent skin, Summer was beautiful. One small hand clutched the ragged Bear, the other a long dark braid. Tears of fright had long since dried, and she slept trustingly and tranquilly.

At Tracy's knee lay Wolfe, his eyes closed, his breathing labored and stentorian. She buried the fingers of her free hand in the thick dark pelt, stroking him with all the love of a breaking heart. He moved slightly, licked her gently, sighed once, and rumbled a farewell deep in his chest.

Long after he was quiet, Tracy sat with her hand curled at his side, tears streaming down her face. Her choice had been made. There could have been no other. She was certain Wolfe had understood.

* * *

By early morning Adam was pacing ceaselessly over the clearing. He had watched and waited, impatient for each ray of light that had crept with agonizing slowness into the starless sky.

A soft breeze rose with the sun, dancing over the valley floor and weaving among the trees. All was still and quiet but for the murmuring of the tall pines. Then, without warning, Tracy stepped from the shade that clung thickly at the edge of the forest. She walked with a sure and unburdened step into the open field. For a heart-wrenching moment Adam thought she was alone, then he saw that she held Summer in her arms.

"Thank God." It was a low, rasping growl, half whisper, half prayer.

"Daddy!" The sweetest voice he had ever heard was followed by a ripple of happy laughter.

Gently Tracy put her down. The child ran three steps, stopped, whirled to race back again to Tracy, who still knelt in the grass. Short, pudgy arms were wrapped fiercely about her as wet, smacking kisses interspersed with giggles were scattered over her face and a small hand stroked the dark braid. Then, with beloved Bear clutched to her, Summer ran into her father's waiting arms.

"Oh, baby, you scared me," Adam said huskily into the blond ringlets as he nuzzled the tender curve of her neck.

"I was scared, too, Daddy. Until Tracy brought me Bear. It was awful dark and we built a fire in a cave." She paused, then with the truthfulness of the very young, added matter of factly, "Maybe I was still a little bit scared, but Tracy held me and Bear and told us funny stories."

"Did she now? And did she tell you not to ever wander out of the yard again?" Relief warred with sternness, and won.

"I won't, Daddy. Besides, Tracy said you'd worry if I did." Summer kissed his cheek again and presented

Bear for his share of loving. With heavy lids shielding his red-rimmed eyes and dampness on his cheeks, Adam hugged them closely, oblivious to the satisfied murmurs of the crowd.

At the edge of the watching group Silas Carpenter murmured in hushed, somber tones of the averted tragedy, of the skilled and beautiful tracker, and of a valiant life given for another. The cameras searched for and found Tracy.

With a tender smile on her face and a sadness deep in her eyes, she had watched father and daughter reunited. Now she had one last painful service to perform. Even as she turned away Summer was speaking innocently and unwittingly of the death.

"Daddy, after he found me, why did Wolfe go to sleep and not wake up, like Mommy?"

"What?" Adam stared blankly down into Summer's frowning face, her words registering dully in his mind. Then he looked up with compassionate understanding, seeking Tracy. He scanned the meadow, but it was empty. A flash of blue shone among the green trees and he knew that she had returned to Shadow.

"Tracy," Adam called, and, setting Summer on her feet, moved toward the path Tracy had taken.

"Let her go, Adam." Jed Halloran moved to his side. "What she has to do she'd rather do alone."

"You know?"

"I do now. Doc Jacobs, the vet from over at Rockville, stopped by late last night. He told me then. I should have guessed myself when she didn't come instantly."

"But what happened? The dog looked in perfect health."

"He was old, Adam. He was her grandfather's dog long before he was hers. His heart just gave out. This last search was too much for him."

"Then she sacrificed Wolfe for Summer." He held his daughter in his arms once more, stroking her hair.

"She had no choice."

"She could have stayed away."

"She tried and couldn't. Remember?"

The silver and the dark heads both turned toward Shadow. The visible trails were empty, but they knew Tracy was there saying good-bye to an old friend.

Late into the night, long after the well-wishers had departed and his sister had arrived, Adam sat holding a drink in his hand, something he did rarely now. Twice he rose to stand in Summer's doorway to watch her as she slept. How beautiful and peaceful she was with the covers tucked beneath her chin and Bear snuggled next to her cheek.

"Adam? Hadn't you better get to bed? You need some rest." Liza in her robe and nightgown, ready for bed herself, watched her brother worriedly. He had been dreadfully quiet all day. Beneath his jubilant elation hovered a darkness that even Summer's gay chatter couldn't penetrate.

"I think I'll stay up for a while yet. You go on. You must be tired from the trip."

"A bit." Liza accepted defeat. "Good night, Adam."

"Good night. Liza?" Adam waited until she turned back toward him, "I'm glad you're here."

"So am I," she murmured, and left him staring into the amber liquid in his glass.

Adam's thoughts were not of this traumatic day but of days ten years past. As if it were only yesterday he could see raven-haired, black-eyed Tracy and his beloved Sharon, blond and blue-eyed. When both had been very young actresses, a wily agent had astutely assessed the value of their difference. He drew attention to it, exploited it. They were Tracy and Sharon, Sharon and Tracy. And through it all they were never competitors, but friends.

At the height of their success, when Adam and Sharon had just begun seeing each other, disaster overtook Tracy. There was an explosion aboard the yacht of a married producer and she was the only survivor, found hours later clinging to a bit of flotsam and grievously injured. For weeks, as she fought for life, she had been the target of much speculation and sly innuendoes. Then she suddenly dropped from sight without a trace.

Adam had watched as Sharon grieved for her friend. She had denied the rumors and remained staunchly loyal while she searched futilely, hoping each day to hear some word. Later, as her own life took new direction, the hurtful memories of Tracy faded into the background. Blissfully in love, Sharon had turned her back on fame, fortune, and all else Hollywood had offered. To be Adam's wife was all that she asked of life.

They had known eight wonderful years, their happiest day when Summer had been born. Two years ago, after sharing a private dinner for two and the lovemaking that was so special between them, Sharon had fallen asleep in Adam's arms. Sometime in the darkest hour, as quietly and as gently as she had lived, she had died.

The doctors, with blank eyes and somber faces, had muttered complicated gibberish about an undetected congenital weakness, a failing heart, and unavoidable circumstance. But all Adam understood was that Sharon had gone from him. For months he had sought solace in a glass, until Summer's growing need for him pierced the alcoholic fog. Through her trust and faith she gave him cause to put aside his shattered dreams and begin again. With Sharon's child as the center of his life, he had learned to live with his memories. Until today. Until Tracy.

A quiet step sounded on the porch, one that he had waited for all evening. Without looking up, he spoke softly.

"Tracy."

"Yes."

"I knew you would come." He turned to face her. She stood in the doorway, quiet and relaxed with no visible sign of the grief that must be lacerating her. Only the slight tautening of the scar at her temple and a dusting of blue beneath her eyes attested to her fatigue.

"How is Summer?" There was an utter stillness about her that was uncanny.

"Please, come in." He rose as she stepped farther into the room. Indicating a chair with a nod, he watched as she walked across the room. She sat and waited.

Long minutes passed as he absorbed her cool composure. At last he answered. "Summer's fine. Thanks to you and Wolfe."

Only a slight flicker of pain surfaced, and it was hidden quickly behind her mask of control. She said nothing.

"Tracy, can you forgive me for the things I said yesterday?"

"You were upset." He could read no more from the flat, stoic words than from her expression and rigid posture.

"That's hardly an excuse."

"It's happened before. Strong people react pretty much the same." She shrugged, meeting his look squarely. "It will happen again."

"Will there be a next time? Will you track again without Wolfe?"

"I suppose I will, if I'm needed. Adam?" She used his first name easily and comfortably. "How is it that you remembered my past?"

"I was there for most of it." He waited for a reaction. There was none.

She studied him closely, but she had no memory of him. And he was not a man to be forgotten. Surely . . . She shook her head slowly. No! She seldom forgot anymore.

"You don't remember?"

"No." She shook her head again, watching him intently. "I'm sorry."

His eyes moved to the mark at her temple, wondering. "You do remember Sharon?"

"Sharon Summers?"

"Sharon was Summer's mother."

Nothing about Tracy changed. Her face lost none of its serenity. She sat perfectly erect with her hands resting lightly on the arms of the chair. Adam's gaze moved carefully over her until his eyes met and held hers. There he found no tranquility. In their dark depths was a raw, primitive pain that nothing could ease. Tears glittered but did not spill, then were hidden by a sweep of lashes.

"Sharon's dead?" The pain in her eyes was also in her voice.

"Yes."

"Two years ago?" Her voice broke slightly, then was controlled determinedly.

"Yes."

"I lost track of her and couldn't find her, but I liked to think of her living each day well and happy." She raised tortured eyes to his. "Was she happy?"

"We were both happy."

"I'm glad." She was hurting, and Adam wanted to take her in his arms to soothe her as he might Summer.

"Adam, I . . ."

"You still don't remember me," he said gently.

"No."

"There's really no reason you should. We never met officially. I was on the other side of the camera."

"I knew all of Sharon's friends," she said in a low voice.

"Sharon and I hadn't had more than a date or two when you had your accident." He watched as Tracy relaxed visibly. "She searched for you after you left the hospital. Where did you go?"

"To another hospital for therapy, then here to be with my grandfather." Old memories hurt alongside the new.

Adam stepped behind her chair, his hand brushing over her brow, then lightly tracing the scar. "This is from the accident."

She nodded, though it was not a question and needed no answer.

"Were there any lasting effects?" Rhythmically he stroked the jagged ridge.

Wondering how he knew it ached, she relaxed beneath his touch. "For a while. But not anymore. There's an occasional headache, some weakness on the right side. The really bad part was the aphasia."

"Was it severe?"

"Yes."

"You couldn't speak?"

"I could speak as well and as clearly as before." An aura of sadness hovered over her as she seemed to draw away to a distant place of hurtful remembrance. Her voice dropped to a softer tone. "Oh, yes, I could speak very well. Very beautifully enunciated gibberish."

"Did you know?"

"I knew it was gibberish. I *always* knew I hadn't said what I intended." She closed her eyes. "I couldn't find the right words. If I called a house a tree, I knew instantly I'd made a mistake. Then, in searching for the right word, I might call it several things, all of them wrong."

"Did you have trouble understanding?"

"Never. Comprehension wasn't a problem. I understood everything that was said or written. I simply couldn't express myself."

Adam's hand at the scar grew still as he understood the devastating effect of her injuries. What agony for a quick, intelligent mind to be trapped in an injured brain. He wished desperately he could stop the flow of her words, but he knew he must hear her out.

"And now?" he said into the silence that had surrounded them.

"When I'm tired or upset, a word might escape me.

Then sometimes there's some agnosia, which means I don't visually recognize things. It doesn't happen often, and it's usually only fleeting."

"You were afraid you hadn't recognized me."

"For a moment." His soothing touch, the gentle timbre of his voice lulled her into a new and easy trust as she spoke a secret thought. "I don't think I'll ever be free of that fear."

Adam silently acknowledged the depth of her uncertainty. "Why did you come back to the mountain?"

"Familiar surroundings were thought to be beneficial for me. My grandfather brought me here to what I knew best."

"What about therapy? Surely you needed quite a bit."

"I did. Twice a week he took me over the mountains to a medical center. The other days he worked with me."

"Your grandfather must have been quite a man."

"He was. Without him I wouldn't have survived."

"You were still that ill?" He was shocked by her grave words. The thought that she had nearly died, and the waste it would have been, made him angry. It was a strange reaction to something long since resolved.

"My body had healed." She touched the scar, her fingertips brushing his and growing still at the moment of contact. A tension crackled between them, and neither moved until Tracy sighed and continued in a steady voice. "My brain was still bruised and battered."

"The aphasia?"

Tracy nodded. "There's no doubt I would have lived, but without him I would have lost myself."

Her words were calm, too calm. He needed to see her eyes. There he would be able to read the truth. He took his hand from her forehead, stroking it down the length of her hair, then touching her shoulder before moving away. The chair he sat in gave him an unrestricted view of her face, palely lit by the single lamp.

She was beautiful . . . and for the first time in two long years Adam realized how lonely he had been.

"And Wolfe helped you too," he said.

"Yes." It was a murmured half whisper. "And now both are gone."

Adam understood the great depths of her loss. Wolfe had been not only her friend and helpmate in her precarious recovery, he had been her last link with her grandfather as well. Looking into her stark gaze, Adam found himself wishing he had known the man and the dog . . . and the younger Tracy.

As if she knew he could see beneath her brave front, Tracy dropped her head, shielding her eyes. Like thick ebony spikes her lashes lay against her cheeks. She drew a long shuddering breath, then faced him again. Needing to deal with all that hurt and have done with it, she broached pain with pain.

"Can you tell me about Sharon?" she asked, her voice trembling only slightly.

For the first time ever, he found that he could speak of his and Sharon's last moments together. "She died while she slept in my arms. The doctors assured me there was no pain. She simply went to sleep and never woke up."

"I'll miss her," Tracy murmured. "It's strange, isn't it? I hadn't seen her in years, but I'll miss her. You must think me mad."

"No. I understand. I think she felt the same way about you. In fact, she spoke of you often at first. To Sharon you were Tracy Brendon."

"Brendon is my middle name. I chose to use it, rather than Walker, for personal reasons."

"Sharon told me once." He could remember now that long-forgotten conversation.

Tracy moved. It was only a subtle shifting, but she seemed, somehow, at ease. "I'm glad Sharon had you. You loved her. I can hear it in your voice. She deserved that."

"I did love her. I still do."

"I know."

"Have I thanked you, Tracy, for giving me back Sharon's child?"

"There no need for thanks. I did only what I had to do. It was my job, nothing more."

"You knew Wolfe couldn't survive, yet you came."

"A child for a dog? It was not a question of choice, Adam." Another grief she had so neatly filed away broke free, ripping through her, raw, wild, and destructive.

"Would you like to see her?" Adam asked, standing up. "She does look like Sharon, doesn't she?" Like a precious gift, he offered healing succor in the form of his daughter.

"I'd like that." Tracy placed her hand in his and he helped her to her feet.

He led her down a narrow hallway to a door that stood partially ajar. A night light burned, filling the room with a dim glow. Unthreatening gray shadows flickered as a tree outside the open window swayed in the night breeze.

A gentle sigh drew their attention to the child who was nestled among the covers. A chubby hand curled at her cheek, while curls, burnished gold by the lamplight, clung damply to her forehead. Bear, lumpy and tattered, stood guard from his place of honor nearby.

A slight smile curved the tiny lips, then was gone, and she burrowed deeper still into the comforting down of the pillow. Only a long, wicked scratch at her wrist recalled the day, but nothing disturbed her peaceful slumber.

Tracy brushed back a ringlet that had fallen over an eyelid. Her finger was brown and strong against the tender white skin.

Was anything as special or as lovely as a sleeping child? Looking at her now, Tracy acknowledged that Summer did look like Sharon, but it had been Adam's gray eyes that had looked so trustingly at her in a cave on the mountain.

"Thank you, Adam," she said softly. Seeing Summer sleeping contentedly did help to ease the pain.

He bent to kiss Summer's tousled hair, then straightened and looked down at her. She was all that he had left of a wonderful dream.

"Sharon was pregnant when she died," he said softly. It was something he had never told another living soul. The dinner and the loving had been a joyful celebration of the long-awaited confirmation. It had been one more special secret that had been his and Sharon's alone, to keep and to savor for a while. Then it had been too late to share their happiness with the world. He spoke of it now, wanting Tracy to understand how very precious her gift of Summer's life had been.

She neither moved nor spoke, and only by the tears that trickled down her cheeks did Adam know that she had heard. No sob sounded in the stillness, no lines of distress marred her face. Yet hers was an infinite sadness.

"Don't, Tracy." He cupped her chin in one hand, tilting her face to his. With his thumbs he wiped away the tears. "Don't cry for me. I learned long ago not to dwell on tragedy. In that way lies madness. We've both lost special loves, but at least we had them for a while. There are those who never have as much in a lifetime. Put your sorrow behind you, darling, and be happy that we still have Summer."

Tracy stood mesmerized by the soothing murmur of his voice, lulled by the warm comfort of his hands, finding solace in the kindness of his eyes. She had an irrational desire to step into those powerful arms, to nestle her head into his shoulder and cling to his strength. She would ask nothing of him but that he hold her, comfort her. It had been so long, and she had been so alone.

"Adam." It was there, trembling in his name, the need and the bitter loneliness.

Carefully, with all the tenderness in him, he drew her into his arms, enfolding her, burrowing his hand into her hair. He didn't speak; he simply let her draw from him the comfort she sought.

Tracy rested her head against his chest, the strong, even beat of his heart sounding in her ear. Its steadiness soothed her. Soon her ragged breathing slowed, then resumed a more natural pace. Her tenseness vanished, and with it the numbing fatigue. She was grateful when his fingers again found the scar at her temple and stroked away a bit of the pain that was pounding there. Warm and secure and, for a time, unburdened by her cares, Tracy sank further into the contentment so freely given. Gradually her eyelids drooped, then closed.

Adam felt the slight relaxing of her body. In one smooth motion he lifted her and carried her to the aged rocker by Summer's bed. Lowering himself into it, he settled Tracy on his lap. A handmade afghan lay on a dresser nearby. He slipped it from its folds and drew it over her to guard against the creeping chill.

She stirred, but only to snuggle closer.

"Better?" he murmured.

Tracy only nodded, her eyes still closed.

She didn't move again as he held her much as she had held Summer the night before. He rested his head against the silk of her hair, breathing deeply of its fragrance. Outside, a night bird sang and then another, and Adam's eyes closed in sleep.

In the first morning hours a figure appeared in Summer's doorway. Liza, her cap of short dark red curls disheveled, looked long and curiously at the sleeping couple.

Driven from her bed by concern for Adam, she had wandered through the house seeking him. She wasn't surprised to find him sleeping by Summer's bedside. It was Tracy who was unexpected.

Having arrived in the midst of the jubilant celebration, Liza had heard repeatedly from one source after

another of the loss, of the fear, of the search and the rescue. She had heard far too much of the skilled and
heroic tracker not to recognize the dusky-skinned
woman who slept so peacefully in Adam's arms.

Tracy was curled in his lap as if it were her true and
rightful place. Her hair spilled in an ebony cascade over
his hand, which rested at her neck. His arm was pressed
against her breast near the open throat of her blouse.
With the easy rise and fall of her breathing, the rippling
cloth displayed a hint of shadowed cleft and softly
rounded fullness.

Moving soundlessly on bare feet, Liza crossed the
room. She picked up the fallen afghan from the floor and
drew it about them. Neither woke. She waited, watching
them for a minute, struck by the contentment on
Adam's face. It was a look she had thought she would
never see again.

Liza turned her gaze back to Tracy. She saw maturity
rather than gay, young innocence; straight dark hair
rather than golden curls; dark skin rather than alabas-
ter; an exotic slenderness rather than voluptuousness.
There was a strength about her that would complement
that of the man who held her.

Tracy was none of the things that Sharon had been.
But Adam had had his Sharon. He did not need another.

Adam shifted in his sleep. His hand slipped to curl
possessively about a full breast, and Liza smiled a slow,
pleased smile. Then, as quietly as she had come, she left
them.

The brilliant glow of the sunrise woke him as it crept
over the room. Disoriented, he watched as the shadows
lost their darkness, faded, then vanished. He was alone
and his arms were strangely empty.

"Tracy!"

He sat up abruptly, spilling the afghan that had been

neatly tucked about him onto the floor. His voice was husky with disuse as he called her name.

The tantalizing aroma of rich coffee wafted through the house. Thinking that he might find her there, he hurried to the kitchen.

"Tracy?"

"She's gone, Adam."

He whirled to face Liza, who emerged from her bedroom dressed in jeans and a pale lavender sweatshirt. Her red hair was neatly brushed.

"When did she go?"

"I don't know," Liza said. "She was still with you when I checked around one o'clock. When I woke later, she was gone."

"It was Tracy who found Summer," he said as if it might answer any questions she would ask.

"She's an unusual woman."

"Yes."

"And beautiful."

"I know." He stood at the window staring down the road Tracy would have taken. Almost to himself he murmured, "I had forgotten what it was like to hold a woman in my arms."

"It's time you had a woman in your life, Adam."

"I think maybe you're right," he agreed softly, never taking his gaze from the dusty road.

Three

The sun had risen well into the sky before Tracy moved, then it was only to flip a stray lock of hair over her shoulder. For hours she had sat on a huge outcropping of granite that projected from a mountainside. With her knees bent and her chin resting on her folded arms she had seen the birth of a new day.

Far below, down a narrow ribbon of twisting road, was Adam's sturdy cabin. Where was he? Had Summer awakened to begin her day? Would she ever see them again, Sharon's lovely child and Adam?

Disturbed by her thoughts and uneasy with her memories of the night, Tracy rose restlessly, stretching her long legs and flexing her cramped shoulders. For a long while she stood at the edge of the stone. A light breeze caressed her face and the sun kissed her cheeks. Here on the mountain she had found peace. What could she find in the valley in Adam's arms? She shivered and turned away, not yet ready to deal with the question.

Tracy forced her mind from the haunting thought as she deliberately turned her eyes to Shadow. Wolfe lay there close beside her grandfather. He had been old and tired and had stayed with her far past his time. Now he was at rest. She would miss him and be lonelier.

"It's time to go home, Tracy," she murmured aloud.

"You can't put it off any longer." She had to fight the dread of facing the familiar places without her friend and loving companion. When her grandfather had died, the grief had nearly destroyed her. But she knew that this time she was stronger and could face the sorrow and the memories. Brushing back her hair and looping it in a loose knot, she retraced her steps to the jeep parked at the roadside. Not allowing herself to look at the empty seat beside her, she revved the engine to life, reversed, then headed down the incline toward home.

Tracy's days assumed a pattern. She rose early from an often sleepless night, did her household chores, tended her small garden, then with her sketch pad under her arm, tramped the fields and the forest. Sometimes she stopped to sketch a bit, sometimes not. Some days she remembered to eat the sandwich she always dutifully packed, some days she didn't. She never returned before dusk, always weary, always spent, hoping to find rest in oblivion.

Tracy lost count of the number of times she looked for Wolfe or turned to speak to him. Every part of her day seemed to bring some thought of him.

As she sat by the creek bank, her memories turned to a young and playful Wolfe who forgot his majestic dignity long enough to chase and tease the fish that darted in and out of the submerged stones. Waiting for a prickly porcupine to waddle across her path, she recalled his look of chagrin when he had chosen to annoy one just as prickly and in no mood to play. She had never seen such outraged pride as when she had dug the broken quills from his snout. While she gave right of way, most respectfully, to a band of prissy skunks, she remembered how he had laughed at her and disdainfully turned his nose away when she had run afoul of one of the pungent striped creatures.

Tracy knew that the people of the valley had stood in

awe of Wolfe, believing his prowess as a tracker to be a supernatural skill. She had heard the whispers that called him strange, a phantom with mythical powers, a devil dog. How shocked they would have been if they could have seen his gentleness and his humor. Wolfe had been a capricious creature at times, gay and charming, teasing her in an almost human fashion, yet always savagely protective because he loved her.

She could not escape the memories of the great dog. They were everywhere around her, woven into the fabric of her life.

Slowly and by degrees she learned to accept her loss, and each day she missed Wolfe less. It was Adam who was constantly in her mind. The craggy, roughhewn features, the shaggy hair that was the exact color of his eyes, and the gentle smile that curved his lips haunted her thoughts and her dreams. In anger she would chide herself for acting like a giddy young girl and bury herself in her work.

"Hi, Tracy," Jed Halloran called as she stopped her jeep in front of the post office. "Haven't see you in a while."

"Yeah, I know." She jumped to the ground, waiting as he crossed the street to her.

"How have you been?" In his concern, Jed rested a hand on her shoulder, bending his head to look down into her upturned face. Tracy knew what he was asking.

"I'm all right, Jed. Every day it gets a little easier."

"Can I do anything to help?"

"No." She shook her head. "It's something I just have to accept."

"Have you thought about getting another dog?"

"No!" The word whipped from her with a harsh vehemence. As soon as she said it she wished she could recall it. Jed meant no harm, only kindness. She grasped his sleeve, her eyes pleading for forgiveness. "I'm sorry, Jed.

I didn't mean to snap. It's just that there could never be another Wolfe."

"I know." He covered her hand with his. "There's a nice way you could apologize to me."

"Oh, yeah?" Laughter was in her voice, answering the chuckle that rumbled beneath his words.

"There's a barn dance over at the MacFarlands tomorrow night. Come with me."

"You know I don't dance, Jed."

"Doesn't matter. I'll just spend the evening looking at you."

"Idiot." Tracy laughed again. "Okay, you win. I'll go."

"Great. I'll pick you up early. How about five?" At her agreement he kissed her cheek and patted her shoulder in a brotherly fashion. "Wear something sexy so the other guys will wish they were me."

Tracy was still laughing as she turned to enter the post office.

"Land sakes," she was greeted when she stepped inside. "Where you been, Tracy? Ain't seen you in a coon's age."

"Hi, Lucy. I've been round and about. Any mail for me?"

"Got another of those letters from that art place in New York."

"Drat! I wish they'd take no for an answer."

"Them lowlanders is persistent, that's fer sure."

"Well, they can just be persistent. I don't intend to leave these mountains, nor send my work." She dropped the offending letter into the trash bin by the door. "See you next week, Lucy."

"Yeah." The large woman chuckled. "To pick up your next letter from those city folk and drop it in the trash again."

"Maybe someday they'll realize that I mean it when I say no, and give up. 'Bye, now." The door banged shut behind her.

"Hello, Tracy."

"Adam!" In her gay chatter with Lucy, she had very nearly run him down. She stopped abruptly, looking up at the fascinating man. "How are you? How is Summer?" The words tumbled from her in a mad, nervous rush. Even if she tried, she couldn't have broken away from his piercing gaze.

"We've both been fine." His eyes released hers as his keen gaze traveled over her body, dwelling on the narrow hips, which looked even narrower than before. "You've lost weight."

"Only a bit."

"Have you been ill?" His voice was terse as concern leaped into his face, and his eyes moved to the scar.

"I've been very well, Adam," she answered firmly with a tinge of an old defensiveness returning. "Just busy."

"I know. I had hoped to see you before now. I came to your cabin several times but never caught you home."

"Was there something special you wanted?"

"I . . . Summer wanted to see you."

"Oh." Disappointment lanced through her and, on its heels, anger. How stupid to be so vulnerable to a man whom she had seen a grand total of three times. One that, once he had finished his research on Shadow, she would most likely never see again. "Summer's well?"

"Yes."

"You already told me, didn't you?" With an agitated hand she pushed the heavy wealth of her hair farther back off her shoulder. It was little more than a nervous reaction.

"Why did you leave me, Tracy?" His eyes had darkened; a frown creased his features.

She made no pretense of not understanding him. "I thought it best to leave while I had a bit of my dignity still intact. I don't make a habit of sleeping in strange men's arms."

"I know that." With the back of his hand he caressed her cheek. "We aren't strangers. We never were."

"Adam—" She stopped, her eyes closed as he traced the line of her jaw with his fingertips.

"Adam, what?" He stepped closer, his voice sinking to a low, musical whisper. "What is it you want, Tracy?"

"I . . ." A fragrance drifted about her, wrapping her in a cocoon of his cologne. It was a clean, woodsy scent that would forever remind her of Adam. Unable to think with him so near, she stepped back, away from his touch, breaking the hypnotic spell. "Nothing, Adam. I have to go."

"No!" His hand at her arm stopped her. "Don't run away from me again. We need to talk."

"What is there left to say? Your daughter was lost. Wolfe and I helped to find her. We *are* hardly more than strangers." Tracy made the point again, this time emphatically.

"Whether you make a habit of it or not, you did sleep in my arms. That makes us a bit more than strangers."

"I was tired. I hadn't slept," she defended herself curtly.

"I know, darling." Again he lifted his hand, this time to stroke the scar. It was as if, in some curious way, he understood that in times of tension or stress the pain could be excruciating. "Was it terrible for you on the mountain?"

"No." Her eyes were held by his. She couldn't look away. "I knew that Wolfe would die there."

"That can't have made it any easier. The people here have told me how he was your constant companion while you were ill. Sarah told me that he seldom left your side."

"Except for my grandfather, he was all that stood between me and insanity."

"Sarah said that your grandfather let you roam Shadow, and that sometimes you got lost."

"I had to have that freedom. Grandfather understood. I was never in any danger. Wolfe always found me."

"Are you lonely without him?"

"Yes." Even the simple word hurt. "Is it foolish to miss a dog like this?"

"Not one who has meant so much to you. Perhaps he did possess those magical powers the villagers hint about."

"No. His only power was love."

"Sometimes I think love has magical powers," he murmured almost to himself, and again he stepped closer. "Tracy . . ."

"Hey, are you two going to stand here all day blocking the doorway?" Jed was standing on the lower step, grinning a friendly greeting. "How are you, Adam? And how's that sweet little charmer?"

"Summer's fine, Jed."

"And the cute little redhead?"

"Liza?"

"Yeah. The gossips say she's your sister."

"For once the gossips have it right," Adam said with a laugh. "She's my kid sister."

"It's plain to see who got all the looks in the family, and it isn't you, my friend." Jed clapped him on the shoulder with a hearty laugh. "You are going to bring her to the dance tomorrow, aren't you?"

"I hadn't thought about it."

"You have to! Can't visit the mountains without attending at least one genuine barn dance. And besides, we wouldn't want that fire-topped city gal to miss her chance at dancing with the master I'll expect you." He grinned confidently. "And you I'll see about five, dark eyes."

With a playful tug of her braid and a jaunty wave to Adam, Jed moved on into the post office.

"You're going with Jed?" The warmth in Adam's eyes had been replaced by a glacier coldness.

"Yes."

"Perhaps I'll see you there." He turned away, dismissing her as if she suddenly no longer mattered.

Tracy could only stare, confused by the lightning-swift change. One minute he had been kind and considerate, almost like a lover, then the next he was coldly aloof and distant. She had no idea what she might have done, but watching his stiff, retreating steps take him farther away from her she knew that she couldn't let him go.

"Adam?"

He slowed only slightly and did not stop. Nor did he acknowledge her call.

"Adam, wait!" Tracy rushed to catch him. For a moment she tried to pace her stride with his, but she was no match for his long legs and could not keep up. He seemed to realize that she couldn't and stopped to look down at her, his face closed and expressionless.

"Well?" The curt word was a demand.

"Hey, look, I don't know what I said that made you so angry. Whatever it was, I'm sorry."

"Why didn't you tell me you were Halloran's property?"

"What?" She looked at him incredulously.

"I said—"

"Never mind," she interrupted, bristling with anger. "I heard what you said. I don't know where you get your ideas, but I can assure you that I'm nobody's property! Nobody owns me. They never have, they never will."

"You're going to the MacFarlands with him."

The man's jealous! Tracy was speechless with the discovery. She looked into the glowering face and did not know if she should laugh, be angry, or feel flattered. One part of her wanted to slap away his arrogance, while another wanted to reassure him and melt the frost in his eyes. Later she wouldn't remember making the decision.

"There's nothing between Jed and me, Adam." She deliberately kept her voice steady with no inflection. "He's a friend, nothing more."

"But you do go out with him."

"Occasionally," she acknowledged. "We enjoy each other's company. The valley's not exactly overrun with single people, you know. Through the years we've just sort of teamed up for some of the parties and the dances."

He relaxed visibly, then a slow, rueful grin spread over his face. "I've been acting like a fool, haven't I?"

"Truth?"

"Of course."

"Then yes. Yes, you have acted like a great, hulking fool," she answered firmly.

"Ouch!" He winced in mock hurt. "You don't mince words, do you?"

"If you don't want to know, don't ask."

His shout of laughter startled her and turned many heads. More than one pleased smile was hidden quickly as one matchmaker after another made note of the couple. A few even nodded their approval when Adam flung an arm about Tracy's shoulders and hugged her to him.

"Arguing is thirsty work. How about a cool drink? I'll buy. In fact, when I left, Summer had just talked Liza into making a fresh pitcher of lemonade, and I have it on the best authority that Aunt Liza's lemonade is t'rrific." The warm laughter was back in his eyes. Tracy could almost fool herself into thinking she had only imagined his swift withdrawal and the hint of a sneer that had hovered beneath the cutting words.

Adam was a man of hidden emotions. He would bear watching and would, indeed, take some careful understanding. Tracy filed the thought away, intending to think about it later. For now she put it aside and smiled her acceptance.

"A tall cool drink would be grand. I had planned to stop by to see Summer anyway."

"Good. I have another errand to do. Why don't you go on ahead and spend some time with her. She's hardly spoken of anything but you for weeks. I won't be long."

Hardly more than a few minutes later Tracy slipped

from her jeep and stood watching Summer while she played under a tree that shaded both yard and cabin. As patches of sunlight broke through the swaying leaves, her bright hair was a poignant reminder of Sharon. Tracy could see why she was life itself to Adam.

"Hello, Summer." Tracy stepped farther into the yard.

"Tracy!" The small child flew across the lawn into her arms. "I kept hoping and hoping you'd come."

"Was there some special reason?" Tracy brushed back the curl that Summer had unsuccessfully tried to push from her face.

"Nope. I just wanted to see you. I told Aunt Liza all about you and Wolfe and the cave and the campfire. She said she'd like to meet you. I told her she couldn't meet Wolfe 'cause he went to sleep like mommy and didn't wake up."

"Summer! You're chattering like a magpie. Slow down." A petite woman who was obviously Adam's sister crossed the lawn toward them. She wiped her hands on the apron that was tied around an impossibly small waist, then grasped both of Tracy's firmly. "I'm Liza, Tracy. I hoped I'd get the opportunity to thank you for all you did for our little rascal here. I don't know what Adam would have done if things had turned out differently. It's not something I like to think about."

A bell-like laugh sounded as she gestured toward some chairs clustered in the shade of the tree. "Gracious, I'm as bad a chatterer as Summer. Come, sit down. I'll get you something to drink. Will lemonade be all right?"

"Lemonade will be fine," Tracy answered, appreciating the sparkle and flair of the young woman. She wasn't beautiful in the strictest sense of the word, but with her coloring and spirit she would be unforgettable. Quite suddenly Tracy found herself thinking of Jed. Liza would be perfect for him. Then just as suddenly she realized she had succumbed to the favorite pastime of the hill women: matchmaking. Heaven forbid that she should be so presumptuous. And yet . . .

"Here we go." Liza set a pitcher and a tray of cookies on the table before them. "Sit. These are pretty good cookies, if I do say so myself. Sit, Tracy, sit."

"Thank you, Liza." Tracy could hardly keep from smiling, for Liza sounded just like Sarah. Oh, Jed, watch out, she thought. Your number has just come up. That thought defeated her. The smile blossomed into a full-blown laugh.

"I said something funny?" Liza asked, looking at Tracy curiously.

"No." Tracy fought to compose herself. "I was just enjoying the day and the company."

"Oh, I see." Liza looked doubtful, but she was far too well-mannered to question anymore.

"Tracy?"

"What, pumpkin?"

"Did Daddy come to your house and tell you to come see me?" Summer reached for a cookie with grubby hands, ignoring the wet cloth Liza had laid by her place.

"I did see your dad, but I was coming to see you anyway."

"Why?" Adam's gray eyes looked at her solemnly from Summer's face.

"I have something for you."

"A present?" An excited smile began to tilt the innocent mouth and there was a happy eagerness in her every feature.

"Umm-hmm." Tracy smiled as she drew a small package from her carryall. It was wrapped in a brilliant yellow paper and tied with a strand of white yarn.

"Can I open it now?" Summer clutched it tightly in her lap.

"Sure you can. Presents are to open, aren't they?"

Summer needed no other invitation. With the glee of an energetic six-year-old, she tore the paper away from the box. When she lifted the lid she grew very quiet and still.

"Don't you like it, Summer?"

"Is it real?" She turned her wondering gaze to Tracy.

"No, it's a carving made out of wood."

"Can I touch it?"

"Of course you can. See?" Tracy lifted the tiny blue butterfly from its wrappings. "Since it's wood, it isn't nearly so fragile as a real one would be."

"Did you catch it?"

"No, honey. When I was a little girl, I liked the blue butterfly too. My grandfather carved this for me when I was just about your age."

"It's for me?" Summer asked wistfully. "I can really keep it?"

"You surely can. I can't think of another person I'd rather have it."

"Hi, how are my girls?" Tracy started at the sudden sound of Adam's voice. He was standing in the bright sunlight, smiling at the three of them. Tracy's heart lurched at the vibrant strength that seemed to emanate from him.

"Daddy!" Summer jumped from her chair and rushed to him, carrying the carving like a precious treasure. "Look what Tracy brung me."

"Brought, darling." Adam corrected her as he lifted her high into his arms.

"Look what Tracy brought me," the child repeated dutifully, displaying her gift proudly to her father.

"Ah, that's nice, Summer."

"It's all right, you can touch it. It's not real. Tracy's grampa carved it for her when she was six too. She liked blue butterflies then."

"I'll bet she didn't chase one up on Shadow and lose herself like somebody else I know," Adam teased as he kissed her.

"I won't do that again, Daddy." Summer's eyes were studiously serious.

"I know you won't, baby. I was just teasing." Adam set her on her feet and turned to Liza. "Could I have a drink too?"

"Of course, Adam. Come along, Summer. You can get out the ice for me." Liza offered her hand to the child.

"Okay. I'll leave my butterfly here till I get back." With great care she set the carving down and skipped away to join her aunt.

Adam looked down at the figure and traced the shape of a delicate wing with a broad finger. "Are you sure you want to give this away? It must be very special to you."

"I have others. I'd like Summer to have it."

"I know she'll take care of it. Thank you, Tracy." He turned to look toward Shadow. "At least something pretty has happened to her here at this godforsaken mountain."

"What happened to Summer was not the mountain's fault." Tracy's voice was firmly controlled, seeking with calmness to stem the rising rage she could sense in him. "It's an inanimate object and only what people make of it."

"You don't believe that any more than I do. That pile of rocks damn near killed my daughter and it did kill your dog. At first I thought all the stories I'd heard about it were exaggerated, but I don't now."

Tracy stood to face him, her hand resting on the back of the chair. "Shadow is just like anything that's different. People don't understand it so they look for reasons for the differences, and they don't always make sense. There are good stories about it, but they're not nearly so exciting to gossip about."

"There's nothing good about that thing. It sits there like the knell of doom, waiting to snatch some poor soul away. How you people can live here is beyond me. If I weren't committed to this book, I wouldn't take a picture or write a single word about it."

"I hate to see you misunderstand how we feel about Shadow. For every tale of horror there's some good.

Haven't you discovered that those of us who live here love Shadow just as much as we hate it? Doesn't that prove something?"

"No." When she shook her head, discouraged by his stubborn refusal to listen to reason, he relented. He took her hand in his, staring down at the long, slender fingers as his thumb caressed her palm. "All right, Tracy. Show me this good and pretty mountain. Spend some time with me and let's explore the legends together. Show me your Shadow."

"I don't know, Adam—"

"You've made your claims, now prove them."

He was issuing a challenge. Tracy had never backed down from a dare in her life, but just now all she could think about was how comforting it was to feel the warm, hard hand holding hers.

"Are you afraid, Tracy?" he taunted, leaning down until the loose tendril of hair at her ear was fanned by his breath. "Are you afraid that you can't prove your point, or are you afraid of me?"

"Don't be ridiculous. Why should I be afraid of you?"

"Not of me, Tracy, but of this attraction that's between us. You know as well as I do that there's something there. Are you afraid to find out what it is?"

"We were talking about Shadow." Tracy futilely tried to curb the shiver that rushed through her. His eyes seemed to hold her captive. She wanted to look away, but did not.

"Um-hm," he murmured as he lifted her palm to his lips. "You had something to prove to me, didn't you?"

"Adam . . . no."

"Didn't you?"

"I—all right."

"You won't regret it, darling." He pressed three lingering kisses to her fevered skin, and smiled.

"Daddy! You almost knocked my butterfly off the table." Summer's plaintive cry broke the spell he had cast about her.

* * *

Many hours later Tracy paced the floor of her cabin. An angry frown marred her smooth forehead. She had been fuming since she realized how neatly she had been manipulated.

"Damn you, Adam Grayson. You tricked me."

She had been well on her way home before the truth had hit her. Adam was far too intelligent to think a mountain evil or to believe the ugliness some liked to spout about Shadow. It had been an act, she was sure of that. But for what purpose? What earthly reason would he have for lying to her, pretending something that was untrue?

"He pegged you right from the first, Miss Tracy," she said aloud. "He knew that if he made it sound like a dare, you'd jump at the chance to prove yourself right. Fool!"

If Tracy were to face the truth, she would have had to admit that she was angrier at herself than at Adam. There had been no contest, but he had been the winner all the same. He had issued a challenge, and she had given him the victory by accepting.

Furious as she was, Tracy knew she would not back down. She never had; she never would. It was the sort of determination that had kept her injuries from destroying her, and it was what made her a good tracker as well. She never gave up. That in itself was victory of a sort.

When the anger had at last worn itself out, Tracy lay in her bed. She stared out the window at the moonlit world, but saw none of the familiar hills or fields. A broad-shouldered man with a wicked smile was the center of her thoughts.

"Go away, Adam. I want to sleep," she muttered as she drew the sheet under her chin and shut her eyes. Determinedly she kept them closed, but it was quite a while before she truly slept.

Four

The sun had long since slid behind the mountain and the lanterns strung through the leafy oaks were glowing in the twilight by the time Jed and Tracy arrived at the MacFarland farm. Music and voices blended into a low murmur punctuated by the shouts and laughter of children.

"It's not exactly five o'clock, is it?" Jed said, grinning at Tracy. He stepped from the open side of his jeep and walked around it to offer Tracy a hand. "Unpredictable hours are all part of the territory that goes with the job. I wouldn't have kept you waiting if I could have avoided it."

"Hey, Tracy," a young boy called as she passed him. "Someone was looking for you earlier."

"Who, Rick?" She stopped, turning slightly, her eyes searching through the crowd for the man who had disrupted her sleep the night before.

"A little girl. The one who was lost up on Shadow a few weeks back."

"Summer."

"Yeah. That was her name."

"Did she say what she wanted?" Tracy fought down a twinge of disappointment that it wasn't Adam who had asked for her.

"Nah. She just asked us if we'd seen you. They were over on the other side of the dance floor."

"Want to go over?" Jed asked. He, too, scanned the crowd, and Tracy wondered if he was seeking Liza.

"I doubt they're still there now," Tracy said. "Why don't we wait? We're bound to see them before the evening's over." She only hoped Jed was convinced by her nonchalance.

"Then let's sit for a while and watch the fun."

"Sounds good. I left our blanket in the jeep. I'll go get it."

"No need. Not when we have the perfect seats right here." Before she could answer, Jed had swung her high onto the tall stone wall that wound through the Mac-Farland property. Built many years ago, when stone and manpower were plentiful and wire was rare, it still served to mark boundaries and fence the numerous dairy cattle that grazed the rolling green pastures.

"What do you think?" He pulled himself up beside her and grinned down at her. "Beats a blanket, doesn't it?"

"A trifle harder but the view's better."

"An old mountain gal like you can take it. You've been rock-sitting for years. In fact, early one morning a couple of weeks ago I thought I saw you up on Raven's Roost."

"You did," Tracy said, remembering as if it were yesterday the morning she had left Adam's arms. "I had some thinking to do."

"Something important?"

"Maybe."

"Tracy." Suddenly Adam was standing by her side, magnificent in the traditional dress of the dance. His white shirt with the sleeves turned back was a stark contrast to his suntanned skin. In the dim light his hair looked almost black again—until he moved and the heavy strands caught a moonbeam. His face was a study of deeply carved shadows and she could read nothing there as he turned toward her companion. "How are you, Jed?"

"Can't complain, Adam. Things going all right with you?" After an answering nod Jed continued pleasantly. "I hope you haven't come this evening without your beautiful women folk."

"No." Adam's eyes were again on Tracy. "Liza and Summer stopped to speak to Hester Calton."

"Do you think your sister would think I'm rude if I went over and introduced myself?"

"I'm sure she wouldn't." Adam seemed to draw himself from distant thoughts. "Summer would like to see you too. You go on. I'll see to Tracy."

"Okay?" Jed hesitated, having the good grace to feel a bit embarrassed that he was about to desert Tracy when he had very nearly coerced her into coming with him.

"I'll be fine, Jed," Tracy assured him, looking into Adam's half-hidden face as intently as he looked at her. Neither saw the quizzical glance Jed gave them.

In the stillness that seemed to surround them, Adam's gaze lingered on the peach-colored flush that stained Tracy's cheeks, then moved on to her lips, seeming to memorize their shape. As if to test their softness, one finger touched them, then was gone.

At the instant of contact, a current of pleasure caught at her, halting her breath, suspending her in another time, another place, banishing the meadow and its people. There was no crowd, no Jed, no Liza, no Summer. There was only Adam, a stranger she had known and waited for all her life.

The shock of her thoughts drew from her a sharp gasp of surprise, its sound breaking his mesmerized gaze from her parted lips. A swift and deep inhaling of a new breath drew his eyes to the rounded fullness of her breasts. For the space of a heartbeat he smiled his appreciation of her womanliness.

With the uncanny acceptance that was hers, Tracy waited, hardly moving, as Adam's gaze roved over her, missing nothing. He was totally absorbed in her, yet she felt not the least bit uneasy by his searching contemplation.

"You're a beautiful woman, Tracy Walker," he said, stepping closer and stroking her brow with the back of his hand. His voice sank to no more than a hint of a whisper. "The most beautiful woman I've ever seen."

"No more beautiful than you."

"Men aren't beautiful." His low laughter was like a kiss.

"You are." Her grave reply left no doubt that she meant every word.

"Don't, Tracy. Don't look at me like that. Not now, not here." Unaware of what he did, he tucked back a bone pin that had escaped from the dark coil of hair resting at the nape of her neck. His fingers paused at the pulse that beat raggedly at the line of her jaw, then curved to frame her chin, lifting her face to the moonlight. In a voice harsh with strain, he said almost to himself, "I think it might be best if we join Jed and Liza for a while."

He stepped back and waited. She clasped his proffered hand, needing no aid to leave the stone wall but seeking his touch. With fingers interlaced, they joined the others. They had just sat down when Melinda approached them shyly. "Mr. Grayson?" she said.

"Hello, Melinda," Adam said. "Are you enjoying the dance?"

"Yes, sir. Mr. Grayson . . . I was wondering . . . I thought . . ." They could see the girl gather her courage, then she spoke in a rush. "Would it be all right if I take Summer over to play the games? I'd take very good care of her. Truly I would."

"Where are they?"

"Over by the barn there are stalls like this one," Tracy explained, "with bingo, toss-a-penny, darts, that sort of thing. Noah Hawkins will probably be there telling stories too. Later the little ones will sleep in the hayloft until their parents are ready to go. She will be well supervised, Adam."

"And I'll help," Melinda added, wanting to make amends and to acquit herself of the guilt she felt. "I promise I won't let Summer be lost again."

"I know you won't, Melinda," Adam assured the girl kindly. He was rewarded with a tremulous smile. "If Summer would like to go . . ."

"You bet!" The child hopped down from her chair, eager to join in the fun. With a wet smack of a kiss planted somewhere in the vicinity of her father's ear and a wave to the others, she raced away hand in hand with Melinda.

In the silence that followed, Tracy's smile was equally as tremulous as she looked gratefully at the man sitting across from her. Both ignored the sounds of the band striking up another rousing square-dance.

"Liza," Jed said, flicking a knowing glance at the two, "is that our song they're playing?"

"Why, Jed." A pleased chuckle accompanied her answer. "I do believe it is." Not bothering with words of parting that would go unheard, they left to join the dancers.

"That was a thoughtful thing to do," Tracy said above the noisy voices and the music that surrounded them. "Melinda's been heartsick for weeks, worrying about what happened to Summer. Trusting her as you have tonight will help to ease some of her guilt."

"I never meant that she should shoulder all the blame," Adam said.

Tracy's hand closed over his where it rested on the rough boards of the table. Her thumb caressed his knuckles. "You're a nice man, Adam Grayson. The nicest I've ever known. Sharon was a lucky woman."

"Thank you, Tracy." Adam was silent for a long while, his thoughts on times past and faraway places. Though the memories were deeply ingrained and unforgettable, they had at last begun to fade because of this woman whose touch warmed him. His lips relaxed in a hint of a smile as he turned his hand up to catch her fingers in his own. "Let's walk a bit and you can tell me more about all this. Surely it's not the customary barn dance."

Later, as Tracy led him from one booth to another, showing him the crafts on display, she answered his question. "You were right. This is actually more a church social than a dance. We gather here fairly often during the year. Usually it's to raise funds for some cause. This time we hope to earn enough to replace the organ in the church."

"Do you always have it here at the MacFarlands?"

"Always." She smiled. "Look, there's Noah Hawkins. He spends a part of every social telling the legends. The children know them nearly as well as he does, yet they always listen as if it's the first time. Would you like to go over and listen?"

"Not tonight." The look he turned to her was teasing, yet tender. "Tonight my mind's far too filled with music and moonlight, and an entrancing woman."

As color rose in Tracy's cheeks he laughed and drew her to the next exhibit. Stringed instruments, carefully handcrafted in wood, were lined against the wall.

"What are these?"

"They're Clayton Tarleton's dulcimers. Listen." Tracy struck the taut strings with the leather-covered hammer, sounding only a few notes. "Pretty, isn't it?"

"Can you play?"

"Not the dulcimer. The guitar's always been my favorite."

"Will you play for me, darling?" He stepped closer, his head inclined as he waited for her answer.

"Yes, Adam." Tracy stared up into eyes that shone with a strange light. "Someday I will."

In that stolen moment, amid the revelry and jostled by the crowd, he wasn't sure what it was he asked, nor she what she had promised. But both knew it was far more than a song.

"Well, land sakes! Are you two going to stand over there lollygaggin' all evening? Or are you going to come over here and sample one of my tea cakes?" Sarah Price glared at them in mock severity, her hands on her hips.

"Have a heart, Sarah." Adam groaned good-naturedly. "We just left Hester's booth. I don't think I could handle two cakes in one night."

"Lord love a duck, Adam!" The tiny woman looked aghast at his ignorance. "A tea cake's not a cake."

"It's not? But you called it—"

"A tea cake is a cookie, Adam," Tracy said, leaning close to speak over the gay chatter of a group of young girls.

"Then why is it called a cake?" he asked matter of factly.

"Because . . ." Tracy searched for an explanation even as she tried to hide her amusement. "It's always . . . uh . . . Because that's it's name, that's why." She put a definite end to the conversation.

"Since you've already spoiled yore appetite over at Hester's," Sarah said, "I'll just send some tea cakes with you. Stay right here and I'll put some in a poke." She scurried to the far end of her booth and rummaged among some papers.

"A poke?" Adam murmured quietly in Tracy's ear.

"A paper bag," she answered as quietly.

"Oh." He nodded. "Of course."

"Here now!" Sarah set the bulging bag before him. "Take these on home for later. I don't aim to toot my own horn, but Tracy can tell you that they're the best in the valley."

"Thanks, Sarah. I'm sure I'll enjoy them."

"I'm sure you will too," Sarah called immodestly after them as they moved back into the mainstream of the milling people. "Adam, be sure to have Tracy show you the special exhibit."

Adam and Tracy laughed and talked, exchanged greetings with friends as they walked, and Adam's hand again found Tracy's.

"I think this is the last," she said later as they stood before a table of delicate embroidery and crocheted doilies. A wizened old woman sat at the table, her eyes staring blankly at them. "Thank you, Opal, for sharing your work with us."

"Tracy?" A gnarled, brown-spotted hand searched toward the sound of her voice.

"Yes. It's Tracy." Young, firm fingers clasped the wrinkled and workworn hand.

"Let me see you. It's been months since you come to the house. Come down," the old woman urged. "Come down."

Quickly Tracy knelt before her. Opal's fingers stroked over her every feature, from her brow, across her eyes, to her cheeks and her lips. Finally they traced the path of the scar at her temple. "Have you kept well, little girl?"

"Very well, Opal."

"No more trouble with the words?"

"Not anymore."

"Good. Good." The gray head bobbed once. "Young man?"

"Yes, ma'am."

"Are you Tracy's man?"

"I . . ."

"Don't dillydally. Ain't no substitute for a straight answer. Either you are or you ain't."

Adam hesitated for a moment, his gaze traveling over the slender form of the kneeling woman. When he spoke, his voice was low and measured. "Yes, I think that perhaps I am."

"Think!" The old woman snorted. "The man who gets Tracy will know he's her man."

"Opal," Tracy interjected mildly, "Adam and I hardly know each other. We're just friends."

"Are you a friend, young man?" The milky white of the cataract-scarred eyes turned toward Adam.

"Yes."

It was only a single word, but Opal tilted her head, listening to its rich tone, savoring its intensity. She seemed to read in it what she wanted to know. Laying a steady hand on either side of Tracy's face, she kissed her forehead and smiled.

"Yore Adam is a good man, Tracy." She fondly patted Tracy's cheek. "Go now and have the fun you young'uns should instead of wasting time with a foolish old woman."

"Never foolish," Tracy murmured as she rose to her feet. "I'll be over to see you soon, Opal."

"You do that. I'd cherish it."

"It's a shame," Adam said as they walked away.

"What?" Tracy looked up at his frowning face.

"It's a shame that anyone who could do such beautiful work has to be handicapped and unable to continue."

Tracy smiled as they moved farther away. "It's a good thing Opal didn't hear that. She's the last person who would consider herself handicapped. Sure, she can't do the embroidery anymore, but she still crochets."

"How could she?" Astonishment was strong in Adam's words. "Some of those pieces were so delicate that they looked like cobwebs. How on earth could she do that when she's blind?"

"The patterns come from her memory and she says she sees with her fingers. I've watched her sit for hours crocheting, creating one lovely piece after another. If she could see, I doubt she would look down as she worked."

"The saddest part is that she can't see how beautiful they are."

"Yes," Tracy agreed, pleased that he understood.

"Couldn't something be done for her eyes?"

"There might have been in the past, but not now."

"With all the advances in medicine, I would think that there's some hope."

"No." Tracy shook her head sadly. "She's ninety-seven

years old and even frailer than she looks. I don't think she could survive any shocks to her system."

"Surely—"

"Adam." Tracy laid her hand on his arm in a gesture of comfort. "Opal would tell you not to fret yourself over her. She said long ago that she had made her peace with the blindness."

"She's a marvelous woman, isn't she?"

"We all think she is."

"These mountains seem to be good at producing magnificent women." Adam smiled and touched her hand. "Magnificent and beautiful."

"Flattery."

"Truth."

A glow suffused her face at his praise. "Do you think we should find Jed and Liza? They're going to think we deserted them."

"They don't need us. And anyway, we haven't seen that special exhibit Sarah told us about. Where is it?"

"It's over by the barn."

He turned to the booth in question. The laughter that lit his eyes faded and was replaced by wonder. "Tracy! What are these?"

Before she could answer, he moved closer to stand before a stunning array of miniature figures that had been carved from wood, then painted with a breathtaking realism. Beside each were the preliminary sketches and a watercolor that mirrored the final product.

"This is absolute genius! Whose work is it?" His hand hovered for an instant over the whimsical figure of a chipmunk curled sleepily on a leaf. "Are they for sale?"

"No."

"How can you be sure?"

"Because they're mine. Or at least they were."

"Yours?" Adam looked at her in surprise, and with the dawning of a new and even greater respect. "Why didn't you tell me? Why haven't I seen some of your work before? Surely you've shown it somewhere."

"Few of my carvings have ever been shown other than right here. These were gifts to my friends here in the valley. This display is their idea."

"You don't sell anything at all?"

"Only a piece of two when it was a necessity." Her finger stroked the colorful wing of a mallard duck, a decoy that had been a gift to Jed.

"It's strange, but I've seen something somewhere that reminds me of this." He looked down at a grouping of a fox and her three cubs tumbling in tall grass. "Tra . . . My God! You're *Trace*!"

"I do sign my work that way," she acknowledged.

"One of the loveliest things I've ever seen was in a small, exclusive gallery in New York. It was titled 'A Vixen at Play.' Even in miniature that fox was so realistic I waited for it to breathe. It carried the signature of Trace. Damn it, Tracy! What are you doing hiding yourself in these hills when you can do something this beautiful?"

"I like the mountains, Adam. They're my home; they always will be. I sketch, I paint, and I carve what I know and what I see around me. I do it for the pleasure it gives me. I never intended that it should be a career. My grandfather was the true artist in the family. If you know woodcarving, you probably know his name. He was called the Forest Walker."

"Of course," Adam muttered to himself. "I should have known." He looked at her as she stood illuminated by the dim light of the lanterns and the moonlight, and the last pieces of an old and unsolved puzzle fell into place. He said nothing, though, and waited for her to continue.

"Actually he started it as a sort of physical therapy for me. With the weaknesses left by my injuries, I could hardly hold the instruments and I cut myself more times than I care to remember. But he pushed and urged until I continued."

"It's a blessing that he did. But as a master carver himself, he would recognize your talent as unique."

Tracy's laugh was mirthless, tinged with the pain of remembered frustration. "You wouldn't say that if you could see my first efforts. Most were unrecognizable, shapeless masses, and often as not painted with my own blood."

"Yet in the face of it all, you never gave up." Adam wanted to take her into his arms, asking nothing but that she let him hold her.

"As my mind healed and I recovered more and more of my coordination, my skill grew. It became easier and easier, until one day I realized that I no longer needed the carving, but that I was doing it for the sheer love of it."

"Each of these has been a gift?"

"Yes." She picked up a lifelike figure of a plump piglet. "This was for Malcolm on his sixty-sixth birthday. The quail was for Bobby Toney. Raising quail was his 4-H project. The coon dog is Ezra's, the hummingbird, Sarah's. I have little I can give to my friends except my carvings, and they seem to appreciate them."

"How many pieces have you sold?"

"Only a few. The New York gallery you mentioned handled Grandfather's work, and they also seem willing to take mine."

"Gladly, I should think. Have they approached you about taking more pieces than you've offered?"

"I receive a letter from them with great regularity. I haven't bothered to open the last few. They all used to say the same thing. I suppose they still do."

"Why won't you listen to what they have to say?"

"Because I don't really want to sell anything. I'd rather give them to the people I know will enjoy them, not just sell to someone who's—who's a collector. And because I don't intend to leave here. This is my *home*."

"Hey, hey, it's all right." He curved his hand around the nape of her neck, drawing her near. "I didn't mean to push."

"I know." She rested her forehead against the muscled wall of his chest. "I'm sorry. I don't usually overreact like that. I guess I'm just tired."

"Would you like to go back to join Jed and Liza now? We could watch the dancers."

"I'd like that." She leaned her head back and smiled up at him as he released her.

"Tracy, Adam," Jed called to them, catching their attention as they neared the platform where a square dance was just ending. He was sitting with Liza, their blanket spread a bit apart from the others. "Come sit with us."

"You two made an evening of it just seeing the exhibits. Did you buy anything?" Liza asked Adam as he sat down and stretched out onto the grass.

"Didn't buy a thing. All I have to show for my study of the mountain crafts is this." He produced the bag of tea cakes. "Sarah made these. Would you like to share?"

"I'd love one. Maybe I could get her recipe." Liza blinked in confusion as all three burst into laughter.

"Now, what did I say that was so funny?" she demanded.

"Nothing, really, Liza." Adam wiped the grin from his face. "It's just that you're a city girl visiting the hills, and you sound like you were born here."

"Is there some law that says I can't enjoy cooking just because I happen to live in the city? You should know that I like to cook. You visit my apartment for dinner often enough."

"At your invitation," Adam reminded her. "If I didn't, you'd probably scour the bushes looking for someone to feed."

"You don't live with Adam and Summer?" Tracy

asked. She was sitting on the far side of the blanket, enjoying the teasing exchange between brother and sister.

"No," Liza said. "I would, but Adam won't hear to it. After Sharon died he insisted on hiring a housekeeper. If I hadn't forced myself on him, he wouldn't have let me come with them to the valley. I had a hard time convincing him that I wanted to see the mountain and that I love spending time with Summer."

"But you'd been ill," Adam protested.

"Adam." Liza looked at him in exasperation. "You know that it was only bronchitis and now I'm as good as new. In fact if you hadn't been so stubborn and hadn't insisted on that final doctor's appointment, I would have been here when—" She stopped short, realizing what she had been about to say. "Oh, Adam, I'm sorry."

"Never mind, Liza. I understand." He ruffled her tumbled curls and smiled.

"Liza," Jed said, stepping in to ease the awkward moment, "the band is back from their break and I'm sure they're going to be playing our song. Can you keep your foot out of your mouth long enough to dance?"

"I certainly hope so." She took his hand and let him help her to her feet as the first chords of the music began.

"C'mon. We're going to miss the first call," Jed said, virtually dragging her away.

"Poor Liza," Tracy murmured as she watched her join Jed in the intricate moves of the dance. "She didn't mean to bring up a painful subject."

"I know," Adam said. "She's a good kid, and whether she'll admit it or not, I couldn't have managed over the past two years without her. She's there when I need her."

"You're lucky to have her."

"Yes." Turning his gaze from Liza to Tracy, Adam was aware of Tracy's wistful look. "Are you sure you wouldn't like to dance?"

"I can't dance, Adam. I used to love it, but not anymore. My recovery has been almost total . . . except for the rhythm. Somehow I can't seem to get it right anymore."

It was a simple admission, but his memories of the vibrant young girl of years ago made it one that tore at his heart. He couldn't help but wonder if her calmness was a cover for her fear that she would make a mistake or that she would forget again. He suddenly realized why she had chosen such a lonely life.

"I'll be right back." In a quick move he was on his feet. He strode to the platform, weaving through the dancers to the leader of the band. The band leader didn't miss a beat as he listened to Adam and nodded his head. As quickly as he had gone, Adam was back by Tracy's side.

"Ladies and gentlemen," the leader announced over the loudspeaker. "We have an unusual request, but we agree that it's time for a change. So here it is, a nice, slow ballad. Here's your chance, fellas. With this one you can hold her close."

As the smooth beat of a gentle love song filled the air, Adam held out his hand to Tracy. "Tracy," he said.

"Adam, I can't."

"Yes, darling, you can."

"No."

"The music's slow, and I'll be with you."

She looked up into his eyes, wanting to take his hand but afraid.

"Come with me, Tracy. I need to hold you in my arms."

Suddenly, completely trusting, she did as he asked. He led her through the crowd to the dance floor. Once there, he waited a moment while she gathered her courage, then opened his arms. He breathed a soft sigh of relief when she stepped into them. Carefully, moving in short, slow steps, he led her through the dance.

At first uncomfortable and afraid, she held herself stiffly erect. Then with only a gentle pressure from his hand at her back, she moved closer until her head was nestled beneath his chin. Neither knew that the band played the song twice, nor that those around the dance floor were watching with silent pleasure.

As the final notes of the song faded away, it seemed natural that they should wander away, arm in arm, among the trees. They stopped by a brook that bubbled and sparkled in the bright moonlight.

"Tracy?" Adam threw an arm around her shoulders and drew her closer. His hard fingers tilted her head so that he could look into her eyes. As though in slow motion, he bent to kiss her. With a seeking hunger he parted her lips in the caress of a lover. He enfolded her body in his strong arms, pulling her hard against himself, letting her know his passion.

Tracy met his need with the fire he had kindled and gave herself up to enchantment. With a force of feeling that was new to her, she welcomed Adam's kiss with her own possessive caress. There was no shock, no outrage when his gentle fingers stroked the fullness of her breast. Nor did she protest when his hand cradled its weight, soothing the haughty nipple with his palm.

Adam groaned, a harsh and frustrated sound. He broke the kiss and dropped his hand. He molded her soft body to his own hard, taut one, resting his chin on her brow. His ragged breath stirred her hair.

"Who are you that you've become the center of my thoughts and my dreams?" he whispered. "Have you bewitched me, Tracy Walker?"

She stirred, then stepped away from his embrace. With her arms crossed, one hand resting at her throat, she stared over the water. "You've said it, Adam. I'm simply Tracy Walker. No more, no less. What I've done is nothing that any concerned human being wouldn't do for another. Be careful. What you feel now might be the result of your ordeal. Summer's safe and you're grateful. Maybe it's even a misguided sense of guilt over Wolfe."

"No! Summer *is* safe, and I'm more grateful than you

could ever know, but it has nothing to do with what I feel now."

"I'd like to believe that." She turned to face him, her eyes dark and secret in the shadows.

"You can, darling."

"No." She shook her head slowly. "It's too soon, our emotions are in a turmoil. We need to regain an even keel before we can know what we really feel for each other."

"Then will you come to Shadow? Will you spend some time there with me? Will you give me a chance to know you?"

"Yes. I'll come. For as long as you want me, or until we understand this attraction between us."

"I couldn't ask for any more than that . . . for now."

Five

"Is this where we'll be camped?"

"No such luck," Tracy said as she pulled supplies from the back of the jeep. "This is just an old logging trail. We have a bit of a walk ahead of us. None of it easy."

"Do you have a campsite chosen?"

She nodded as she shifted the frame of her heavily loaded pack. "We need to be near water and where there's a break in the underbrush. About midway up there's a small clearing that should serve our needs nicely. It has a stream that's more rock than anything else, but the water's clean and plentiful."

"Sounds good."

"The stream isn't very deep, and if you want to take a bath you have to sit on a rock in the middle. Even then the water would hardly come to your waist." Her laugh carried a far happier note than Adam had ever heard before. "But that should be more than enough, unless you enjoy frigid baths."

"I'm sure I can manage a quick dip no matter how icy, but since I don't relish the thought of a cold shave, I might use this as the excuse to grow the beard I've been considering."

"There is a small lake over on the other side of the

mountain that's fed by a hot spring, but it would be quite a walk."

"That sounds like it might be another of the unexplained oddities of Shadow."

"One of them," Tracy agreed, engrossed in checking her first aid kit one more time. She snapped it closed and turned. For a moment she stared at Adam, a half smile on her lips. "I wonder if it will be gray."

"What?"

"The beard."

"What beard?"

"The one you're going to grow."

"I was only teasing." He laughed as he shouldered his pack.

"I don't see why," she said as she did the same. "I think it would look most distinguished. Unless . . ." She gave him an impish grin and an enticing wink, then walked away.

"Hey! Wait." He rushed to catch up with her, sparing a quick look of admiration for her trim hips hugged so snugly by the heavy denim. "Don't leave me in suspense. When would my beard not be distinguished?"

"What beard?"

"The one I'm going to grow."

"Are you going to grow a beard, Adam?" She turned to look at him in mock surprise, a barely suppressed grin twitching her lips.

"Yes. A distinguished one, remember?" He was delighted as he fell willing prey to her quick tongue, loving the bright cheerfulness that lit her face.

"And maybe a red one."

"Red!" They had begun to move again, but now he stopped abruptly, an expression of absolute horror on his face. "A red beard?"

"Um-hm. The same color as Liza's hair. Gorgeous!"

"Gorgeous!" he choked on the word, watching Tracy as she climbed the slope, following a trail that was barely visible. As a low-hanging branch hid her from view, he started to chuckle, the sound quickly growing into a full, rolling laugh. "Where but on a crazy mountain like this would I find a woman who thinks I should grow a flaming red beard and calls it gorgeous?"

"Adam?" Her voice drifted back through the dense foliage of oak and evergreen. "Don't you think you look a bit silly standing by yourself on a mountainside talking when there's no one to listen except maybe a squirrel or a polecat or two?"

"Polecat as in skunk?"

"Would you quit stalling like a tenderfooted flatlander and come on?" Her voice was growing progressively distant. "I'm your leader, but I can't lead if you won't follow. Adam? Are you coming?"

"Coming, fearless leader. But I wonder if you'll be any more fearless than I if we do meet that polecat."

"Still talking to yourself, Adam?"

He gingerly pushed aside the prickly branch of a blackberry bush and found her waiting for him. She was leaning against a straight, skinny pine, her arms folded beneath her breasts, one foot crossed over the other. Dressed for the mountain and with her hair in its customary braid, she looked much as she had the first day he had seen her. Yet she was infinitely different.

Her aloof restraint had softened. A quiet spark of laughter and lightheartedness seemed to hover just beneath the surface. It had not been there when she had met him earlier that morning. She had been subdued and thoroughly efficient as she checked both his clothing and his equipment, from the high boots he wore at her insistence to the flashlight in his pack.

The change in her, slow and subtle yet clearly evident, was something to ponder. But for now he would simply appreciate it.

"Waiting for me, darling?" he said, teasing, giving her a slow, lingering look.

"Waiting and listening to you mutter."

"I was muttering, as you call it, to you."

"And what was it you were muttering to me?" She straightened from the tree, obviously enjoying the exchange.

"I was wondering if you would protect me with your wily woodsman's knowledge if we should meet with the aforementioned polecat."

"Sorry." She turned to continue up the trail. "If we meet one, you're on your own. I have a healthy respect for all wild animals, but the little creature in the striped suit strikes fear in the heart of any woodsman or woman, wily or otherwise."

"In other words, to put it bluntly, you'd run."

"Like a shot."

"Some leader you turned out to be."

"Wanna trade me in?" Climbing surefootedly, she didn't spare a glance in his direction.

"Not on your life."

"That's what I thought." This time her voice was softer, the hint of laughter gone. "Better save your breath, tenderfoot. The climb gets rough from here on."

"Yes'm." Adam applied himself to negotiating the twists and turns of the thorny, rock-cluttered path. It did, indeed, grow rougher and at times impassable. Agile and strong, a man used to strenuous and vigorous activity, he needed only to move with care. The pack on his back, heavy but well balanced, presented no problem, and his mind was free to roam to the woman ahead.

Tracy. She was an enigma, and Adam was intrigued by the multifaceted personality that was emerging. On the first day he had been struck by her cool competence and the studied confidence of every deliberate movement or word. She had met his anger with the understanding and kindness of a rare sensitivity. Then quietly, without fanfare or furor, she had traded one life for another.

He had shared with her the grieving for a loyal friend, Wolfe. And a lost friend, Sharon. In the deep of the night, buffeted and racked by loss, she had slept trustingly in his arms, only to disappear as quickly as she had come.

Tracy. She was a woman of many moods. He had been burned by the fire of her temper and cut by her truthful tongue. He had felt her kinship with his motherless child and watched her loving patience with the blind Opal. He had learned of her talent and her generosity with her carvings. And he had seen her fear.

When he had led her onto the dance floor the night before, he had also gained her trust. In the face of overwhelming self-doubt she had given herself into his care. It was a step toward the future, sealed by the kiss they had shared beside the brook.

Adam had no illusions that the way to his goal would be without its problems. Watching her that morning, seeing her mood lighten, he had been astounded by the effect the mountain had on her. At first he had doubted the strange thought that had begun to form in his mind. But now he believed. In some way Shadow was her confidence. Here she knew peace. For the first time he began to understand the strength of the hold Shadow had on her. A frown crossed his face. He nodded once slowly, then moved forward again.

At one point the terrain flattened into a small plateau before rising again. The trees nearer the crest had grown more stunted and sparse, offering a view of the gentle peaks of the flanking mountains.

"This is beautiful," Adam said as he stood by Tracy, gazing out at the panorama before him. For as far as the eye could see, rolling tree-covered lands stretched toward the horizon. "I don't see the valley and the village."

"We're on the far side of the mountain. The valleys to the east were never settled."

"Then we've been climbing around as we've climbed up."

"Right. The logging camp was about halfway up. That

was where we left the jeep. The path we took was used by the loggers as they came up from the sawmill."

"What did they log? This wood doesn't look like it would be worth the effort."

"It wasn't."

"Is that why the trail is so faint? It was never traveled much?"

"It was hardly used at all. Shadow didn't want them here. For every tree that was cut down, a man died."

Adam turned to her, shocked by the conviction in her voice. "You don't believe that."

"In the days before automation, logging was slower and harder. More men were needed. Nine trees were cut; nine men died. Finally no one would work here. The business ended before it was started. None of the trees cut were ever taken completely away from Shadow. The project was abandoned before they could be."

"Is that the basis for a legend?"

"Yes. The old-timers say that if you listen carefully, you can hear the sound of the axes. There's no sound in the world quite like that of wood being chopped."

"The axes are supposed to belong to the dead men, I suppose."

"They spend eternity cutting trees that never fall."

"Have you heard them?"

"Yes." She turned her back on the scene, facing the starkness of the mountain. "We'll be camping just beyond that patch of woods. There's a clearing there and the stream I told you about."

Adam rapidly took some pictures of the plateau for his book. The loggers and the faint trail that remained would be of interest to his publisher. Surreptitiously he also shot two photographs of Tracy. After replacing the lens cover, he put the camera away and shouldered his pack again. "Ready."

Tracy moved from the sunlight into the shade of the dark pines. Brambles and briars were thick on the ground, but a narrow path cut cleanly through them.

Adam was startled when, without warning, they entered a tiny clearing.

The land was perfectly flat. Grass, lush and green, carpeted the meadow. A wide but shallow and slow-moving brook wound and looped among the scattered trees. There was none of the raw starkness of the rest of the mountain that Adam had seen, and it didn't fit his image of Shadow.

"We'll cross the brook," Tracy said. "The best campsite is on the other side." She led him to the bank and they looked down at the sparkling water.

"Boy! You weren't kidding when you said this would be mostly rocks." Adam laughed as he surveyed the piles and clusters of smooth gray granite stones. "There's not a sharp edge here."

"Over the years the water has tumbled them about, wearing their edges smooth. There are rocks all along this stream, but for some reason more seem to have accumulated here."

"A legend?"

"None that I know of. It's just Rocky Creek. There's no significance to the rocks or the name, appropriate though it is." Tracy slipped free of her pack. "Let's cross and find the best spot to set up camp first. Then we can take our supplies over. We might decide that this would be best. I haven't been here in a while, and things do change in the mountains."

Adam gratefully shrugged off his own pack and flexed his shoulders. Feeling more cramped than tired, he stretched and muffled a yawn.

"Sleepy?" Tracy asked. "It's the altitude. It affects some people that way."

"I'm accustomed to the altitude," Adam contradicted her. "It's lack of sleep. I lay awake into the small hours of the morning thinking of you. Remembering how you felt in my arms as we danced, and how your lips trembled when I kissed you. Did you sleep well, Tracy?"

"I slept like the proverbial log," she lied, feeling his

gaze on her lips, recalling the power of his kiss. She turned away abruptly. "We'd better decide on a campsite soon. Sunset comes with little warning up here. I'd like to get set up and gather firewood while there's still light. It's safer that way."

"Rattlesnakes?"

"Among other things."

He lifted a quizzical eyebrow. "Such as?"

"Bears, mountain lions, raccoons, deer. Shall I go on?"

"I'll worry about the snakes and the bears and the lions, but why the raccoon and the deer?"

"They wouldn't hurt us, but both the 'coon and the deer are notorious for foraging in camping supplies. So are the lion and bear for that matter."

"Then we set up camp, do our chores, finish with our supplies, and before we turn in for the night we hang anything interesting by a rope from a high tree limb. Right?"

"You've got it. But let me warn you, an enterprising 'coon wouldn't be defeated by that." Tracy laughed. "Hopefully, one that hungry or just that curious won't find us."

Adam checked his watch, then looked at the sky, which had begun to darken. "If we plan to get all that done before nightfall, we need to get started, don't we?"

"Right. Maybe you'd better wait here while I go over to check the old campsite to make sure that it's safe. Rest a minute."

Tracy stepped carefully onto one of the many rocks that lay partially submerged in the crystal-clear stream. Scattered randomly through the water like hundreds of steppingstones, they formed a natural path to the opposite side. She was halfway across when Adam spoke.

"There's no need for me to sit here doing nothing. I'll come too.

"Adam. Wait!" She was turning around as she spoke. "These rocks are—"

Splash!

"—slippery."

Her last word was little more than a gasp. The water that showered over her head and shoulders was so frigid that she lost her breath. For an instant her lashes were weighted by the fine spray and she couldn't see. When she blinked the moisture away she was greeted by the spectacle of Adam sitting waist-deep in the swirling water.

He sat calmly, with one arm leaning against his bent knee. His face was blank, registering neither shock nor outrage. From his unruffled manner, one could almost believe that to be sitting fully clothed in an icy mountain stream was a common occurrence for him.

"Are you hurt, Adam?"

"No."

"Are you sure?"

"Positive."

"Then, I have to tell you"—she choked slightly on the words and her lips refused to obey her efforts at keeping a solemn expression—"that was the poorest imitation of a windmill I've ever seen."

"You think so, huh?" Adam still didn't move.

Her battle was lost. From only a hint of a grin, to a muffled chuckle, the laughter rose in her until it flowed over him. A happy laugh, a carefree laugh, and she was again the young, exciting Tracy of years ago.

Charmed by the lightning-swift transformation, he sat transfixed. His only reaction to her amusement was a good-natured grin. He didn't want to move, afraid that if he did, the moment would be lost.

"Oh, Adam." Her laughter rose and fell with each new breath. "You are truly an amazing man."

"I am?"

"Yes, indeed."

"How so?"

"No one else could carry this off with such dignity. The sitting, not the falling." Her merriment at last subsided, only to erupt again in a fit of giggles at the memory of his flailing arms and flying legs. She fought to regain her composure, then, striving for a serious tone, spoke with exaggerated gravity. "You do know that you'll be very uncomfortable if you don't change soon?"

"I know."

"You did bring a change of clothes, didn't you?"

"As instructed." He nodded but made no attempt to rise.

Tracy stepped carefully onto the rock that had been Adam's downfall and leaned over to offer him her hand. A puzzled look crossed her face as his gaze moved over her and his expression altered subtly. Still, he did not move, nor did he accept her help.

"Adam." She rested her hands on her hips and looked down at him sternly. "Are you going to sit there all day?"

"I might."

His tone was level, almost casual, but there was something in his eyes. A spark of hidden excitement? Tracy wondered, even more perplexed.

"Aren't you cold?"

"I really hadn't given it much thought." He looked down at the water as if just becoming aware of it. "I've been too busy admiring the view to pay it much attention."

"Oh, dear." Tracy's words were a low moan of realization. In her first concern that he might be hurt, then in the midst of her hilarity, she had given no thought to herself.

She had dressed that morning as always when climbing Shadow. Her clothing had to be durable, but also comfortable. A rough fabric that chafed or rubbed could become agony on the trail. Her heavy cotton shirt was both thick and soft and afforded the greatest protection, except when it was drenched. Now it molded and clung to her, leaving no doubt that she had forgone one article of clothing—the one that could cause her untold misery when she carried a heavy pack.

Tracy knew that Adam saw, beyond a doubt, that beneath her blouse she wore nothing.

"I—I'm sorry" she stammered, flustered by his stare. "It's just that with the heavy . . ." She stopped as his gaze again traveled over her.

"Don't apologize to me." His smile caressed her, deepening her embarrassment when she realized she had made no effort to turn away. "Seeing you like this makes falling in the creek worthwhile."

Something in his voice took her breath away as surely and as sharply as the cold water had. She turned and hurried heedlessly across the stones. "I'll check that site now. You can change while I'm gone."

When she reached the other side, Adam rose from the water, watching her as she walked through a patch of knee-high grass.

"Are you frightened, Tracy?" he murmured. "Or only confused?" Not until she had moved out of sight did he wade back to the bank to change and wait.

Tracy spent longer than she had intended in surveying the campsite, and finally ended up at a small tributary of the stream. As she tossed stones into the rippling water, her mind was filled with conflicting thoughts. She was at once disturbed by the unwitting display of her body and pleased that Adam had found her desirable.

She was astonished by the strength of her own surging response and wondered if she could cope with an attraction so powerful. After her words of caution the night before, she was dismayed to find his teasing on a sunlit day created the same tantalizing excitement as an intimate caress in the moonlight.

Trying to untangle her turbulent thoughts, she asked herself the inevitable questions. What part in her limited life was Adam destined to play? What of herself could she give to him and survive?

He was a virile man, one who had perhaps known many women, and had loved one deeply. A woman's body held no mysteries for him and yet . . . what was it about the way he looked at her? What was it she saw in his eyes?

In the peace of the meadow she searched in vain for answers. Only when dusk began to fall rapidly did she turn back to the stream. By the time she had recrossed the path of stones, her shirt had dried enough to restore her modesty. Tracy wished ruefully that her sense of perspective could be restored as easily.

When she stepped on shore, she saw that Adam had dressed. He was lounging against a large boulder, his face upturned to the waning light, his eyes closed. Nothing about him moved but the blade of grass between his lips.

Walking with her naturally quiet step, she had a precious moment to observe him. With a sudden clarity that brought the serenity that had eluded her, she realized that the answer to her questions lay in the future. She must for now simply accept what each day might bring.

"Are you all right?" His quiet words broke into her thoughts. Lost in them, she hadn't been aware that he had opened his eyes.

"What?"

"Are you all right?" he repeated as gently, his gaze filled with tender concern.

"I'm fine, Adam."

"Then hadn't we better make camp?"

"Yes." She forcibly drew in her wandering thoughts. "It will be dark soon. We'd better get a move on."

"Where to?"

"The other side." She tilted her head in mock earnestness. "That is, *if* you think you can make it."

"You just lead the way, darlin'," he drawled. "I'll be right behind you, taking every step you do."

"Good enough. Shall we?" She hefted her pack onto her shoulders, waited until he had adjusted his own, then, carefully picking her path, led him over the slick stones.

Darkness has fallen over the mountain by the time their camp had been set up and supper done. Adam had hoisted the remaining foodstuffs over a tree limb while Tracy washed the last of their dishes in the creek.

He was sitting before the fire as she tucked them away in her pack. "Doesn't it bother you?"

"What?" On her knees by the pack, she paused to look up at him.

"There's just the two of us here. The valley's a small community. Won't there be talk?"

"Why should there be?" She finished in one quick move, then sat down by the fire and looked into the flames. "I'm a guide and a tracker, simply doing my job. I've been alone in the company of men many times. As far as I know, no one's ever said anything. But"—she shrugged—"it wouldn't matter if they did."

"The liberated woman?"

"If doing what I enjoy to the best of my ability regardless of my sex means that I'm liberated, then yes, I suppose I am," she said, not looking away from the dancing fire.

"Do you act as a guide often?"

"If I like the person or the party, and if I'm not involved in something else."

He frowned at the thought of the possible danger in which this could put her. "How can you judge whether or not someone is trustworthy?"

"Mostly instinct."

"Then you're never afraid, not even of the mountain."

"I love this mountain. There's nothing evil here. She just demands more respect than the foolhardy realize."

"She?"

"Yes, Shadow's a woman," she murmured more to

herself than to Adam. Silence stretched between them again, but it was not uncomfortable.

A night bird called; a mountain lion screamed in the distance. Adam stirred and leaned toward the fire. "There's about one more cup of coffee left. Would you like to share it?"

"Yes, I would." She watched his strong profile silhouetted by the flames as he filled their cups and set the pot aside. Short dark hairs glistened on his wrist as he handed the cup to her. Their fingers brushed as she took it from him. Her free hand clasped his, turning it over to look at the callused palm. "A rugged hand for a photographer. You're very strong, Adam."

He turned his hand over to twine his fingers with hers and took a sip of coffee. "My photography takes me many places. I learned very early in my career that studio work was not for me. I suppose I'm a bit of a hunter, but my weapon is my camera. I have to be fit to go the places I do."

"Tell me about your work." Tracy was contented as she had never been before, simply sitting beneath Shadow's summit with Adam's hand warm and strong over hers.

"Mostly I've done adventure series, things like rafting down white water. I've been in the desert and the rain forest. Once I photographed an erupting volcano. Another time I flew with a hurricane-watch crew. Those were fantastic pictures that have been compiled into a book. Shadow will be a feature in my next one. It'll deal with strange and beautiful phenomena of America. I'll take the pictures, then write a short text on each."

"It sounds exciting."

"It has been."

"You've traveled a great deal and to some interesting places."

"Umm." He paused, then answered her unasked question. "Sharon traveled with me most of the time. If she couldn't go on the actual location, she stayed nearby. We were never apart for more than a few weeks, if that much."

"What did you do after Summer was born?"

"For a while I didn't take any long-range assignments. Later, she stayed with Sharon's mother. She still does if I have to be away for a time. I try to keep my absences short. As an only parent, I feel it's imperative that I spend as much time as possible with her. But I don't know what I would have done without Marjorie. She loves being a grandmother and she's been a life saver."

"Liza said you had a housekeeper."

"I do. Cora takes care of the house and the shopping. She watches Summer after school and on the weekends some. But when I'm away for long, I want a member of the family with her. It's important that she feel a sense of security."

"Security is a very necessary thing. She'll be the stronger for it." Tracy said no more as she tossed away the last of her coffee, then sat mesmerized by the dying fire.

Adam wondered if, perhaps, she spoke of a frightened young woman whose speech and memory had been impaired, and who had found her security on Shadow. He tightened his hold on her hand. "It's been a long day. Do you think we should build the fire up a bit, then turn in?"

"I am tired. I didn't know how much until now. I'll spread out the sleeping bags while you add the wood."

The crackle of the burning limbs, the faint smell of wood smoke that drifted on the breeze, and the welcome comfort of the soft sleeping bags slowly lulled them to sleep. Tracy had laid their bags on either side of the fire. After the climb they had welcomed the rest for their tired bodies, and a whispered good night was hardly finished or hardly heard as heavy lids closed with fatigue.

A soft, happy sound filled the meadow, floating like

the smoke on the playful breeze that still teased the leaves of the trees. It trilled through the air again, starting low, then rising to a gay, bell-like note. Adam bolted upright, pushing his sleeping bag aside.

"What was that?"

"Umm?" Tracy turned toward him.

"There must be a raccoon into our food. I heard him chatter." He looked up at the swaying bundle of their supplies. Nothing had disturbed it. There was no sign that anything had been near. "I must have scared it away."

"I don't think so. I mean, I don't think it was a 'coon. It was probably Alice."

"Who's Alice?"

"We'll know for sure in the morning if it was her. Good night, Adam." She pulled the cover up under her chin. Soon her even breathing told him that she had again drifted to sleep.

He sat as he was for quite some time. He scanned the trees and the clearing about them. There was nothing there. At last he lay back down, settling himself comfortably for the night. "Good night, my darling Tracy," he whispered. "And good night, Alice . . . whoever you are."

In a matter of seconds his breathing matched Tracy's. The stream babbled its way down the mountain. A rabbit feasted on the succulent grass, an owl hooted, a whippoorwill called. The bright flame of the fire sank to the red-gray hue of dying embers.

Somewhere far in the forest a sound rose and fell like the giggle of a happy child.

Six

The tantalizing aroma of coffee and bacon teased his nostrils. Adam woke slowly, not abruptly nor startled, but with an instant awareness of time and place. Rolling to his side, he watched Tracy as she tended the fire and the heavy pans that rested on the rack above it. By the frying pan a small pot gave off a cloud of steam.

Adam was completely captivated by her fresh loveliness, and by the memory of how she had looked the night before—like an Indian woman who saw to the needs of her mate. The thought that he might belong to her was infinitely satisfying. He stretched leisurely, folded his hands beneath his head, and allowed himself the luxury of listening, feeling, and appreciating.

"If you want this while it's at least edible, you'd better crawl out and hop to," Tracy called suddenly.

"Hop to?"

"It means, simply, that you'd better get busy, buster."

"Yes'm." Adam slipped from the sleeping bag, chuckling at the colorful idioms of the local speech.

Naked to the waist and on bare feet, he dashed to the stream and splashed water over his face and hands. Tracy watched him kneeling there with water gleaming like jewels in his hair and on his skin. Not one brisk move nor shivering breath escaped her rapt attention.

As he began to rise she quickly turned away and busied herself with the fire.

When he returned and huddled before its warmth, she was already dishing up the eggs she had scrambled. After he had shrugged into his shirt, she handed him the plate and cup.

"This looks terrific," he said eagerly. "I can't remember when I've been so hungry. What's in the pot on the fire?"

"Water for you to shave."

"Ah, then you've decided against my beard?"

"On the contrary," she said. "I think you would be quite handsome in it, even if it were red. I put the water on in case you decided you wanted it."

He rubbed his hand across his chin, grinning at the roughness. If it was a beard she wanted, she would get one. "Then for now I think I'll forgo the shave."

"Good." She deftly lifted the pot and tipped the steaming water over the campfire. "This should be completely cold by the time we're ready to move out."

This time Adam did the dishes in the creek while Tracy packed away their sleeping bags. These, too, were put out of the way of any curious roaming animals. They would spend the day ranging over the mountain, with Tracy showing Adam the interesting points of Shadow. Before nightfall they would return to this base camp. Though neither mentioned it, they each looked forward to being unencumbered by the weight of packs.

"That's the last of them. My dishpan hands and I are ready to go whenever you are."

"You don't make it a practice of doing dishes, I assume." Tracy grinned at him, eyeing his fingers, which were red from the cold water.

"That's what I have a housekeeper for at home. But in my work and in the wilds I've done my share."

"And quite well," she said, thinking how comfortably he had adjusted to the trek up the mountain.

"Thank you, my sweet. I do try." He bowed low in exaggerated servility that the wicked glint in his eyes belied.

"If you're really ready, what we had better try is to get started with this little jaunt. We have a lot of territory to cover today."

"Before we go, aren't you going to tell me about the sound we heard last night?"

"Alice was playing in the meadow. What we heard was her laughter."

"How can you tell and who the devil is Alice?"

"I'll show you on the way out of camp. But first, do you have what you need?" Tracy studied him carefully. The attire of a mountain man suited him well, enhancing his already rugged masculinity. As she appreciated Adam the man, she realized that only a fool would doubt his virile appeal. Her gaze slowly traced the long, lean lines of his body, then came to rest on his face.

His skin had grown darker in his days in the valley. When he smiled at her as he did now, he was a man of irresistible charm.

The promised beard was only a stubble of no discernible color. Tracy laughed aloud as she remembered his horror that it might be red. The sound broke her trance, and she became acutely aware that she had been staring at Adam.

Giving herself a mental shake and wondering why she found the sight of him so seductive, she forced her thoughts to the moment. "Do you have your knife and your canteen?"

"Both." For emphasis, he shook the canvas-covered canteen and his left hand came to rest on the hilt of the knife at his belt.

"Good. I have the first aid kit and some chocolate bars."

"What about lunch?"

She laughed again at his worried expression. "Hungry already, Adam?"

"After a morning of hiking in this rarefied atmosphere, I'm sure to be, and soon. If I grow faint from hunger, will you comfort me, darlin'?" The teasing in his voice did not reach his eyes.

Tracy quickly turned away for fear that he would read her thoughts in her face. Though she must speak of practical things, her mind was creating images of Adam, hard and strong, held against her breasts . . . but in desire rather than comfort.

"Don't worry." She fought to subdue a startling quiver of anticipation. "I won't let you starve. We should be back here by lunch. If not, the candy should suffice."

"Too bad. Suddenly, starving begins to have its merits. I was hoping to get your arms around me with less drastic measures, but . . ."

"Idiot!" Tracy smiled, glad for his lighthearted changing of the mood, his banishing of the serious note that seemed to lie beneath every flip comment. "If you've quite finished with your foolishness, we'd better move on, or we won't make it back by lunch."

She kicked at the dead fire with the toe of her boot. Once assured that there was no danger of a spark igniting, she faced him. "Shall we go, Adam?"

He followed her, observing that she also wore a sheathed knife at her waist, as she had the day before. When she wasn't wearing it, it was never far from her reach. Here on Shadow it seemed to have become an essential part of her. He wondered why.

"Careful," Tracy warned. "The rocks will be even slicker from the dew. Step exactly where I do. When we get to the other side, I have something pretty to show you. Ready?"

At his nod she stepped onto the low, flat rocks, picking her path very slowly and with meticulous care. Adam did as she had instructed, not relishing the thought of another dunking in the icy water. Precisely fitting his footsteps to hers, he joined her where she waited on the opposite shore.

She touched his arm lightly. "Look, Adam."

His gaze followed the direction her gesture indicated. The meadow was filled with clumps of tiny flowers, their purple and yellow petals drenched with shimmering dewdrops. There were hundreds of the small clumps clustered closely together.

Tracy had been guilty of understatement when she had called it pretty. The flower-strewn meadow was breathtaking, Adam mused.

"Beautiful," he murmured. "I've never seen anything like it. What are they?"

Tracy smiled, pleased that he found pleasure in something of Shadow. "These are Alice's flowers. They bloom in the foothills in the spring and some people call them Johnny-Jump-ups. But to those of us who live in the valley, they've always been Alice's flowers."

"Why?"

"Many years ago a small child lived at the base of the mountain. These were her favorite flowers. She would spend hours gathering them, then she wove them into chains to make bracelets and crowns.

"On an early spring day she was on Shadow gathering them when a terrible storm rose. There was thunder and lightning and a strong wind. Trees were blown over and small landslides obliterated the paths. Alice was lost."

She looked away from the multitude of flowers, wanting to see Adam's face as she finished the legend. "The mother was inconsolable, for Alice was her last surviving child. The old-timers say that they thought she would die from grief. Then one day as she wandered the paths her little girl had loved, she heard the laughter and saw the flowers, and her hurt was eased. Shadow had shown her that the child was happy here among the flowers. Everywhere Alice goes they appear, no matter what time of year."

To Adam, it was a beautiful story told by an even more beautiful voice. He knew Tracy wanted him to believe, but his practical mind could not accept the legend. As he adjusted his camera, he offered his logical argument.

"The temperatures we had last night were more like spring than summer or fall. That must have stimulated their growth out of season."

"Don't you see that the flowers are growing exactly where a small child's footsteps would fall?" It was her only hope of disputing his reasoning.

"Only a random pattern. Coincidental." Taking picture after picture of the flowers, he failed to see the flash of disappointment that crossed her face.

Tracy remained silent, waiting until he had taken all the shots he wanted. Why, she wondered, was it so important that he see Shadow as she did? Why did she need him to understand that Alice's flowers had been a gift of kindness? For this man to feel as she did about the mountain meant far more to her than anything had in a long time. But perhaps it was too soon. She offered herself this straw of hope.

When he put his camera away she moved silently on through the clearing. Careful not to crush the tiny, violetlike flowers, she led him to the path that would take them higher onto the peak.

It wasn't long before the gradual slope of the trail grew steeper and, at times, nearly impassable. There could be little doubt that few came here. Adam's muscles began to ache from the sharp incline, but Tracy showed no sign of tiring. Her pace was as steady as it had been at the first. She seemed to draw strength from the mountain, its ruggedness no obstacle.

The sun bore down on them intermittently as it broke through the rustling leaves of oak and poplar. At a point where the path widened, a small patch of color caught Adam's attention and he paused in his climbing.

"Tracy." His voice was low, but she heard him and turned back.

He was kneeling at the edge of the trail, his hands half hidden in the tall grass. She couldn't see what he was doing and took a step toward him. When he rose he was holding a flower, and he quickly walked over to her. Even standing on the downward slope he had to bend to her.

"Alice has been here too," he said. With deliberate care he slipped his fingers under the V of her blouse, then threaded the fragile stem of the flower through the buttonhole. The backs of his fingers brushed her bare skin, resting for a moment in the cleft between her breasts.

Intent on his task he bent nearer, his warm breath caressing her. Tracy wondered if he knew that he was touching her or if he was feeling any of the unfamiliar sensations that were exploding within her. Surely he could sense how feverish she had become and that her heart was racing like mad beneath his hand, leaving her drained of any will of her own.

When she thought she could stand no more, he finished his task and moved away, slipping his fingers slowly from within her blouse. Freed from his touch, her body was again hers to command.

Totally oblivious of his overwhelming effect on her, Adam looked down into eyes that had grown even blacker as she looked up at him in question. In innocence he misinterpreted her expression.

"It's a beautiful flower and a beautiful story. One doesn't have to believe the legend to appreciate it. I like Alice. She reminds me of you, for you both love Shadow." He smoothed a loose tendril of hair back from Tracy's face, then brushed her lips lightly with his. "Now, what's on the agenda of mysteries for the day?"

Shaken to the very essence of her soul by his inadvertent touch and light kiss, Tracy couldn't gather her wits. No thoughts, serene or deliberate, were forthcoming.

She was caught in a web of awakening desire that had little to do with reason or logic.

This wasn't the dark, despairing forgetfulness of the past, but speechless delight. The panic that lurked behind every forgotten word had no place amid what Adam offered. The sight of him was pleasing. His voice was soothing. His kiss was magic and his hands on her body brought enchantment. But now he only smiled down at her.

You were going to accept serenely what each day brought, she chided herself in that part of her mind that still functioned rationally.

"Tracy, darlin'." Adam touched her cheek with the back of his hand. "If you keep looking at me like you did at the dance, I might think you've begun to fall in love with me." His hand closed gently about her chin, then moved down to circle her neck. His arm rested against her full breasts. In a voice hoarse with hope, he whispered, "Have you, sweet Tracy? Do you love me?"

"I don't know." The words were low, murmured through trembling lips.

"Could it just be that here on Shadow you're more relaxed and your guard is down?"

"I've been on Shadow with men before. Many times." Though she offered no explanation, Adam knew that it had never before been like this.

He was almost certain that this Tracy did care for him. But once they left Shadow, would she grow aloof and distant? Would she again cloak her uncertainties in that calm deliberation that made her unapproachable? She had friends in the valley, friends who loved her, but no one truly knew her. Not Jed, nor Sarah and Ezra. Not the amazing Opal, nor even himself. But he would, he vowed. Somewhere in the reconciliation of the two Tracys he would find the whole woman.

And she would be his. He respected the mystique of the mountain even as he rejected it and knew he must go cautiously. What might be his for the taking could be lost, should he move too soon. He must have all of her—both the valley's Tracy and Shadow's Tracy.

A squirrel, impatient that they should move on, chattered fiercely and a smile lightened Tracy's face as she turned toward him. Adam chuckled at the almost comic figure that was glaring down at them from the gnarled limb of a tree.

"If I looked silly standing by myself yesterday, then the two of us must be a riot," he said. "Do you think that little fellow thinks we're crazy?"

"Undoubtedly," Tracy said. "We could be standing too near his cache of winter nuts. Something's making him distinctively nervous. Anyway, we should move on if we're to stay on schedule."

"Not just yet." Adam drew her to him. Holding her thus, he felt as if some part of himself—one that he had not known existed—had come home. No matter that he teased about standing so long and so still on the lonely trail, it seemed very right to hold her here on the face of Shadow.

Stroking her sleek hair, he looked up at the crest of the mountain barely visible through the leaves. Its hold on Tracy was strong and far-reaching. It was as a moving force in the life of this woman, whom Adam now realized he loved passionately and unendingly. As he stared at the bleak, rocky face of the peak, Adam mentally issued a challenge. *I must woo her from you, old woman. I must do it slowly and with infinite care. . . . but I will win.*

The squirrel chattered stridently and Adam put Tracy from him. "I think we'd better move on before the little fellow attacks us."

"You needn't worry. The natives are friendly."

"Tracy! Wait." He caught her hand as she had turned to continue up the trail. "Neither of us are fools. We both know that something powerful is happening between us. If we're careful and move cautiously, it could become a beautiful thing. But right now it's so explosive, the wrong move, the wrong word, could destroy it. Let's leave it for a while. Let it sit in the back of our minds and our hearts until we understand it better."

She stared directly into his serious eyes. "How do we come to understand it, Adam? And how do we keep it in the background?"

"We learn to understand it, whatever *it* is, by learning about each other. We keep it in the background by strength of will, and let's hope I have the discipline to do it."

"You can. You're a strong man, Adam."

"Not where you're concerned, Tracy. It won't be true strength that will keep me from you, but fear. I'm afraid I'll lose you before you're ever really mine."

"Then we must be very careful, mustn't we?"

"You do know, don't you, Tracy, that the real decision rests with you?"

"Yes. I know."

For the remainder of their climb their resolution was not mentioned again. While the sights and the tales of Shadow might have been uppermost in their minds, thoughts of their relationship, and what it might become, were never far away.

As they neared the top, Tracy veered onto a less evident trail, pushing her way through dense, unbending undergrowth. Suddenly the brush gave way to a clearer but still rugged path that led straight to the mouth of a cave. Mounds of dirt and loose rocks nearly obscured its entrance.

"Wait here while I check to be sure the cave isn't inhabited," Tracy said. "I'd rather not blunder in on a bear or a wildcat, or even a rattlesnake that might have set up residence since I was here last."

"I'll go with you," Adam said instantly.

"No!" Tracy was adamant. "If I need to move fast, I'd rather not have to worry about anyone but myself."

"Damn it, Tracy. If there's a chance you might be in danger, I should be with you."

"Please." She touched his hand lightly. "I'm accustomed to doing this sort of thing. You aren't. I couldn't bear it if I let you go in there and you were hurt."

"Then we'll skip it. I can get enough material for my book without risking that you might be harmed."

"No. I want you to see this. If you don't, the whole climb will have been for nothing. I've been in this cave many times, Adam. I'll be careful."

Tracy turned away, allowing him no chance to argue further. She agilely scaled the rocks, slipping only once as the dirt shifted under her weight. Before he could call out, she disappeared into the yawning blackness of the cave.

For what seemed like an eternity, Adam waited. The day was not hot, but drops of perspiration beaded on his forehead. Twice he looked at his watch. The hands had barely moved, but he would have sworn that an hour had passed. With his camera still slung over his shoulder, he paced back and forth before the gaping hole. With each step his worry grew until he was near panic.

Abruptly he turned. He had one foot on the mound of debris, meaning to go after her, when Tracy stepped from the darkness into the light.

"My God, darling! Are you all right? You were gone for so long, I was afraid you might be hurt."

"Adam." Her hand on his arm eased his agitation a bit. "You can see for yourself I'm perfectly fine. It's a fairly deep cave. It took me a while to check it out. I'm sorry. I didn't mean to worry you."

"I was coming in after you." Hearing the hoarse strain in his voice, she knew he was still far from calm.

"There was no need." She leaned forward to brush a pine needle from his hair. "There was truly no danger," she said softly, soothingly, "but I'm glad you cared."

Her fingers in his hair rekindled the very thing Adam had sworn to himself he would control. He wanted to snatch her from that pile of ugly dirt and draw her close against himself, to protect her from any harm. Instead, with fists clenched and teeth gritted, he willed his mind to accept.

This was Tracy's territory. She had lived here for many years. She knew the vagaries of Shadow. In truth, she was probably far safer here than anyone else would be. Still, he couldn't repress the insidious thought that in some way Shadow would take her from him. Adam knew he was being irrational, but his clear, orderly mind was helpless before this malignant fear.

"Tracy," he said finally, "I never meant to doubt your skill. I do understand that you know what you're doing. It's just that—"

"Hush, Adam." She laid a hand across his lips. "I know. Now, come with me." Lacing her fingers through his, she drew him up and over the mound, then into the cave.

By the time they had taken only a few steps they were engulfed in a pitch-black darkness that was totally unrelieved by any spark of light. Until his eyes adjusted from the brightness of day to the dark void, he could only follow where Tracy led. She moved carefully but easily through the cave.

"How the devil can you see?"

"I can't," she replied with a laugh. "I'm relying on memory."

"Do you mean to tell me that you came into this utter darkness not knowing what you might find, and you couldn't see?" Adam was quickly and fearfully angry at what he considered to be a foolish risk.

"No, Adam," Tracy said reasonably. "I had a flashlight."

"Then why on earth aren't we using it now?"

"Because I want the cave to be a surprise. Stop. Stay here for a second and close your eyes."

"Close my eyes in this? Whatever for? I can't see anything with them open."

"Please? Just do as I ask."

"Okay. If you insist, but what surprise could a cave hold?"

"You'll see. Are they closed?"

"As requested." Adam grinned in the darkness, thinking that she sounded much as Summer did when she shared a pretty rock or a wildflower with him.

"Don't move. I'll be right back."

Adam obeyed. He heard the soft sound of her step growing gradually fainter. Twice he heard the chink of glass bumping against something and twice he heard the rasp of a match being struck. There was nothing more until Tracy spoke from nearby.

"You can open your eyes now."

The sight that greeted him was astonishing. The sounds he had heard were the matches lighting two oil lamps. Their pale glow lit what appeared to be a small, comfortable room. The walls were dry and hung with intricate needlepoint designs. Handmade furniture that had been cut and fitted precisely, then rubbed and polished to a rich patina, was scattered about. Cushions of a heavy material were tied to the seats of the chair. Small, bright pillows added a splash of color. In the center of the table was a chipped glass vase of fresh wildflowers. On the dirt floor were colorful braided rag rugs. Someone had, with great care, created a home.

"I had no idea anyone lived on Shadow."

"No one does."

"Then why all this?" He gestured about the cozy room. "Someone has been here, and from the looks of the flowers, no later than yesterday."

"Are you sure?"

"Of course." He touched a flower with the tips of his fingers. "Good grief! These flowers have been preserved."

"Yes, they have, but naturally. They've been sitting on that table for nearly a hundred years."

"That's impossible."

"The tables and the chairs, even the cushions and the pillows are older than that. This is the cave of the MacLaren."

Adam was drawing his camera from its case and loading it with the proper film as she spoke. When he had made his adjustments and settings, he began to shoot rapidly and expertly, recording this room and its furnishings for his book. Once he touched a dirt wall, dusted off his fingers, then returned to his photographs. Finally satisfied that he had all he needed, he put his equipment away.

"Can you tell me about the MacLaren?"

Tracy nodded. "Come and sit."

"If the cushions are that old, won't we hurt them?"

"No." She waited while Adam laid aside his camera, then lowered himself cautiously into the chair beside her.

"If the MacLaren no longer lives here, does someone come to take care of it?"

"The only care any of us takes of it is to leave it alone."

"Who was MacLaren and why did he live up here on Shadow? Surely he would rather be in the valley among friends." As Tracy slowly shook her head, he leaned back into the surprising comfort of the old chair. Patiently he waited for her to begin her story.

"Nobody knew who he was, or when he came, or even where he came from. He was seldom in the valley, so no one knew how long he'd been here before they saw him. He shunned the company of others and rarely spoke. When he needed coffee or sugar, or any other staples, he came down off the mountain, wearing the tattered blue and green plaid of his clan. Children cried when they saw him, pregnant women hid their eyes, and even men turned away.

"He was a giant of a man and obviously very strong, but he was hideously scarred. The settlers in the valley speculated that he'd been burned and tortured, but no one ever really knew for certain. For years he lived here in squalor, with hardly the barest necessities, until he found his Laura.

"When he was checking his traps late one evening, he found her wandering in a heavy snow. She had no memory of who she was, except that her name was Laura. She couldn't remember where she had been or where she was going, but she must have been lost for a long time. Because of the constant glare of light on the snow, she was blind.

"MacLaren took her first to his cave, this cave. He treated her for frostbite, and then later for pneumonia. For two days he cared for her. When he realized he needed help, he took her into the valley to an herb woman. No one ever understood how he got her down the mountain alive, but he did. He stayed for days with the healer, doing exactly as she asked.

"Laura was conscious for short periods of time. She would cling to his hand and refuse to let him leave her side. When she lapsed into unconsciousness, she called constantly for Dougal. The people in the valley learned later that this was the MacLaren's Christian name."

Tracy shifted in her seat, looked slowly about the room, then continued with her narrative. "When Laura's fever finally broke, the MacLaren made his preparations to leave. She cried and pleaded with him to stay with her. At first he was adamant that he must go, then in the face of her tears, he relented.

"For three more days he stayed with her, baring his ugliness to those who came and went. He fed her, changed her bed, and brushed her long black hair. When he knew she was regaining her strength, he again made ready to return to Shadow. Laura didn't cry and plead for him to stay with her this time. Instead, she insisted that he let her come back to the mountain with him. He refused, and Laura told him she loved him.

"The legend says that he knelt by her bedside, stroking her hair with his big, mutilated hands. There were tears streaming down his face as he told her how ugly he was, and that when she could see she would hate him. Laura listened very patiently and didn't interrupt, but waited for him to finish.

"When he left her side and shouldered his pack, she watched him until he reached the door. Then she spoke for the first time since he had refused to take her with him."

"What did she say?" Adam prompted when Tracy paused.

'I've been able to see for the past three days, and you're the most beautiful man I've ever known.' "

"Surely he couldn't leave her then."

"No. He married her that very day, and when the snow melted and the trails were clear again, he brought her here. There were those who swore that over the next three years the MacLaren did change. Perhaps he wasn't as beautiful as Laura thought him, but he was less ugly.

"When the weather permitted he brought her down to the valley to shop, for dances, or simply to visit. Laura was a gay little thing, and even he began to fit in.

"Then in the dead of night, during a bitter cold winter, the MacLaren came down from Shadow without Laura. He carried a very small bundle in his arms. He stopped at Jenny Brown's house. When she answered his knock, he very gently placed the bundle in her arms. There were tears on his face and in his voice when he said, 'Keep her well until I return.' Then he turned and walked away.

"There was a tiny baby wrapped inside a delicate handmade quilt. She was dressed only in a nightshirt and a diaper. A locket was wrapped around her wrist. Jenny took her in and cared for her with all the love of a childless woman, and all the while she waited for his return. But no one ever saw him again."

"What do you think happened?"

"No one knows. Perhaps Laura was lost or taken and the MacLaren went after her. We do know that loving him as she did, she would never have left him willingly. We know, too, that he would search until he found her.

"Now Shadow keeps their home as they left it. Waiting for their return."

"But the flowers . . . it was winter."

"No one can explain that. Perhaps the MacLaren came back for a time in the spring, or perhaps . . ." Tracy shrugged and stopped.

Adam had listened spellbound; now he felt a need to move, to shake off the last sad note. As he walked about the room his gaze fell on the bright plaid and shiny wood of bagpipes. He didn't touch them. "His, of course."

"Yes. He played them for Laura."

"I see." Adam wandered restlessly again, then paused. "You never said what happened to the child."

"She was well cared for. Jenny Brown had lost all her children in an epidemic the year before. The baby was a godsend. She grew to womanhood, married, and had children without ever leaving the valley. She's still living, but she's quite old and completely blind."

"Opal."

"Yes."

Again, Adam prowled the room. Tracy watched but said nothing. Twice he touched the smooth dry walls of the cave, and once the floor. She heard him mutter, "It must be the dry air and the altitude that's preserved it so well."

Prudently Tracy offered no comment.

The trek back down the trail was easier and much quieter. Adam was withdrawn and introspective, as he had been since putting away his camera after taking a few last photographs of the cave, and Tracy was reluctant to break into his thoughts.

Lunch was a quick but hearty affair. Each ate with good appetite, then they stretched out side by side on a blanket Adam had spread by the stream. A pale sun bore down on them and the water sang as it rushed over its rocky bed. It wasn't long before Tracy drifted into a restful but light sleep.

The softest of caresses drew her from her dreams. When she opened her eyes Adam was leaning over her, his smile filling her world. "I always wanted to wake a sleeping beauty with a kiss. Or should I say lazy beauty?"

Tracy's mouth curved into a smile. "I think I've just been given a left-handed compliment."

"Of course. I'm left-handed, hadn't you noticed?"

"I've noticed."

"If you knew what I've been noticing, you'd consider getting up from your bed of leisure and getting on with the business of this trip. What have you planned?" he asked as he helped her up.

"There's one more thing I want to show you." Tracy folded the blanket and carried it back to the camp. "It isn't far, and the climb's not half so bad as the one to the crest. You needn't bother with refilling your canteen. There'll be plenty of fresh cold water."

"How long will it take to see it?"

"Not long."

"Another cave?"

"No."

"Another legend?"

"No."

"You aren't going to tell me, are you?"

"Nope."

"You do love a good mystery, don't you?"

"Don't you know that the way to a man's heart is through a good mystery?"

"Uh . . . I don't think you've got that quite right."

"Haven't I?" Tracy winked and set off across the meadow in the opposite direction from the one they had taken earlier. She skipped lightly over a stone, then began to whistle a happy, tuneless melody.

Adam stood as he was, gladness rising within him. Then he crossed the meadow after her.

Seven

"This is it?"

"Sure is." Tracy ducked her head to hide her grin.

"Do you mean you brought me all the way over the trail and through that infernal briar patch to show me another trail?" Adam loftily ignored her giggle at his use of one of Sarah's favorite words. "Even as trails go, this one is particularly nondescript."

"For heaven's sake, Adam!" Tracy scolded playfully. "Stop growling like a bear with a sore toe and take your pictures. You'll be glad you did."

"Do you promise?"

"I solemnly promise."

"I'll hold you to that. But I don't think anything will make me glad to have shots of that misbegotten place."

"Have I steered you wrong yet?"

"No."

"Then trust me."

"I do, darlin'. With my life." Adam grinned at her and began to photograph the path from varied angles.

Leaning against a large smooth boulder that dwarfed her, Tracy lifted her face to the light, absorbing the warm rays that filtered through the low-growing trees. Totally relaxed, with one foot firmly on the ground and the other resting against the stone, she listened to the familiar sounds of Adam at work.

With my life. His words were in the whispered sounds of the swaying pine and the rustle of the oak. The softest of smiles crept over her face.

Choosing his composition, judging the light and using shadows for contrast, Adam carefully photographed the terrain. The ugliness of the surroundings wouldn't matter; they would be interesting. He had only been gruffly teasing and he knew Tracy understood. In their time together on the mountain, an easy camaraderie had grown between them. More than anything he liked to see the slow, teasing smile light her eyes, followed by a low, husky chuckle. This was the Tracy of whom he hoped to see more, the one he feared he would lose when they left the mountain. Tomorrow was their last day, and a slow dread was beginning to build within him.

He swung his camera toward what had rapidly become his favorite subject. How many women, he wondered, could be so lovely or so desirable dressed in heavy jeans and a plaid hunter's shirt? Despite the boots that could not by any stretch of the imagination be called dainty, she seemed fragile. A smudge of dirt marked her cheek and a leaf was caught in the braid that lay against her breast.

His eyes were drawn to her slender waist, the narrow hips, then again upward to the full breasts that pushed against the soft fabric of her shirt. With each slow indrawn breath her shapeliness was evident. He was certain her breasts were bare, but the shirt was nothing if not concealing. The image of how she might look with it open, then discarded, was something of which dreams were made.

Two more shots, then he closed the shutter and quietly walked over to her. He lifted the braid and with its end he traced down her forehead to the tip of her nose. Tracy smiled but didn't open her eyes or move.

"You've been gathering leaves with your braid."

"Have I?"

"Just one, but it was quite fetching. Like an emerald clinging to black silk."

"Shadow brings out the poet in you," she said with a soft laugh.

"Not Shadow. You."

Tracy opened her eyes. Adam was leaning against the stone, looking down at her. "Am I fetching, Adam?"

"Very! Particularly with this smudge right here." With his thumb he brushed away the loose dirt. "There. Now you look almost presentable again. What would you do without me?"

"I don't know." The words were not a whisper, but they were said in such a low voice, Adam wasn't sure he understood.

He searched her face gravely, hoping against hope that he could believe what he saw. Shaken, his desire for her an almost tangible thing; he wanted desperately to draw her away from the stone, to hold her close, to make love to her. He wanted it as he had never wanted anything before, but he knew he mustn't. Instead he leaned forward, kissed her lightly on her upturned nose, then moved away.

"Do I get to see what's on this pitiful trail sometime today, or do you plan to become a lady of leisure, basking in the sun?"

Tracy instantly accepted his change of mood. Her expression was mischievous as she straightened away from her resting place. "I don't think that's the way any self-respecting leadee should speak to his leader. He might get left behind."

"Perish the thought. But, 'leadee'?"

"I didn't forget." She laughed at his frowning, questioning look. "I simply made it up."

Subconsciously Adam had tensed at her use of the word. Now he relaxed and his laughter joined hers. "You're a sharp little cookie, aren't you?"

"If you say so." Still laughing, she moved around him and up the trail.

Adam was unashamed of the sudden restriction in his throat. For the first time, Tracy had teased about her disability. Perhaps it was a sign that her paralyzing fear of its return was lessening. Perhaps she was one step closer to becoming the whole woman, a combination of the kind and generous tracker he had met in the valley and the enchanting, desirable Tracy he had discovered on Shadow. For her own happiness and his as well, he hoped he wasn't mistaken.

"Now who's standing about like a lazy layabout?" she called back to him. "If you want to see what's beyond here, now's the time."

"I believe my lady of leisure has become my fearless leader again," he answered lightly. "Never let it be said that this leadee didn't follow his leader into the rigors of yon dull, drab pathway."

"If that's some sort of quote, I think I missed something."

"Nothing to worry yourself about." Adam knew she didn't realize what she had said, that her teasing had been spontaneous. His step was buoyant as the spark of happy hope that had glowed faintly in his heart burst into full flame. With patience she would be his.

At the edge of the path, he stopped to stand just below where she waited. "You remind me of Summer when she has some surprise for me," he said. "There have been several times here on Shadow when I've seen flashes of the child you must have been. And each is more enchanting than the last."

"Just don't pat me on the head and call me a good girl." She wrinkled her nose, but her eyes held a light-hearted amusement.

"Never! But I would like to take you to bed and kiss you goodnight."

"Take?"

"Tuck."

"That's better."

"A slip of the tongue." Adam smothered a grin.

"Of course," Tracy replied airily, then turned and with a quick step raced to the top of the dusty track. From her lofty stand she looked down at him. "Now that you've managed to untangle your tongue, come on up. There's something I'd like to show you."

"Right behind you." As nimbly as she had, he scaled the rocky path and joined her on the ridge.

"Look." Tracy turned and extended her arm in a sweeping gesture.

Following the motion of her hand, Adam saw a part of Shadow unlike any he had seen before. At his feet lay a tiny valleylike hollow. Tall, lush grass undulated as the mountain breeze rippled over it. Except for the dusty track that wandered in and among the scattered trees, this place was as richly green as all else had been bleak and bare.

Adam reached for his camera as Tracy explained the hidden valley. "The Applachians are a mature chain of mountains and quite old. Most have rounded peaks and are densely covered by trees. Shadow was probably just like all the others until something happened—an earthquake, a massive landslide. Something nearly ripped her apart, defacing her, leaving her as we know her."

"Except this part."

"Yes. This small section was spared. From it you can see that Shadow was once a beautiful woman." Tracy turned toward him. "There's more. Would you like to go down now?"

"Okay." He slid his camera back into its case and took her hand. "Shall we?"

Like young lovers, they wandered hand in hand down the path and through this highland vale. The trees were tall and straight, the trunks of the hardwoods greater than a man's arm span.

"This is as far as we go," Tracy said as they rounded the last turn.

The trail ended abruptly at a sturdy wooden railing. When Adam stepped closer he was looking down into a deep gorge that was wild and untamed. A river of white water clawed and churned through the chasm, twisting and turning and taking with it everything that stood in its path. Even trees and boulders were swept away. With jagged cliffs and deeply carved walls, it was a primordial scene.

"This is how the world must have looked in the beginning," he murmured, automatically reaching for his camera.

"It's like time stood still," Tracy said, then, not wishing to distract him, she stepped away. She sat down on a flat stone that looked like a natural bench.

"Do many people come here?"

"Only an occasional hiker, or maybe a hunter. It's not exactly in the flow of traffic."

"Then why this guard rail?"

"Because even the valley has its share of foolish people who do foolish things."

Something in her tone disturbed him. He carefully set his camera aside and sat by her on the stone. Taking her hand in his and weaving his fingers through hers, he held her arm against his side.

Tracy looked down at his broad, strong hand and the lean fingers that had caressed her. "Maybe the altitude has gotten to us." Her laugh was wobbly and not quite believable.

"How so?"

"Already today you've compared me to a child. Then we spend the afternoon holding hands like a couple of teenagers."

"More of us should rediscover the child in ourselves, Tracy. And I like the feel of your hand in mine." Refusing to be diverted, he then asked softly, "What happened here?"

She would have drawn away from him, but he refused to release her. "The purpose of this trip was to show you something unique and beautiful, not to drag out old stories better forgotten."

"I'd like to know," Adam said gently, persuasively. He brushed his thumb over her wrist in a slow stroke that was as exciting as it was soothing.

The slight nod of her head was followed by a deep shuddering sigh as she yielded. "Years ago a careless young teenager wandered too near the brink of this ravine. Before she could catch hold or regain her balance, she slipped over the edge."

"You, Tracy?"

"Yes. I was seventeen and this was one of my favorite places. No one knew I came here and I could dream the dreams of a young girl."

"Were you hurt?"

"No. There's a ledge just below. Not so far down that the fall did more than bruise me, but too far for me to climb out. There were no plant or roots, and the soil was so hard, it might have been granite. My hands were the only tools I had. For what seemed like an eternity I tried to claw my way out."

A sound of distress rumbled in Adam's throat. He had no need for her to tell him of fear and desperation, or of torn nails and bleeding fingers. His hand tightened protectively around hers.

"There was no use in calling out. No one would have ever heard. It could've easily been days before I was found . . . or even never.

"When I was exhausted, when I thought there was nothing left for me to do, I found the knife. It was wedged between two stones at my feet. It was old and rusty, but the most wonderful thing I'd ever seen. Using it to make handholds, I literally carved my way up the face of the cliff."

She lifted her head, her eyes meeting his for the first time since she had begun her story. Memories of the terror were as vivid as if it had happened a day ago.

"Oh, God." Adam drew her to him, holding her close,

resting his head against hers. "Sometimes I wonder how you've survived this monster."

"Shadow's no monster," she said firmly. "What I needed she gave to me. She always has."

Accepting, for now, Adam said no more. His hands moved gently over her back, stroking her braid down to her waist.

Tracy's arms stole about him, her fingers caressing the hard swell of his muscles. Her head rested against his heart and her disquieting memories were tempered by its steady beat. The trauma and the fear of that experience still had the power to unnerve her. Except for the accident that had very nearly taken her life and mind, it had been her closest brush with death.

"I wonder if Shadow would give me what I need?" His voice was deeply resonant in her ear.

"And what might that be?"

"A kiss."

"Perhaps Shadow wouldn't, but I will. But what of our resolution?"

"Resolutions were made to be broken," he muttered as he tilted her chin so he could look down into her face. His eyes had grown smoky with desire and he leaned close to her. "Kiss me, Tracy," he murmured against her lips. "Kiss me as if you mean it."

Tracy needed no other invitation. Her arms closed tighter about him, her fingers crumpling the fabric of his shirt. Her lips parted eagerly, even as he was seeking the sweetness of her mouth. Resolutions were, indeed, made to be broken and cast to the wind, she decided, as she and Adam joined together in a wild enchantment.

Adam's hand slipped slowly from the scar down her body. At her breast he paused to brush lightly over its fullness, then with shaking fingers he unbuttoned her shirt. His hands slipped inside and closed over her warm flesh. With a soft sigh Tracy moved instinctively to give him free access to her body.

A joy like none she had ever known surged through

her at his first intimate touch. His hands were a sweet caress to the ache growing inside her. Sweeter still were the softer touch of his lips and the rasp of his tongue as he kissed a proud nipple. Her fingers laced through his hair to cradle him to her, to offer him herself.

He moved away from her with deliberate slowness, his eyes seeking hers. Never looking away, he traced the contours of her face with his fingers, lingering at her trembling mouth. He drew her close and kissed her gently—once, twice—then moved away again. His thumbs met at the base of her throat where her pulse beat raggedly, then he slid his hands down her bare skin. As they closed reverently over her breasts, he stared at her intently, needing to know that her desire matched his. He was rewarded by a sudden flaring in her dark eyes and a soft sigh. A shiver of delight rippled through her body and her breathing quickened. Then, as he caressed the sensitive breasts, she drew in a sharp breath.

"Tracy?" He drew back quickly, his eyes seeking what his fingers had found. Small red marks marred her dusky skin. "My beard! I hurt you! Why didn't you tell me?"

Tracy looked down at herself in surprise, feeling no shame that he was looking hungrily at her even in his concern. "I—I didn't know."

"Damn beard! I'll shave it first thing when we get back to camp."

"No!" She rubbed the coarse stubble with the palm of her hand. "It'll soften as it grows. You didn't hurt me, Adam. Really, you didn't."

"Perhaps not." He drew the edges of her shirt together and began to button it. "But I would if we continued as we were."

"Adam?" She looked at him with such pleading that his resolve was almost destroyed.

"No, love, not yet. This is a special place for you; you're feeling the backlash of your memories. I offered comfort and, perhaps, security, and you're grateful. I don't want gratitude from you, Tracy. It wouldn't be enough."

She remembered her own words from the night of the dance—that it was too soon, that their emotions were in turmoil—and realized that he was right. She was almost sure she could cope with having the little that could be hers before Adam left Shadow. But almost wasn't good enough. She must be certain, or this could destroy her.

"If you're ready," he said, lifting her face to his, "now that I have my sanity restored, what's next for the day?"

"Nothing on the legends," Tracy whispered, still in the grip of her own emotions. "But there's a place I'd like to check before we go down to camp."

"All right," he agreed.

"I should warn you, it'll be a long hike and there's nothing you could use in your book." She paused. "Maybe I should leave it for another time. I could, you know."

"Shh, Tracy love. Just who is it that you're trying to discourage? Yourself or me?"

"A little of both, I guess," she admitted ruefully.

"You obviously do want to see this place, or you wouldn't have brought it up, and I don't mind, so what's the problem?"

"Not anything, I suppose." She stood up, feeling lost without his touch. "We should leave now if we expect to make camp by nightfall."

The only visible signs that the old derelict had once been a home were part of a roofline and an old stone chimney that was still standing. Tons of rock and dirt had been torn away from the mountain and buried it. A flower bed in what had once been the yard had been weeded. Though no one lived there, someone still came and cared for the area.

"I had no idea that anyone had lived on Shadow so recently," Adam said. "Did you know them?"

"I lived here," Tracy answered. "With Grandfather."

Her tone was perfectly level and completely emotionless, but Adam could feel her loss. "When?"

"Three years ago." She stared at the ruin that had been her home for many years. "He's still there. I like to think he's sitting in his favorite chair where he sat every evening." With a faraway look in her eyes she gazed up at the mountain. "He would've been resting there when the mountain came down on him."

"Then Shadow took your grandfather?"

"No. She *kept* him." Tracy turned away. With her back to the cabin she relaxed. "He was very ill, Adam. He had been for quite some time. For the last year he was in almost unbearable pain. At first the drugs helped some, but he'd reached the stage where they no longer did anything. He never complained, but each day was a great agony. So Shadow gathered him to her and ended his suffering."

"You still miss him." Adam didn't need to ask. He simply read her face.

"Yes." She summoned her strength and faced the cabin again. "I'll always miss him. He taught me all I knew as a child. Then he became my courage and my salvation after the accident. But I could let him go, Adam. He'd lived a full, happy life. By sheer willpower he had stayed with me longer than we expected he could."

"Where were you when it happened?"

"He'd sent me across the valley to the workshop. He wanted me to do a carving that day. I think he knew what was coming, and he was ready. He felt I'd recovered enough that he could leave me."

"The workshop wasn't here?"

"It had been for a long time. Then he had an inexplicable desire to move it away from Shadow. He gave me no reason. He simply wanted it moved. I'm sure he knew the slide was coming and was saving his carving tools for me.

"The cabin and buildings at the other side of the valley

had been his. He lived there until my grandmother died; then he came to Shadow."

"Have you ever thought about returning yourself?"

"No. When Wolfe and I left here, I knew that I would never live on Shadow again."

"Where is Wolfe now?"

"He's here with my grandfather." Tracy turned toward a pile of small stones. "I brought him back to the person and the place he loved best. Wolfe loved me and took care of me, but he was truly the dog of the Forest Walker. They were two of a kind. Grandfather left him here only to watch after me a bit longer. Wolfe saw me through my grief and helped me accept Grandfather's death. He had been tired for a long time."

Adam took her cool, dry hand in his. "You've been fortunate in many ways."

"I know." Her fingers clung to his, but she said no more.

He waited patiently, watching her carefully. He could almost read her thoughts as she looked once more at the cabin, then at the grave of the dog, then at the flowers. He knew she had planted them. He could see her love in each blossom.

"Are you ready to return to camp?"

"Yes." She clasped his hand more firmly in her own. "I'm ready."

The sun had begun to sink beyond the mountain when they arrived back at the meadow. The stones in the stream bed glistened with the fresh moisture of the cool day. Tracy again instructed Adam to follow her path, stepping exactly where she did as they crossed.

With the ease of experience she crossed without mishap. Adam was not so fortunate. When the opposite shore was nearly within his reach, his foot slipped. Amid an inelegant waving of arms and a frantic search for firm footing, he fell with more splash and less dignity than before.

"Adam! Not again!" Tracy put her hands on her hips. "This is becoming a habit. Too busy protecting your cameras to catch yourself?"

"So it would seem," he replied dryly.

"Are you hurt this time?"

"Only my pride."

"Then aren't you going to get up?"

"Not for a minute." His gaze moved over her slowly. Instinctively, though she knew she had been well beyond the reach of the scattering water, she looked down at her shirt.

A flush spread over her cheeks as she realized that Adam had read her thoughts. To hide her embarrassment she said quickly, "Are you going to sit there all evening?"

"No."

"Then what on earth are you doing?"

"I'm thinking."

"You *like* to sit in cold water to think?"

"Shh. I'm creating a legend."

"A legend!"

"Um-hm. One that says when a flatlander photographer falls into the creek for the second time in two days, he must sit there until he's kissed by a pretty, dark-haired woman."

"Adam, don't be ridiculous. Get up before you freeze."

"Can't."

"Come on. This isn't a joking matter. You might catch cold."

"I'm not joking. The legend says I can't get up until you kiss me."

Tracy's suppressed laughter broke free. "I think Shadow's finally gotten to you."

Adam only smiled, crossed his arms over his chest, and waited. Water swirled and eddied about him, but he paid no attention to it.

Accepting defeat, Tracy walked back across the stones. When she reached him she sat on the one closest to him. Without a trace of a smile she cupped his cheek in her palm and touched his lips softly with her own. Drawing back, she brushed a strand of hair from his forehead and regarded him intently. She whispered his name as she leaned forward to kiss him again.

Her mouth was warm and seeking against his. Her tongue caressed him fleetingly, like rough velvet, then she moved away. Her eyes never left his as she rose and held out her hand.

Adam was as bemused as she as he accepted her help. Together they crossed the stream to the campsite.

For the first time since they had come to Shadow, Adam could see that Tracy was tired. Though she didn't limp, she did move her right leg carefully. At supper her hand had trembled so badly, she had put down her cup and hadn't take it up again. She disappeared for a quick bath and shampoo in the stream, and by the time she reappeared, wearing her sweatsuit, and with a towel wrapped around her hair, she moved with a marked slowness that worried Adam. Strain showed in her face and dark smudges had appeared under her eyes.

While she'd been gone Adam had built the fire to a strong, warm blaze, for there was the promise of fall in the night. He was concerned that the toll of the day, both emotional and physical, might make her easy prey for a chill.

"Hi," he said as she approached the fire. "Feeling better?"

"Much. It always helps to wash away the trail dust."

"Come sit by the fire." He patted the sleeping bags he had spread out side by side while she'd been gone.

If Tracy considered it strange that they would not be sleeping as they had the night before, she made no comment and sat down beside him.

"Are you warm enough?" he asked in a voice low with worry.

"The fire's nice. I'm very comfortable, Adam."

"Then rest, love. I'll be back before you know it." He gathered up his own soap and towel and quickly disappeared in the direction Tracy had come from.

Long after he had gone she sat staring into the fire, fascinated by the dancing flames. Her thoughts were on the day and Adam. She remembered how he had looked kneeling by the stream in the early morning light, how he had likened her to Alice, and his gift of a flower. Even now it rested, safe and protected, in her first aid kit.

She remembered, also, his worry for her at the MacLaren's cave and his lovemaking at the ravine. *With my life.* The phrase leaped into her mind, softening a bit of the tired strain in her face.

"Tracy?" Adam stood across the fire from her. His chest was bare, the curling black hair showing none of the silver she had expected. His fresh dry jeans were beltless and rode low over his lean hips. His dark skin seemed darker still because of the pristine white towel hanging about his neck. His eyes still held the same caring concern she had seen at the cabin and by Wolfe's grave.

"I'm all right, Adam," she assured him. "I'm only tired."

With a start she realized she'd made no move to take the towel from her hair, nor to comb out the tangles. How long, she wondered, had she been staring into the fire thinking of Adam?

"You're sure?" he asked.

"Absolutely." To prove her point, she unwrapped the towel and shook her hair free, then began combing it.

"Wait." Adam quickly shrugged into a lightweight sweatshirt. "Let me."

He settled himself behind her, drawing her back between his bent legs. He took the comb from her and carefully worked through each tangle. Once he left her to stack more wood on the fire, then returned to his self-appointed task. Long after the snarls had been controlled, he continued to comb the flowing strands in long sweeping strokes.

Tracy grew visibly less tense and more rested. When her hair was dry, Adam put away the comb. With his fingertips he began to massage her temples, then down her jaw to the base of her neck and across her shoulders.

"Mmm, nice."

"Always at your service, my lady." The pressure of his touch remained unchanged as he worked the corded muscles of her neck. Only her soft sighs of pleasure and the crackle of the fire could be heard.

Tracy was never really aware of when it changed. She never knew when the contentment became a wild longing. Suddenly she desperately wanted him to answer the surging cry of her body. More than anything in her life, she needed Adam.

But could she love him and let him go? Could she return to her cloistered life unscathed if she listened to her heart? Could there be life for her after Adam?

"Better?" His voice broke into her thoughts and when she looked at him, she knew her decision must come soon.

"Yes. Much better. Thank you."

"You seemed so far away. What were you thinking?"

"I . . . Not really anything." She hated to dissemble, but would he understand the direction of her thoughts? Did she understand?

She leaned forward and picked up a large chip of wood. Without thinking, she reached to her belt for her knife. Old habits died hard. In the past when she had been troubled, she'd turned to the soothing and restful carving. If the strength in her hand seemed in danger of faltering, as it did tonight, she denied its weakness by plying her knife. In concise strokes, she created from the chunky block of wood a crude but delicate flower. It would take hours for it to become the finished product, but for now it was simply her therapy.

"Alice's flower?" Adam asked.

"It will be, but not for a while yet."

"It looks good already to me."

"The shape is barely there," she said with a slight smile.

"This is the knife you found on the ledge."

"I've kept it with me since that day." she continued working the wood with the knife, but twice she nearly dropped it.

"Let it go for the night, darling." His hand closed over hers, stopping it. "It's late. Why don't we turn in? We're making an early start in the morning, aren't we?"

Tracy sheathed her knife and put away the flower. "You're right. Tomorrow will be a long day."

He kissed her lightly on her cheek, then stood and smoothed his sleeping bag.

"Adam." She waited until he looked at her. "I am tired, but it's been a nice day."

"A beautiful day," he agreed, but knew that she had been the beauty of it.

Eight

The fire had died to dusty gray embers and still Adam was awake. The night was clear and through the trees he could see stars that seemed near enough to touch. The sounds of the forest had grown strangely muted in the thickening dark. Only Tracy, who lay close by him, was reality.

"Adam?" His name, as she said it, was a beautiful sound.

"I thought you were asleep."

"Only resting. You haven't slept?"

"No. I was watching the night."

There was no answer, only the slow, even rise and fall of her breathing. He wondered if she had at last fallen asleep.

"I've been meaning to thank you." Her voice filled the darkness.

"Thank me?" He turned his head to look blankly at her. "For what, Tracy?"

"For not judging me as others have. You knew of the accident and the rumors, yet you never condemned me."

"I wish that were completely true. I'm afraid I have my feet of clay too. I had my doubts. Don't you remember? I acted like a thirty-six-year-old child."

"You mean about Jed." The day at the post office and Adam's strange reaction rushed through her mind.

"I thought you might be his mistress."

"What changed your mind?"

"You did. You told me quite bluntly that you belonged to no one, and that there was nothing but friendship between you."

"Just like that? You believed me?"

"Yes."

Tracy was quiet for a long while, savoring the gift of his trust, yet wondering how he had dealt with her past. "Have you been curious about what happened years ago?"

"At first I was," he admitted truthfully, "but when I learned your grandfather's identity, I understood."

"So you know about my parents?"

"Anyone who's ever been involved in the movie industry knows their story. The young actress, daughter of a prominent filmmaker, who was becoming a person of note in her own right. Her love for a man of Indian descent, the son of a famous artist, one who had little use for the trappings of her public life. They married, and though she still made an occasional film, she was never a part of the Hollywood scene. Then ten or twelve years ago they perished together in a private plane crash." Adam shifted restlessly. "We all knew their story, or thought we did. Nobody ever knew there was a child."

"I was a well-kept secret. Mother had grown up being so constantly in the public eye that she wanted to protect me from it. We lived here in the valley, where I spent a happy, uneventful childhood, free of the circus atmosphere so many show-business children face."

"Yet you became an actress yourself."

"I was young and impressionable, Adam. I had this glorious idea that I would continue in my mother's footsteps, but without the benefit and help of her name. I chose to use my middle name for anonymity."

"Why wasn't your identity revealed later? It could've

answered so many of the rumors. The public would've understood that your relationship with the producer was innocent, that he was your mother's brother."

"At first those who knew were more concerned with whether I would live than with the gossip. When I started to recover it was too late to bother. The furor had died down and no one wanted to stir it up again for any reason. We simply lived from day to day, and when he could, Grandfather brought me back here to Shadow.

"The valley people knew about me, and they understood. It was all that mattered—until you came." Tracy's voice trembled and broke on the last words.

"Come here." Adam lifted her, bag and all, to bring her closer to him. She made no protest, but quietly accepted the warmth of his embrace.

"Comfortable?" he asked.

"Mmm." Tracy moved closer into the curve of his shoulder. "But are you?"

"How could I not be when I have you in my arms?" He smoothed a strand of hair from her face with his lips. "You say the people of the valley understood about you. Did they understand the aphasia?"

"Not at first. Grandfather explained to them what it was, how it would affect me, and what my recovery would be like. They learned even more by being with me and listening to me. I'm sure I tried their patience, but no one was ever unkind to me."

"Still, it must've been terrible."

"It was. I won't deny that. It was painfully frustrating, and above all, frightening. I was a prisoner of my own mind. I knew what I meant, what I wanted to say, but the words wouldn't come. Even with the speech therapy and the physical therapy, my progress seemed slow. I would've given up without Grandfather and Wolfe.

"Each day, with their help, the words became less elusive. With the carving my hand grew stronger. On my walks with Wolfe my step became surer. Gradually the agnosia faded. I relearned the landmarks and he had to lead me home less and less often, until finally he became my companion rather than my guide.

"I'll never be as strong on the right side as I was, and I'll always have to speak slower, but I'm considered to be recovered. I've stabilized at this level, and I'm fortunate. Some aphasics never recover at all."

By habit, Adam's hand had found the scar. His fingers brushed over it absently, then down the white streak of hair that met it. "Do you think that the concentration the carving required might've stimulated your thought processes?"

"That's my reasoning, though the doctors have never ventured any sort of opinion. Their only comment is that due to some circumstances I've achieved an amazing recovery, far better than they ever hoped for."

"Over the years you must've accumulated quite a number of carvings."

"I have a veritable workshop full of them," Tracy said with a pleasant laugh. "They range from worse than the flower you saw a while ago to those displayed at the dance."

"I'd like to see them."

"They're at the cabin, but you can see them whenever you like."

"Few people outside the valley ever see them, do they, Tracy?"

"No."

"Why not?" he asked gently. "Why won't you share your talent? To have something as beautiful as one of your carvings would bring one a great deal of pleasure."

"I've shown and sold a few pieces in the past. Grandfather's needs were simple, so he kept very little of what he earned over the years. When he became so ill and the bills mounted, I sent a sampling of my carvings to the gallery where you saw 'A Vixen at Play.' They earned enough to keep him as comfortable as possible for as long as he lived. That was enough."

"Talent such as yours shouldn't be kept hidden," he

said, his tone almost clipped. "If you won't sell any of them, why won't you at least show them?"

"I can't." Tracy pulled away from him and sat up, staring into the dying coals. "I have no desire to spend long hours confined in a gallery."

"You wouldn't have to be there." Adam leaned forward to sit shoulder to shoulder with her. "The artist needn't be present when the work is shown."

"No! I couldn't do that! Each piece represents the regaining of some part of myself. They aren't just blocks of wood that've been whittled into some cute, little shape." Tracy's bitter tone matched her expression. "I couldn't just send them for strangers to stare at and not understand what they mean. I couldn't stand for them to be gaped at. It would be too much like baring my soul to the world."

"Tracy, Tracy." He rested a comforting hand on her shoulder. "No one could look at your work and feel as cold as that. Show the carvings. Come and watch the faces of those who see them. I think you'll be surprised at the emotions you inspire."

"No!" She shrugged his hand away. "That's impossible. I'm not leaving here for any art show."

Adam was startled by her vehemence. She was wrong and he knew it. She had no concept of the power of her own work. In time he would show her, he promised himself. He would share with her the pleasure of knowing her artistry was appreciated and treasured. Someday he would, but not yet. As with his love, this, too, would take time.

"Come, love." He firmly drew her stiff, resisting body back into his arms. "We won't speak of it anymore!"

Slowly, with a soft sigh she relaxed against him. Neither knew how long he held her. The last glowing coal had long since died and the sky had begun to brighten with the hint of false dawn before Adam spoke.

"Tomorrow we go the other side of Shadow."

"Yes. Many of her legends are tinged with sadness. Tomorrow I'll show you a happy one."

"Will the trail be difficult?"

"Yes."

"Then we both should get some rest."

"I know."

Neither moved. Adam was reluctant to relinquish her even for the needed sleep. Tracy had found a comfort in his arms that nothing could match.

"Could you sleep now?"

"Perhaps."

"If I hold you, could you?"

"Yes."

Adam pulled the rumpled sleeping bag around them and leaned farther back against his makeshift pillow of clothes. Tracy's long body curled into his longer one. Her head was pillowed by his chest. Before sleep overtook him, Adam sensed when she slipped into drowsy oblivion. He smiled to himself in the darkness, thinking how well she suited him in every way.

Five lonely and anguished days later Adam climbed Shadow again, alone. The path was as he remembered, climbing slowly upward in a crazy, distorted angle. It meandered around bends and by precipices for two miles, always obliquely rising. In direct contrast to the other side of Shadow, with its rocky slopes, this way was steeper and dotted by cliffs. Small chasms lined by shattered rock broke the trail repeatedly, forcing travelers to use an indirect route.

He was heading for the waterfall that Tracy had shown him that last day, drawn to it irresistibly. It was like a long, gleaming ribbon and could easily be seen from a great distance. It leaped from a high cliff and fell several hundred feet, then rushed again down the mountain. An outcropping of massive stone on the face of the cliff split it apart, channeling a small stream away and down a separate slope. Leaping from stone to stone in gentle cascades, it fell to a basin in a small plateau of its own.

The clear lake it formed was framed by stone worn smooth with age. The fronds of giant ferns dipped their leaves in rippling water that reflected rhododendron, tall and stately in their antiquity.

Tracy had laughed with childish delight at his speechless wonder when he had first glimpsed the lake. Again he had been reminded of the difference between this lively mountain woman and the remote valley woman. When they had left Shadow later that day, he had waited in dread for the reappearance of the aloof, withdrawn Tracy. He had watched for the calculated moves and the precise words, but they never came. She had, instead, remained the lighthearted woman who recognized her disabilities, but was not afraid. Even as they had bumped across the valley floor in her jeep, she had been the woman he'd discovered on Shadow. Adam had been exultant in his certainty that he had won.

After depositing him and his equipment at his cabin door, Tracy had blown him a kiss, waved jauntily, and left him.

In the days that followed, he had waited impatiently, listening for her familiar step on his porch. He had tried not to give in to the feeling that he had lost her, and today, frustrated and angry and restless from inactivity, he had come back to Shadow. With cameras and supplies he struggled toward the lake, intending to appease the caldron of seething emotions with work. Today he would continue alone the study that with Tracy had been exciting. More than once, when limbs slapped and briars clawed, he cursed himself, his cameras, and his own fertile mind for undertaking this project. Who was he to wrest from the mountain its secrets? How could he expect it to yield to him?

Another branch snapped back to graze his cheek above the beard. A sharp expletive broke from him, and again he wondered what he was doing there. He was a flatlander photographer who should stick to level ground. His legs ached, and he was hot and tired and irritable, his mood even blacker than when he had begun. Gradually the sharp incline began to lessen. Adam dodged under one last low-hanging branch and stepped into the clearing. He lowered his equipment to the ground, noting how the clear water sparkled in the bright sun and the echoing roar of the larger fall enveloped the plateau in a cocoon of muted sound.

As he swept this secret paradise with his sharp gaze, Adam realized that it was here that he had first seen the mountain through Tracy's eyes.

Beneath her harsh exterior, Shadow offered too many places of secret beauty to be ugly. But could he reconcile himself to the legends? He thought of the cave of the MacLaren, waiting safe and undisturbed; a rock-covered cabin where an old man's suffering had ended; an old and rusty knife that had saved Tracy's life. A soft smile replaced his scowl as he bent to pick a tiny flower. When he straightened he could almost believe he heard Alice laugh.

A splash of scarlet caught his attention. Barely visible at the foot of a huge boulder was a blanket. Stacked neatly on it were a sketch pad and charcoal. Eagerly he searched the shore and pathway for Tracy. Thinking that she might have scaled the rocky face of the wall to the top of Indian Maid Fall, he scanned the rock that jutted and tilted to form a natural stairway. The summit was deserted and only the sound of the falls broke the silence. His gaze was drawn downward, following the path of the water. It was then he saw her.

From beneath the fall she emerged, stepping lightly from one slippery stone to another. She stood poised before it, more a fairy creature than real. The rising mists of the water met the midday sun, wrapping her in a rainbow. Her long black hair fell wet over her shoulder and one bare breast. With a slow, leisurely brush of her hand, she flicked it back and in a fluid, arching dive cut cleanly through the lake water.

Adam walked to the water's edge. He watched spell-bound as she weaved her way in and out of the sunken rocks. Appearing, vanishing, reappearing, she had become a dusky-skinned mermaid, seductive yet strangely innocent.

A gentle splash and a quiet laugh sounded as she surfaced. Her arms flashed brown and strong as she swam to a large stone that hovered at the moss-covered banks. She shook back her hair as she rose from the water, then stepped onto the flat granite.

For a lingering moment she smiled down at her own image, then bent to shatter the reflection with the tip of her finger. Her husky laugh drifted through the air as she caught up a length of printed silk and knotted it low over her hips.

"Tracy," Adam said, stepping away from the concealing leaves of a huge fern.

She turned to him, making no move to cover herself. His eyes devoured her, sweeping over a face made more beautiful by its imperfections. Her breasts, with darkened crests taut from the chill of drying water, were firm yet full. A slender rib cage seemed far too frail to bear their weight. From a small waist, her body flared slowly, and the bare hip and thigh he glimpsed beneath the silk enticed him with their elegance.

"Adam."

His name on her lips broke the spell. Though he relaxed, he was no less bewitched by the sight of her. He knew there was sunlight in her hair, that a bird called. He heard the leaves rustle in the light breeze. The grass whispered and a cricket chirped, but it was not of his world. There was only Tracy as she moved to him. She stopped only a step away, waiting, soft-eyed and wistful.

The time was now, the moment that from the first day they had both known was inevitable. Adam gave a low, hoarse cry as he buried his hand in her hair, bunching it in his fist, reveling in the feel of it as he drew her to him. He filled his arms with her sleek loveliness, whispering soft words of promise and love.

Tracy's low murmuring answer was lost to him as she burrowed her face into his shirt. Her arms clung to him drawing him nearer, crushing her breasts against his chest.

"Your hair smells like wildflowers," he said.

"I was washing it."

"Under the falls?"

"Yes."

"I've missed you, Tracy."

"I know."

"Where did you go?"

"Back on the mountain, to think."

"About what?"

"This."

"And did you decide?" His heart seemed to stop as he waited an agonized eternity for her answer.

"I was coming to you."

"Now?"

"Yes." She drew away, her head tilted back, her eyes were held by his.

It was there at last. She had become the complete woman.

Tenderly, as if she would break, he touched her. Loving fingers stroked the jagged scar that was so much a part of her, then trailed down her cheek to her neck. The heel of his hand rested for a fleeting second at the first gentle swell of her breast, then he cupped the breast in his palm, molding the nipple in its hollow.

"Before you continue," she said, "I think I should tell you I've never made love before." Her tone, despite its halting breathlessness, was almost conversational.

The words hit him with the impact of an earthquake. Tremors of astonishment shook the hand at her breast. His fingers ceased their adoring stroke. His eyes were filled with wonder.

"Then the liberated woman was only the cloak worn by the shy young maiden." His hand moved lightly over her heart. Its cadence was strong and vigorous, and quickened beneath his touch.

"Not shy," she said gently. "Liberated. Most liberated. And confident enough in myself to feel no need to prove it." Her dark eyes glistened with warmth and love. "I have no fears of my body's needs," she half whispered.

"Then why?" Adam stared at her intently. She was beautiful. She was woman. She was bewilderment.

"There has never been anyone in my life before whose touch I wanted and needed. Desire alone was never enough, Adam."

She stood motionless before him, her tall, slender body proud and bare but for the scarflike silk that swayed alluringly about her. With a shuddering groan he reached for her, eager for the gift she offered.

His fingers sought again the soft perfection of her breasts, then traced the curve of her waist to the gentle swell of her hips. As he swept her up into his arms to carry her to the blanket, the colorful silk blew away in the breeze.

As she lay darkly inviting against the scarlet, Adam shrugged from his clothing. With skin as tawny as hers, he was her counterpart in silver. When he was naked, he stood transfixed by the treasure that was his for the taking. Much as he loved her and wanted her, he couldn't take that final step until he had one last sign that this was truly what she wanted.

"Adam." As though she understood his hesitancy, Tracy opened her arms to him.

With a ragged groan he sank down beside her. As his body touched hers, a sigh trembled through her. There was no need for more. With kisses and caresses he taught her the first of love. Slowly and with infinite care he awakened the passion that had been sleeping within her. Then with a soft sigh of his own he drew her beneath him.

"Oh, God." The low groan tore from his lips in agony. He tensed and would have pulled away, but Tracy's arms held him fast. "I can't, darling. I mustn't. You have no protec—"

"Shh." Her fingers at his lips stopped him. "It will be all right. I don't care."

"No! You could conceive."

"I don't care. Love me, Adam. Love me."

When he still would have resisted, she seduced him with an expertise that was astonishing. Having no understanding of the instincts that guided her, she lovingly tempted him beyond refusal.

"My love," he whispered as he answered her desire.

"Adam, I love you." Her words were lost in the mist and the rumble of the falls, but he heard and answered with body, heart, and soul.

Warmed by sunlight, Tracy turned, murmured a soft sound, then sought again the hard but comfortable slope of his broad chest. The chuckle that rumbled like a low growl against her ears was all part of a wonderful dream. A sleepy smile lifted her lips as she curled quite naturally against the long, lean body at her side. Her mouth brushed lightly over the bare skin.

There was no other sound as with loving hands Adam caressed her. He leaned over her, his free hand tangling in the long, shining black hair that spilled gloriously over the blanket. One kiss was given to each eyelid, one was brushed lightly over her cheek, then he whispered her name against her lips and took her once again to their own world of enchantment.

"Do you think she knows we're here?" Adam asked. He had awakened only minutes ago, and had spent the time watching Tracy sleeping with her head pillowed on his shoulder. When the ebony lashes had lifted to reveal her softly glowing dark eyes, he had kissed her flushed cheeks and asked his question.

"Do you mean Shadow?"

"No. The Indian maiden who came to the falls to bathe and found her true love. Do you think she knows we found each other here too?"

"I'd like to think that she does and that she's happy for us." Tracy leaned on her elbow and traced patterns in the pelt of dark hair that grew thickly on his chest. "It's the same color."

"Mmm?" Adam's silver eyes had turned to darkened steel as he quickened with desire.

"Your beard and your chest. Neither are red." Tracy sounded disappointed as she concentrated on the swirling thatch that narrowed to a line that reached beyond his waist.

"Tracy." Adam captured her wrist in his grasp. "I don't think you quite understand your own power yet. Perhaps we should have a swim, then go home."

He chuckled when her face clouded and her smile faded. He pulled her down to him, wrapping his arms about her. "You need time, love. Time for your body to heal."

"But you . . ." She blushed, dropped her eyes from his and mumbled, "Well, it only hurt for a moment."

His happy laughter rang out through the forest, startling a rabbit that was feeding at the edge of the glade. Adam rolled her onto the blanket, pinning her beneath him. His hands held each wrist above her head and he smiled down at her. "I love you, Tracy Walker. I love your heart and your body, but most of all your fighting spirit. To be brief, I love everything about you."

"I love you, Adam." Her look nearly made a mockery of his strength.

"Damn! If we don't go for a swim, it's very likely that I'll find myself doing exactly what I just said I shouldn't. Too bad the water's heated. I feel a definite need for a cold shower."

"There's always the waterfall," Tracy suggested, then laughed at his horrified look. She pushed him away in an unexpected move and bounded to her feet. "Last one in the lake is a lazy lover."

"Ah-ha!" Adam surged up to give chase. With the advantage of his longer legs he could overtake but not surpass her. Simultaneously they cut through the water in perfect dives.

Adam surfaced instantly. Turning all around, he searched the clear water for Tracy. Before he could find her she rose in front of him with a great splattering of water.

"So." He took her into his arms, pressing her hips close to his own. "Now that you have me in the lake, you plan to drown me."

"Never!" Tracy brushed the water from his face, then kissed him. "I have plans for you, but they have nothing to do with drowning." Her hands strayed over his ribs and down the curve of his hip.

He released her abruptly. "I think I *will* make use of the waterfall."

"I'll come with you."

"No!" He pointed an accusing finger at her. "You, you little witch, should get dressed immediately if you know what's good for both of us." He swam away toward the fall, muttering under his breath with every stroke he made.

Tracy watched him with her heart full of pride. He was a beautiful man, inside and out. And he could be hers for a time. Her smile was suddenly tinged with sadness as she turned toward the bank.

Two days of enchantment followed. The waterfall became their haven, and each time they loved, it was with a new intensity. On the third day they joined Jed and Liza on a picnic that had been planned long ago as a special treat for Summer.

"That's nice, Summer," Tracy said to the little girl. Tracy was sitting by the creek bank watching Summer sail the boats she had made out of hickory nut half shells, with leaves as their sails. "Your daughter's quite good at improvising, Adam."

"Of course. She gets it from her father."

"Is she as modest too?"

With his head resting in Tracy's lap, Adam was far too comfortable to rise to the bait of her teasing. He simply agreed. "Yes, that too."

Tracy laughed. "You're an idiot. But I love you."

Adam's eyes opened then. "I know. But it's like hearing it for the first time each time you say it." His voice grew husky. "Say it again."

"I love you." She whispered the words so none but he could hear.

"Tracy!" Summer stood before them, her hands on her hips in a childish imitation of Liza. "I've called you and called you. You're not paying any 'tention to me."

"I'm sorry, sweetheart. What did you want?"

"I wanted to know if we could go fishing now." Again, as the child spoke patiently, Tracy could almost hear her red-haired aunt saying the same words.

"I think we can. That is, if your father can do without a pillow for a while."

"It'll be difficult, but I suppose I can rough it if I must." He rolled away from Tracy and onto his feet in one smooth motion. He ruffled a curl that fell over Summer's eye. "Are you going to catch our supper for us, muffin?"

"Could I?" Her gray eyes that were so much like her father's sparkled with excitement. She turned to Tracy. "Could I really catch a fish for supper?"

"You might. There are some pretty big trout and catfish in the creek. Why don't we get started? Maybe we'll have a nice string of fish in time for supper. You catch them, your daddy can clean them, and I'll cook them. Deal?"

"Deal." Summer laughed and scampered to the tree where the fishing rods rested. "Which one can I use?"

"Why don't you take the shorter one. It fits you better."

"Tracy," Adam said softly. "I have news for you. I don't think I have the proper tools for cleaning a fish."

"Not to worry." Tracy looked toward her cabin that was barely visible through the heavy foliage of the oaks. "I have all you need."

"You're a woman of many talents, Tracy darlin'. A matchless tracker, an artist, a good cook, a true friend, a wonderful lover . . ."

"Adam! Hush, they'll hear you." Tracy glanced toward the couple who had just come from a trail that led through the woods. "Hello, Liza, Jed. Did you have a good walk?"

"It was wonderful," Liza said. "Jed showed me several plants that I might use for dye when I do my next weaving. It would be interesting to try to duplicate some of the old colors." Liza stopped short at Adam and Tracy's laughter. "*Now* what did I say?"

"Nothing, Liza," Adam said. "You just always shock me when you sound so much like you belong here."

"Maybe she does," Jed said, smiling brilliantly at Liza.

"We'll see," she said, a faint blush suffusing her face.

Looking from one to the other, Tracy realized that she had missed something. She had been so wrapped up in Adam for the past few days, she hadn't recognized the signs that were so obvious. Jed was in love with Liza, and if Tracy's eyes weren't deceiving her, his love was returned.

Tracy found herself wishing fervently that Jed and Liza would marry. Then Adam would come back to the mountain at least for visits. The thought lightened the small dark ray of sadness that edged every part of her days with him. Her gaze met his, and she found that he was watching her with a puzzled expression.

"I've got one! I've got one!" Summer's excited call

broke into the silence that had fallen between all of them. "Help! I can't hold him."

Adam and Jed ran to the child's side. Adam placed his hands on Summer's and helped her reel in her catch.

"He's a big one, muffin. Hold on. We'll get him in together." Carefully guiding the child and adding his strength to hers, he helped her wind the line, bringing her catch closer and closer to shore.

"Here's the net." Jed handed it to Adam, who scooped the fish from the water.

"My fish!" Summer wailed. "It's a turtle."

"Indeed it is, and a big one too. Do you feel like turtle soup tonight instead of trout?"

"Daddy! We can't eat this turtle. It might be somebody's mommy."

"And the fish wouldn't?" Adam cut the line and set it free.

"I hadn't thought of that," Summer admitted. "But anyway, a fish doesn't look as much like a mommy as a turtle does."

Tracy's sputtering laughter joined with Liza's and Jed's. Adam fought the smile that quirked his lips in spite of himself.

"Does your daughter get that sort of logic from her father too?" Tracy asked tongue-in-cheek.

"Heaven help me, I have no idea where that came from," Adam said quietly, so that Summer couldn't hear. "Do you think the mountain has gotten to her as it has her father . . . in a bit of a different way?"

Tracy prudently chose to ignore the remark. "What did you use for bait, Summer?"

"The rest of my peanut butter sandwich."

"Peanut but—" Tracy smothered a smile. "You really should have waited for one of us to bait your hook. You could've gotten a barb in your finger."

"That's all right. I didn't have any trouble. I just squeezed it on."

"Adam," Jed managed to say amid gasps of hilarity, "I

think your daughter has just invented a whole new way to fish. Who knows, maybe next time she'll catch one."

"This is fun," Summer said. "I wish we didn't have to leave tomorrow."

Adam instantly looked at Tracy. She had grown quite pale beneath her tan. The time they had been avoiding thinking about had come. They were faced with the specter that had loomed over these last intense days. Though his schedule had been set from the beginning, Adam and Tracy had futilely denied the inevitable by not speaking of it. Now, with the words of an innocent child, they could pretend no longer, and Adam could feel the hurt he saw in Tracy's eyes.

"Come on, Jed," Liza murmured. "Let's put away the picnic supplies."

Tracy realized in some dim recess of her mind that she and Adam were alone. Summer had returned to building sailboats, and Jed and Liza were making a pretense of being absorbed in repacking the picnic basket. But all Tracy knew was that she was hurting as she had never known she could. Tomorrow Adam would be gone from her life.

"Tracy. Darling. It'll only be for a few weeks." He dried away the tears she hadn't known were falling. "Summer's due in school the next day. I'll stay for a while to be sure she's settled, then I'll be back." Catching her hands in his, he lifted them to his lips and kissed her fingertips. "I'm not fool enough to say the time will pass before we know it."

"Don't!"

"It might be only a week or two." He hated the hopelessness he heard in her single word. "Tracy, Summer needs me."

"I know."

"She's a well-adjusted child. In two weeks or so she should be perfectly attuned to the class. First grade shouldn't be so different from kindergarten. Luckily she knows the teacher. That should help." Adam cursed himself for babbling inanely. There was a deep sadness about Tracy that no words he might offer could wipe away.

"Tracy? I have to go now," Summer said. She was subdued, much of her excitement dimmed. "Jed's going to take Liza and me home."

"I'll walk back to the car with you." Tracy took the child's hand and they followed Jed and Liza toward her cabin. Adam walked behind, aware of how his daughter clung to Tracy.

By the car Tracy knelt before Summer. "I'll miss you. Maybe if you study hard and do well, your daddy will bring you back for a holiday."

"Can we, Daddy?" Summer's solemn eyes pleaded with him.

"I'm sure we can."

"Then give me a kiss," Tracy said, "And I'll see you soon." Summer's pudgy arms wound tightly around her neck and a kiss that was sticky with peanut butter was pressed to her cheek.

"I love you, Tracy."

"And I love you, Summer. Good-bye, Liza, Jed. Come again soon."

Tracy stood perfectly still as Jed's car left her drive. It had gone completely from sight before she faced Adam. "I know you have to go and I'm sorry I've acted such a fool."

"I never meant for it to happen like this. We both know we had to talk about it before the day was over, but I'd hoped to find an easier way."

"Is there an easy way?"

"No." Adam was stricken by the loneliness he could already see in her face. "We still have the rest of this evening."

"Yes. We do." Tracy clasped his hand in hers. Very slowly she led him up the steps and into her cabin.

Nine

There was a sharp rap at the workshop door. Deep in concentration, Tracy frowned but did not consciously acknowledge it. With great care and delicate precision she changed the flow of a line by trimming away a single sliver. The rapping sounded again, this time penetrating her thoughts.

She put down the fragile figure and her tools and rose from her chair. Still looking at the carving that had so engrossed her, she brushed woodchips from her jeans and wiped her hands on a towel hanging from the table.

"Tracy." The muffled call broke the total absorption in her work.

"Coming." Absently pushing aside her unbraided hair, she walked to the door and opened it. "Jed, you're early—Adam!"

"Good morning, Tracy." He straightened from the doorframe, lifted a long curl to his lips, and breathed deeply. "Nice."

She looked up at him in complete surprise, moving only to tuck back the strand of hair he had kissed.

"Your mouth's open, darling." He grinned down at her.

"What're you doing here? You're supposed to be half-way to New York City by now."

"Whatever happened to Good morning Adam. How are you?"

"Oh—uh, yes, well. Good morning, Adam."

"Is this always your early morning voice, or do you just stutter on the odd days?"

Tracy laughed then and relaxed. "I only stutter when I find a man who shouldn't be there standing on my doorstep."

"If I think about it a minute, I might make some sense of that."

"Adam, what are you doing here?" A whimper sounded behind him and Tracy looked past him into the yard. "Is Summer with you? Where's Liza? And Jed? Aren't you going to miss your plane?"

"Taking your questions in order, I'm here to bring you something. No. Gone to the airport. With Liza and Summer. No. There, does that take care of all of them?" He ran his finger down her forehead and tapped her gently on the nose. "If so, then I have a question for you."

"Oh, yeah?" Tracy was so happy to see him that she failed to notice that he didn't say what he had brought her. "And just what question might that be?"

"Well, I was wondering if you were planning to make me stand here all day, or are you going to invite me in?"

"Of course, sir, and welcome to my humble workshop." She stepped from the door and bowed low in flamboyant courtesy. "Won't you have a seat?"

"First things first," he muttered as he drew her into his arms. "Were you going to make me wait all day for this too?"

"No." On tiptoe, Tracy met his kiss eagerly. Her arms locked tightly about his neck, her body molded to his. When his lips met hers, she sighed softly in pleasure.

Reluctantly Adam lifted his head from hers. With one arm still around her he walked her to the work table. "Something new?" he asked, indicating the rough figure on the table.

"Yes. Something to keep me busy while you're away."

"What is it?"

"It's a surprise."

"For me?"

"Yes. It should be ready by the time you return."

Adam only nodded and released her. He prowled the room, looking at her carvings that were scattered about in profusion. "Do you know, even though I've seen these a dozen times, it's always astonishing to see what you can make a block of wood portray. There's too much beauty here for it to be hidden away."

"Thank you, Adam." Tracy knew where this was leading and firmly changed the subject. "Would you like some coffee? It's still warm."

"No, thanks." He accepted defeat, but only for the moment.

Tracy leaned against the table and watched him as he moved from one carving to another. "You still haven't said why you're here."

"You weren't listening, love. I answered that question first. I brought you something." He stepped outside the cabin and returned immediately. "This."

Before she could react he placed a wriggling brown and black ball of fur into her arms.

"What?" Tracy looked blankly at the fuzzy puppy he had given her. "No! Here." She tried to push it back at him. "I don't want this. Take it back!"

"Can't." Adam backed away, refusing to take the dog from her. "He's yours."

"He's not! I don't want another dog."

"Want and need can be two different things."

"Then"—Tracy gritted her teeth—"I don't *need* another dog. There's no place in my life for another one."

"Obviously he thinks differently." Adam grinned as a pink tongue licked Tracy's finger.

"I said no!" She gently set the dog outside. Even in her anger she couldn't bring herself to hurt it by simply dropping it. Before she could straighten, though, the puppy scampered back to her side as quickly as his short legs could carry him.

"Adam, take it away."

"I can't. My plane leaves in less than an hour and I'll have to drive like a bat out of hell to make it now."

"Adam, please take it."

"His name is Bear. Summer thought it fit."

"I won't keep him."

"That's up to you. Where Bear belongs is something the two of you are going to have to settle between you. But it looks as if his decision's made." Adam nodded to the puppy, who was now sleeping contentedly on an extra shirt of Tracy's that had dropped on the floor. "He may not be yours, but he thinks you're his. Now, kiss me again. I have to go."

She had no time for further protest. He swept her into his arms and kissed her thoroughly. As he drew away he said almost sternly, "Remember, I love you, and I'll be back as soon as I can."

Then he was gone. Long after his car had disappeared and the dust had settled, she stared after him, her fingers pressed to her lips. In a pain-filled daze she walked to the front porch steps and sank down on them. With her knees drawn up and her fists clenched, she huddled there.

"Fool," she said aloud. "If it hurts this badly when he leaves for only a short while, how will you survive when he's gone for good?" Tortured by her thoughts, she wasn't aware that tears were streaming down her face until a small, warm body crept into her lap and a rough little tongue started licking her chin.

"Go away. I don't want you." She pushed the dog from her lap.

Bear whimpered, tilted his head curiously, then wagged his stub of a tail with zest. Tracy didn't see his attempt at friendship; her head was buried in her arms as silent sobs shook her. Sensing that something was wrong, but unable to understand what, the puppy crept as close to her as he could. He was still there when she rose. She returned to her workshop and shut the door firmly in his face.

Tracy had no idea how long the scratching had been going on, for she had been involved in a particularly tedious part of her carving. At such times she could easily block everything but the figure before her from her mind. Now that she was satisfied with her accomplishment, she was again aware of her surroundings. Once she noticed the sound, she found it impossible to ignore. Angrily tossing her knife on the table, she pushed back her chair and went to the door. Throwing it open, she glared down at the dog.

"Now, look. I've given you food and water. You're not ill; you have a place to sleep. There's nothing more I can give you. I know you're lonesome, but I can't let you in here. I don't want you to get attached to me because as soon as I have time I'm going to find you a home."

Bear only looked up at her, thumped his tail, and Tracy could have sworn he smiled.

"Don't you ply your charms on me. It won't do you a bit of good. As soon as possible, you're leaving. That's final." Again she shut the door, blocking out his wistful expression.

For nearly a week it had been the same. Tracy saw to his needs, promised herself that soon she would find him a home, then firmly shut herself away from him.

"What now?" Tracy tossed aside her brush, closed up the pot of paint, and stalked to the door. The incessant barking had been a minor irritant for the past ten minutes. Now there was a shrill, urgent quality about it that she could no longer ignore.

As she crossed the yard, seeking the source of her trouble and meaning to scold him severely, she heard the sound that no one from the valley could mistake—the angry, rapid buzzing of a rattlesnake. It was followed by a soft thump and a yelp from Bear. After a split-second, the buzzing resumed.

Tracy knew what she would see before she rounded the corner of her cabin. Bear had discovered a rattler. It had struck and recoiled again, but had it found its mark? Bear's barking was little assurance, for she knew he might be staggering and ill in a matter of minutes.

She stopped short, fear roiling in the pit of her stomach. On her porch, its tail high, its rattles moving faster than the eye could follow, and its head drawn back prepared to strike again, was one of the largest snakes she had ever seen. Bear was dancing and prancing just beyond its reach, his shrill bark sliding into bass now and then. He teased the snake with all the enthusiasm of a playful puppy.

Her first instinct was to call out, but common sense told her that to distract him could bring disaster. Her hand went by habit to the knife at her belt. To get a clear target, she knew she would have to circle behind Bear, hoping that she wouldn't draw his attention.

So began one of the most agonizing journeys Tracy had ever taken. Carefully placing one foot in front of the other, she edged her way through the yard. Every move was slow and calculated. Once again the snake struck and Bear danced out of its range. Tracy had to force herself not to scream her warning. Beads of perspiration were on her forehead, and her cheeks were flushed by the time she had come half circle to the other side of the cabin. Praying that Bear would not make an unexpected move, she drew back the knife, aimed, and threw it with all her strength.

For one long, anguished moment, she thought she had missed. The rattling grew even angrier, rising to a fevered pitch, then abruptly ceased. She couldn't look. Sinking down on the grass, she buried her face in her hands. Her whole body was trembling from the tension.

The grass whispered and the patter of feet stopped. She knew he was there waiting. She lifted her head and looked into golden-brown eyes. "Okay, mutt, you win."

Bear's body seemed to vibrate with love at the sound of her voice, but still he didn't move.

"Well, don't be shy at this late date." Tracy laughed and pulled him into her lap. Bear snuggled closer, burrowed his nose into her hair, and with a gusty sigh relaxed against her. "So you're going to be a lover, are you? Before you get too comfortable, let me look at you."

She held the pup from her and truly looked at him for the first time. "Now, let's see just exactly what you are. Airedale? Maybe some collie and even hound? You are a mutt, did you know?" She shook him playfully and was rewarded with a wet kiss.

"Now I know you're an airedale, and exactly like your father. Noah Hawkins's Rebel is the biggest lover in the valley, and you look and act just like him. I wonder who he visited this time? What staid and proper lady dog did he woo then leave with his little bastards?" Bear barked at that. "Sorry, didn't mean to hurt your feelings.

"Adam was right, you seem to have chosen me and there's not a thing I can do about it. So, since it's to be you and I, suppose we both go attend to an unpleasant matter."

Pushing Bear off her lap, she stood and for the first time looked at the dead snake. A shiver ran through her when she remembered how the pup had cornered it. She looked down at him. "Bear, I believe you have more courage than you have sense. Come on. There's no need in putting it off. We have a snake to dispose of."

Tracy looked up and smiled as Bear stirred restlessly and growled. "Something out there interests you, does it? Just make sure you don't find any more rattlesnakes. One was more than enough."

Bear rose and wagged his whole body as he was prone

to do when she spoke to him in such a teasing way. She laughed, rubbed his ears, and pushed him toward the door. "Go on. You might as well investigate. You won't be happy until you do."

She smiled indulgently as he slipped and stumbled over his own feet in his haste to leave. With her back to the open door, Tracy resumed the last of the painting of the exquisite carving. She always worked now with the door open so Bear could come and go as he wished, though he very seldom strayed from her side. There must have been something of great interest out there, Tracy thought as she again became immersed in the painting.

When she heard him return, she didn't bother to look up. "That didn't take long."

"That's strange. I thought it took forever."

"Adam!" She dropped her brush, spattering paint on her shirt. Her chair fell with a crash as she leaped up to face him.

He stood in the doorway, the reality of her love. His tie was loose and his shirt-sleeves rolled up. The navy blazer hung from a crooked finger across his shoulder. With the sun behind him he was a shadowy figure, but to Tracy he was the light of her day. Her throat was dry, her lips parched, and her feet seemed to be nailed to the floor.

"If I can come nonstop all the way from New York, do you think the woman in my life could cross the room for me?"

"Adam! I thought you'd never come." Tracy was in his arms before she finished speaking. When his lips met hers, with his short-clipped and luxuriant beard brushing her face, it was as if her life had begun again.

Adam wound her flowing hair about his hands as he drew away. "How have you been?" he asked, his voice a husky whisper.

"Lonely."

"Have you been working too hard?"

"Not really." She searched his face intently, seeing an underlying strain. She frowned in concern. "Are you ill?"

"Only tired. I've been busier than I expected."

"Adam! Is something wrong? Is it Summer or Liza."

"No, they're both fine. There were some technical problems about the book. Most of them have been worked out."

"Most, but not all?"

"I'm afraid not." He rested his weary head against her hair.

"Then you shouldn't be here. You should've stayed where you needed to be."

"Tracy, this *is* the place I most need to be. You wouldn't believe how I've missed you. I couldn't work for thinking of you. So I—what the hell!"

They both heard the ferocious growl just before Adam's shoe was attacked. Never one to be left out of anything, Bear chose this method to join in. Adam bent to look him in the eye.

"And just who do you think you are to interrupt when I finally have my woman in my arms? Hasn't anyone taught you that it's bad manners?"

"You're now looking at my other shadow," Tracy said, grinning. "Don't look at me like that; he was your idea."

"But"—Adam rose and took her back into his arms—"he was to keep you company when I was gone, not while I'm here."

"Tell him that . . . and lots of luck. You said Bear had decided I was his and you were right."

"Maybe I'd best try to find him a lady of his own."

"I think he's a bit too young just yet. But if his father's who I think he is, he won't need your help."

"Hester Calton had him. She said something about Noah Hawkins's Rebel had been visiting."

"That's what I thought. Rebel gets around. You can see his mark on more than half the young dogs in the valley."

Bear barked and wagged his tail.

"Go find your own girl. This one's mine," Adam said, then laughed when the puppy wagged everything. "He's enthusiastic, to say the least."

Even though he laughed and teased, Tracy could see the fatigue in the deep creases around Adam's mouth. "Have you had your dinner?"

"It was served on the plane, but I was working and didn't eat."

"I have some spaghetti on the stove, and a salad. Would you like some?"

"That sounds like heaven. I've been so eager to get back here that even before I left I skipped a meal or two and stayed at my desk."

"Then why don't you go on to the house and wash up? I'll be there in a minute."

"You won't be long?" His eyes seemed hungry for more of her.

"No, I'll only be a minute. I promise."

"I'll hold you to that. Only a minute."

The last of the dishes were done; the kitchen was all in order. Adam leaned against the counter with a glass of wine in his hand, watching Tracy put away the last pieces of silverware.

"That was the best meal I've had in a long time," he said.

"I'm glad you liked it."

"I really should be going." He set his glass on the counter.

"Have you been back to your cabin?" Tracy concentrated fiercely on the flowers she was rearranging in a small vase.

"I came straight to you, Tracy, but now I suppose I'd better go along."

"Don't go." Her trembling voice hardly rose above a whisper.

"Tracy?" Adam was afraid to trust himself, afraid that he had heard only what he wanted to hear.

"I asked you not to go." She turned to face him, her eyes were wide with desire. "Stay with me. I need you."

"You need me?" He pulled her to him with an urgency that was almost painful. "Do you know how I've ached for you? I've been trying all evening to think of some way to ask you if I could stay here with you. Then you look at me so honestly and cut right to the heart of the matter in the most enchanting way."

"Where else would I want you to be, Adam?" she asked matter-of-factly. "Why don't you get your bag from the car while I see to Bear? I'll put a fresh towel in the spare bath for you."

While he was gone, Tracy readied the bathroom for him. She laid out a towel and fresh soap, and the grooming kit she had bought for him. She had no idea how he cared for his beard and mustache, but hopefully anything he might need would be there. Before he returned she was back in the kitchen.

"Did you say the spare bath?" he asked.

"Yes. Then you won't have to fight my clutter."

"Okay, but I wouldn't mind clutter that was yours."

"That's what you think. You haven't been slapped in the face with drying 'unmentionables.' "

"I look forward to the day," he said, laughing as he walked down the hall to the assigned bath.

Tracy busied herself in the kitchen, fussing over nothing. She gave Bear his supper and saw that he was settled for the night. It wasn't until she heard the water running that she made her way to her own bath.

Tracy stepped from the shower, dried herself vigorously, then slipped the ribbon from her hair. From her closet she took a sheer robe that fastened at the waist with a satin belt. She slipped her arms into it, belted it tightly, then crossed the carpeted floor to her dressing table. First she applied a touch of fragrance to her earlobes, the hollow of her throat, and the cleft between her breasts. Next she began to brush her heavy mane of hair. Lost in her memories of Adam and how he had looked today, she did not hear his quiet tread. It wasn't until he took the brush from her hand that she saw his image in the mirror.

In a short navy robe, water glistening in his hair, he was an image of contrasts, dark and light. When he set the brush on the dresser and offered her his hand, Tracy did not demur. She let him lift her from the chair and waited while his eyes traveled over her as if seeing her body for the first time.

He untied the sash slowly. The harsh sound of his indrawn breath broke the silence of the room. The sheer fabric swung open to reveal the shadowy valley between her breasts and the inner flesh of one thigh.

Tracy waited, calm beneath his adoring gaze. When his rough hands rasped against her bare shoulders, she did not move. Gently Adam slipped the robe from her, letting it fall neglected to the floor.

Only then did she touch him. With a strange calm she untied his own belt and, moving nearer, pushed the robe from his shoulders. Her memory had been faithful, for he was beautiful.

"This is the moment I've dreamed of for days," he whispered as he took both her hands in his. "There were times when I could almost feel your touch." He turned to the quilt-covered bed, swept back the blankets, turned off the lamp on the night table, and all was in darkness.

Lightning flashed in the sky. Thunder answered in a low, deep rumble over mountaintops and through the low-hanging clouds. One minute all was an empty black, then a blue-white blaze bathed every object, every shadow in an eerie glow. This was the world outside Tracy's cabin. A symphony of sound surrounded them, muted by the steady drone of rain beating down on the tin roof, giving back a soft melody of its own.

The two who lay curled amid the covers of the massive antique bed found a responsive chord in the storm. Their arms were entwined, Tracy's head was pillowed on Adam's shoulder, and his hand curled possessively at her hip. The storm was little more that an overt expression of what they had shared.

The gentle rain that had been left by the dying furor was also like this time together. The startling roar of electric excitement, the wild fury, and the sweet, quiet gentleness had all been theirs.

Passion had come to them with little warning, its ferocity and intensity a consuming thing. It had unleashed a wild, primitive love that knew no conventional bounds. Only two who loved equally could have withstood its force, with neither absorbing nor destroying the other.

Each had met the fierceness of the other with a matching spirit, the wildness with a tender savagery, the sweet and the quiet with a gentleness that held no less passion than the first. It had been the rejoining of two who loved and who had found being separate beyond bearing.

Inch by inch, moving with an agonizing care, Tracy slid from the bed. Her robe lay in a tangle on the braided rug. She slipped into it and belted it securely, then glided on bare feet across the floor. A moonbeam caught her in its web, turning the silk to a bright iridescence. For long, quiet moments she stared out at the familiar shape that always loomed before her.

Shadow—benevolent and jealous. Which was it to be with her? As though searching for an answer, she watched the moon cast its glow over the dark mountain.

Adam stirred in his sleep, his arm seeking her giving warmth. With no more thought to her silent question,

Tracy dropped the robe to the floor and slipped quickly into the bed. Her only desire was to be where Adam needed her—at least while she could.

He drew her hard against him, holding her as though he felt threatened.

"Tracy," he muttered as he bound her to him with her hair, his lips resting against the scar. Soon his breathing settled to a soft, easy rhythm as, even in sleep, he drew contentment from her.

Finally Tracy slept for what little of the night was left.

"What was that?" Adam sat upright, realizing that he was alone as he pushed the covers from his body. He was unmindful of his complete—and to Tracy totally beautiful—nakedness.

"That, my beloved, was Livingston, my own personal, dependable alarm clock. What—"

"Say that again!" Adam's voice held the huskiness of sleep and more.

"That was Livingston, a rooster who thinks—"

"No! Not that. The first part."

"Let's see. What was it I said?" Tracy crossed one bare foot over the other and leaned against the doorframe, her head cocked in a pretense of thought. "If it wasn't about Livingston and it wasn't about alarm clocks, what could it be?"

"Tracy!" A playful menace laced his words.

"Ah-ha!" She launched herself at him. "I suddenly remember." From her place, cradled so protectively in his arms, she stroked the short, silken beard. Her voice sank to a loving whisper. "You are my beloved."

"Oh, God." An unusual light shimmered in his eyes as he kissed her forehead. "Only you could make or destroy me with a single word. Beloved. Who would have thought such an old-fashioned word could be the key to the world of my dreams? Say it again, Tracy. Please."

"Beloved Adam. *My* beloved." Her dark eyes shone with a glow he had come to recognize.

His hand stole beneath the loose fabric of her sweatshirt, finding and caressing her bare breasts. "Surely we aren't backpacking today after this rain," he teased.

"Not unless you'd like to experience a mud slide or two firsthand."

"Then why this?" His hands again stroked her breasts and teased the rising nipples.

"I thought . . . I . . ." She blushed furiously.

"That we might make love? Did you leave your body bare so that I might touch you like this?" His fingertips drew from her a shiver of delight. "Don't be ashamed of wanting me, darling. Don't you know that the greatest compliment you could pay me is to want me as much as I want you?"

"Am I that obvious?"

"Only to me, thank God." He drew her farther into his embrace.

She snuggled against him, reveling in his caress. Her fingers curled into the thick hair of his chest as she rested there contentedly. After a while she drew away and stared solemnly into his eyes.

"Adam?"

"Mmm?"

"We have a problem."

"We do?"

"I'm afraid so."

"What is it, love?"

"Your breakfast is burning."

"My what is what?" Adam's mind was clearly not on breakfast.

"Your breakfast. It's burning." She bounded off the bed and was out the door as his laughter rose.

The day was a comfortable one. They built a fire in the old grate to ward off the chill of the early fall day.

Adam sat on the sofa, his papers scattered about him, his pad on his knee. In frowning concentration he composed, destroyed, then recomposed the text that would accompany the photographs of Shadow.

Tracy was hunched over a small table in the corner, her back to Adam and the fire, with Bear at her side. At each crumpled page and the colorful expletives, she smiled but did not halt in her work. Bear only raised a lazy eye as if to say, what now?

"Dammit it all to hell and back again!"

Only Tracy's rollicking laughter and Bear's puzzled thump of his stubby tail followed yet another rattle of crumpling paper.

"Don't laugh," Adam said, looking balefully at her. "It isn't funny. I have all this material that promises to be a marvelous story and it *won't* come together." He stared at the fire. "No matter how I try, it's flat! I can't make it come to life. Somewhere down the line I haven't captured the essence of it. Tracy, I want those who read this to see and to feel the mountain as a . . . a . . . a living thing."

"Perhaps tomorrow when the roads are clear we can begin our research among the old people. Some of them have actually lived a part of the legends. Talking to those who know firsthand should help," Tracy said hopefully.

"Maybe you're right." Adam's fingers stabbed repeatedly through his hair, making it more untidy. "It would probably be best just to put it away for now. I'm certainly making no headway."

"A sensible idea," Tracy murmured, then returned to her own task.

Adam began to straighten his work into some semblance of order, then sat watching the flames. Bear left his place by Tracy to go to him. He leaned heavily against Adam's knee, signaling that he had been neglected long enough and should have his head scratched.

"Spoiled mutt." Adam chuckled as he did as he was required. "I think this should be your lady's job, except she does look a mite busy." He chuckled again, delighted with his own use of one of the local idioms. "Let's find out what it is that keeps her from sharing our laziness. A good idea? I thought so."

Adam turned again to face Tracy. "In case you missed that brilliant one-sided conversation and need an interpretation, darlin', we two lonely males need your company. What could be keeping you from our irresistible presence?"

"Not a thing." Tracy rose, holding the finished carving behind her back. She walked across the room to stand before him. "In fact, I was only waiting until you finished with your work to give you something."

"What?" He looked up at her curiously.

"This." She set the figurine on the table at his side.

"Dear God."

Tracy had heard many harsh words tumble from his lips in his growing frustration, but these were a reverent prayer. He said nothing more, only looked at the carving through eyes that glittered.

In the flicker of the firelight, the tiny figure of mother and child seemed to take on a life of its own. The mother, her blond and fragile head bent over the golden ringlets of the child, throbbed with a vibrant love. Only a fool would not know that a contented child was being sweetly sung to sleep.

"Summer and Sharon." He could hardly say the names. "How did you know? How could you?"

"You told me the first day we met."

"Yes. I remember now." He never took his gaze from the figures. "I told you how Summer loved to be sung to sleep, but not since Sharon died."

"Sharon had a lovely voice."

Adam took a deep breath and looked up at Tracy. "This is beautiful, but I've never known you to carve people."

"I never had until now."

"Why this time?"

"Because you've given me so much. I wanted to give you something in return."

"You've given me far more." Adam lifted her hand to his mouth and kissed each fingertip lingeringly. "You've given me my daughter's life, and my own."

"No . . ."

"Shh." With a gentle tug he drew her down to his lap. "Summer would've died on Shadow if not for you, and for Wolfe. And I would have died with her. Perhaps not physically, but life without meaning is a sort of death."

"Then I'm doubly glad I found her." She settled comfortably into the curve of his shoulder.

As the fire danced, casting its warmth into every corner, they retreated into their thoughts, remembering a woman with hair like new gold and a smile just as bright. Adam was the first to stir as he pulled Tracy nearer his heart.

"We need to speak of Sharon, darling."

"I know."

Quiet hovered again in the room. Neither knew where to start. A coal popped and hissed. At his place near the hearth Bear whimpered and growled, playing some fierce game in his puppy dream. In the light the carved figures seemed to live.

Adam's voice at last broke the silence, rippling through it, deep timbred yet steady. "When we met and fell in love, Sharon was the perfect woman for me. Her soothing calm was the foil for my pent-up restlessness, and I loved her so completely it was frightening. Even when we made love I had to hold a part of myself in check. She wouldn't have understood any but the gentlest love. Had she lived, it would have been enough.

"But the man her death created, the man I am today, must have more. I need the fire and excitement you bring to me. Each of us loved her in our own way. Our lives have been enriched by her short time with us, and I'd like to keep her memory alive for Summer." He picked up the carving and caressed the blond heads lovingly, then set it back down. "But for us, I'd like to put her to rest."

Tracy murmured something indistinguishable and turned her face into his shirt.

"I'll always love her memory," he continued. "It's something precious and inviolate, but still only a memory. A new Adam has risen from the ashes and pain of her death. A richer, wiser, and a far stronger Adam. I love you, Tracy."

She lifted her head to gaze into his eyes. "I know," she said, her hand stroking his cheek at the line of his beard. "I understand, but you needn't worry. I have no guilt about Sharon. Instead I think that wherever she is, she's happy that we had this time together."

"I think you're right. Sharon would like her best fellow and best friend to find a love together. She was an incurable matchmaker. If you hadn't . . ."

"If I hadn't had the accident," she supplied. "It's all right, Adam. That should also be put to rest. We both need to lock those closets and throw away the key." She straightened abruptly. "Now, what sort of matchmaking did Sharon have in mind for me? Was he handsome? Devilishly charming? A lady-killer? Hmm, on second thought, he doesn't sound half bad. You wouldn't happen to still have his phone number, would you? I have use of a good man around here every now and then."

"Oh, you do, do you?" The gleam in his eye warned her.

"No, Adam, no. You wouldn't. You know I'm ticklish."

"Oh, wouldn't I?" His imitation of a wicked leer threw her further into fits of merriment. "Just watch."

"No! Oh, no. Please. My grandfather always warned me to remain a mystery. Never to let a man know my weaknesses or my secrets."

"Ah, but you did, and I do. So what will you do about it?"

"Anything, anything. Just don't tickle me."

"Did I hear the lady cry uncle?"

"Uncle. Uncle."

"Who is it that needs a man?"

"I do."

"And who is that man?"

"You, Adam, only you."

"Prove it."

"Like this?" A tiny kiss grazed his cheek.

"Another."

"This?" The second lingered deliciously on his lips.

"You're getting the hang of it."

"Shall I try again?"

"Practice makes perfect."

"Then never let it be said I didn't strive for perfection."

Bear had watched this human game with a puppy's interest. Now he cocked his head at the sudden silence. After a moment he laid his head between his paws and returned to the field of clover, where rabbits played in abundance.

"Adam, I love you."

"I know, love, I know."

Only the sounds of the fire and the soft sighs of the sleeping dog were heard for a long time.

Ten

"Are you sure?"

"Positive."

"How can you be so positive?"

"Because I'm *positive!*"

"Tell me how."

"Look, Adam." Tracy leaned against the jeep, struggling to hide her grin. "We aren't going to get stuck and you're not going to have to walk out of some deep, dank quagmire. The water runs off these hills in a hurry. You are familiar with their slight slope, I hope."

"Slight slope?" Adam grinned at her marvelous understatement.

"Come on," she said, "hop in the jeep. We're wasting most of the morning with this chit-chat."

"Chit-chat she calls it. All right," Adam grumbled as he climbed over the dented door. "*But* I'm not above saying I told you so if we get stuck."

"Good." Tracy put the jeep in gear and moved slowly out of the rutted drive. "You can tell me with every stroke while you're digging us out of your anticipated mud hole."

"We'll see," he said, still unconvinced. "Who's first?"

It was the sort of day Tracy had predicted. The visits were many, the tales fascinating, the food plentiful and delicious, and the host always reluctant to let them go. At day's end they were greeted by a lonely Bear and were as glad to be home as he was to see them. There was no pretense that Adam should stay anywhere but with Tracy.

In the early pre-dawn hours Tracy stood alone before the window, staring silently at the moonlit Shadow.

"Okay. You've made a believer of me. I won't argue *anything*," Adam said. Dressed in jeans and a heavy sweater, he was standing by the jeep, ready for the day's excursion.

"I'll believe that when I don't see it." This sort of badinage had become commonplace between them, as natural as breathing.

"There's not one steep incline, one deep gulley, or one sheer drop that's going to worry me. *And* I refuse to turn my head into a punching bag today. You drive. I'll relax."

"Terrific. Except today's different. We're going to the other side of the valley to visit the only Indian family that still has a farm here."

"Across the valley?"

"Yep."

"Across the *flat* valley?"

"Very flat."

Adam sighed. "Then, in that case, I'll drive."

"Revenge?"

"No, love. Just reasserting my bruised male ego."

"Show me the bruise, I'll kiss it well."

"Ah, but then we wouldn't make today's visit." He held out his hand for the keys.

"Spoil-sport!" Tracy laughed and dropped them into his waiting grasp.

*　　*　　*

Jimmy Black Hawk's family was a large one, spanning four generations. It was a true blending of the old and the new, and each member of the family had his or her own contribution about the legend of the waterfall. After they had waved good-bye and promised to visit again soon, Adam drove back to Tracy's, not speaking.

"What are you thinking, Adam?" Tracy's soft question drew him back to the present.

"That you were right. The legend about Indian Maid Fall is beautiful. Until I heard Jimmy describing it, I hadn't realized how dangerous internal strife could be for the Indian tribes."

She nodded her agreement. "They had troubles enough without fighting among themselves."

"If those two young people hadn't met at the fall, and if their love hadn't been strong enough to overcome their differences, there might never have been peace."

"The entire tribe could easily have been decimated. Then there would've been no beautiful Black Hawk family," Tracy added.

"They are a handsome people, aren't they? I wonder if the lovers were as handsome."

"Does it matter?"

"No." Adam glanced at her. "It doesn't matter at all. But such a strong love had to make them proud and beautiful."

"Yes," Tracy said. "Proud and very beautiful."

The days passed far too quickly. With each visit, Adam added to his store of knowledge. With each conversation he learned and understood more and more about the legends. He learned how each had come to be, how they had been kept alive, and how they had been protected. No one had been reticent about speaking with him. It was as if he bore Tracy's stamp of approval, and that was enough.

The day arrived, as they knew it must, when all the

visits had been made but one. Tracy had deliberately saved it for last. It was the legend that was most special to her.

"Is Opal expecting us?" Adam asked her.

"Yes. I told Noah Hawkins that we'd be over that way at the first of this week. Opal has no telephone, but the grapevine's a wonderful thing. I wonder if smoke signals could've been any quicker."

"From what I've seen, I doubt it."

They were quiet for the remainder of the long, rough drive. The day was lovely, but for Tracy it held a touch of sadness. Soon there would be no reason for Adam to remain in the valley. Already the dread of the coming confrontation was chilling her heart.

A gaggle of geese greeted them as they drove into the yard of the tiniest cabin Adam had seen yet.

"It is small, isn't it?" Tracy said, reading his thoughts. "Opal feels more secure in small areas."

"Because of her blindness?"

"She's never said, but I think it's probably so." She swung down from the jeep and waited while he did the same. "If you're wondering about the geese, they're her watchdogs."

"Watchdogs!" Then remembering the furor they had caused, he understood. "I can see very well where they would be excellent for the job."

"Why don't you sit here on the porch? I'll go inside and bring her out. She loves to feel the sunlight on her face."

When Tracy returned, the old woman clung to her arm as she walked to a battered rocker.

"Good day, young man," she said once she was seated.

"How are you, Opal?"

"Tolerable, just tolerable. Tracy says you want to ask about Dougal MacLaren."

"I've seen his cave and I'd like to know more about him, and his Laura."

"I don't know much of the MacLaren hisself, but I know a mite about the clan. They took to being soldiers

for pay and 'tis that answer I favor for the MacLaren.
Why else would he be in this country, and why else
marked so terrible?

"I know naught of his Laura. None ever know'd her
beginnings or why she was lost and alone in the snow.
The best I know of my mother and father is that theirs
was a great love. It could span all earth and time."

Opal's blank gaze fixed itself on Adam's face. For a dis-
concerting moment he forgot she couldn't see. "Have
you heard the MacLaren's pipes yet, lad?"

"No." Adam was curious. In all that had been said
about the MacLaren and his legend, no one had mentioned that the pipes might still be heard. "When would I
hear them, Opal? Would it be on the mountain, or near
the cave?"

"It could be, but you can hear them anywhere. On the
mountain, in the valley. Where you are don't matter. It's
who you're with that counts."

"I couldn't hear the pipes alone?"

"No. You only hear them when you're with your last
and true love."

"Have you heard them, Opal?" Adam asked softly.

"Aye, but not for a long spell. Not since my Joshua
died."

"Do you think I'll hear them?"

"You're a stubborn flatlander and you refuse the
believing of our legends, but you will believe . . . and
someday you'll hear the pipes." Opal grew silent. It was
obvious that this short talk had taxed her strength.

"You're tired," Tracy said. She had remained standing
by the rocker. "Let me take you back inside."

"No. Thank you, but I think I'll sit a time in the sun."
Her wrinkled old hand patted Tracy's as it rested on her
shoulder. "You and yore young man go on along. Harvey
will be from the field soon. I'll go in then."

"You'll be all right?"

"Of course. Take yore man and go. But Tracy, I'll look
to be seeing you again real soon."

"I'll be here." Tracy kissed Opal's withered cheek, then walked back to the jeep with Adam.

They spent the rest of the day rambling over the trails of Shadow. It was nearly dark before they returned to Tracy's cabin. Dinner was quiet, both subdued by the realization that an interlude had come to an end. Adam's research was complete. It was time that he moved on.

Their loving that night was an untamed and all-consuming thing. Amid their soft whispers they spoke with their bodies and hearts. They were lovers who could drink from the well, but they had a thirst that could never be slaked. Dawn had begun to lighten the sky before their needs were momentarily fulfilled.

Adam woke slowly. He knew that Tracy wasn't with him, and he instinctively looked to the window. She stood there, wrapped in a quilt, staring up at Shadow.

"Good morning, love."

"Adam! I didn't know you were awake." She turned to him.

"I haven't been for long." He saw the sad, serious look on her face. "What are you thinking, Tracy?"

"That you'll be leaving soon."

"Yes, and I'll miss the mountain and the valley." He shifted the pillows behind him in order to sit erect. "I thought I'd spend a few days at the shore getting the material in sequence before I try to write the actual copy. Summer's so excited. She has it all planned out. When I told her that this time when I came home you'd be with me, she was beside herself. I—" Adam stopped short, startled by the sudden pallor on Tracy's face.

"Damn my impatient tongue!" he said, his voice filled with irritation. He got out of the bed and walked over to her. With his hands on her shoulders he drew her near.

"I'm sorry, darling. I meant to wait to do this with a bit more style. Flowers, candlelight, soft music, and even bended knee." His rueful laugh flowed over her. He started to speak again, but stopped when he saw the shattered look on her face. His gaze traveled over her, seeking the softness he had come to love.

Tracy turned and fled from his touch, taking refuge in the huge bed, the place of her happiest moments. She was lovely there in the tangled covers, with her hair tumbling about her shoulders and the quilt clutched to her bare breasts. The knuckles of her right hand were white with strain, and the hand shook with a barely noticeable tremor. Her eyes were dull, fathomless pits—too deep for any light to reach their darkness.

Pain like none he had ever known clutched at Adam, banding his heart with the cold of bitter premonition. He turned away to stare out the window. Drawing a shallow breath, he forced a calmness into his voice that hid the shock that ravaged him.

"You're not going with me, are you, Tracy? You're not going to marry me."

"No."

"Why?" He couldn't turn, couldn't face what he might see. "Have you decided that you don't love me after all?"

"Yes." She tried to lie, but seeing the flinching of the muscles in his taut back, she found she couldn't. "No!" Her voice sank to a soft urgent whisper. "You know I love you."

"Then why? For God's sake, tell me why!"

"I can't go with you because I can't function in your world." Beneath the flat, blunt statement lurked a plea for understanding, but Adam didn't hear it.

"Dammit, Tracy." He turned to her, his face a desolate mask. "It wouldn't be *my* world. It's *ours.*"

Tracy sat as she was, unmoving, yet stricken by the powerful longing to take him in her arms and smooth away the slashing furrows by his mouth. Somewhere in the deepest well of her soul her own pain blended with his, promising her a living hell. But because she loved him, she had to send him away.

"Adam." That love trembled in the sound of her voice, his name becoming an endearment. "It could never be our world. I thought it could be. I dreamed it. I wished it. I willed it, but . . . it can never be."

She looked away, unable to bear the despair in his empty eyes. From the window she could see Shadow looming. Shadow, the massive and powerful force that had shaped her life, was her destiny. Her own eyes were bleak when they met and held his. "This is my world, Adam. My only world."

"Then I'll come back to Shadow. If you can't share what you consider mine, I'll share yours. We'll build something together here."

"It wouldn't work." She shook her head in despair. "You have your own obligations to meet. Your photography, Summer—"

"Summer can be a part of our lives no matter where we are," he interrupted harshly, then added softly, "She loves you."

"I know, and I love her." Now the pain rose from that dark, hidden place, cutting like broken glass through her voice. A stray strand of white hair fell against her cheek as she dropped her head and stared blindly at the ancient pattern of the quilt. "I love you both. That's why I can't tie you to me. What kind of lives could you have, either of you, hidden away here with an emotional cripple? I can't . . . I *won't* let you live your lives half in the real world, half with me."

"And if we want to?"

"No! You both lost so much when Sharon died, yet you've built lives that are vibrant and full of meaning. I can't let you throw that away." She lifted her head. The dull, dry eyes now glistened with gathering tears.

Adam wanted to hold her, to still her trembling lips with his own. He wanted to quiet the pain-filled, probing words. But he didn't dare. Her control was too tenuous, the break too near. How could he explain that without her there would be existence, but not life? Yet had he the power to explain, she wouldn't listen. He said nothing.

"You were happy before you came to Shadow, weren't you, Adam?"

"Yes."

"Then you will be again."

No! Never again. Not without you.

"Between the three of you, you and Liza and Marjorie have made Summer into a beautiful, well-adjusted child. She'll forget me in time, just as you must. It's best we let this be our last good-bye."

"No!" The word was ripped from his aching throat.

"Please don't make this more difficult than it is already. If you'll only listen to me, you'll know I'm right." Her gaze faltered and she looked again at Shadow. "I can't ask you to live scurrying from one place to another, from one agonizing good-bye to another. Each of us would be hurting, opening and reopening the wounds of loss until neither of us would see the other as anything but a source of torment."

He made a low sound of pain and disbelief, and she looked up at him. Her face reflected her own pain. "How could either of us live with the uncertainty?" she said. "You with never knowing what you would find each time you return—love or hate. And me wondering which time you'd find you couldn't face another good-bye." Her voice throbbed with a muted and distant sorrow, as if she were already in that far and desolate future. Adam had to bend near to hear her whisper, "Which time wouldn't you return?"

"It wouldn't have to be like that, darling," he said. "Others live very separate lives, yet together."

"Could we? Wouldn't we spend our time together dreading our next parting? How long would it be before that overshadowed any joy we might find?"

"You love me, Tracy."

"Yes!" The word was a vehement profession of what Adam had never doubted.

"Yet not enough to come with me. Not enough to leave Shadow."

"I can't! Adam, I can't!" Tears spilled over her cheeks, looking like liquid opals against the chalky hue of her skin.

"And if there should be a child?"

"Oh, God!" Tracy bent nearly double, her arms clutching her abdomen. "I must've been mad."

"What if there's a child, Tracy?" Adam prodded, but gently, kindly.

"There is no child, Adam. I'm sure."

"Not from the mountain, perhaps, but what about now? What about this very minute? The fruit of last night could be growing in your body even as we speak."

"No. There's no child. The timing's wrong." This lie she let stand as a fervid yearning was born.

"My poor darling." Adam sat on the bed and drew her into his arms. "This has all happened too fast. You're frightened and confused."

His hand found its way under her heavy hair. Gentle fingers soothed the tense muscles of her neck. "We've shared too much in too little time. You're still off balance and reeling from the shock of it all.

"You've come from a world of careful words and calculated moves to one of abandon in one fell swoop." He brushed a tangled lock from her shoulder, then smoothed it down her back. "It's a new world for you, with new emotions and new love. In the past you lost everyone you ever loved. Now you're sending me away before you get hurt again." His voice broke and dropped to a deeper note. "It's too late, darling. Far too late."

A shake of her head drew a patient sigh from him. Tenderly he held her unresisting body closer.

"What you don't realize is that all the partings in the world could never hurt as much as a final farewell, the one that would mean we'd never see each other again. A hundred good-byes, a million, none would matter as long as they were followed by one more loving hello. I'd never like being apart from you, Tracy, but knowing I'd soon be seeing you would make each separation bearable."

"You're wrong! It would destroy us. You'd come to hate me for tying you to the mountain, for interrupting your life with my insecurities."

"Only losing each other could destroy us, darling."

"Adam . . ."

"Shh." He tilted her chin up and kissed each eyelid. "I won't argue or push. All I can do is prove my point." He stood abruptly and crossed the room. With his back to the window, blocking Shadow from her view, he absorbed the picture of her heartbreaking confusion.

"I'll leave today. I'm not due back in New York until later in the week, but if I go now, I can sneak in an extra day or two with Summer."

Tracy's heart shattered. He was going away. It was exactly what she wanted, what she had convinced herself was best. Yet it still hurt.

"I'll catch an afternoon plane." He walked back to the bed again and looked down at her. With a compelling hand he lifted her chin. "Six months from now, on the first day of spring, I'll be on the first plane back. Then if you still feel the same, if you still want me to go, I'll step out of your life."

He leaned to kiss her. "If I'm going to make that plane, I'd better grab a shower and pack."

Before Tracy could think of a sensible response he was gone. Soon the wonderfully familiar sound of his off-key whistle blended with the drone of running water. It was more than she could stand. Slipping quickly from the bed, she dressed in jeans and a shirt, then hurried from the house, seeking shelter and comfort in her workshop.

* * *

Nearly an hour later, as she sat staring blankly at the virgin block of wood, she heard his footsteps on the porch. Her hands gripped her knife so tightly, the handle itself threatened to harm her.

"Tracy."

She made no response. Only the tensing of her body showed that she had heard.

"Darling, it's time."

She faced him then. He was standing just inside the room dressed in the navy blazer that enhanced the silver of his hair and the dignity of his carriage. He was, indeed, a man of great attraction, if not true beauty. There were so many pictures of him that she would carry in her heart, and this was another.

"My plane leaves in just under two hours."

"That soon?" It was a soft question that fooled neither one with its calmness.

"Yes. It seemed best to get on home. I know you hate good-byes, but I couldn't leave without saying it." He moved easily through the room and lifted her from the chair. His kiss was warm and tender, but asked nothing. When the kiss ended, she felt lost and bereft.

He twined his fingers through her hair, staring at her so intently, he seemed to be memorizing her every feature. In barely more than a whisper he said, "I'll be back, darling. On the first day of spring. Watch for me."

He had almost reached the door when she found her voice. "Don't come back, Adam. Not in the spring. Not ever. Find someone who can walk in the sunlight with you."

"I have found her." He hadn't turned. Tracy could only see the strong angle of his shoulders and the handsome shape of his neck and head. "I've walked with her on Shadow. Someday she'll be ready to walk with me into the sun. And in the spring I'll come for her."

The sound of his car had long since faded before Tracy

turned from the door. In a trance she returned to her worktable and took up her tools again. For a long while she stared at the wood, then she lifted her knife and made the first cut. She knew now what this carving would be.

She worked steadily, without respite. To the observer there would have been no form or reason to the mis-shapen block, but in her torn heart and mind it had assumed the shape of a treasured memory.

As Tracy sat working in the solitude of her shop, a small car drew to a halt at the point where the road would take one last turn, blocking the valley from view. The man who sat behind the wheel stared up at Shadow.

"I'm leaving now," he said to the mountain. "But I'll be back. You've had her for years, but your time's over. Tracy doesn't know it yet, but she doesn't belong to you, just as she doesn't belong to me. Which of us will she choose?"

Slow minutes ticked away before he spoke again. "I'm going to beat you, Shadow. I'll be her choice. Not out of fear or emotional need, but because she loves me. By setting her free I can make her mine. Can you?"

He started his engine and released the brake. As he drove onto the pavement, he paused with one parting remark. "I'll be back for her in the spring."

Twice Bear looked in on Tracy, whimpered, then went away. As dusk began to fall he returned again. Padding over to her, he nudged her gently, a puzzled look in his eyes. His low worried whine finally penetrated her deep thought.

"Bear?" She looked up in surprise, finding that she had worked long past her usual time. "I see what you mean." She scratched him behind the ears. "It is too dark to work. Why don't we see what we have for supper that's quick and easy?"

She stood up, then looked down at the largest piece she had ever attempted. It would be hard, even likely to be beyond her skill. But it was a carving she had to do. She lovingly patted the shapeless mass, then, whistling for Bear, left the workshop.

Days flowed into weeks and then months. Tracy worked constantly on the figures of her carving. She cried her loneliest tears the day she knew there would be no child, that she had nothing left of Adam.

For the first time in her life she found the mountain lacking. With Bear close on her heels she wandered the roughest trails to return physically exhausted, but never at peace.

The people of the valley seldom saw her and when they did, each expressed shock at her look of fatigue. Tracy only shrugged away their concern and muttered that she was working very hard.

In the mail there was an occasional letter from Liza or a drawing from Summer. From Adam there was nothing. Since the day he had walked out of her workshop, he had virtually vanished from her life, but never from her thoughts.

Jed, good friend that he was, became her only link with Adam. Though he could barely afford it, he flew to New York City twice each month to see Liza. When he returned, Tracy battered him with questions almost faster than he could answer them.

Was Adam all right? Yes.

Was he sure? Absolutely!

Was Adam working too hard? Yes.

Had Adam shaved his beard? Yes.

And the mustache? No.

Did Adam ask about her? Yes.

* * *

Christmas came and went. There was a scarf from Summer but nothing from Adam. Summer's card of thanks only casually said that Daddy had liked Alice's flower. There was no word from Adam.

January was a dreadfully cold month. Tracy moved her carving into the house for the sake of conserving fuel. Consequently she worked even longer hours. During her frequent sleepless nights she found herself picking up her carving tools and beginning again on the wood.

Bear was her constant companion. She spoke to him of Adam. Her tears fell on his fur when she held him, wishing for someone to hold her. He became her link with reality, always there to remind her when it was time to eat or time to rest. He was the friend that Wolfe had been.

On the first day of February she made her decision. Because the lines were down in the valley, she drove to the next town. Shivering in a public phone booth, she dialed the number of the gallery that had contacted her with regularity since they had sold her "A Vixen at Play."

"This is Tracy Walker," she said when the phone was answered. "I'd like to speak with Barry Carrington, please." She waited, then a man identified himself as Carrington and asked if he could help her.

"Your gallery has been asking me to arrange a showing of my work." She paused and took a long, deep breath. "I've decided to give my consent."

The voice at the other end demurred until, with a sudden surge of confidence, Tracy interrupted.

"Perhaps I should have introduced myself as Trace."

The voice immediately changed tone. Of course the gallery would be more than pleased to display her work. A pause to check the calendar. April?

"No. That's too late," Tracy said resolutely. "It must be before spring."

Impossible. There wasn't enough time to make the

arrangements. Publicity and promotional campaigns took time.

"No publicity," Tracy said. "Private invitation only, until after the opening . . . in March."

March! Impossible.

"Thank you for your time, Mr. Carrington. Perhaps another gallery—"

The voice hastily capitulated. The show would be by private invitation and would open on March seventeenth. Would Trace be present?

"Yes."

Would any of the works be for immediate sale?

"Yes."

The call ended with the arrangements complete, and profuse apologies for not recognizing her at first.

Tracy had six busy weeks ahead of her. But with Jed's help she could do it.

"For heaven's sake, Adam. Stop fidgeting. It can't hurt you to wear that tuxedo for a few hours." Liza paced to the window, looked out, then paced back to the chair where Adam sat.

"Why should he want me to come to dinner with you, and why wear this stupid monkey suit?" Adam asked irritably.

"More like a penguin, I'd say," Liza said as she tried to stifle a smile.

The doorbell silenced any reply Adam might have made. Liza fairly flew to answer it. When she opened it Jed was waiting there, smiling and impressive in a tuxedo of his own. After a long, loving kiss for Liza, he greeted Adam.

"After that kiss," Adam said, "why would the two of you want me along as excess baggage?" He began to loosen his tie. "I think I'll stay home with a good book."

"No!" Jed and Liza said in unison.

"What on earth is wrong with the two of you? You're

both acting like you're walking on eggshells. If my not going makes you so nervous, then I'll go."

They were halfway across town before Adam showed any great curiosity about their destination. "What restaurants are in this part of town? I'm not familiar with any."

"Jed has another stop to make first." Liza looked worriedly at Jed for support.

"Yes. A friend of mine asked me to stop by the Carrington Gallery and look at a painting for him."

Adam was puzzled about which friend of Jed's had a penchant for art, but he asked no more questions. When the car was parked and Jed had helped Liza out of the car, Adam suggested that he wait for them there.

"No," Jed and Liza said again in unison.

"Are the two of you practicing to become a chorus?"

"No," Jed said. "But we'd both like your opinion on this work. It won't take but a minute."

Most ungraciously Adam consented and joined them on the sidewalk. The moment they entered the door he stopped in shock. When he turned to Jed and Liza they had mysteriously disappeared. The room was filled with elegantly dressed men and women, but it wasn't the people who interested Adam.

On tables draped with green velvet, on stands of walnut, on blocks of glass, and even on rough stone were graceful and lifelike carvings, each bearing the name Trace. Sarah's hummingbird was there and Ezra's dog. Jed's mallard shared a spot with a majestic eagle. A blue butterfly like Summer's rested on a delicate rose, and the chipmunk still slept curled on his leaf.

Adam's heart began to pound as he understood the meaning of this display. Urgently he searched the crowd for her . . . and she was there.

Dressed in a simple gray dress with her long hair coiled at the nape of her neck, she was the picture of composure. Her back was to him and she was chatting in a most relaxed way with a man who obviously appreciated her looks as well as her talent. A swift unreasonable jealousy surged through Adam, then she moved and he saw the carving.

"Tracy." He whispered her name as he absorbed the full impact of her work. There, captured in wood and painted with a breathtaking realism, were two people. A woman reclined on the mossy ground, clad only in a piece of sheer silk tied low over her hips. Her dark hair hid one breast. The man who bent over her and caressed her had hair of silver and the first beginnings of a dark beard. It bore the title "The Promise of Shadow, a Gift of Sunlight."

The card beneath the title stated in a bold black script that the carving was the property of Adam Grayson and not for sale. Adam was hardly aware of the crowd that moved about him. He was frozen, unable to move, until Tracy half turned and blocked the carving from view. Then he began to wend his way through the crowd.

Snatches of conversation floated about him, though nothing but Tracy penetrated his thoughts.

"Did you see that precious 'possum hanging by his tail?"

"The kitten tangled in a ball of yarn was my favorite."

"Her sketches are almost as breathtaking."

"I liked the skunk with the pink ribbon around his neck."

"Have you noticed that only one carving is of people."

"I asked James to buy that one for me, but it's most emphatically *not* for sale."

"My daughter lost her dog last week. She'll like the little beagle."

"I don't care how much you've been offered, Mr. Carrington. 'Sunlight' isn't mine to sell."

"Darling."

Tracy turned slowly toward him. Her eyes misted with a happy radiance

"Adam." His name on her lips was a healing balm for the aching loneliness of past months. Her gaze moved slowly over him. As if to assure herself that he was true and not her constant dream, she touched him. Her trembling fingers moved lightly over his clean-shaven jaw, barely brushing the edge of his mustache, and lingered for a fleeting second beneath his lips before falling away.

Adam could only look at her. She was thinner; there were dark smudges beneath her eyes from lack of sleep, but she was nonetheless lovely. He saw the glow that flushed her face and the light in her eyes, and knew it was meant for him. Yet none of the pretty speeches he had rehearsed would come.

"You never played your guitar for me," he said. It was a nonsensical thought that had appeared from nowhere.

"I know." Her husky voice was little more than a quiet whisper in the static air about them. "But I will, Adam. Anytime, and anywhere."

"Oh, love. Come here." With a rasping, shuddering groan, he drew her into his arms, forgetting the crowd around them. At this moment there was only Tracy, who with two words had given herself to him.

Anywhere and anytime. With these words she had made his life complete.

"Damn!" he muttered. "How long do you have to stay here?"

"Not one minute longer than you do."

"But your carvings? You wouldn't leave them."

"I would, for you."

"Tracy?"

"They don't matter like they did. I could never be careless about them, or callous, but nothing really matters but you."

"And Shadow?"

"She's a lovely mountain and I'd like to go back, but only with you, and only to visit."

"You're sure?" Nothing about him moved as he waited for her answer.

"Positive. My world is where you are."

"How would you like to go back to Shadow tonight?"

"Could we?"

"My bags have been packed for three days."

"But it's not the first of spring."

"How well I know. I don't think I would've made it."

"I've missed you, Adam."

"Don't look at me like that, Tracy, or we won't make it to Shadow." He took her arm and started walking to the exit.

"But how else can I look at you?"

"Oh, hell. Let's get out of here. By the way, how many bridesmaids do you want?"

"Well, let's see." She paused and thought. "There's Sarah, and Hester and Opal, and Liza, and Summer, and . . ."

"On second thought, maybe we'd better just elope."

"Sounds great to me."

"What?" Adam stopped abruptly in front of the door.

"I said to elope would be perfectly all right with me."

"Tracy, do you mean that?"

"I want *you*, Adam, not a fancy wedding."

"Then we'd better hurry. We have a detour to make on our way back to Shadow."

"Summer?"

"She's spending a few days with Marjorie." He laughed as a subtle hand began to show. "Guess who arranged it?"

"Liza?"

"Devious, isn't she?"

"Yes. Bless her."

Among the astonished crowd two people looked at each other and smiled as Adam and Tracy vanished through the exit. No one seemed to notice when the tall dark man dried tears from the cheeks of his red-haired companion and kissed the finger of her left hand that wore a sparkling diamond.

*   *   *

As moonlight filtered through the trees, casting patterns on the walls of the cabin, Adam stirred sleepily and drew Tracy to him. His hand wandered down her body to the slight swell of her abdomen.

"Are you sure?"

"Positive."

"How long?"

"Six weeks."

"Our first night back to Shadow."

"So it would seem."

"Will you be all right?"

"There's nothing to worry about."

"Darling, I . . ." Adam's breath caught in his throat. "Did you hear that?"

"Did I hear what, love?"

"It sounded like bagpipes."

Tracy laughed delightedly as she leaned over him. "At last you've heard the MacLaren's pipes."

"You've heard them?" he asked softly as he looked up at her.

"Yes."

"When?"

"The night I slept in your arms by Summer's bed."

"But you left me."

"I was frightened."

"And now?"

"Never again, Adam. Not as long as I have you."

"My last love, my true love."

"And mine," she whispered.

"Play, MacLaren, play." Adam drew her gently down to him.

Bear, who slept by the foot of their bed, hardly moved. He had in recent weeks grown accustomed to the strange behavior of his favorite humans. With a slight wag of his tail he settled back down to his dreams.

Far into the night Tracy slept in Adam's arms. Her dreams were of the silver-haired man who loved her; of

Summer who was sleeping contentedly nearby; and of the child who would be her Christmas gift for Adam.

Tomorrow this visit would end. But they would return, she, Adam, and their children. Someday she would tell them of Shadow, who had given her life and love.

EDITOR'S CORNER

Don't be surprised when you see our LOVESWEPT romances next month. No April Fool's joke . . . but we do hope to make you smile when you see our books on the racks. We've had a makeover! Our cover design has been revamped for our upcoming second year anniversary of the publication of LOVESWEPT. Ours is a svelte and lovely new look that doesn't just keep up with the times, but charges ahead of them. And the new colors are exquisite. We believe our new image is sophisticated and modern and we hope you enjoy it. Do let us know what you think.

We've other anniversary surprises in store for you . . . but not the least of them is some delightful romantic reading!

Warm and witty Billie Green leads off next month's LOVESWEPT list with her unforgettable love story, **DREAMS OF JOE,** LOVESWEPT #87. Imagine a famous hunk of a professional quarterback coming to live in a small town to coach the high school football team. Then add a beautiful young widow with two children . . . and a town full of the most warmhearted matchmakers. Now you have the delightful premise of **DREAMS OF JOE.** And for a long time, poor Abby thinks all she *will* be able to do with Joe is dream about him . . . because all those well-meaning folks who are throwing them at one another are also forever on hand! Oh, utter frustration! Oh, the resourcefulness needed to get a little privacy for some ordinary courtin'. We're sure you'll love every minute of Billie's high-spirited love story and that it will inspire a few dreams of your own.

Showing remarkable versatility, Joan Bramsch, noted

for her humor, has given us a heart-wrenchingly beautiful and sensual love story in **AT NIGHTFALL**, LOVESWEPT #88. Hero Matthew is a man with a handicap that is new to him, frightening, and cuts him off from all he loves best to do in the world. Then suddenly heroine Billy Theodore, a warm and honest woman, intrudes into his life . . . and lights it up! She adds a sense of fun and play to his existence while he frees her to know a new and delicious sensual awareness. But for both of them there seems a time on the horizon when they must part—especially when a miracle occurs! **AT NIGHTFALL** is a truly memorable romance.

We're very pleased to introduce you to the work of Anne and Ed Kolaczyk, a long and happily married couple, whose writing you've enjoyed in other romance lines and mainstream novels as well. But before they've always published under pen names. You'll read all about how they came to write together in their biographical sketch next month, but now let me hurry to a description of their charming debut book for us. **CAPTAIN WONDER,** LOVESWEPT #89, features a hero who *is* a hero! Mike Taylor is an actor who has achieved vast fame as television's Captain Wonder. Fleeing a mob of fans, he is befriended by heroine Sara Delaney's twin daughters. Those little girls are just as wild for the muscular marvel as others, even insisting their mom wear a Captain Wonder nightshirt, yet they are soothed in his presence. Not so Mom! Mike has a most unsettling effect on her. And, as circumstances draw them together on a trek that ends at Mike's California home, they find their attraction to one another irresistible! But, there's a key question: can an ordinary smalltown woman face up to a life in the fast lane with a famous television star? The answer is heartwarming in this love story you won't want to miss!

Joan Elliott Pickart is becoming a regular on the LOVESWEPT list, as well as a real favorite! No where is her talent in creating riveting romances more evident than in her offering next month, **LOOK FOR THE SEA GULLS,** LOVESWEPT #90. Record temperatures prevail when Tracey Tate arrives in Texas to write a story on Matt Ramsey's Rocking R ranch. Immediately, too, the temperature soars within his air-conditioned house as these two fiery personalities clash . . . and learn to love. But like his father, Matt cherishes his land which he has always put ahead of everything else in life. And Tracey finds herself to be a very possessive woman where her heart is concerned. How these two sensual, emotional people resolve their conflicts makes for the very best in romance reading!

We hope you'll agree with those of us who work on the LOVESWEPT line that we've provided you with four equally wonderful romances next month. And of course we're sure you won't miss any of them—even with that high-fashion new look on our covers!

Sincerely,

Carolyn Nichols

Carolyn Nichols
  Editor
LOVESWEPT
Bantam Books, Inc.
666 Fifth Avenue
New York, NY 10103

Dear Loveswept Readers,

On the pages that follow you will find an excerpt from my new Bantam novel, PROMISES & LIES. Publication of this is an exciting event for me, and I thought I'd share with you a little of the story and how I came to write it.

I think the development of a person is fascinating, like taking a blank canvas and watching design and color create form. I wanted to do this with a young woman, and Valerie Cardell, the heroine of PROMISES & LIES, became this young woman. Three men at different stages of her life influence and help shape the woman she becomes because I believe that without romance and love, no woman's development is ever complete! I also have long been fascinated by sibling rivalry, especially between sisters, and in PROMISES & LIES, Valerie's road to happiness is often made rocky and treacherous as a result of her sister.

I set out to write a modern-day Cinderella story because I still believe in fairy tales, especially one with love, romance, danger—and of course, a happy ending. Like you and me, the heroine of this novel has her fantasies, and the fun of writing the story was that I could make sure all her dreams came true!

Happy Reading!

Susanne Jaffe

Susanne Jaffe

They drove in silence, Valerie pretending to herself that she did not know what was about to happen. He was taking her to his apartment and he was going to make love to her. That's what she wanted too, wasn't it? He would kiss her, whisper encouraging love words to her, and touch her and touch her and touch her until her skin was on fire. He would find out she was a virgin. She had to tell him. Would that turn him off? No, he would be proud that she was giving him such a special gift. And he would be gentle with her. But he might also be disappointed and she could not bear the thought of that.

Valerie had gone out with Teddy for more than three months, and had considered getting married, but had not been able to have sex with him. She had known Roger Monash for less than two weeks and she was worrying about not being able to please him in bed. She never questioned her feelings for him or what the outcome of this intimacy would be. Irrational, illogical, uncharacteristically impetuous as it might be, Valerie knew she loved him. She could not conceive of his feeling differently. The very intensity of her emotion bespoke its rightness. She did not think she was being naïve, only truer to herself than she had ever been before. And she was too innocent and inexperienced to understand the vast difference between longing and loving. She had no qualms, therefore, about doing the right thing, only about doing it right.

"Is this where you live?" she asked tremulously as they climbed the stairs of a small apartment building near downtown Dallas.

"Uh, no, this belongs to a friend of mine."

"Why can't we go to your place?"

"I loaned it out to a buddy. I wasn't sure you and I would be using it, and besides, he's married, so if I can help the poor sucker out, why not?"

Valerie nodded her understanding, but her stomach gave a funny little lurch.

"Roger, maybe we should wait," she said when they entered the apartment. It was a dismal place, with a hodgepodge of dusty furniture and a view of a parking lot. "I'm sure your place is much nicer and—"

"Who gives a shit about nice. All I care about is that I want you." He crushed her against him and kissed her deeply. "Now tell me," he whispered against her ear, "do you really want to wait?"

She shook her head and smiled up at him, eyes glistening with love. "Roger," she said softly, stepping slightly out of the circle of his arms. "I'm a virgin."

His laugh was a crude, harsh snort that Valerie pretended not to hear. "Sure. And I'm Santa Claus. Come on, get serious. If there was ever a stew who was a virgin she'd be kicked out for poor job performance."

"It's true," she said, ignoring the quick stab of hurt.

He looked hard at her. "You're telling me the truth, aren't you?" She nodded. "Why me?"

She tilted her head, surprise evident on her face. "Because I love you."

Roger Monash did not answer immediately, but a frown flashed across his Kennedy-like face, as if he was considering just how much of a bastard he really was. What he saw as he looked at Valerie was a lovely young face filled with trust, and a body that had been tormenting his dreams for a week. She had to lose it sometime, he thought selfishly, it might as well be to him.

"I love you too, baby," he said as he took her back in his arms. "And I won't hurt you. I promise."

"Could I have a drink?"

"Sure."

She followed him into a sliver of kitchen and watched him fumble around looking for the liquor and glasses. Without asking what she wanted, he poured her a glass of Scotch, neat, and she gulped it down, grateful for its warmth. She was beginning to feel chilled, as if only now the cold reality of the situation was dawning on her.

Then she was being led into a bedroom, and Roger was kissing her, his tongue prying her lips apart, his hands roaming over her back, to her shoulders, down to her hips. "Val, oh, Val, you feel so good, baby," he murmured against her ear. His hands were on the cool skin of her back as he pushed up her sweater; then he was unhooking her bra, lifting it away. He lowered his head, and his tongue caressed first one nipple, then the other, his breath scorching her as much as his touch.

"Take off your clothes. I can't stand this another minute."

"Roger, maybe—"

"I said get undressed." He turned away and took off his clothes, unaware that Valerie had not moved. She tried to unbutton her skirt, but her fingers were trembling so badly that she could not grip the button. Her sweater and bra were still bunched up over her breasts, her hands dangling by her sides. She felt miserable, foolish, incapable of doing anything to help herself.

When Roger was naked, he faced her. Whatever embarrassment and awkwardness she might have experienced during her first encounter with a naked man was mitigated by her awe at his physical beauty. His muscles rippled like those of a thoroughbred stallion. Shoulders, chest, tapering waist; lean, firm thighs: this was a body of power, a body almost audacious in its perfection. Her eyes followed the mat of sandy hair on his chest to its thinning trail, then darted up again to meet the grin on his face.

"Come on, honey, don't be shy," he said softly. "I'll help you."

Seconds later she was naked, on her back, willing herself to feel the warmth that Roger's kisses and touch usually inspired in her. But she felt oddly dispassionate as he murmured in her ear, kissed her neck and breasts and nipples and stomach, touched her in secret places and sacred places. Was it fear that had taken control, or was it something deeper, more vital? Thoughts suddenly fled as she felt him throbbing against her thigh, and then he hoisted himself above her.

"It'll hurt for a second and then it'll be fine," he assured her, and she kept her eyes wide open, nodded, wishing it was over, wishing more that she would feel something, even the pain.

* * *

It was from three this morning until five that Valerie had permitted herself to dwell on what she had done. Until then, she had found things to occupy her thoughts, to keep her from remembering how pleasureless Saturday night had been, and how a repetition of the sex Sunday afternoon and evening had left her similarly unmoved. She told herself that it was her fault; she was inexperienced and therefore scared, inhibited, inept, inadequate. She still loved Roger, she told herself; he had been kind and thoughtful each time. If it bothered her that Sunday they had gone straight to his friend's apartment and had stayed there all day, she let herself be convinced that Roger's needs were more urgent than her own, and that once the newness became part of a practiced routine, they would do things together, things that had nothing to do with sex. She told herself that he would never grow bored with her as he had with Wanda Eberle. She told herself that she had not been used.

In those two hours when night was at its

unfriendliest and morning seemed a light at the end of an infinite tunnel, when time turned threatening and thoughts turned to unavoidable truths, Valerie was thankful that Linda was sleeping. Whatever she was telling herself, she knew she would not be able to say it to Linda with any conviction. But now, as they walked together silently to get their uniforms, she had a feeling that the confrontation was imminent.

"Should I start or will you?" Linda asked quietly, keeping her eyes straight ahead.

"I suppose it will have to be you because I have nothing to say." Valerie despised herself for acting this way. She did not resent her friend's prying because she knew it came from caring. She was scared of Linda—scared to hear her speak with knowledge that Valerie would refute without sincerity.

Linda stopped and reached out to hold Valerie back from walking ahead. The two girls faced each other, Valerie's expression challenging and proud. Linda's eyes shone with anger.

"You went to bed with him, didn't you?"

"Who?"

"Who! How many could there be?"

"If you mean Roger, the answer is yes."

Linda shook her head in amazement. "Didn't I warn you? Didn't I tell you what he did to Wanda? How could you be so stupid, Val? How?"

"If you think it's stupid for two people in love to do what comes naturally, that's your problem, and I'm sincerely sorry for you," she said haughtily.

"In love! You're an even bigger fool than I thought," Linda yelled.

"I don't have to listen to this!" Valerie started to walk away, but Linda's hand was on her arm.

"Do you really think he's in love with you? Be honest, do you?"

"He said so and I believe him."

" 'He said so and I believe him.' You're incredible, you really are."

"I would appreciate your not repeating everything I say. And I suggest that we save this little chat for another time. We're going to be late."

"We have plenty of time, and besides, this won't wait. You've been deliberately avoiding me since Saturday and I—"

"I haven't noticed you trying to be with me, either," Valerie cut in.

"Of course not, you idiot. What did you want me to do, rush up and ask for a blow-by-blow description! I figured that you would *want* to talk with me—that what happened to you was important and you would want to share it with a friend. Obviously, you're so ashamed you can't even face me. That's why I knew I had to bring it up first."

"I am *not* ashamed!" Valerie retorted hotly. "What Roger and I did was beautiful and special. We're in love with each other. Why won't you believe me?"

Linda took a deep breath, briefly shut her eyes, and said: "I do believe you, Val. I believe that you love him and that you think he loves you. But let me just ask a few questions, okay?"

Valerie nodded, dreading what was coming.

"Did he take you to a friend's apartment, saying his was too far or that he had loaned it to a married friend? Did he tell you that he couldn't fly for wanting you so badly? Did he take you to bed Sunday and stay there with you all day? Did he say he can't make plans for when he'll see you next, it depends on his schedule? Did he—"

"Stop it, stop it!" Valerie shrieked, covering her ears with her hands. Gently, Linda lowered them and took Valerie in her arms. Soundlessly, Valerie sobbed, for being a fool and a coward.

"I'm sorry," Linda said softly. "I didn't want to have to hurt you this way, but I didn't know what else to do. You had to see what was going on, what kind of bastard you were getting involved with."

"How did you know he said those things to me? How did you know about his friend's apartment?"

"The answer to the first question is easy. He used the same lines on both me and Wanda. As for the second, while you've been out of it these past few days, I asked around a little. It seems that Mr. Swinging Singles Monash shares an apartment with three other guys, two to a bedroom. When he's in Dallas, he hits on anyone he knows who has a place to himself."

For a moment Valerie said nothing, staring at her roommate but seeing beyond her to the dingy, dreary, unkempt apartment with its parking-lot view. "What am I going to do?" she whispered.

"What do you want to do?"

"I *don't* want to go to bed with him again."

"Not good, huh?"

"Well, I'm sure it's my fault, but no, not too good."

"Why do you think it was your fault?"

"I'm not very experienced, after all, so I probably don't know what I'm doing."

"Your pleasure comes from *his* knowing what to do, kiddo, not you."

"Well, still, I think I'll save sex for another time."

"Another man, Val, not another time. Roger Monash simply was not the right man. Not for someone like you."

"Why *not* someone like me?" Valerie demanded, tired of being different, of being unable to do what other grown women did. What made her so special? What made her so unable to pretend?

"Because your innocence won't disappear no matter how many men you have, even if they're all like Roger Monash," Linda said with a small smile. "You deserve someone who can appreciate that innocence. I'm not saying he has to love you, Val, but there are men who will recognize your purity and admire it. If you want to experiment with sex, do it with them, not with selfish bastards like Monash."

Valerie thought about what Linda said. "You're not like that, are you?" she asked gently. Linda shook her head. "Why not? What makes me this way, and why am I so embarrassed by it?"

"Oh, Val, don't ask me questions like that. I'm not smart enough to answer them."

"You're smarter than I'll ever be," Valerie said miserably.

"No, just not as nice."

The girls looked at each other and broke into laughter, but for Valerie the sound was bittersweet. She would be seeing Roger the next night and she did not know how to tell him there would be no sex. She had a feeling that telling him she did not love him would not matter as much to him.

Murdock's motives for pursuing her? Guilt? Pity? Casey had to choose. She could live with doubt and fear . . . or learn a lesson in love.

#7 A TRYST WITH MR. LINCOLN?
By Billie Green
When Jiggs O'Malley awakened in a strange hotel room, all she saw were the laughing eyes of stranger Matt Brady . . . all she heard were his teasing taunts about their "night together" . . . and all she remembered was nothing! They evaded the passions that intoxicated them until . . . there was nowhere to flee but into each other's arms.

#8 TEMPTATION'S STING
By Helen Conrad
Taylor Winfield likened Rachel Davidson to a Conus shell, contradictory and impenetrable. Rachel battled for independence, torn by her need for Taylor's embraces and her impassioned desire to be her own woman. Could they both succumb to the temptation of the tropical paradise and still be true to their hearts?

#9 DECEMBER 32nd . . . AND ALWAYS
By Marie Michael
Blaise Hamilton made her feel like the most desirable woman on earth. Pat opened herself to emotions she'd thought buried with her late husband. Together they were unbeatable as they worked to build the jet of her late husband's dreams. Time seemed to be running out and yet—would ALWAYS be long enough?

#10 HARD DRIVIN' MAN
By Nancy Carlson
Sabrina sensed Jacy in hot pursuit, as she maneuvered her truck around the racetrack, and recalled his arms clasping her to him. Was he only using her feelings so he could take over her trucking company? Their passion knew no limits as they raced full speed toward love.

#11 BELOVED INTRUDER
By Noelle Berry McCue
Shannon Douglas hated

Michael Brady from the moment he brought the breezes of life into her shadowy existence. Yet a specter of the past remained to torment her and threaten their future. Could he subdue the demons that haunted her, and carry her to true happiness?

lar. But Maggie Sims and Mark Wilding were anything but perfectly matched. Maggie wanted to prove he was wrong about her. She knew they didn't belong together, but when he caressed her, she was swept up in a passion that promised a lifetime of love.

#17 TEMPEST AT SEA
By Iris Johansen
Jane Smith sneaked aboard playboy-director Jake Dominic's yacht on a dare. The muscled arms that captured her were inescapable—and suddenly Jane found herself agreeing to a month-long cruise of the Caribbean. Jane had never given much thought to love, but under Jake's tutelage she discovered its magic . . . and its torment.

#18 AUTUMN FLAMES
By Sara Orwig
Lily Dunbar had ventured too far into the wilderness of Reece Wakefield's vast Chilean ranch; now an oncoming storm thrust her into his arms . . . and he refused to let her go. Could he lure her, step by seductive step, away from the life she had forged for herself, to find her real home in his arms?

#19 PFARR LAKE AFFAIR
By Joan J. Domning
Leslie Pfarr hadn't been back at her father's resort for an hour before she was pitched into the lake by Eric Nordstrom! The brash teenager who'd made her childhood a constant torment had grown into a handsome man. But when he began persuading her to fall in love, Leslie wondered if she was courting disaster.

#20 HEART ON A STRING
By Carla Neggers
One look at heart surgeon Paul Houghton Welling told JoAnna Radcliff he belonged in the stuffy society world she'd escaped for a cottage in Pigeon Cove. She firmly believed she'd never fit into his life, but he set out to show her she was wrong. She was the puppet master, but he knew how to keep her heart on a string.

#21 THE SEDUCTION OF JASON
By Fayrene Preston
On vacation in Martinique, Morgan Saunders found Jason Falco. When a misunderstanding drove him away, she had to win him back. She played the seductress to tempt him to return; she sent him tropical flowers to tantalize him; she wrote her love in letters twenty feet high—on a billboard that echoed the words in her heart.

#22 BREAKFAST IN BED
By Sandra Brown
For all Sloan Fairchild knew, Hollywood had moved to San Francisco when mystery writer Carter Madison stepped into her bed-and-breakfast inn. In his arms the forbidden longing that throbbed between them erupted. Sloan had to choose—between her love for him and her loyalty to a friend . . .

#23 TAKING SAVANNAH
By Becky Combs
The Mercedes was headed straight for her! Cassie hurled a rock that smashed the antique car's taillight. The price driver Jake Kilrain exacted was a passionate kiss, and he set out to woo the Southern lady, Cassie, but discovered that his efforts to conquer the lady might end in his own surrender . . .

#24 THE RELUCTANT LARK
By Iris Johansen
Her haunting voice had earned Sheena Reardon fame as Ireland's mournful dove. Yet to Rand Challon the young singer was not just a lark but a woman whom he desired with all his heart. Rand knew he could teach her to spread her wings and fly free, but would her flight take her from him or into his arms forever?

#25 LIGHTNING THAT LINGERS
By Sharon and Tom Curtis
He was the Cougar Club's star attraction, mesmerizing hundreds of women with hips that swayed in the provocative motions

of love. Jennifer Hamilton offered her heart to the kindred spirit, the tender poet in him. But Philip's worldly side was alien to her, threatening to unravel the magical threads binding them . . .

#26 ONCE IN A BLUE MOON
By Billie Green
Arlie was reckless, wild, a little naughty—but in the nicest way! Whenever she got into a scrape, Dan was always there to rescue her. But this time Arlie wanted a very *personal* bailout that only *he* could provide. Dan never could say no to her. After all, the special favor she wanted was his own secret wish—wasn't it?

#27 THE BRONZED HAWK
By Iris Johansen
Kelly would get her story even if it meant using a bit of blackmail. She'd try anything to get inventor-genius Nick O'Brien to take her along in his experimental balloon. Nick had always trusted his fate to the four winds and the seven seas . . . until a feisty lady clipped his wings by losing herself in his arms . . .

#28 LOVE, CATCH A WILD BIRD
By Anne Reisser
Daredevil and dreamer, Bree Graeme collided with Cane Taylor on her family's farm—and there was an instant intimacy between them. Bree's wild years came to a halt, for when she looked into Cane's eyes, she knew she'd found love at last. But what price freedom to dare when the man she loved could rest only as she lay safe in his arms?

#29 THE LADY AND THE UNICORN
By Iris Johansen
Janna Cannon scaled the walls of Rafe Santine's estate, determined to appeal to the man who could save her animal preserve. She bewitched his guard dogs, then cast a spell over him as well. She offered him a gift he'd never dared risk reaching for before—but could he trust his emotions enough to open himself to her love?

 **LOVESWEPT**

Love Stories you'll never forget by authors you'll always remember

☐	21603	**Heaven's Price** #1 Sandra Brown	$1.95
☐	21604	**Surrender** #2 Helen Mittermeyer	$1.95
☐	21600	**The Joining Stone** #3 Noelle Berry McCue	$1.95
☐	21601	**Silver Miracles** #4 Fayrene Preston	$1.95
☐	21605	**Matching Wits** #5 Carla Neggers	$1.95
☐	21606	**A Love for All Time** #6 Dorothy Garlock	$1.95
☐	21609	**Hard Drivin' Man** #10 Nancy Carlson	$1.95
☐	21610	**Beloved Intruder** #11 Noelle Berry McCue	$1.95
☐	21611	**Hunter's Payne** #12 Joan J. Domning	$1.95
☐	21618	**Tiger Lady** #13 Joan Domning	$1.95
☐	21613	**Stormy Vows** #14 Iris Johansen	$1.95
☐	21614	**Brief Delight** #15 Helen Mittermeyer	$1.95
☐	21616	**A Very Reluctant Knight** #16 Billie Green	$1.95
☐	21617	**Tempest at Sea** #17 Iris Johansen	$1.95
☐	21619	**Autumn Flames** #18 Sara Orwig	$1.95
☐	21620	**Pfarr Lake Affair** #19 Joan Domning	$1.95
☐	21621	**Heart on a String** #20 Carla Neggars	$1.95
☐	21622	**The Seduction of Jason** #21 Fayrene Preston	$1.95
☐	21623	**Breakfast In Bed** #22 Sandra Brown	$1.95
☐	21624	**Taking Savannah** #23 Becky Combs	$1.95
☐	21625	**The Reluctant Lark** #24 Iris Johansen	$1.95

Prices and availability subject to change without notice.

Buy them at your local bookstore or use this handy coupon for ordering:

Bantam Books, Inc., Dept. SW, 414 East Golf Road, Des Plaines, Ill. 60016

Please send me the books I have checked above. I am enclosing $_____ (please add $1.25 to cover postage and handling). Send check or money order—no cash or C.O.D.'s please.

Mr/Ms_____

Address _____

City/State_____ Zip_____

SW—3/85

Please allow four to six weeks for delivery. This offer expires 9/85.

LOVESWEPT

Love Stories you'll never forget by authors you'll always remember